Love's Journey

By

Nancy Kabakoff

All of the characters and events in this book are fictitious, and any resemblance to actual persons, living or dead, is purely coincidental.

ISBN 978-0-9794946-8-0

Copyright ©2017 by Nancy Kabakoff

All rights reserved

Losantiville Press, Inc. maintains full ownership and or/legal rights to publish this work.

Cover design and production by Randall Zimmerman

This book may not be reproduced, transmitted, or stored by any means without the expressed written consent of the publisher.

Love's Journey Synopsis

Forty-eight-year-old Rachel Blum has every intention of keeping her heart locked away from love forever. Marriage to her college sweetheart, Steve, ended in divorce. He had been unfaithful, and his actions left Rachel emotionally scarred. Steve is unhappily married to Linda, the selfish woman with whom he had the affair. Rachel's focus is on raising two attitude-laced teenage daughters, Sarah and Rebecca an amiable son, David, and making frequent, self-imposed dutiful visits to the upscale retirement home where her uncaring mother, Delores, resides.

One rainy day brings Rachel into the retirement home to see her mother. After criticizing her daughter's wet locks, Delores notices Don, whose father, Ben, lives in the retirement home. She feels that Rachel should meet Don and go out with him. Considering Rachel is still recovering from the emotional scars left by her ex-husband, she doesn't understand why her mother isn't more compassionate regarding her wounded heart.

However, Rachel is soon introduced to kind and handsome Don, and they continue to encounter each other during visits to their respective parents. As they gradually become acquainted, Don asks Rachel if she'll go to lunch with him. She agrees, knowing that Don merely wants company as he is new to the area. Surprisingly, she discovers that they have more in common than she would have ever guessed.

As Don and Rachel begin a relationship, she becomes stronger and happier than she has been in a long time. Don is caring and supportive, and Rachel is happy to become part of his life. She is there for him, and eventually Rachel realizes that she can let down her guard and find happiness.

Through family issues, Rachel's insecurities and the happy resolution of problems, both Rachel and Don heal their emotional wounds together, and find that love is possible at any point in life.

Nancy lives in Montgomery, Ohio with her husband, Ron.
They enjoy travel, reading, theater and movies.
Nancy also has fun spending time with friends and family as
well as cooking and playing with cats.

*I dedicate this to my loving, supportive and
funny husband Ron.
We have our own loving journey!*

Acknowledgements

Thanks to my dear friend, Valerie Lim, who was the first to read
and to edit the story, encouraging me to have it published.

Also to Susan Dygert for her loving friendship and for
her help with the computer aspects.

To wonderful friend, Amy McPike, who has been so
supportive and made very helpful suggestions.

Also to friend and cover designer Randy Zimmerman,
whose help brought the story to the amazing Losantiville Press.

And much appreciation and gratitude to the delightful, kind and
so helpful Deanna Ashing of the Losantiville Press, who did an
extraordinary job of editing, coaching and bringing this story to
the public. Many thanks to all my family and friends!

Chapter One

The charcoal gray sky had opened wide, and the spiking rain was pelting Rachel's car, making it very difficult for her to see the road. The windshield wipers couldn't keep pace with this spring rain. Dealing with the tailgating car behind her wasn't making life any easier. Why, in lousy weather, did some people think that they were driving in the Indy 500? The deluge was a welcome relief from the hot, dry weather that the city had been wilting under, but this was overkill as far as Rachel was concerned. She had experienced quite a day already, and she knew that it was only going to get more challenging before night came to take her away into a refreshing bath and a comfortable, albeit lonely bed.

Her daughters, Sarah and Rebecca, were grumpy from the moment the day began. At sixteen and fourteen it shouldn't have come as a surprise that this would be what Rachel had in store for herself during the next several years. Being teenagers, and not being thrilled that Rachel and their father's marriage went south, had given them quite an attitude. Still, it would be nice every now and then to have a "Good morning, Mom! Love you!" At this point, Rachel would gladly accept silence instead of raised voices, slamming doors and rolling eyes.

Rachel's twelve-year-old son, David, was far more endearing, and he had the good sense to steer away from his belligerent sisters when they got into their bad moods. His nature was more happy and upbeat than either of theirs, and he was quick to show a smile and give a hug. That might not last much longer, although Rachel felt confident that her relationship with David would be more pleasant than the current one she had with her "charming" teen girls.

Because this was the weekend their father had visitation, the kids would be at his house, and Rachel would get some quiet time and do whatever she pleased without the constant criticisms from her all-knowing daughters. She loved her children with all

1

of her heart and soul, but the girls did try her patience. Rachel was forty-eight, and she was quickly running out of that quality. She knew that yelling wasn't the answer, and considering how she felt during her own teen years with her mother, she tried to avoid constant tensions.

Rachel's grip tightened on the steering wheel, willing the car to behave and get her safely to the retirement home where her seventy-three-year old mother resided. Heaven forbid if Rachel would be late; she'd hear plenty of complaining, and she didn't think it would be a good idea to strangle her mother right in front of everyone at the home. It might be in bad taste. Rachel gave a little chuckle with that thought. "Hey, I haven't lost my sense of humor yet! However, I am now talking to myself." In times like these, she'd do whatever it took to gain some comfort.

As she approached the lush entrance to the retirement complex, she took a deep, cleansing breath. The setting for this renowned facility was gorgeous. It was always impeccably maintained, and it felt like one was entering a resort. The landscape's healthy green grass was combined with flowers of every color and shape. The grounds housed various fountains as well as lovely displays of marble sculptures depicting wildlife. There were numerous walking paths, although with the torrential downpour, there wasn't a soul to be seen taking advantage of them.

Rachel saw a few cars coming from the opposite direction. She wondered if they were happy to be leaving or if they were already missing their loved ones. She knew how she felt upon her departure, and sometimes she wondered why she bothered coming as often as she did. Good 'ole Jewish guilt. That's what her beloved sister, who had the good fortune to live a plane ride away, always told her. Leah was her own person, never influenced by what anyone ever thought about her. She did as she pleased, but she had a sympathetic ear when Rachel would call and purge herself of life's events. As was the case with most siblings, they weren't the same in personality or lifestyle, but the two had a deep love for each other that had existed from the moment Leah was brought home from the hospital when Rachel was five years old.

As she approached the parking lot, she took one more deep breath and parked her car in a spot facing out. She didn't like backing up when she left any parking place, and the home's parking lot was no exception. After a visit with her mother, she could just zip right out. Generally, after seeing her mother, she needed to get her freedom as quickly as possible.

Rachel shut off the wipers and turned off the vehicle. She glanced at the floor on the passenger side in front then craned her neck to see the floor in the back. "Damn!" No umbrella. She could never remember where the seemingly dozen or so umbrellas were that she was sure she had purchased over the years. Probably in the garage or used by the girls' friends when they went out for their gossipy walks, even in the rain. They didn't want Mom to overhear one word of their important conversations.

Oh, well, I'll just have to make a dash for the door. I won't melt, even if that's what Sarah and Rebecca would think would happen to me. Rachel opened the car door, key in hand, and stepped out. The downpour of rain flattened her hair, and the water dripped down her face. She locked the door and then ran with her head down, as though the rain would decide to avoid her because she wasn't acknowledging the deluge.

Within seconds, she was under the green awning, grateful to be protected from the elements. The sliding door made a whooshing sound as it automatically opened, and she gazed at the pretty, softly lit lobby. Even on a gloomy morning such as this one, it was illuminated. The ceiling glowed with its crystal chandeliers. The elegant light enveloped the lobby which had a large, thick patterned carpet, artistically representing sweeping floral designs done in dusty rose, light yellow, grass green and beige with a cream background. Perfect for its residents, making it not only cheerful but safe to use a walker or wheelchair if necessary. No slipping on marble or wood floors here. The walls were painted a neutral beige color and proudly displayed various paintings; some floral, some wildlife, and one rather imposing portrait of the elderly female benefactor whose money had founded the entire home.

Sitting at the reception desk was a young lady of around thirty who was dressed very conservatively in a gray pinstripe suit with a crisp white blouse. Her hair was light brown, and fell on her shoulders. She wore just a hint of pink lipstick and blush to give her some color. She was on the phone and, upon seeing Rachel, she smiled and waved in acknowledgment. Rachel watched a few people walking to some destination. Others were sitting on burgundy colored velvet chairs, and there were a few sitting in groups on the comfortable matching plush couches. There were vignettes of spaces, making each area feel as though it could be someone's living room, complete with simple brass lamps sitting on carved cherry wood tables as well as books and magazines scattered around crystal containers filled with potpourri.

Rachel smiled and waved to a few residents whom she had known since her mother moved there two years ago. There were a number of visitors, some possibly friends still residing in their own homes, but others must have been relatives, probably sons and daughters. These individuals were younger and most bore some resemblance to their parents, whether in facial appearance and/or mannerisms. It was interesting to see the guest's expressions as each spoke to their retired friends and loved ones who were very privileged to be living in such idyllic surroundings. The visiting friends appeared happy to sit and chat with their longtime friends. Some daughters listened patiently to their mothers, and one was laughing and talking animatedly with her mom. Others displayed an anxious appearance with a lack of focus, indicating that they may have other pressing matters to attend. The sons, some dressed in suits, might be making a pit stop on the way to the office or to their next business meeting. They would lean forward, listening to their mothers, but looking as though they were ready to leap out of the seat at any moment. Talk about multitasking! There was one man who looked a bit more casual, and as she noticed him, he looked at her as well. They locked eyes for a split second, each giving the other a polite smile.

Out of the corner of her eye, she saw someone with an arm extending in the air, giving almost a queenly wave. Ah, yes, there was Delores. She was sitting in one of the richly upholstered chairs, looking like the royalty she thought she was. Rachel waved back. She plastered a smile on her face and walked towards her mother.

Delores was a lovely woman who looked as though she belonged in the luxurious residence. She had beautiful, shiny brunette hair, colored of course, which was always pulled back into a tight and tidy bun. Rachel realized that her mother's hair style hadn't changed for at least twenty years. Her face, fair skinned and oval in shape, was only slightly lined, mostly around her thin lips. Maybe that was due to all of the irritated lip pursing

4

she had done throughout her many years. Her eyes had a light to them, even though they were the darkest brown that Rachel had ever seen. Delores always used cosmetics, although very tastefully. A little eye makeup, slight peach blush and a hint of lipstick, which was her favorite cosmetic. She must have had a hundred different colors, depending upon her mood or what color of fabric she was wearing for the day. Her clothes were of the finest cut, designer made and lasted forever. Rachel's mother wasn't a major shopper; rather she wanted good clothing that would see her through the years. With her lifelong petite figure, she never needed alterations.

Rachel walked towards her mother, who was dressed in navy linen slacks with a matching jacket and a red blouse. She was wearing a delicate gold flower brooch on her lapel that her husband, Aaron, had given her on their first wedding anniversary. Rachel caught a gentle whiff of the light perfume that her mother always wore; Chanel No 5. Not a full blast of it, like some ladies did, just a spritz. Her mother didn't rise to greet her. She never did. As always, Rachel leaned in and kissed her mother's soft cheek. Delores took great care to moisturize and have the occasional facial from the home's salon.

As Rachel sat down in the chair set diagonally in front of her mother, she greeted her. "Hi, Mom!" Rachel always tried to sound upbeat. "How are you?" That was not normally a good question to ask, but she had to be polite.

"Hello, Rachel." Her mom's voice was clear and strong. Never really happy or excited, though. "I'm okay. I have my aches and pains, but that's nothing new." All of this was said as it was always said, just matter-of-fact.

"Well, I guess that's the way it is." Rachel never knew quite what to say to this comment. She knew she couldn't help her mother feel better, although it's not like Delores was in dire pain either. Her mom was a lucky lady. Here she was, sitting very pretty at a nice and costly retirement home. It was hard for Rachel to get out the violin and start playing it for her mother.

Rachel motioned towards the sliding glass door. "It's really raining out there." She wasn't sure she could muster up anything more than small talk.

Her mother eyed Rachel's wet appearance. "Hmm. I can tell by looking at your hair."

Never mind, Rachel thought with annoyance, *that I am wearing nicely tailored tan slacks with a white twin set, cute shoes and the pretty strand of delicate pearls that her parents had given her for her sixteenth birthday. Nope, she HAS to notice my lackluster wet hair.*

"What can I tell you? It's a wet day out there, and I forgot my umbrella. But I'm here," Rachel said with a phony chipper voice and a phony smile. What she WANTED to say was, *You're lucky I'm here, you #@&%,* but once again, sanity prevailed. It's not as though her mother had hundreds of visitors, so she should be grateful that Rachel visited, damp hair or not. Her mother didn't say another word.

"Soooo, anything going on here?" Rachel was getting desperate. She had only been with her mother for a minute, and it already seemed like an eternity.

"There are things going on here and there. I don't know, I'm not all that interested in the activities. I just read and I sit. Sometimes, if I feel up to it, I go for a little walk." Once again, everything was said without any emotion.

"Have you been eating okay?" Rachel thought her mom looked perfectly fit, but she wanted to make sure that she did have her appetite.

"Yes, I guess so. The food here isn't exactly gourmet, as you know."

Rachel sighed at that comment. Well, actually, it was gourmet food from what she knew. She had been there every now and then for a lunch or a dinner. Maybe it wasn't like going to a five-star restaurant, but it was far better than anything her mother had ever prepared. She didn't know how her mom could be so picky.

Suddenly, her mother perked up. "I saw Betty's daughter the other day." Betty was a friend of Delores's from years back. Their husbands had worked together at the same business consulting company, both making their way quickly up the corporate ladder, enjoying the financial rewards.

"Oh? Did she say hello to you?" Rachel realized how stupid her response was, but she honestly didn't know what to say at this point.

Her mother looked at her incredulously. "Of course she said hello to me!" Like, *duh Rachel, couldn't you have guessed that, you idiot?* "Lisa took HER out to lunch."

Okay, here we go. I should have seen this coming, thought Rachel.

"That's very nice." Rachel didn't want to pursue this topic. She knew that her mother probably thought that she should be taken out to eat as well, although nothing was ever said. Maybe if her mother wasn't such a pain, it would be nicer to go out with her. But her mother just wasn't pleasant. She sucked the life out of Rachel.

Delores leaned forward in her chair, her long hands with their perfectly manicured red fingernails clasped together. "They had a nice lunch together. Betty told me all about it." Delores nodded her head as if she held all of the secrets that had been divulged by her friend.

I just bet she did, thought Rachel. *More like bragged about everything going on in her life. She probably went on and on about her perfect daughter, with her 2.5 children and her handsome husband, all living happily together with a dog in their 5,000 square foot mansion.* Rachel didn't know what to say. She heard a man's voice from behind, which was a welcome relief to the tension that was building in her body.

"Hi, Delores, how are you today? I see you have a visitor here with you." He sounded very energetic and friendly. Rachel turned to look at him, and then he stood beside their chairs. Rachel started to get up.

"No, no, don't get up. I was just walking back to my apartment, and I thought I'd say hello."

Delores, without even a smile said, "Rachel, this is Mr. Rosen. This is my daughter, Rachel."

Rachel did get up, looked at him with a smile and said hello. She noticed that he was a nice looking man of average height, slightly bent over, but otherwise looking fine. He had thick white hair, and smiling blue eyes.

"Well, I'll let you two talk amongst yourselves. Have a nice day!" And off he went, as though he had other important matters to attend during the day.

"He seems nice," said Rachel.

"Yes, he is. He's always talking with people, and he seems very happy here."

There was a moment where neither mother nor daughter uttered a word. Rachel noticed that, as always, her mother never

7

asked anything about her or her children. She couldn't figure out why Delores didn't want to know anything about her life. Rachel decided that any news about her sister would be a topic that would appeal to her mother.

"I spoke with Leah yesterday."

Delores raised her perfectly plucked eyebrows. "Oh? What did she have to say?" For the first time during this visit, Delores smiled slightly. Not a big smile by any stretch of the imagination, but she was interested in this part of the conversation.

"Well, not much. She couldn't talk for too long."

"I'm sure that's true. She's always very busy." This was said with pride more than irritation.

"She, Bob and the kids are fine. She's helping with a fundraiser at the school. Bob went on a business trip to Arizona, but he'll only be gone for a few days. Aaron is playing baseball, and Amy is in a production of "My Fair Lady" at school. Guess who she's portraying?"

Delores smiled broadly this time, thinking about Leah's family. She adored her grandchildren. Her grandson was named after her husband, who had passed away suddenly at age sixty-four. Leah was pregnant with Aaron at the time, and she knew that if she had a son, he would be named after his grandfather. Amy was also the light of her grandmother's eyes. She was somewhat like Delores in her appearance, although thankfully not her personality. Now, as a teenager, she wasn't gawky or odd, just tall, graceful and full of charm.

"I'm sure she's playing Audrey Hepburn's part. No question about that!" She was gleeful about this.

"You got it. I think Amy's most excited about the pretty clothes she'll get to wear." Amy and Aaron both went to a very nice private school, and the plays performed there were incredible. No expense was spared in any production or activity at this school.

"Naturally. She's so particular about everything she wears. And everything she does." Delores sounded very boastful.

Rachel debated, for one second whether or not she should talk about her kids. Sadly, she believed that she would only become upset if she did. Her mother never reacted positively about her brood. She would listen half-heartedly, and she never said anything to praise them.

"Yep, Amy's a great kid." At this point, Rachel felt that she

8

was totally out of anything more to say.

Rachel heard a blast of laughter coming from another part of the room. She wished that she could have that kind of fun with her own mother. Just to be able to sit, share secrets, gossip and laugh. She wasn't asking for much, merely a little fun.

Even Delores must have wanted more from their time together, so she decided to take the initiative and say something. She shifted a bit in her chair and crossed her legs. "You may not know him," she said, pointing to the man whom Rachel had locked eyes with upon her entrance into the lobby, "but that's Don Levy."

Rachel turned to see where her mother was pointing. She shook her head back and forth, indicating that she did not know him. She wondered where this conversation was going.

"Well, he's a nice fellow. He came here from New York. His dad is Ben Levy. You know him, right?"

"No, I don't think that I do." Rachel wondered where her mother was headed with her comments.

"It doesn't matter. Anyway, Ben introduced me to his son the other day. Ben's a nice man, too. His son has never been married. He decided to come here to be closer to his father. He uses a computer to help companies with advertising, and he figured he could do that anywhere."

Okay, well, what do I care? Rachel didn't know why her mother brought up these two men at all. However, she felt the need to fill the gap of sudden silence. "That's great. I'm sure Ben must be happy to have his son nearby." *What else could she possibly say to her mother?*

"Yes, he is." Delores looked expectantly at her daughter, and then went silent again.

Clearly, this conversation was going nowhere. Rachel decided that she wasn't in the mood to pretend today. Enough was enough. If her mother didn't want to know anything about her or her children, or to talk about anything of significance, then Rachel had other things she could be doing. She had to get everything together for her kids to take to their dad's, and she wanted other chores to be done so that she didn't have anything to deal with over the weekend. This was going to be her relaxing weekend, and she didn't want to continue on with this pointless visit. She could tell that her mother was being her mother, she was fine, and that was that.

"Mom, I have quite a bit to do today, so I should head out now." Rachel couldn't think of anything else to say. Just goodbye would suffice at this moment as far as she was concerned.

Delores looked a bit surprised. She realized that she hadn't made her previous point clear enough to her daughter. "Well, okay, but I wondered if you might want to have dinner sometime with that nice man?"

Rachel was very glad that she hadn't stood up yet. If she had, she was convinced that the floor would have swallowed her whole. She wouldn't be able see her way out of the crater that had been created because she wouldn't have been conscious enough to get that far.

"What?" That was all Rachel could muster at the moment.

In spite of Rachel's obvious displeasure, her mother actually thought that Rachel hadn't heard her. She was a bit annoyed realizing she'd have to repeat herself. "I SAID that I wondered if you might want to have dinner sometime with Don?"

Rachel was now mortified. *What in the world was her mother thinking?* "Why would you even ask me that?"

Her mother didn't seem to see any problem. "I just thought it would be a nice thing for you to do. He's single, you're single. He seems like a decent fellow. He's new in town, and he's certainly good looking enough for you."

Well, darn it if her mom didn't know how to warm the cockles of her daughter's heart. *He's certainly good looking enough for you.* Rachel wanted to smack her mother. Not that she was a violent person, but she could change into one if necessary. *I'm not hideous Mom,* Rachel thought to herself. She glanced over at Don, who appeared to be engrossed in a conversation with his dad. He had a smile on his face, and he was saying something. To be honest, Rachel thought he was quite attractive. After a moment, she came back to reality.

"Mom, thanks but no thanks. I'm not interested." Rachel had had enough. She stood up, leaned into her mother, kissed her cheek and told her she'd see her soon. Unfortunately. But she didn't say that to her mother.

Delores looked perplexed by Rachel's reaction. "I don't know what the big deal is. I'm just talking about the two of you having dinner together. Two lonely people eating a meal with each other. Goodness!" Delores was put off by her daughter's attitude.

10

Rachel was beyond annoyed at this point. "Well, it IS a big deal Mom. I'm divorced and still reeling from everything that happened. I have three children who take up most of my time. And there are a million other reasons that I don't want to do this, the least of which is that I'M not asking any man out. If he asked me, MAYBE I'd go." Rachel said all of this with her hands on her hips, disgusted that she'd even have to speak about any of this to her mother. *Shouldn't Delores already know this? Shouldn't she realize what I've been through, what I'm dealing with now?*

Still not quite understanding what Rachel was upset about, Delores continued. As far as she was concerned, she had the perfect solution to the problem. "Oh. Well, if it's a matter of HIM asking YOU out, I'm sure that could be arranged. I would just talk to Ben about this." She said it as if it could be a done deal.

Rachel felt like screaming. She didn't, but instead she lowered her voice while she was seething. "Please Mom, don't help me. I don't want to go out with him. I don't want you and Ben conspiring to set up anything. Let it go, will you?"

Delores looked at her, and put her hands in the air, as though she was going to surrender. "Okay, okay. Whatever you say. I don't understand the problem, but I won't say anything. Rachel, you're too sensitive. No wonder you've had your issues." Delores looked away with a cold expression on her face.

Rachel felt as though her mother had punched her in the stomach. She couldn't believe how cruel Delores could be. *Maybe I have issues because you were a lousy mother who never took an interest in me.* She didn't say it out loud, but she wanted to. She wanted to hurt her mother, just as her mother had hurt her. Not just now, but many times before.

"Thanks. Have a nice day." That was all Rachel could say. She turned from her mother, and started to walk back to the sliding doors. Her faced burned with anger, but she tried to calm herself and put a weak smile back on her face.

As she walked across the lobby, she saw Ben and Don. Although they were still conversing, they both looked at her and smiled. Rachel nodded her head once to acknowledge them and walked through the glass doors.

The rain had dissipated slightly, but Rachel's anger had not. She grabbed the car key out of her purse, walked quickly to her car, and unlocked the door. She sat in the driver's seat, and closed

11

her eyes for a moment. *How could her mother be so insensitive? And why do I keep putting myself in the emotional line of fire with her?* Rachel wondered if she needed to have some time away from seeing her mother.

On the drive home, Rachel decided that it was best to just not think about anything that happened with her mother. She turned on the radio, and listened to her oldies music.

Chapter Two

Within ten minutes, Rachel was pulling into her driveway and into the garage. As she got out, she noticed two umbrellas on a shelf. *It figures.*

Rachel unlocked the door to the garage which led into her laundry room. Fortunately, the laundry was all done, so the space was clear. She went into her gourmet kitchen. It was a space that she treasured. Two years before the divorce, she had remodeled the large kitchen. Cooking was a hobby, even if her kids didn't always express their appreciation for what she prepared. The room had recessed lighting, and modern frosted glass pendant lights hanging over the granite countertop, which was tan with flecks of black and white. The natural stone was gorgeous and functional, and she had plenty of space to do her prep work. The stainless steel range was the crowning jewel where she sautéed garlic with olive oil, as well as many other delights, to make lots of tasty creations. For Rachel, cooking wasn't drudgery; it was pure joy, her outlet. Rachel knew that she was lucky that, although her ex was a jerk, he had made good money. Rachel's father had also included she and her sister in a healthy inheritance. So she didn't have to work, and she could concentrate on her children and her passion for cooking.

Rachel slammed her purse down on the counter, and took a glass from the cherry wood cabinet. She went to the large stainless steel refrigerator, pushed the lever for crushed ice, and then poured water into her glass. After taking a long swig, she placed the glass on the counter. Rachel glanced at the time displayed on her range, and debated calling her sister. Leah lived in La Jolla, an upscale part of California. It was a bit early there, but Leah had probably already seen her kids off to school. As Rachel reached for the phone, it rang. She looked at the Caller ID display.

"Crap!" It was Rachel's ex-husband calling from his office. She was NOT in the mood to talk with him, so she decided to let his call go into the answering service. *The last thing I need right now is to have Steve ask questions or request something*, thought Rachel.

She went into the family room, where she collapsed on the red leather sofa. Oh, how she loved this couch! The color was just the right shade of red, one of her top color choices, and it felt like she was reclining on a cloud. Rachel had purchased the comfortable piece of furniture right after her divorce was finalized. She needed something that was fresh and new. After waiting a couple of minutes Rachel listened to find out what message her ex left.

She picked up the phone and heard the familiar beeping sound. After punching in her code, and pressing a couple of buttons, she heard Steve's voice. "Hey, Rache, it's Steve." He always called her "Rache." That casual way of speaking with her never changed. He didn't need to say who he was. She was well aware of his office number. Still, that was easy-going Steve. "Just wanted to confirm that you're dropping the kids off at the house right after they get home from school. I'm sure you know that. I just want to make sure everything is in order. Maybe call before you leave so Linda knows you're coming. I'll try to be home at a reasonable hour, but I want them settled in as soon as possible. Thanks. Bye!"

There wasn't any need to verify the plan. Steve knew that Rachel handled everything efficiently. She may not have been too sharp some years back, especially considering that she had no clue about his affair, but she wasn't totally brain dead now. Rachel sat for a moment, thinking about the life that she had shared with Steve. Most of the time they had spent with each other had been great, but somehow things went wrong.

Steve and Rachel had been together since their college days. He was cute with his brown hair cut conservatively short and brushed to the side. He had beautiful blue eyes and a dimpled smile. He was also a very smart young man, and Rachel adored him from the moment they met at a party in the dorm. Steve liked to talk and laugh. It was fun to be with him, and although he was always intense about his studies, he still found time to go out and explore life.

Rachel liked college and her classes, but her real interest was Steve. They were nearly inseparable for their four undergrad years with the exception of summers away from the campus. Rachel went home to Illinois to be with her family. She spent her days

14

employed at her aunt's clothing boutique, helping with anything and everything. Steve returned to Maine where he worked at an inn on the water, educating himself about the business of running a summer resort. Both were getting work experience and earning some money in the process. They wanted to be together during these few months, but they knew that this was their only option. Neither set of parents would ever have allowed them to spend their summers together. They felt that their children should be responsible and not only focus on each other.

Rachel didn't argue. She knew what she had to do, and she felt that she would just bide her time until college ended. Her mother in particular, wasn't as fond of Steve. She felt that he had an "East coast attitude," believing that he was too slick and sure of himself. Well, Steve was sure of himself, but he wasn't trying to charm or deceive anyone. At least not at that time. Rachel wasn't thrilled to hear her mother disparage her boyfriend, so she tried to ignore her as much as possible. Rachel's dad just wanted her to be happy. He liked Steve, and he believed that Rachel's boyfriend was simply an agreeable young man who liked people and was working hard at his studies. Clearly, considering how understanding her father was about her life choices, Rachel chose to spend more time with him than with her mother.

After graduating from college, Steve and Rachel both ended up getting jobs, surprisingly at the same firm. Steve knew Rachel would want to live in her hometown, so he applied to companies there. He was in sales and she was an office assistant. They didn't even realize that they had both applied to the same company. So, when they told each other that they had received job offers at the same place, they screamed with laughter and joy. It was hard to believe that they could be this lucky.

The two decided to marry right after graduation. They would be living close to Rachel's parents' house in Illinois. Neither would be starting with the company until the middle of July, so they could take a honeymoon and not have to take time away from work once they started. Although Rachel's mother wasn't happy about their alliance, she accepted her daughter's decision and decided to throw a big, expensive wedding. Rachel didn't feel the need to have either of those things, but she knew that this was her mother's desire. So she went along with all of the bells and whistles that her mother wanted. Delores chose the

15

wedding dress, although Rachel chose the lavender colored satin bridesmaids' dresses. The wedding was to be held at the end of June, so her mother had to plan everything very quickly. The invitations, the flowers, the photographer, the caterer and the music were all chosen within a week of Steve and Rachel's announcement of their engagement. No time was wasted. The ceremony would be held at the temple where the Weinstein's belonged, and the reception would take place at a nearby country club.

Replies from the invitations came flooding in quickly because the guests were given only two weeks to respond. Most of the invited out of town guests were coming, so a number of rooms in a hotel were set aside for all of them. Steve had been getting things in order back home in Maine, but he came to Illinois for a weekend so that he and Rachel could take a day to register for gifts, deciding on one department store to supply them with all of their household needs. This was an exciting part of the process for both of them. These presents would be things that would be used in their new home. They would temporarily be staying in an apartment, but they planned on looking for a house as soon as possible. In the meantime, Rachel's parents would store the wedding gifts in their home.

As the wedding day approached, the flurry of activities was almost overwhelming. Rachel's friends from her high school days threw her a very nice wedding shower. One of her friends was already married, and living in a house, so she hosted the gathering, which also included Rachel's college friends. Delicious finger food was served, which included Rachel's favorite stuffed mushrooms and other tasty treats. Wrapping paper was strewn all over as Rachel unwrapped the gifts that had been lovingly given to her. Bows were placed on a paper plate, which would be used as the "wedding bouquet" for the wedding rehearsal. Rachel had a lovely day, and her friend's house echoed with laughter and a lot of "oohs and ahhs."

Steve's bachelor party was less elaborate but equally fun. When he returned to Maine, his boyhood friends took him out for dinner. He wasn't interested in going to a bar or a strip joint, although a couple of his buddies would have loved that idea. Steve just wanted a nice meal with his friends. None of them were married yet, and they teased him about how his life would change after he was tied to 'the ball and chain.' He took it in the good natured way that it was meant. He was very happy to know that he would soon be sharing his life with his best friend.

Everything had come together, and on the morning of the wedding, Rachel woke up to see the sun shining. She stretched and leapt out of bed with a smile on her face. She could hear her mom and dad chattering away downstairs, and then she heard the voices of her aunt and uncle. Her mother insisted that her sister and brother-in-law stay at the house so that they could be an integral part of everything for a couple of nights. Rachel was delighted to have them there. Not just because she loved them and enjoyed their company, but because they would spend time with Delores. Rachel tried to avoid her mother as much as possible. Rachel was a happy bride-to-be, and she didn't want her mother spoiling her good mood. She showered and dressed in jeans and a t-shirt, and practically skipped down the carpeted stairs, heading straight for the kitchen where all the action was taking place.

Her smiling Aunt Viv reached out her loving arms to Rachel. "Good morning, sweetie! How are you doing this morning?" She put her arm around Rachel's shoulder and gave her a smacking kiss on the cheek. "I'm feeling great and I couldn't be happier." Rachel meant every word of that statement.

Her Uncle Gary winked at her. "We're so happy for you, kiddo. You look terrific."

"Thanks! So, what are all of you gabbing about?"

Delores piped in. "Just remembering the old days. Have some breakfast."

Rachel wondered if anyone noticed how her mother behaved towards her. There was no hug or a kiss, no words of love. Only a cold shoulder.

Rachel's dad went to her and gave her a fatherly squeeze. He picked up a plate for her, and she started placing her breakfast items on the china. Her mother hadn't cooked anything. There was a basket of bakery made croissants, some scrambled eggs that she knew her father had made, and some butter and jam. She also picked up a banana. That and some orange juice made up her morning meal. She talked and ate, appreciating the good conversation she was having with her aunt and uncle.

Rachel spent the rest of the day talking with her sister, who was to be her maid of honor, and packing for her honeymoon to

Oregon and Seattle. Neither she nor Steve had ever been to that part of the country, and they thought this would be a nice time of year to enjoy the sights.

The time finally came for everyone to drive to the temple. The clothes for the wedding were meticulously put in the car, and for the first time, Rachel felt a twinge of nerves. As her father started the car and began driving, she stared out the window of the vehicle and realized that her life was about to take a dramatic turn. A good turn, but a turn nonetheless.

The group arrived at the temple, and they noticed a couple of other cars in the parking lot. The groom and his family and groomsmen must have arrived. Rachel got out of the car, and she carefully removed her wedding dress. Everyone followed her from the parking lot to the brick paved path that invited congregants into the modern temple. The expansive wood floor was flawless, polished to the highest gleam. There were photos of the rabbis placed around the entryway, as well as numerous brass plaques inscribed with names of the temple's generous benefactors. Her parents had bestowed the temple with a substantial gift several years back, and her mother was delighted by the brass recognition. She had strutted like a peacock to their plaque, beaming from ear-to-ear when she first viewed their names.

The wedding party made their way into the dressing room designated for the bride. Rachel's bridesmaids helped her put on the beautiful wedding gown, and after she was buttoned up the back, she gazed at herself in the full-length mirror. The sleeves of the white dress were a satin capped style, and the bodice was a simple satin scoop neck that narrowed at the waist. The remainder of the satin dress was studded with flowers designed in seed pearls, giving the appearance of embroidery. Rachel felt a shiver run up her arms. She couldn't believe the vision she witnessed in the mirror. Rachel had thought of herself as a kid, not incredibly mature. Today, she felt like a woman. Her mother had chosen this dress, and Rachel had to admit that she liked it very much. She hadn't thought about her dress at the time of the purchase and the fitting because there were so many other plans that filled her mind. Now, it was all about her. Rachel could really admire herself and appreciate what was in store for her today and in the future. She glided out of the dressing room, and heard a collective gasp. Everyone stood still, looking at her with love in their eyes.

Her mother eyes even moistened.

Rachel's aunt was the first to speak. "Rachel, my dearest, you look lovely!" Everyone murmured in agreement.

Rachel looked expectantly at her mother. She didn't want to say a word to encourage a loving comment, but she certainly felt that her mom should say something. Her mother finally took her visual cue. "Yes, Rachel. You DO look lovely." That was it. No flowery sentiments or words of affection. Rachel's aunt even turned to her own sister giving a look of surprise and uncertainty. She didn't understand either why Delores couldn't be more expressive at a time like this. *Oh, well*, thought Rachel. *I'm moving forward with my life, loving mother or no loving mother.*

Photos were taken, the ketubah was signed, and it was show time. The sanctuary was decorated with red, pink and white roses. The orchestra sounded, and the wedding party began the march down the aisle. After they all reached the chuppah, the music changed, and everyone stood. Rachel walked down the aisle on the arm of her loving father. He gave her to Steve, and within minutes they became Mr. and Mrs. Steven Blum.

After the ceremony was over, and photos were taken of the beaming wedding party, they all jumped into the limos like they were celebrities, and were whisked off to start the party at the country club. The room was large and beautiful. Round-shaped tables were set with white linen tablecloths, and the centerpieces were red and white roses in crystal vases. Quartz crystals had been placed in the vases, and white tea candles were lit around them. Music was playing and guests were already dancing. The room crackled with laughter and chatter. The delicious dinner of mixed salad greens garnished with grated carrots, cranberries and sliced almonds and tossed with champagne vinaigrette as well as roasted chicken with mushrooms and wine sauce was a big hit. Glasses of champagne were clinked, and the bride and groom danced. The massive vanilla wedding cake was decorated with white fondant, roses made of icing, and filled with layers alternating between chocolate and vanilla cream. Rachel and Steve cut the cake which was devoured within minutes of the slices being served to the eager guests. Toasts had been made, and at the end of the festivities, Rachel tossed her bouquet, which ended up in her sister's outreached hands. The evening was a whirlwind of excitement and pure joy.

19

Rachel and Steve spent their wedding night at a hotel near the airport before departing for their trip. The honeymoon was glorious, and it seemed that they both appreciated that life together would be more special than they could ever have imagined. This was what they had hoped for as they had gone through their college years together. They were two young people, in love and ready to start their lives with work and play intermingled.

Oh, how Rachel loved those days. She and Steve had waited a decade before having children. They wanted to travel and just spend time together. Their college years, marriage, work, exploring the world and then the early years with the children all seemed like a hazy memory now. She couldn't quite believe how much they had lived during their years together.

Well, Rachel could dwell some other time on the challenges that she had faced since those glorious years. She decided that she needed to talk with Leah. Between the rain, her mother, the message from Steve and her mind wandering back to her earlier happier days, she needed a friendly ear to listen to her. Rachel pressed the numbers that she had pressed so many times before.

After two rings, Leah, who had Caller ID, answered the phone. "Hey, Rachel, how's it going?" Leah always sounded chipper.

"Hey, how are you doing?" Rachel inquired.

"I'm fine, but what's up with you? I know we talk all the time, but it's still early and I just spoke with you yesterday. What's going on with my dear sis? Is Mom making you nuts?" Rachel told Leah that she would be visiting Delores today, and Leah was no fool. She was always perceptive and she cared deeply for Rachel. If Rachel needed to talk now, that meant she was having some problem.

"Boy, you just cut right to the chase. I do have some stuff to tell you, but I want to know how life is going for you."

"Things are fine here. Nothing has changed all that much since we chatted yesterday. So, TELL me, girl, what is it?"

"Okay, okay. I am fine, just a bit annoyed. It has been a long day already." Leah chuckled at the other end of the line. "It's not funny, Leah, today really has been a bear."

"I didn't mean to laugh. I just know that this HAS to be about your visit with Mom. I don't know how you put up with her as much as you do. You're a better daughter than I am, that's for sure. You dutifully go there, at least three times a week, and she

20

treats you like garbage." Leah was always disturbed by how mean her mother could be to Rachel. She never understood why she acted this way towards her.

"I know. I'm crazy to subject myself to her slings and arrows. I guess I'm a glutton for punishment. I feel like I'm doing this for Dad. He wouldn't want her to be alone all the time."

"It's a shame she doesn't get that. I don't know how Dad put up with her, but you and I have had this conversation many times. So, tell me already! Enough stalling! What did she do now?" Leah wanted the details and pronto.

"Where to begin? Hmm. Okay, well, it started when I came into the lobby. My hair was a mess from the pouring rain. No, I didn't have an umbrella, so don't even ask."

"I wasn't going to say anything. I just want to know what Mom did."

"First, she commented on my ruined locks. Oh, we did talk about you, Bob and the kids. That made her happy."

"Good, Lord. Okay, cut to the good stuff. I have to leave in fifteen minutes. I could talk with you for hours, you know that. It's just that I have a meeting at the school." Rachel had told Delores that Leah was busy. She wasn't kidding.

"Okay, here goes. Mom started talking about the son of a resident."

Leah interrupted her story. "Oh no, oh no, don't tell me. She didn't?" Apparently, Leah knew exactly where this was headed.

"Oh yes she did. She told me that the son is single, never been married as a matter-of-fact. He's new to the area, and would I like to have dinner with him."

"What did you say?" Leah sounded shocked and intrigued at the same time.

"I told her no. There's no way I'm asking this guy to dinner. Then she said that she could tell her friend to tell his son to ask me out. I told her not to do that. Mom thought I was nuts and didn't see the problem, but I think she's going to butt out." Rachel felt a slight weight go off her shoulders now that she had relayed this information to Leah. It always felt cathartic to discuss life with her sister.

"Well good for you. You told her. I think she will respect your wishes, although she won't be happy about it. By the way, have you seen the guy?"

21

"I have."

"And?" Leah wanted details.

"And what?"

"And, is he attractive?" Leah was curious now.

"Yes, he is, but I don't care. Remember, I went through a divorce. I'm dealing with two obnoxious daughters and only one loveable child. I don't have time for some stupid relationship."

"Okay, I was just asking. I understand. I know you've been put through the wringer. I wouldn't want you to go through any other crap, so if you don't want to go out on a nice date, then don't." Leah meant every word, but Rachel wasn't sure that she liked her way of saying this.

"I have no way of knowing if this would be a nice date or not. Just because a guy owns his own business and is attractive doesn't mean he'll be nice or anything else."

"I know. I didn't mean to make you angry. I'm on your side, you know that." Leah almost sounded a little hurt.

"You didn't make me angry." Rachel sounded apologetic. "Believe me, you've been the ONLY one in this family who's been on my side. I won't ever forget that." Rachel was very sincere in her remark. Her sister was her comrade. "I just wanted to let you know the joys of my life." Rachel said that in a sarcastic tone, which her sister knew all too well. She was well aware that Rachel wasn't feeling much happiness these days, but she hoped that, in time, that would change.

"I'm glad that you called to tell me this. I feel for you, sis. Dealing with Mom has never been a treat, and with everything else that you have to manage, you now have her trying to play matchmaker. What fun, huh?"

"You know me. I'll survive." Rachel laughed when she said this. Although she knew she really would be okay. She wasn't being funny.

"That's true. You WILL survive. And maybe I can come in for a short visit soon. I'll check my calendar and see what I can do. I miss you." The last sentence was said so wistfully, it almost made Rachel want to cry.

"I miss you, too. I'd love it if you could come and stay with the kids and me for a while. Maybe we could visit Mom together. Oh, and we could also have fun." They both laughed at that comment. Being with Delores wasn't the fun part of a visit, and at least they

22

both understood that.

"Okay, well, I'll let you know ASAP. I have to make sure that Bob will be home for a while, at least long enough for me to escape for a long weekend or something. I'll see what I can do."

"Sounds great to me. I can't wait." They said goodbye to each other, and Rachel felt better. She let out a happy sigh after she clicked off her phone. Her sister was always there for her, and she felt blessed. Rachel had great friends as well, but when it came to thoughts about Delores, she sometimes needed to talk with the only person who knew what she had dealt with since childhood.

Chapter Three

The time had come for Rachel to get everything together for her daughters and son. This would not be a fun project, but she did get some pleasure out of knowing that she would have some time to herself. It was only for a weekend, but it would seem like a mini vacation. Rachel would miss them, would wonder what they were doing, but at the same time, she could use the weekend to just think and do anything she wanted to do. Not that she had any particular plans. But still, it would be nice to have the house all to herself for a couple of days.

Rachel packed some of their basic items, knowing full well that the girls would be picky about their clothes. She would place most of their items in their weekend bags, but not everything. They'd have to finish packing. Rachel could pack everything for David. He'd be fine with anything she chose. She grabbed their bags from the hall closet, and got to work.

After completing that task, she ate lunch. Just a sandwich would do for now. Maybe she'd make some interesting meals this weekend, things that she would enjoy eating, and not have to worry if the kids liked the food or not. It was a nice feeling to concentrate on what she wanted.

After lunch, she sat down on the couch. Rachel's day must have taken a lot out of her because she was startled awake from a nap. She heard the front door unlock and open. Rachel looked through bleary eyes at her watch. *It's 3:30 already? Gosh*! Rachel jumped up from the comfortable couch, patted her hair a bit, and went to the foyer. She couldn't believe she had slept for two hours.

Rebecca and Sarah came bounding in, dumping their backpacks on the floor of the foyer. David's backpack was still attached to him when he gave Rachel a quick hug and then ran to the kitchen.

"Girls, please put your backpacks in your rooms." She hated having to say that as often as she did. *Will they ever listen*?

Simultaneously they rolled their eyes at her. It was as if she was just asking too much from them to not leave their backpacks on the floor. They picked them up and thudded upstairs. She could hear the backpacks fall on their bedroom floors. Then they came back downstairs, and went right into the family room, sat down and turned on the television.

"Well, hello to you too. Oh, my day was fine, thanks for asking. I hope you two had a nice day." Rachel's sarcasm was leaking out.

The girls glanced at each other, and gave a look. Without saying anything, they were thinking, *what is her problem?*

David came in from the kitchen, snacking on a chocolate chip cookie. "Hi Mom!"

"Hi, sweetie, how was your day?" Rachel was always happy to hear any news that her son would tell her.

"Fine, I guess. Just work and lunch with my friends." That almost sounded like what her husband sometimes said when he'd come home from a long day at the office.

"So, everything is fine at school and you're doing well with your classes?"

"Yep." David sat down on one of the chairs in the family room and proceeded to watch television with his sisters.

Rachel decided it was time for them to leave. "Hey, guys, you know you're off to your dad's house this weekend, so let's get moving. I'm going to call Linda and tell her that we're on our way." There was no response from the girls, but David got up immediately.

"Uh, hellloooo, anybody listening?" Rebecca and Sarah looked at each other again, which for Rachel, was becoming an annoying habit, and they sighed. However, they did get up, folded their arms, and started walking towards the garage.

"Halt just one minute." Her daughters stopped and looked at her wondering what her problem was now.

"I did pack most of your things, but you might want to make sure everything is set to go, and then you can bring down your own bags. If it wouldn't be too much trouble of course." The last part was stated a bit sarcastically, but Rachel couldn't help it.

Once again, without one word to their mother, upstairs they went. Rachel got the phone to call her ex-husband's wife.

The phone rang three times, and then it was picked up. "Hello, Rachel." They had Caller ID, so there was never the chance of talking to a mysterious stranger.

25

"Hi Linda, how are you?" Why Rachel felt the need to be polite, she wasn't quite sure, although her voice implied that the question didn't really require an answer.

"I'm fine. Are you bringing the kids over now?" Linda wasn't Miss Warm and Friendly, at least not with Rachel.

"Yes I am. Okay with you I assume?" Rachel's tone indicated that she wasn't feeling like being very pleasant either right now.

"I'll see you soon." Linda hung up the phone. Rachel gave a look of "okkaaayy", and hung up her phone. She didn't like Linda one bit. But that didn't matter right now. She needed to get her kids off to their dad's house. Rachel shouted up the stairs. "You guys ready to rock and roll? Let's go!"

The girls came down, looking a little annoyed, David just content as usual. Rachel grabbed her keys, went to the garage and pushed the button to open the door. They all got into the car and off they went. It was still early enough that the traffic wasn't too bad. The weather had cleared up a bit, so that made the drive a bit easier. Rebecca and Sarah just gazed out of the windows, and David chattered away about what he anticipated he'd do this weekend.

"I hope dad wants to go out with just me at some point." He turned to look at his sisters in the back seat as he said, "And not even with you two. Just with me." There was no question that David needed a relationship with his father. There was no man in his life other than a teacher.

Rachel looked briefly at David in the passenger seat. "I'm sure he'd be happy to spend some time with just you. Maybe a meal out or a walk somewhere. Definitely ask him about that." Rachel hoped that Steve would comply.

Rachel drove into the little neighborhood where her ex lived. Even though it was just Steve and Linda living in the house, the place was quite large. That did help when the kids came for a visit, but they didn't buy it for anyone but themselves. Rachel meandered down Meadow Lane, and then into the circular driveway. She stopped the car in front of the large limestone porch. There were gorgeous flowers everywhere, including some in huge decorative pots. The imposing wood door opened, and out came Linda. She and Steve had been married for less than two years, but she commanded the household.

Linda was tall, with long wavy blond hair. She had her thin

26

arms folded around her tiny stomach. She was dressed in yellow Capri pants and a gauzy light pink blouse. She had that phony, no teeth showing, smile that Rachel despised. Rachel knew that, although Steve had never confirmed her thoughts, his wife hated the weekends with the kids. Well, Linda knew what she was getting into when she married Steve. Heck, she knew that well before when she had the affair with him. If she wanted him that much, she would have to accept his children as well.

Rachel and the kids got out of the car. The three got their own bags, and went inside, all without even a hello to their stepmother. Rachel didn't want to say anything either, but Linda spoke first anyway.

"Steve told me he'd be home a little earlier today. Are you picking them up on Sunday?" *Wow, she was already getting ready to boot the kids out the door.*

"Steve called me this afternoon." With that truly innocent comment, Linda briefly raised her eyebrows. Rachel continued on with the rest of her statement. "I don't know about Sunday. I'm thinking that he can bring them home because I may have other plans." Rachel didn't have any plans, but she wanted to give herself some flexibility.

"Okay. That should be fine. He'll have them home by dinnertime."

Rachel felt the desire to make things a little uncomfortable for Linda. "Oh, there's no need for Steve to worry about the timing. He's more than welcome to have dinner with the kids. I think it would be nice for all of them. I'll be in touch with him this weekend, and I'll let him know that he can spend as much time as he wants with his children. After all, he's their dad." Rachel ended that with her own phony smile. *Why did that feel SO good?*

Linda looked a bit put out by this, but she nodded. "Well, I guess that's it, right? See ya." And with that, Linda went inside and shut the door.

Rachel realized that she hadn't even said goodbye to her kids. For one moment she considering ringing the doorbell and going in to give the children a hug, but she decided not to bother. Her daughters would only be irritated with her, and David might be okay with it, but Rachel didn't want to disrupt their time in their dad's house. So, she got back in the car, and drove home. She pulled into the garage, went into the empty family room, and sank into the couch. Then, sitting there in total quiet, Rachel wondered what in the world she WAS going to do with her free time.

"I have NO plans!" Rachel was now talking out loud to herself. She debated calling her sister, but she thought it would be crazy talking with her again so soon. Besides, being three hours earlier, she was probably out and about, busy as always. All of Rachel's friends were still married some with children still at home; so they had their own lives this weekend.

She began to have this nagging feeling that she should take her mother out for dinner. Why, she didn't know. She had already had a difficult time with her this morning. Maybe she would offer to take Delores out on Sunday, the day the kids were coming back. That way, Steve would have to drop them off at home while she wasn't there. That would be nice. She'd try to be home soon after the kids got back, but she honestly didn't want to see Steve, or have him think that she didn't have anything going on in her life. Oh sure, spending time with her mother would really seem like Rachel had quite the life going for herself. Nothing is more exciting than spending time with a complaining, critical woman. Rachel picked up the phone and called her mother. The answering machine came on, so Rachel left a message.

"Hi Mom, it's Rachel. Hope you're having fun right now. I wondered if you and I could go to dinner on Sunday night. Let me know what you think. Bye." Rachel put the phone back in the cradle.

It seemed, by the way Delores talked, that she was never doing anything interesting. Rachel wondered where she could be now. Rachel turned on the television and flipped channels for a while, but she wasn't able to concentrate on watching anything. After about five minutes, the phone rang. The Caller ID showed that it was her mother. Rachel snatched the phone and hit talk.

"Hello?"

"Hello Rachel. It's your mother."

"Yes, hi Mom, how's it going?" Rachel wasn't sure if that was a good question to ask, but she tried to be polite.

"I was just freshening up for dinner tonight. I got your message." Then, Delores was silent.

"Okay, well, what do think? Would you like to go somewhere for dinner on Sunday?"

"I suppose so, if you'd like." *Please, don't get too excited*

Mom, thought Rachel. She decided to put this back on her mother.

"Well, would YOU like to go out? It's totally up to you, Mom." Rachel wanted to hear some enthusiasm from her mother. Did she want to have dinner with her daughter or not?

"So, you're not busy on Sunday?" Now Delores wanted to start questioning her life. Okay, Rachel was getting tired of this already. Her mother's tone always grated on her nerves. She was feeling her sarcastic ways leaking out of her.

"I would be busy if you'd want to go out with me. However, if you're not interested, I understand. Like I said, it's up to you." Rachel could hear the irritation in her own voice.

"I'm just surprised that you'd be available to go out with me on a weekend. For dinner." *Why couldn't their conversations ever be normal and pleasant?*

"The kids are with Steve, so I just thought it would be nice to have dinner with you." Who was Rachel kidding? *NICE? To have dinner with Delores? Come on*!

"Oh, I see. So, there's no one around right now." Delores had a matter-of-fact tone. Like, now it's obvious to me, I get it.

"Mom, I'm happy having a little time to myself. It's so rare what with the kids and all. But, this isn't about me. I called to see if YOU want to go out. Can you just say yes or no?" Rachel was at the end of her rope.

"Well, of course I can keep you company, whatever you'd like, dear." Still, Delores could not say, "Yes, I'd love to have dinner with you." Rachel felt like screaming.

"As long as it's what YOU'D like, I'd be happy to take you out." Rachel was going to make sure that she had the final say as to how this conversation would play out. She needed to make it clear that she wasn't desperate for company.

"Okay, then. What time will you come here?"

"About 5:30 or so. Is that okay?"

"Yes. Whatever is best for you." How is it that Delores constantly deflected from herself to make everything seem to be about Rachel? Rachel was not the self-centered one here.

"As long as it works for you, I'll be there at 5:30. If you need to change the time or cancel just let me know." At this point, Rachel was praying for the call to cancel.

"Okay, I'll see you then." And with that, Delores hung up the phone. There was no *Thanks Rachel,* or *Have a nice evening.*

29

Looking forward to see you Sunday. How about a goodbye?

Rachel hung up the phone, wondering why on earth she bothered. *What was it about her that she was almost always treated like she was garbage?* Her husband had cheated on her, her daughters looked at her like Rachel was something they stepped in, and her mother, the one who was supposed to love her unconditionally, practically spat on her. She didn't get it. She was a kind and considerate person. Rachel always tried to put others' needs in front of her own. Maybe that was the problem. She needed to respect herself more.

Rachel got up from the couch and went to the kitchen. She made herself some wonderful comfort food of linguine with olives, tomatoes, garlic and olive oil. She sat in front of the television and enjoyed every bit of her creation. This was the life!

Later in the evening, after Rachel had a refreshing bath, she laid down on the couch in her pajamas. It did feel good to be able to do whatever she wanted, especially in her own home. It was quiet without the kids being around, but she planned to relish every moment.

At eleven o'clock the phone rang. The sound startled her, and she felt her heart thumping inside her chest. *Who in the world would be calling her this late?* Rachel tried not to panic, but she stumbled to the phone. She breathed a massive sigh of relief when she saw that it was her sister. Of course, it was only eight there. Rachel picked up the phone.

"Hello? Leah?"

"Hello. Sorry it's so late, but you know it's only eight here."

"Hey, no problem. You know I'm always happy to hear from you. What's up?"

"You sounded overwhelmed this morning, so I worked it out to come and visit everyone next weekend. I hope that sounds good to you."

"Yes! That sounds perfect! Wow, you worked fast."

"I knew my sister needed me. I assume I can stay with you?"

"Yes, I insist that you do. What would I do without you?"

'I feel the same way about you. I asked Bob if this would work out, and he was cool about it. They'll all manage without me. Can you let Mom know that I'll be coming for a visit? It's too late to call her now, and I don't feel like talking with her anyway." Leah did things her way for sure. If she didn't want to talk, she wouldn't, and she didn't care.

"Yeah, I'll tell her. I'll be taking her out for dinner on Sunday." Rachel thought she would just drop that little bomb for her sister.

"You're taking our mother out for dinner? Okay. Why?"

"Because your sister is an idiot, that's why. I don't know what I was thinking, but I'm stuck now."

"Yes, indeed you are. Don't tell me that she laid the guilt-trip on you into this night out?" Leah didn't want to hear that at all.

"Well, not exactly. I don't know. The kids are with their dad this weekend, and I don't have anything going on. So, what the heck? This wasn't the best decision I've ever made, but I hope she appreciates my gesture."

"Ha! Yeah, right. Delores appreciating anyone's efforts? You're kidding, right? I hope it works for you. Maybe you should have told her that you would go out with that man's son. Then, you'd be doing something fun."

"Very, VERY funny! Oh, you are such a hoot, aren't you? Yes, and I'm just so sure that this wonderful man wants to date a woman who was cheated on and has three kids, two of whom might drive him insane. Ah, yes, that's every man's dream."

"Okay, okay, I understand. I was just kidding. I think it's sweet, although crazy, that you want to take Mom out. Just be prepared that you're going to be beyond miserable by the end of the night."

"By the end of the night? Try the moment I have her in the car on the way to the restaurant. Which reminds me that I had better make a reservation for dinner. Maybe that place that she always went to with Daddy."

"Oh, that would be nice. At least you know that she'll like it. Fine French food. Can't go wrong with that. Fancy schmancy, huh?" The menu was good, but it was a somewhat casual restaurant.

"Nothing but the best for Delores, you know that. What are you up to this weekend?"

"Taking the kids all over the place. Bob and I are going out to dinner with friends. Just the usual." Leah's "usual" was an on-the-go pace. It was nice that she and Bob could always spend some quality time together. She chose a great husband.

"Well, enjoy. And thanks for arranging to come in town. We're all going to be glad to see you. Let me know your timing, and I'll pick you up at the airport."

31

'Okay, thanks. And good luck with Mom. Let me know how it goes!"

"Will do. Talk to you soon."

"Bye!" They both hung up their phones, and Rachel, once again, felt better now. She went to bed.

Chapter Four

Rachel woke up to a lovely Saturday. She slept in a little then showered and went downstairs to consume a breakfast of a banana and some coffee. That was all she felt like eating right now. There would be no rules as to what she ate or when she ate. She didn't have to set any wonderful examples for her children.

Rachel called during the day to make the 6:00 dinner reservation at Bistro Marseille.. She went out to do a little shopping, but she spent most of Saturday at home. She figured that she'd better take advantage of having the house to herself. Rachel did this whenever her kids were at their dad's house. It felt good to be there without the noise and without having to be the adult. Rachel called Steve to let him know that she would be out with her mother on Sunday night. When he and the kids were finished with dinner, Steve could drop them off at home. He agreed that would be fine, and that was the end of their conversation.

Sunday rolled around, and Rachel relaxed at home again. She made up the spare bedroom for Leah's visit because she wanted to be completely ready for her stay. Rachel was already looking forward to seeing her sister. They would enjoy every moment of their time together, and Leah would join Rachel with a visit to their mother. Thankfully Leah would also visit Delores by herself during her stay. Talk about a break for Rachel!

Before she knew it, Rachel had to get herself ready to take her mother to dinner. She dressed in a comfortable pink and lilac spring dress. The sleeves were short, and the dress draped nicely over her body. She wore a pair of sandals, and put on her pearls. Hopefully her mother wouldn't say anything about Rachel's appearance. Rachel looked good, but it was better to not hear anything than to be criticized again. Her mother could always find some reason to be nasty.

Rachel made her way to the retirement home. This time there wasn't a drop of rain to dampen her. She walked into the lobby, looking for Delores. She perused the room and she saw Ben's son sitting close by. He smiled at her, and glanced at her pretty outfit. She gave a quick smile, and then looked for her mother. She felt like a fool just standing there, and because she was uncomfortable, she thought she needed to say something. She looked at Don. "I was just looking for my mother. "We're going out for dinner." Why she felt the need to explain herself, she didn't know. Don stood up and placed his hands in his pockets.

"I'm waiting for my dad. We're going out also." Rachel smiled. She didn't know what else to say and fortunately, at that moment, she saw her mother walking towards the lobby. Rachel waved at her mother, but her mother didn't wave back. However, she smiled a little when she saw Don. Rachel walked towards Delores. Instead of her mother saying hello or hugging her, Delores went over to Don.

"Hello Don. How are you this evening?"

"I'm doing well, Mrs. Weinstein, how are you?"

"I'm fine. Don, have you met my daughter Rachel?" Rachel wasn't too concerned. It was normal for people to be introduced to other people. She told herself that this is how one behaves in society.

"No, not formally." Don looked at Rachel with fondness.

"Don, this is my daughter, Rachel Blum. Rachel this is Don Levy." Don shook Rachel's hand. Hmm, a very nice handshake. Don defined tall, dark and handsome. His hair was almost black with a bit of a curl to it. He had broad shoulders and was very fit. Well, whatever. Rachel didn't care. She wasn't interested, and she was sure he wouldn't be either.

"Nice to meet you." Don said very smoothly.

Rachel smiled. "Nice to meet you too." She looked at her mother. "Mom, we had better get going. I have reservations at your favorite French restaurant."

"Oh, really?" Delores actually seemed interested.

"Yes. I thought you might enjoy eating there again."

Delores said goodbye to Don and he said goodbye to her. He waved at Rachel, and she returned the gesture, and then Rachel and her mother walked outside. After opening the passenger side of the car for Delores and shutting it, Rachel made her way to the driver's side and got in. Delores started talking.

"Didn't I tell that you he was a nice man?" Rachel didn't care what her mother told her, but she knew she did not want to have this conversation with her.

"He seems friendly, but it's hard to tell with just a mini introduction. So, what have you been doing this weekend, Mom?" Rachel wanted to move on.

"Not much." Delores wasn't interested in talking about her activities. "I'm telling you, he's very sweet. His father is a charming man, and I believe Don is like his father. He's got a good job, and he's a good looking fellow." *Oh, no, the evening wasn't off to a good start,* thought Rachel, so she decided to nip this in the bud.

"Mom, please." Rachel was now ready to plead.

"Well, it can't hurt you to be a little interested." Delores was clearly annoyed by Rachel's attitude.

"Actually, yes it can. I don't need to be interested. This is supposed to be an evening for the two of us. A chance to go out to a nice restaurant. Can't we just do this?"

"Fine." Delores seemed to be done talking, but it turned out that she had more to say. "Mothers and daughters should be able to discuss these things." Now Delores was in a huff. Rachel thought this statement was quite amusing. Since when did her mother ever want to discuss anything with Rachel, let alone relationships?

"Yes, maybe they should, but not tonight." Rachel concentrated on driving to the nearby restaurant. Her mother didn't speak, and Rachel was grateful for the silence.

They arrived at the quaint restaurant. The parking lot was half full, so Rachel had no problem finding a spot. She got out of the car, and then helped her mother out as well. Delores could manage perfectly well getting out by herself, but she liked the attention. It was a small price to pay as far as Rachel was concerned. If Delores liked the assistance, she'd have it.

Rachel opened the heavy oak door to the restaurant, and let her mother go in first. Then Rachel went up to the reception desk. The charming restaurant had a rustic wood entrance and antique sconces on the wall, dimly lighting the entry. A lovely young woman greeted them with a sweet smile. "How may I help you this evening?"

"I have a reservation for Blum."

The lady looked at her list and smiled. She took a pen and made a mark. "One moment please."

35

A young man walked up to the desk, and the hostess handed him two menus.

"Right this way please." He sounded very formal.

The man led them just beyond the entryway to their table. The restaurant had a comfortable bistro feel to it. There were photos of France along the walls, and the tables were wooden with lovely patinas. Delores and Rachel were seated, and he gave them their menus and walked away. They both looked at the menus without speaking. Rachel became uncomfortable, so she started talking.

"Mom, I've talked with Leah, and she's coming into town next weekend. Exciting, huh?"

"Oh, that is nice. Why is she coming in now? I'm really surprised that she has any time to get away."

"I think she wants to visit and see what's going on around here. She'll be staying at my home while she's in town."

"That should be very nice for the two of you. I'm sure that the kids will be happy to spend some time with her as well. It will be good for all of you." The last sentence sounded loaded, but Rachel knew that she was being ultra-sensitive at the moment. Besides, she didn't have the strength to figure out her mother's thought process right now.

"Well, I couldn't be happier that Leah will be here. She'll also be visiting with you quite a bit."

A waiter came over to tell them about the dinner specials. He took their drink orders, which consisted of sparkling water for both of them. When he returned with the beverages, he wrote down their dinner orders. Delores chose a chicken breast with lemon butter sauce, and Rachel, a true seafood lover, chose the bouillabaisse. Moments later, he brought some warm crusty bread and creamy butter. If nothing else good came of this evening, the food was sure to be a hit.

The waiter brought their salads, and they began to enjoy those, eating in silence. Rachel knew that she and her mother should be able to talk and enjoy each other's company. She never understood why their relationship had been so strained over the years. Rachel didn't recall behaving badly, and yet her earliest memories were of a cold, standoffish mother. It seemed that Delores never approved of anything Rachel did.

Rachel glanced around the room, taking in the ambiance. "So, Mom, what do you think of the restaurant now? Does it seem the same as when you would come here with Daddy?" Rachel wasn't sure whether asking her mother this question was a good idea or a bad idea, but she didn't know what else to say at the moment.

Delores stopped eating and looked around the room. "I guess it seems the same. I don't think anything looks too different. I hope the food is as good as it used to be. The salad is fine." Delores resumed eating.

Rachel was quickly done with that subject, so she moved on. "The kids will be home tonight. Would you like to come to the house and see them before I take you back to the residence?" Rachel wasn't sure if she'd just entered the Twilight Zone because she couldn't believe the words she heard coming out of her own mouth.

Delores looked up at her, almost startled. "Well, I guess that would be fine. It's been a while since I've seen them." She said this like she was questioning the decision in her own mind.

"Okay, then, it's settled. You can sit with them for a few minutes and chat. The kids will be out of school soon, and they'll be very busy. They'll visit when they have the chance, but spending some time with them tonight would be great." Rachel looked at her mother hopefully.

"Yes, I'm sure it would be fine to talk with them for a little bit. I know they have school tomorrow, so you won't keep me there long, right?" Rachel wasn't quite sure if her mother just didn't want to stay too long for her own sake or if she was actually being considerate of the children's sleep schedule.

"That's right," she reassured her mother, "just for a little while."

After a few minutes, their salad plates were cleared. This was going to be a long meal if they couldn't find anything interesting to say to one another. Rachel filled the void with information about what her kids would be doing during the summer. At least that way, her mother would have some knowledge of their upcoming activities when she was with the kids tonight.

Rebecca was going to be taking art classes. She was an incredible painter, creating landscapes and almost anything from the outdoors. She had won some competitions during the several years that she had been expressing her creative side with canvas and a paint brush. Rachel was thrilled to frame those pieces, and she placed them on walls all over the house.

37

Sarah, because she could now drive, was going to be working at a store in the mall. She loved clothes, and a place where she shopped with a bit too much frequency, was more than willing to give her a summer job when she applied. Despite her teenager attitude with Rachel, she was smart, had a good eye for fashion, and she had a pleasant nature when she was doing what made her happy. The store was also giving her a discount for her purchases. So, Sarah was beside herself with joy when she told Rachel about this position. Rachel had not seen her so animated in a long time.

David was going to be at summer camp for one month. It wasn't an overnight camp, but he would be gone the entire day. He was excited about going, and his friends were also attending this camp. This would be the perfect summer for him. He was already talking about the activities that the camp would have each day.

So, Rachel filled her mother in on some of the details, Delores listened, and they consumed their entrees. She nodded at some of the things that Rachel told her, but she didn't interject with any comments. Finally, their entrees had been consumed, and they both agreed that the meal had been terrific. Rachel asked Delores if she would like any dessert or some tea or coffee. Her mother graciously declined the offers, so Rachel merely asked for the check. She paid the bill, and they stood up to leave.

As they were departing from the restaurant, the waiter and the hostess thanked them for coming. Delores even told them what a nice meal she had, and the staff told her that they hoped she'd be back soon. Rachel felt a momentary panic set in thinking that she might have to bring her mother back, but she pretended that she didn't hear them as she was opening the door for her mother. They walked to the car, and Rachel gratefully drove home. The meal had been perfect, but the company left a little bit to be desired.

They drove the short distance to the house, and Rachel steered the car into the garage. She and her mother got out of the car and went into the house. The television in the family room was blaring. *This is just great*, thought Rachel. *Mom can see how well disciplined my children are.*

"Hey kids!" Rachel shouted over the television noise. They didn't hear her at all. Rachel saw the remote sitting on the table, scurried over and grabbed it, turning off the television. The three of them looked at her with perplexed expressions. Delores merely stood watching them at the entrance of the room.

"Mom, what are you doing? We were watching that!" Rebecca expressed her ire at her mother for turning off a favorite show.

"I KNOW that, but your grandmother is here, and she'd like to chat with you guys. I also want to know how your weekend went. If that's okay with you?" Rachel prayed that her children would hear the desperation in her voice. She wanted the kids to make a good impression.

"Grandma's here?" The three of them turned their heads and saw her standing there.

Delores smiled at them and said hello. Rachel motioned her over to the seating area. The kids were not used to her visiting, except on holidays. They didn't say a word.

"So, how was your weekend? What did you do?" Rachel looked at the three of them, hoping that at least one of her children would say something. She knew that they were not usually this mute.

Finally, David began speaking. "Um, we hung around with Dad. We went out to eat, and we even went to a movie. Dad and I went for a walk this morning while Rebecca and Sarah were still sleeping." David was looking at his grandmother seemingly curious as to why she was there.

Surprisingly, Delores spoke and did so with what appeared to be a genuine smile. "It sounds like you had a nice time with your father."

"Yeah. It was great." David still stared at her, eyes wide.

"And did you two have fun?" Rachel wanted to make sure that her daughters had a nice weekend. She knew it wasn't easy for any of her kids to be without their dad for days on end.

"Uh, huh." That was all Sarah could say.

Rachel realized that she wasn't going to get anything else out of them right now, possibly not at all. She decided to give her mother a chance to be alone with the kids.

"Mom, I have a call to make, so you should chat with the kids for a little while. Then, I'll get you back home."

"Okay, that's fine." Delores looked at her and smiled. Rachel assumed that the cheerier disposition was for the benefit of her kids, but she was more than happy to accept it.

Rachel didn't really HAVE to make a call, but she decided to call Leah. It was always nice to bend her sister's ear, so she went upstairs to her bedroom and picked up the phone. Amy, Leah's fifteen-year-old daughter answered the phone.

"Hi, Aunt Rachel! How are you?" Now, THIS child was happy to hear from her. What a concept. A young lady who wanted to be civil to her. "Hi, Amy, I'm fine. How are you doing?"

"I'm doing GREAT! Did Mom tell you that I'm in "My Fair Lady" at school? I'm Eliza!" She sounded very proud of herself.

"Yes, she did tell me, and I think that's terrific. I bet you're having a wonderful time with this production. When is the play?"

"It's in three weeks. I am SO excited! My drama teacher thinks I'm a natural." And Rachel believed that as well. Amy loved being the center of attention, and at least she found a healthy and constructive way to make it work for herself.

"Well, I'm excited for you! I'm sure you'll be a big hit." Rachel was truly happy for Amy. She was a sweet girl. Leah had been a good, nurturing mother to her and to her brother. *I guess it helps to have a home where there's a mom and a dad and a lot of love*, thought Rachel.

"Thanks! I'll let you know how it goes. Do you want to talk with Mom?"

"Yes I do. Good luck with your performance!"

"Thanks, Aunt Rachel. I'll get Mom. Hang on just a second." A moment later, Leah had grabbed the phone.

"Hi again! How's life? Did you and Mom have your dinner together?"

"Yes, we did. I think she enjoyed it, at least the meal part. I brought her over here to see the kids for a bit. She's downstairs with them right now. By the way, I did tell her that you're coming into town. That made her happy."

"Wow, it sounds like it's been quite an evening. I guess you needed a quick escape, so that's why you called, huh?" Leah's voice sounded amused.

Rachel laughed. "Well, kind of. I figured she should have some time with her grandchildren. They looked shocked to see her. It's kind of weird. Am I a lousy daughter and mother not to bring them together more often?" Rachel oozed guilt.

"No, you're not a lousy anybody. You're a wonderful mom and a good daughter. Mom hasn't been the best mother, and you've had a lot on your plate with the kids. Give yourself a break, Rachel."

"Yeah, sure. You seem to have done things a whole lot better than I have. You have a great husband, and your kids are polite. I wish I knew your secret."

"It's called 'luck.' Pure and simple."

"I wish I had some 'luck' if that's all it takes. Anyway, to be continued when you get here. I just wanted to let you know how everything went and that Mom knows you'll be here soon. I better get back downstairs."

"Good luck with everything. I'll let you know my flight time soon, and I'll meet you at the baggage claim area."

"Sounds great to me. Leah, I can't wait to see you!" Rachel felt like a kid waiting for her birthday to arrive.

"I'm looking forward to seeing you and the kids. Love you!"

"Love you too! Bye!"

Rachel went back downstairs. She found her mother sitting on the couch with the three kids, and the television was not on which was a good sign. David was chattering away, and his sisters and Delores were listening. It was nice to see some normal family interaction.

They all turned to look at Rachel, and David started to speak. "Mom! Grandma said that she'll be happy to come over here during the summer and spend some time with us! Cool, huh?" His eyes were practically dancing with joy. *Oh, yes, that's VERY cool* thought Rachel. *What happened while I was upstairs for two second*s? Rachel supposed that she should be happy about this. If her mom wanted to hang out with the kids, that would be very nice.

"Oh, yes, that IS nice!" Rachel wasn't sure if she could say much more.

Then, Delores piped up. "Yes, David and the girls seem to want me to come over every now and then. Maybe for some meals and we can all eat together. I assume that's okay with you, dear?" Maybe Delores did want to be part of her daughter's family.

Rachel attempted to muster up some enthusiasm "Of course it is Mom. That will be great!" *Oh, boy, that will be just SO great!* Delores smiled, almost like the cat that swallowed the canary. Rachel tried to figure out if the kids really did invite Delores or if Delores hinted at something. She was surprised that her mother was showing this much interest in her family, but she'd go with it. If this was all nice and sincere, maybe she and her mother could have a better relationship. This was the only family Delores

41

had in town. There weren't that many friends either. Most were couples who she and Aaron saw socially, but when he died, so many things changed.

"Mom, are you ready for me to take you back home now?"

"I think that would be a good idea. The kids have to get some good sleep before school tomorrow." Delores smiled at them.

So, Delores got up and the kids did as well. She hugged them all and said she'd see them soon. It was a nice picture. Everyone seemed happy. Rachel and Delores got in the car and drove back to the home.

Rachel parked the car, helped her mother out, and walked with her into the building. Things were pretty quiet now as it was getting late. They stood in the lobby to say goodbye.

"Thank you, Rachel. The meal was very nice and I'm glad I had a chance to spend some time with you and my dear grandchildren." Rachel was stunned. Her mother was being so nice. *What DID happen in her family room while she was upstairs?*

"You're welcome, Mom. I'm glad you had such a good time. The glass doors slid open, and in walked Ben and Don Levy. They were returning from their dinner.

"Hi, Ben! How are you? Did you and Don have a nice dinner?" Delores was as happy as a clam. Ben greeted them.

"Hello, Delores. Dinner was great! Don and I had some tasty Italian food tonight." Ben had obviously enjoyed a nice evening with his son.

"Ben, I don't believe you've met my daughter, Rachel. Rachel, this is Don's father Ben." Rachel thought Ben seemed like a pleasant man. Like his son, he was quick to smile. He had white hair with touches of gray and his eyes were brown. He was of average height and build, and had a very cheerful manner.

Ben held out his hand to shake Rachel's. "How wonderful to meet you!" Rachel responded in kind.

"How was your meal?" Don looked at Rachel.

"Oh, it was great. Mom and I had a nice time. Everything was good." Rachel hurried along with her answer. She wasn't sure she wanted to start having a conversation. She was ready to go home. "Well, it was nice seeing both of you, and Mom, get some good sleep." Rachel was already moving towards the door.

Delores wasn't thrilled that Rachel was leaving while there was an opportunity for her to talk with Don. "Okay, well, good bye." Delores sounded a bit disappointed, but Rachel was happily on her way home.

Chapter Five

During the week, as the kids were in school, Rachel would take her time after they left. She would sit down for a quiet breakfast, and then she used her treadmill. Oh, the joy of that experience, but she had to exercise. After she tortured herself using the monster, she would shower, and go about her life. Because of the alimony and the inheritance from her father, she was financially secure. She could visit friends, shop and sometimes even take adult learning classes. The subjects that she preferred were cooking, gardening and travel.

It had been a while since she had taken her mother out for dinner, so Rachel decided she should call and find out about visiting.

"Hello?"

"Hi Mom. I was wondering if I could come for a visit."

"Sure, I'm here."

"Okay, I'm on my way." Rachel put the phone back in its cradle, picked up her purse and headed for her car.

Rachel arrived at the home within ten minutes. The traffic was light and the weather was nice. So far so good. She just hoped that her mother would be in a good mood. Things went well the last time they saw each other, but one never knew. She parked her car and went inside. Rachel didn't see her mother, but there was Don Levy, sitting by himself. *Was this guy always here? I thought he worked. It is a weekday after all.* He saw her, smiled, and got up and walked towards her. *Oh, no, here we go!*

"Hi. Rachel."

Rachel put on her best smile. "How are you, Don?"

"Fine thanks. I guess you're here to see your mom?"

"Yep, that's right. And you're here to see your dad?" *Wow, this is really stimulating conversation*!

"Yes, I am. So, do you come here almost every day?"

"Uh, well, I get here as often as I can. I'm pretty busy. With three kids, I always have stuff going on." Rachel wanted to make sure this guy knew that she was a mom and had no time.

"I think it's great that you do make the time to see your mom. I'm sure she appreciates it. Do your kids get to see her much?"

"Sometimes. They're pretty busy, but every now and then they see her." Rachel wanted this to end. She really didn't want to share anything about her life with him. He seemed pleasant enough, but she didn't want to encourage any relationship. Not even a slight friendship.

"How old are your kids?"

"I have two daughters who are fourteen and sixteen and a son who is twelve." *Please, no more questions!*

"Wow, teenagers! You must have been pretty young when you had them."

Rachel laughed. "Not really." *Come on, he's got to be kidding! I know that I don't look that young.* Internally Rachel struggled. She felt she should be polite and ask him something about himself. Not that she wanted to, but Rachel decided to ask a question that she was pretty sure she knew the answer to because of what Delores had already told her about Don. It seemed like an appropriate query considering the current conversation. "Do you have kids?"

"No. I don't have any kids. Actually, I've never been married." Don seemed a bit uncomfortable answering that, almost like he felt embarrassed by not ever having lived the domestic life. Rachel suddenly felt awful about asking that question. She certainly didn't want to make him feel ashamed or anything. She decided to put a positive spin on that so he would feel better.

"Oh, well, then your life has probably been a bit more interesting. Kids can be wonderful, but they can also put a little damper on life here and there." *THAT comment made her seem like an evil woman. She didn't want him thinking she didn't want or love her own children.*

"Well, I don't know how interesting my life has been, but I've been happy I guess."

"I'm sure you have been." Rachel prayed for this moment to end.

"Does your husband ever come with you when you visit your mom? I haven't seen you with him, and I've heard that some spouses don't want to have to deal with the in-laws all the time."

Rachel wanted to sink into the floor. Of course, she had no

45

choice but to answer the innocent question. She could feel herself turning slightly red. "I'm divorced." There was really no other way to say it.

Don looked surprised by her admission "Oh, I'm sorry. I didn't mean to pry." He seemed genuinely concerned that he might have stepped over the line.

"No, no, that's okay. You had no way of knowing." *Or DID he?* She knew things about him because of Delores. His father could have told Don tidbits about Rachel too.

"Well, still..." He seemed at a loss for words, so Rachel thought that perhaps he really didn't know anything about her.

"It's fine. It's not a secret, so no harm done." Rachel wanted to put his mind at ease.

"I have another question for you. I was wondering if…" In the nick of time, Rachel saw her mother walking towards her.

"Hi Mom!" Rachel had never been so grateful to see her mother in all her life. She even sounded too elated to her own ears. She didn't want Don to continue wondering about anything.

"Hi Rachel. Hi Don! How are you today?" Delores was always friendly with him. Don smiled at her.

"I'm doing great today. How 'bout you?" He was so nice to Delores. It was quite sweet.

"I'm feeling wonderful." *Wow, wonderful?* Rachel's couldn't believe what she heard.

"I'm glad. I was just getting ready to ask Rachel if she knew of any plans that the home has here for summer fun. Maybe you could tell me if there are any particular activities that my dad might enjoy?"

So THAT was what he was wondering? Rachel felt like an idiot for even thinking that Don was interested in her and was wondering if she would like to go out with him. *How self-centered could she be?* He just heard, from her own lips, that she was divorced with three children. *Of course he's not interested!* Not that it mattered to her. *What a relief,* thought Rachel.

"Well, I don't think there are any particular plans, although they do have nice picnics depending upon the weather. There's also the opportunity to see an incredible display of fireworks on Independence Day. I'm sure your dad can get a list or ask someone about anything." Delores tried to be helpful.

"Okay, well, thanks. I appreciate that information." He looked at Rachel as though he was thinking something, although she had no idea what. Rachel really didn't care. She was ready, oddly enough, to spend time with her mother.

"Mom, should we go sit down somewhere?" Rachel didn't want to be rude, but she didn't want to wait around until Ben came to join his son.

Delores spoke to Rachel while looking at Don. "Why don't we sit here with Don, at least until his father comes to talk with him." This wasn't really a question that Delores posed. It was more a statement of fact. This is what Delores intended to do, and Rachel had to comply.

"If that's okay with Don?" Rachel looked at him, questioning what would work for him at the moment.

"Sure, if you'd like to sit with me, it would be fine." Don led the way to the couches. Rachel hoped that Ben would show up soon. Sitting with Don and her mother could only lead to disaster. Maybe she was being overly dramatic in her own mind, but she knew that her mother wanted to play matchmaker, and Rachel not only didn't want to date anyone, she was sure that Don didn't want to date her either.

"So, Don, how has your work been coming along? Do you like living here and being able to do your job from home?" Delores was totally focused on Don.

Rachel couldn't believe that her mother could speak so easily to this man. She never seemed to be too concerned about what her own daughter was doing. *Why did she care at all about somebody else's child? Not that Don was a child. Rachel didn't feel that way at all. She couldn't help but think that he was quite an adult male specimen.*

"Oh, it's been great. I'm happy to be here. I've just been working and visiting dad, but it's going well."

"Just working and coming here? That's ALL? You need a bit more of a life than that, Don. You should be out having some fun."

Rachel was mortified. Her mother sounded too enthusiastic. *How could she push like this?* Rachel knew that her mother wanted the two of them to go out, but this was ridiculous.

"Truly, I'm doing well. I'm just getting adjusted to living here. There's plenty to keep me occupied." Don was very kind to respond so graciously to Delores.

47

"I'm glad that your life is going well, but I think it's important for a nice young man to get out and socialize a bit." *Would she never stop*? Rachel didn't know what to say so she sat there, paralyzed.

"I'm sure I will soon enough. I'm just happy to spend some time with my dad." And just as Don said that, Rachel noticed Ben walking towards them.

"Hi, all! Nice to see you Rachel!" Rachel stood to greet him, as did Don.

"It's very nice to see you. I hope you're doing well?" Rachel was genuinely glad to see him.

"I'm wonderful, thank you. Other than seeing your lovely mother, what have you been up to these days?" Delores smiled from ear-to-ear upon hearing the compliment.

"Oh, I'm keeping busy. I'm excited because my sister will be coming in town soon. You'll probably get to see her too." Rachel wanted to keep this short and sweet. It was time for Don and his dad to have some father and son time.

"Well, that is nice! Your mother has mentioned her. She lives in California, right?"

"Yes, that's right. She's been there for many years now."

Maybe Don could sense that Rachel was uneasy because he looked at her with that nice smile that was always ready to shine. "Dad, we should let the ladies have their conversation. Why don't we go to another area and talk?"

"Well, if that's what you want to do, that's fine with me. Hope I'll see you soon Rachel."

"Oh, I'm sure you will. Have fun!" The two men departed and started talking with each other.

Rachel looked at her mother in disgust. Under her breath, she began to lecture her mother. "I cannot BELIEVE you! What WERE you thinking?"

Delores looked somewhat shocked by Rachel's ire. "What are you talking about?"

"What am I talking about? Oh, sure, you have no clue as to what you did." Rachel was officially pissed, and she had no intention of letting her mother off the hook on this one.

"Rachel, I really don't know what I did. Goodness, why are you so angry with me?" She stared at her daughter as if she had just shouted profanities at her, and Rachel felt tempted to do just that.

"Okay." Rachel folded her arms in defiance. "You want to play dumb, fine. I'll spell it out for you."

Delores's jaw dropped. She couldn't believe that Rachel would be this rude to her. "Rachel! Honestly, you are out of line here!" Rachel may have been angry with her mother, but now Delores was aghast at Rachel's behavior towards her.

"I'M out of line? You've got to be kidding me! Mother, you said some things that should not have been said." Rachel realized that she was raising her voice, so she turned down the volume. They were sitting in the lobby, and she noticed a couple of older people glancing over at the two of them.

"What did I say that was so bad?" Delores was still flabbergasted by Rachel's anger.

Rachel leaned in towards her mother so that she could more quietly lecture her. She didn't need anyone over hearing their conversation. "I didn't think it was appropriate that you told Don to go out and socialize. Telling him that a nice young man should be going out? Why did you say that to him?"

"Because he should be having fun. Why do you care that I said that to him?"

"Listen, Mom. You never care what I'M doing, so why would you care what he's doing? I know that you want him to go out with me, but that isn't going to happen. You practically told him that the two of us should go out."

"Rachel, that's terrible. I do care about what you're doing, you know that." Rachel gave her a very skeptical look. Delores didn't like that one bit. "Rachel, I mean it, I DO care. And I wasn't insinuating that he should ask you out. I was only telling him to have a life. That's all. There was no ulterior motive here." Delores was annoyed now, and she folded her arms across her chest. Rachel knew there was no winning this battle. Her mother would not admit any wrong doing, and all that happened was they were both mad at each other. *So, why did I bother coming here again?* Rachel was angry with herself now.

"Okay, Mom, whatever you say. I just think you need to stay out of Don's personal life."

Delores answered her very flippantly. "He doesn't have one, so don't worry." Rachel thought that was funny, so she gave a

49

little laugh at that.

Delores looked at her with surprise. "What's so funny?"

"I just got a kick out of you saying that you weren't going to worry about Don's personal life because he doesn't have one." Delores didn't seem to get her own joke, so she obviously didn't intend for her statement to be considered amusing. Rachel couldn't win.

Delores was still peeved at Rachel. "I don't want to talk about this anymore." She paused for only a couple of seconds. "I still don't know why you would refuse to date him."

"I thought you said you didn't want to talk about this anymore." Rachel scowled at her.

"Well, so what would YOU like to discuss? Maybe how I don't care about you?" Delores looked at Rachel with defiantly raised brows.

"No, I don't think we should go down that road right now. Let's just talk about the rest of the family."

"I can't believe that you think I don't care about you. You're my daughter. Of course I care about you."

"I guess. I mean, you NEVER ask about me OR the kids. It's always Leah and her family. I'm glad that you're interested in them, but I'm not sure you're so inclined to talk about my life. But really, this isn't the place to discuss this right now. Let's just try to have a pleasant conversation." Rachel didn't know what got into her. Confronting her mother like this? Well, her mother was pushing things, so she really only had herself to blame for Rachel's outburst.

"Trust me. I DO care about you and your children. It's just that you've never talked with me about your life. I had no idea that you were having a problem in your marriage until you told me that you were getting a divorce."

"Truly mom, I don't want to discuss this right now." Rachel said this in a whisper.

"Okay, but obviously, we need to clear the air at some point; probably even before Leah comes in town. I don't want this hanging over our heads."

Rachel realized that the visit with her mom had not lasted very long, but she looked at her watch and decided it was time to go. She was exhausted and irritated. She would come back tomorrow. "Mom, I do need to go right now, but I'll come back tomorrow.

50

Maybe we can talk in your apartment. If we're going to have a heart to heart, privacy will be necessary. Is that okay with you?" Rachel hoped that her mother would be amenable to the idea.

"Yes, it is. Apparently, there are things that need to be discussed. What time would you like to come?"

"I guess I could join you for lunch here, and then we could chat more after eating. What do you think?" Rachel wanted to try to smooth things over. There was no point in them both being so upset.

"Yes, that would be very nice." Delores probably needed some cooling off time as well.

Rachel said goodbye, and left. She felt as though she had been pummeled. She couldn't keep putting herself through this, but she had to visit her mother. *Maybe Delores really did care about her? I'll find out more tomorrow*, thought Rachel. She was just relieved to get in her car and drive home.

Rachel was happily puttering around the house when the phone rang. It was her sister. They certainly had been talking a lot recently, and that made Rachel happy.

"Hi Leah!"

"Hey Rachel, how's life!"

"I visited with Mom again." Rachel stated this in a downcast way.

"Uh, oh. Not so good?"

"It's a long story. Anyway, I can tell you that we're all looking forward to your visit."

"So am I. That's why I'm calling. My flight will be in at 5:18 your time. I hope that works for you. It was the best I could do with short notice."

"That's fine. I'll be at baggage claim to get you. Everything else okay I assume?"

"Everything is great. We'll get caught up on life when I see you. By the way, Mom is okay, yes?"

"She's fine. I'm going to have lunch with her tomorrow, and then we'll have a bit of a talk. It's been interesting around here, and I think some things will come out."

"Okay, what does that mean?" Leah sounded confused and concerned.

"It's really not that big of a deal. We'll discuss it all when you get here. Really, things are fine, so don't worry." Rachel wanted

51

to reassure her sister that there was nothing to be concerned about. Maybe she needed to convince herself as well.

"All right. If you say so." Leah still sounded uncertain.

"I do. So, I'll see you Saturday."

"You got it. Take it easy, sis."

"Okay, you too. Bye!" Leah said goodbye also, and Rachel let out a sigh. It would be a huge relief to have her sister in town even for just a little while.

Rachel's kids came home from school, and she tried talking with them. Her daughters were a little more open with her, which was nice. She did tell them all about their aunt coming in on Saturday afternoon. The girls wanted to accompany Rachel to the airport, and that pleased her. She knew they were doing this so that they could greet Leah immediately, and not because they wanted to spend more time with their mother. Still, it would be fun for all of them.

They had dinner, the kids did their homework, and Rachel watched television. It was a nice calm evening, and she knew she needed that. Tomorrow with her mother would be taxing.

Chapter Six

The next morning, after the kids went to school, Rachel felt almost queasy. She really didn't want to have any confrontation with her mother. Even though things weren't great, they were managing with the status quo. Opening the flood gates could be brutal for both of them. Well, Rachel would just have to keep her chin up and deal with whatever happened.

She drove to the home, clutching the steering wheel. The drive there was always more stressful than the drive home but today was even more nerve wracking. She wondered if her mother felt the same way about their visits. Did she dread them? Did SHE feel obligated to see Rachel? It was highly possible that it didn't thrill Delores to have these frequent visits from her daughter. Forget thrill. It was probable that she didn't want to see her at all. It didn't do any good to think like this now. She needed to concentrate on trying to have a nice afternoon with her mother.

She arrived at the home and walked through the sliding doors. She didn't see Delores yet, but Rachel had come there early by about ten minutes. She saw Don again. He was seated, his hands in a steeple position across his chest as he was sitting back in a chair. He seemed very relaxed as he was waiting for his dad. Rachel couldn't believe he was here at the same time as she was. Again. She realized that she was staring at him. He must have sensed her presence because he looked up at her. He waved at her and nodded politely. She waved back. *Should she go over and say hello? Interesting that he wasn't getting up to come over to her. I shouldn't be analyzing this. Oh, I'll just go over and say a quick hello.*

As Rachel approached him, Don stood up.

"Just wanted to say hello. How are you?" Rachel tried to sound light and comfortable.

"I'm doing well, how are you?" He was always amiable.

"I'm okay. I'm here to have lunch with my mom." Rachel gave herself something to do by looking at her watch." I'm a little early."

53

"I'm going to be having lunch with my dad. I don't know if you and your mom would want to sit with us in the dining room?" Don looked at her hopefully.

"Uh, okay. I guess that would be fine. I'm sure my mom would like that." Rachel wasn't overly keen on the idea, but she hoped this would all be harmless. But, Don had asked, and she felt it would be rude to say no. Maybe he and his dad would be a nice buffer at the table. This could work to her advantage provided her mom didn't go in a bad direction. Rachel felt that she had admonished her mother enough on the dating topic, so there shouldn't be anything to be concerned about at the moment.

"Great! I think it's nice to have other company sometimes when dealing with parents, don't you?" Don chuckled at his own comment. Rachel was surprised that HE felt that way. She thought that he and his father had a comfortable relationship. "Indeed I do! Your dad seems easy enough to deal with, though, so I'm surprised to hear YOU say that. My mother can make life interesting for me, but I didn't think others had it sooo... how shall I put this, challenging perhaps?"

Don laughed again. Gosh, Rachel really loved that smile. His eyes even smiled when he laughed. "My dad is a great guy. It's just that he has his expectations in life. Especially regarding MY life, I don't think he's perfectly satisfied with me on every level."

"Really? I wouldn't have guessed that either. You seem to have it pretty together. I mean, you care about him and you have your own business. That's any parent's dream."

"Yes, that's all true. But there are missing pieces." He lost a bit of his smile. He seemed a little melancholy.

Rachel was just about ready to ask him what he meant when she heard both her mother's voice and Ben's voice. She turned to see them looking at Rachel and Don, both smiling like they had just won the lottery. She and Don said hello to their parents.

"Dad, I've asked Rachel and Mrs. Weinstein to join us for lunch. I assume that's okay with you?"

Delores was so happy, and she looked directly at Don. "Please call me Delores. Mrs. Weinstein sounds so formal."

"Okay, Delores. Thank you."

"Of course! I'd love to have the four of us eat together!" Ben joyously looked at Rachel and Delores.

So, off they went to the dining room. It was a pleasant room, decorated in the same vein as the lobby. One really did feel as though he or she was dining at a top restaurant. There were tables with white tablecloths, and wood paneling on the walls. The lighting was perfect, not too harsh but bright enough to be able to see the menu choices. It almost seemed like a wedding party was about to come into the room. It was a nicely appointed, elegant eating area.

Rachel, her mom, Don and Ben came into the room, and Don lead them all to a table. He pulled out a chair for Rachel, and Ben pulled out one for Delores. Rachel was impressed by their chivalry. Maybe it wasn't dead after all! After Don pulled out the seat for Rachel, and she sat down, he then sat next to her. Delores was on her other side, and Ben sat next to her. After a moment, two more women came to their table, and both Don and Ben stood and helped them in their seats. Both women seemed to know Ben, but he had to introduce them to Delores. He also introduced them to Rachel.

The waiter brought their menus, and took their drink orders. They all glanced at the available entrees and made their decisions. The waiter returned quickly and took their orders.

"Isn't this nice, Ben, being able to spend mealtime with our children!" Delores was almost giddy.

"Indeed it is! What a treat!" Ben winked at Don and Rachel. "I hope the two of you feel the same way.

"Oh, yes, this is very special." Rachel, at least at the moment, really did mean that.

"Yes, Dad, this is great." Don smiled at his father and then at Rachel.

One of the ladies leaned forward and looked eagerly at Don. "Don, it's always so nice to see you! How darling of you to spend so much time with your sweet father."

"It's my pleasure, really. I know that Rachel visits her mom a lot as well." It seemed that Don wanted the focus off of himself and to acknowledge Rachel's kind ways towards her mother.

The lady looked at Rachel with understanding. "Of course she does. We do see her frequently also." She smiled sweetly at Rachel. Rachel chose not to say anything. She only smiled.

Then, unexpectedly, Delores lovingly grabbed Rachel's hand. Rachel nearly jumped out of her seat. "Yes, she's very good to me. I know not everyone gets visitors, but my Rachel sees me all the time." Delores looked at Rachel as though she meant what she said. Rachel was speechless. She had always been told, by friends whose parents were in retirement homes, that there was a lot of competition between the residents as to how many visitors they received. The parents always felt quite proud of themselves when their children came to see them. It was like, *Look at me! Look how much they love me! Was her mother behaving this way as well?*

In moments, their first courses were placed on the table. They all ate their salads, which consisted of Romaine lettuce with pears, walnuts and blue cheese tossed with vinaigrette. A few comments were made here and there, but nothing of significance.

Their entrées were served shortly after their salad plates were removed. Rachel had ordered salmon with dill sauce, which was very good. She wasn't sure she'd need much for dinner. This was a dinner! Delores was chatting a bit with Ben, and the other ladies were talking with each other. They were leaning into each other, gossiping away.

"This food is really something." Don looked at Rachel figuring they would start a little conversation.

"Yes, I was thinking that this isn't lunch, this is really dinner."

Don laughed at that and nodded his head in agreement. "Very true, I don't think I've ever eaten this well for lunch. Maybe I should come here more often. I'm sure Dad wouldn't mind."

"I like to cook, so maybe I should start fixing lunches like this for myself."

"Really? What do you like to cook?" Don seemed very interested.

"Oh, I don't know. I like making pasta and fish. I make soup every now and then. Even though I'm not a huge meat eater, I prepare a good brisket." Rachel was comfortable talking about her kitchen skills.

"Brisket? Wow, I love brisket. When I was a kid, my mom used to make it."

"Do you ever cook it?"

"No, I can't say that I have. I probably should, but Mom made it so well. I doubt that I could ever to justice to it."

"I assume you do cook. I mean, you have to eat. You don't go out all the time, do you?"

"I cook, but the food that I make is just okay. My 'specialties' are chicken and steak. Just kind of basic food. I do like going out, though. Do you get to go out much? You mentioned you're divorced with three kids. I guess it's not that easy to have much of a social life."

Rachel found herself tensing up with his comment. Not that he had said anything wrong. It's just that anytime her divorce was brought up in any conversation, it made her a little uneasy. Perhaps especially when Don mentioned it. "I do get out here and there with friends and sometimes with my kids."

"That's great. You need to be good to yourself. You seem to do a lot for everyone else. I've always heard that many women can be like that. You know, doing so much for the people around them but never enough for themselves."

"Oh, I do enough for myself, although it is true that my kids have to be a priority for me, and, of course, my mother as well. But you know how that goes because of your dad." Don nodded his head.

"That was a wonderful meal, wasn't it Rachel?" Delores had finished her lunch. Her positive nature baffled Rachel, although she suspected her mother wanted to seem pleasant and happy for everyone's benefit at the table. Rachel figured she should play along.

"Yes, Mom, it was very nice." Rachel looked at her watch. "Mom, we probably should go to your apartment soon if we're going to have a nice chat. I don't have a lot of time today."

"I'm finished, so we can go now if you want."

Rachel and Delores said their goodbyes to everyone at the table. When they both stood up, so did Ben and Don.

"It was nice chatting with you, Rachel. I hope you and your mom have a nice day." Don was certainly a very kind and polite man. Rachel had to admire that.

"Thank you. I enjoyed talking with you also. I hope you and your father have fun." Don always seemed very pleased to converse with her. He gave a little smile.

Delores and Rachel walked slowly and silently to Delores's apartment. It wasn't too far from the lobby, which was nice for Delores. She had her key in her pocket and opened the door. It was a pretty and comfortable place. She had a small kitchen, which was rarely used because meals were served in the dining room. Her dining room, which housed an antique carved wooden table and four matching chairs with blue cushions, opened into the living room, which was bright and cheerful. The walls were painted a pale yellow, and there were family photos and artwork on the walls. Rachel and Leah had helped her arrange everything when she moved in. There was a couch with a floral design and a few upholstered chairs all surrounding a glass coffee table. A television was situated by the wall near the balcony. Each of these pieces was in the house where Delores had lived with her husband. There was one bedroom, which was decorated very simply with a queen-sized bed (how appropriate!), and a wooden dresser with an oval gold-leaf framed mirror hung over it. The balcony ran across the entire area, so her view was that of a fountain and lovely flowers. There was one bathroom right outside her bedroom. The vanity held antique perfume bottles, and Delores had plenty of storage space for cosmetics and everything she needed.

Rachel closed the door, and she and her mother took seats in the living room. Delores seemed to be a bit more distant. She wouldn't look at Rachel, so she fixed her gaze towards the glass doors leading to the balcony. Rachel decided to speak.

"So, Mom, you wanted to talk?" Rachel was not looking forward to this, but perhaps her mother was correct. The air needed to be cleared.

Delores looked at her, and sighed. "Yes, I suppose. I think we should talk. Considering that you don't think I care about you or your children. I must say, I don't understand that at all." Delores looked at her with resignation, as though there was just no hope if Rachel had these ridiculous feelings. Rachel's heart began to pound, both with nervousness and agitation.

"Mom, I'm not quite sure what it is that you don't understand. It is a fact that you NEVER ask about me or my kids. You always seem annoyed with me. I'm glad that you like to talk about Leah and her family. I love them very much, so it's nice to discuss them. I just wish that you'd at least pretend to be more interested in my children and of course in me as well." Rachel set her mouth firmly as though she had nothing more to say.

"I honestly don't know how to respond to this, Rachel." *Of course you don't. You can't admit that this is true.* Delores continued. "You never seem to want to tell me anything. I certainly don't want to stick my nose in where it doesn't belong. I have chosen to respect your privacy."

Oh, please, she's got to be kidding! Rachel was sure that she had a skeptical look on her face. "I never intended to keep you out of the loop, Mom."

"Then why on earth didn't you ever mention to me that you were having marital problems? All of the sudden, you were telling me that you and Steve were getting a divorce." Delores had a very intense look on her face. She seemed offended not to have known all the details.

"Mom, the truth of the matter was that I didn't KNOW that we were having problems. I thought things were okay until I learned that Steve was having the affair with Linda. The moment I found out, I told Steve that I wanted a divorce. That's how it happened." Rachel hated having to relive the past. This was always a difficult topic for her to discuss.

"Oh, so you really didn't know that there were issues?" Now Delores had the skeptical look on HER face.

"No, Mom, I really didn't." Rachel had the feeling that Delores couldn't figure out how her daughter could be so stupid. *Sorry, but I didn't have a clue here!*

"If you HAD suspected something, would you have confided in me?"

That stopped Rachel dead in her tracks. She couldn't speak for a moment. "Uh, well." Rachel slumped back a bit in her chair. "I don't know." Rachel wasn't happy that she had to admit that there was a possibility that she wouldn't have felt comfortable sharing her problems with her mother. Delores looked a bit hurt.

Then Delores nodded her head up and down as if affirming what she already knew. "So you don't know. Interesting, and you wonder why I don't ask you anything." That wasn't a question that was said as fact. "My own daughter isn't sure if she would tell me her most important thoughts and concerns. This is not good, Rachel."

Now Rachel was angry. She didn't believe that her lack of meaningful conversations with Delores was her fault. It was her mother's fault. She let it rip. "Mom, I'm sorry. It's just that, in all my life, you've never treated me with much more than disdain. No hugs, no warmth, nothing. How do you expect me to relate to you when we've barely had a relationship?" The solid flood gates were beginning to crack.

Delores looked like she had been slapped. "Disdain? You really think I've been that evil?"

Rachel looked at her and shrugged. "Can you deny this Mother? Have you ever hugged me or been happy with me?" Rachel looked at her very seriously.

Delores wouldn't look her in the eye. She merely seemed defensive. "I don't know whether or not I hugged you. Maybe I didn't. My family was never very demonstrative when I was growing up. But that didn't mean that I didn't care. Besides, you always seemed much closer to your father than to me."

"Mom, it wasn't a contest. I could have been close to both of you. Dad did seem to care about me, so naturally, I probably did lean more towards him, like a plant leans into the sunshine. What else would you expect?"

"You say that I talk more about Leah and her family. SHE must feel close to me." Delores was getting defiant.

"You'd have to ask her. Mom, I'm not trying to be nasty. I really didn't want to talk like this. It's just that I've never seemed to do anything right by you. My marriage and my whole life. Maybe I did make a huge mistake marrying Steve. However, I have three children whom I love. That has to count for something." Rachel bowed her head in despair.

Delores softened her tone a bit. "We all make mistakes. That's part of life, Rachel. Your kids are important, although I've heard you complain about those girls of yours."

"They're teenagers. It's going to be this way for a while. But they still matter, and as their grandmother, you should show some interest in them. I know we're not like Leah's family. Bob is a wonderful husband, and their kids are nice and polite. Leah has

60

done everything well, and I couldn't be happier for her." Rachel paused for a moment. "Maybe we should just let this go and move on." Rachel was worn out.

"I guess we could talk more at some other point. I will try to be a better mother and grandmother. I don't want to fail in anyone's eyes." Delores was playing the martyr role now. Rachel hated that.

Rachel was ready to wave the white flag and surrender. "Whatever. We all do the best that we can." Rachel got up from her chair. She needed to get out and go home. Delores stood as well.

"So, will I see you tomorrow?" If Delores wanted to see her, Rachel would come.

"Sure Mom. I'll be here. Around ten or so?"

"That would be nice. And I'm so glad you were able to come for lunch."

"Me too." Rachel had lost any feeling of enthusiasm.

Delores walked Rachel to the door. Rachel was ready to just say goodbye, but Delores put her arms out to her and hugged her. It wasn't just a quick, limp hug. She embraced her daughter for several seconds, and then she let Rachel go. Her eyes misted just a little, and Rachel was truly touched. Maybe they did have a chance at a better relationship.

"Thanks Mom. That was nice." Rachel gave her a weak smile and Delores smiled as well.

"Okay, dear, see you tomorrow morning." Rachel nodded, appreciating her mother's efforts.

Rachel made her way down the hall to the lobby. She was taking her keys out of her purse when she heard a man say something to her.

"Bye, Rachel!" It was Don. He was waving at her. Ben also waved.

"Bye! Have a great day!" She didn't feel like stopping for a conversation. Rachel felt all talked out at this point, so she left through the glass doors, headed to her car and drove out of the parking lot.

After Rachel arrived home, she started preparing dinner. She decided to make a nice meal that required chopping, marinating and sautéing. Those activities always helped her clear her mind and put her more at ease. The day had been a decent one, but she

61

needed time to be calm and functioning for when her kids came home from school.

After getting everything done for the day, her kids bounded through the door. School was coming to a close very soon, and they were getting excited. They'd all still be able to see their friends and do their activities, but the pressure of homework and tests would be over for a few months. They would also be spending a lot more time with their dad, staying at his house.

All three were willing to talk with her, the girls gossiping about friends and teachers. Which ones they liked, which ones were a pain. Her son gave his opinions on different matters. The cacophony of voices and discussions of everything under the sun were constant, and Rachel was enjoying every minute of it. She realized that her children faced different pressures in life, just as she did. She wanted to make sure that she showed them as much love as possible, and she would always listen and try to be helpful whenever she could. The thought of having the same conversation in the future with her kids as she just had with her mother made her want to be an even better parent.

Sarah, Rebecca and David had studying to do, so they went upstairs and closed their doors. Rachel finished cleaning the kitchen and was sitting down to look at the mail. The phone rang and startled her. She looked at the Caller ID, and saw the name Levy Donald. *Oh, what is this about?* Her heart did a flip flop, and she debated answering the phone. She realized he'd have to know she was home, so she pressed talk.

"Hello?" Rachel spoke tentatively.

"Hello, Rachel? This is Don Levy. How are you?"

"I'm fine thank you, and you?" She tried to sound calm.

"I'm fine. I hope you don't mind that I phoned you, especially at this hour. Your name is listed in the phone book, so I figured it would be all right if I called you. I have a question to ask you." He sounded hesitant, and she was praying his question would be a simple general one that she could answer.

"Oh, sure, it's no problem. What can I help you with?" Rachel was doing her best to sound ultra-casual. And yet she was very nervous.

"I was curious if there are activities that your mom does that my dad could do? They get along so well, and although he's an outgoing guy, I think it would help him get involved in things a bit

62

more if he knew someone. You know, like if there's some social thing going on that he would feel comfortable doing because a friend was also involved."

Rachel thought it was sweet that he was so concerned about his father's well-being, but she realized she had jumped the gun in thinking that he was going to ask her out. "Well, I know my mom isn't as active as she should be. However, I could look into things a bit more, and find out if there is something that would work for both of them. Your way of looking at this makes sense. Get them both involved and they'll be more likely to do the activities that the home offers. That's smart."

"I don't want you to have to research this. I didn't mean to put this on you at all. I only thought that I'd ask if you were aware of anything in particular." Don sounded guilty about mentioning this idea to Rachel.

"Really, it's no trouble at all. I honestly don't mind. I should have done this quite a while back for my mother. You're a good son to care so much." Rachel was happy to help. Getting her mother into retirement home life would be good for her. And if Ben could find some happiness with it, so much the better.

"That's really sweet of you. Like I said, I don't want to make this challenging, so please, don't spend too much time on this."

"Believe me, Don, I'm fine with doing some research. It will give me something constructive to do."

"It's not like you don't have a lot on your plate already. Being a single mom takes most of your time, I'm sure." Don was being very understanding, and Rachel appreciated his consideration of her life.

"I'll let you know if I have any challenges in figuring this out. If I find out something, I'll share the information with you. We'll both work on this project. I guess I should have your phone number so that I can call you if I learn anything." Rachel did not want him to know that she already had his number through Caller ID.

"Sure." Don happily gave her his number, and thanked her for her help. After they said goodbye, Rachel gave a contented sigh. Don was a really decent person, from what she could gather.

She knew now that she shouldn't have panicked when he called her. Clearly, he wasn't going to be asking her out, so there was no need to worry about that thought. Don kept mentioning the fact that she was a single mother, so he seemed to be making it clear that he wouldn't want to bother with that kind of mess. He was a good, kind man who loved and cared for this father. And he was quite attractive with that fabulous smile and those sweet eyes. He was also well spoken and had a charming presence about him.

Suddenly, Rachel was jarred out of her dream world.

"Mom! I forgot to tell you that I need cookies for tomorrow. Our class is celebrating the end of school, and we're all bringing something." David was shouting down the stairs at Rachel.

"You're telling me this NOW? When did you first know about this, David?" Rachel didn't like his lack of consideration for time.

"Um, well, I don't remember. I just need them. Sorry Mom." No man was going to deal with this, especially if these kids were not his own flesh and blood. *Who could blame a person?* Rachel got up and went to the kitchen. She didn't bake very often, but she'd get something together. She found a cookie mix in the kitchen cabinet, and used that. Soon after the cookies were baking in the oven, she realized the kids must have smelled the sweet aroma. She heard them coming down the stairs like a herd of buffalo.

"Mmm. Cookies!" Rebecca's eyes gleamed with pleasure.

"Nope, not for YOU. This is for David's class at school. Besides, it's way too late for you guys to be munching away on cookies. Have you all finished your homework?" The happy expressions on their faces sank.

"Bummer!" Rebecca wanted a darn cookie.

"Sorry, but maybe I'll make some cookies for all of you very soon. Anyway, why don't you finish up with everything and get ready for bed." They all left the kitchen and slowly made their way back upstairs. Rachel let the cookies cool, and then she went upstairs to say goodnight to the kids. She knocked on Sarah's door first.

"Yes?"

"It's Mom. I want to come in and say goodnight." Although Rachel did not receive a verbal response, she did hear some noise. Within a few seconds, her older teenage daughter opened her door. She looked somewhat sullen, as was usual for her most of the time, at least when she was dealing with her mother.

"Okay, goodnight." Sarah didn't say it with any love at all. More like, *fine, is that enough for you or what?* It was such a shame that as lovely a young lady as Sarah was, she just didn't have the personality to go with her being. She was lanky and had nice cheekbones like her father. Her hair was the color of chestnuts, parted in the middle, and flowed in waves around her neck. She had blue eyes that were beautifully framed by perfectly plucked arched eyebrows. Sarah tilted her head, giving a questioning look, wondering if there was more that her mother needed.

"I assume everything is good, right?"

"Yep." It appeared that would be the end of the responses.

"Okay, sleep well." Sarah shut her door. Rachel went down the hall, and knocked on Rebecca's door. She didn't say anything, she just opened the door.

"Hi. What's up, Mom?" At least Rebecca was a little more upbeat than her sister. She was more the picture of Rachel. Rebecca was a little shorter than her older sister, although she was two years younger as well. She had a slightly rounder face that was more expressive. Her hair was a bit darker than her sister's, and the cut was straight, parted to the side and above her shoulders. Her hazel eyes were bright and she could actually smile every now and then.

"I just wanted to say goodnight and see how things were going."

"Everything's cool."

"Well, goodnight then." Rachel smiled at her, and her daughter gave her a little smile as well. Rachel went to David's door and knocked.

"David, I want to say goodnight." Rachel shouted at his door. David instantly opened his door wide open.

"Hey, Mom, goodnight." He gave her a nice hug as well as his ever present smile. He was a cute kid whose dark brown hair had a very slight curl to it. His blue eyes always lit up when he was with his mother. "Thanks for making the cookies."

"You are very welcome. I'm going to put them in a tin."

"Great!" At least David was an appreciative child.

"Get some sleep."

David closed his door, and Rachel went back downstairs to the kitchen. She put the cookies in a blue tin, just like she told David she would do. She tried a cookie only to be sure they were good. Rachel watched some television, and decided she should hit the sack as well.

Chapter Seven

The next morning, Rachel's kids were quite animated. Each day brought them closer to summer fun, so they couldn't help but be excited. She didn't blame them. Rachel remembered those days as well herself. They all grabbed their backpacks, and David held onto his prized tin. He'd probably come home very hyper after a day of sugary snacks.

The bus came, and off they went. Rachel got herself ready to go to see her mother. She'd probably take a little break from the frequent visits, just until her sister came in on the weekend. She'd go with her maybe once, and then she'd let Leah take over for a bit. Rachel put on a pair of navy Capri pants and a short sleeve white top. She was casual, but the outfit was cute and summery. She put on some silver bangles and her sandals, and went to the retirement home.

The drive was pleasant, and it seemed that the rain that had left them so soggy was finally over. The sky was blue with white billowy clouds, and the grass was a lush green. Everything looked fresh and pretty. She opened her car windows to take in the light breeze. The air was sweetly aromatic with its earthy scent.

Rachel arrived at the retirement complex and noticed a number of people walking along the pretty paths, taking advantage of such a gorgeous day. Water spouted from the different creatures' mouths in the various fountains that adorned the acres of land. Rachel could never forget how fortunate her mother was to be able to live in such an ideal setting. Aaron had done very well by his wife. He had done well by his whole family.

Rachel parked her car and went inside the building. Once again, she had arrived a bit early, so she sat down on one of the upholstered chairs. She was going to pick up a magazine, but a voice interrupted her plan.

"Rachel! Hi!" Don appeared in front of her. She stood to greet him.

"Hi, Don. As always, I'm here early. I guess you're here to see your dad."

"Yes, although I arrived a little early myself. I thought I should talk with someone here about the activities with which my father could involve himself. I was told that the activities director would send me something, and I could call her if I need more information. I appreciate your willingness to help, but I thought that I should try to find out something also. I'll let you know what happens."

"That would be great. I'll discuss it with my mother and see if she knows of anything going on right now. One way or another, we'll get our parents involved in something around here."

"I didn't mean to bother you. You looked like you were ready to relax for a moment." Don seemed a bit sheepish about disturbing her.

"You're not bothering me." Don looked a little uncertain and a bit uncomfortable. Rachel was somewhat concerned. "Is everything okay? Rachel eyed him quizzically.

"Oh, yeah, sure, everything is fine. Please, sit back down." He motioned to the chair she had taken when she arrived. Rachel sat down, and Don sat next to her in a matching chair. Rachel was still in doubt over whatever was going on with him.

"You're sure you're okay?" Rachel was curious to know if he was really okay.

Don gave a look of resignation, and began to speak. "Rachel, the truth is that I have something to ask you. I know that you're a busy lady, and that you've probably been through quite a bit in recent times. I just thought it would be fun to go to dinner with you sometime, if you want." Don looked at her as though he had asked something monumental from her. Rachel could tell that he didn't want to impose his time on her, but that he simply wanted to go out. She had been afraid of this kind of confrontation, but it should be okay now. Besides, they had lunch together in the home's dining room. And, really, he wasn't using the word 'date.' *A fun time out couldn't really hurt, could it?*

"I guess it would be okay. What did you have in mind?"

Don looked relieved and he smiled. "I'd be happy to go wherever you'd want to go. We could even go out for lunch if you'd like. Being new in town, I feel like I've been kind of stuck either here or at home. I'm not the type who is comfortable eating out alone, so I thought that you and I could enjoy some time out

67

and about. If there's some place that you really like, we could go there."

"There's a little café near here. It's quaint and the food is pretty good. Maybe we could go there for lunch." Rachel thought that would be simple enough.

Don's eyes lit up. "Fantastic! I'd love that. Would you like to go there today after we see our parents?"

Rachel wasn't sure. She didn't want her mother to see her leave with Don. That would put way too many ideas in her head. "Um, well, let me see." She tried to think quickly as to how she would handle this. "I know. My house isn't far from here. Maybe I could take my car home, and you could pick me up, and we'll go from there? Is that okay with you?"

"Sure, sure, that would be great. Just give me your address and I can come over after spending time with my dad. Maybe about 12:30 or so? Does that sound good?"

"Yes, that would work out very well." She had no intention whatsoever about letting Delores in on her plans. She'd leave when her mother had lunch, and head home. Simple, simple, simple! Delores and Ben saw the two of them and picked up their paces as they approached their children. Both Don and Rachel stood up.

"Hello you two! How are you?" Ben smiled at Don and gave him a big hug. Delores looked at Rachel, smiled and gave her a little hug.

"Hello, Ben. How are you today?" Rachel was always happy to see Don's father.

"I'm fabulous! Always glad to see you, that's for sure." Rachel gave a little laugh, and said how pleased she was to see him. Rachel looked at Don, and she realized that she hadn't given him her address yet.

"Well, Don, it was nice seeing you. Just check out that information I was telling you about. You can look it up in the phone book. The address to the place is sure to be in there." *Talk about a covert mission!* She hoped he understood. She also hoped neither Ben nor Delores would clue in to anything or ask any questions.

Don looked at her as though he didn't quite understand. Then, she saw the look of a light bulb going off in his head. He nodded his head. "Yeah, thanks. I'll check it out." Rachel hoped he didn't mind her subterfuge. She didn't mean to be difficult or unkind, but she couldn't risk either parent knowing that the two of them were having lunch together. There was nothing to this outing, and she didn't want them thinking there was. Rachel said goodbye to Ben and Don.

"Mom, do you want to sit in your apartment or somewhere else?"

"What was that all about? What did Don need to know?" Delores looked inquisitively at Rachel.

Uh, oh, thought Rachel. *Think fast!* "Oh, it was nothing important." She was buying time.

"Nothing important? Then you can tell me." Delores was always persistent.

"Just something about stuff with his house. Really, it was nothing." Rachel shoed the questioning away like it was inconsequential.

They went to Delores's apartment and made small talk for a little while. Rachel and her mother discussed aspects of Leah's upcoming visit. Delores asked about the children. They had a pleasant conversation, and even a few laughs. It was almost noon, and Rachel knew she needed to get going.

"Mom, I need to get back home. Leah and I will be visiting you on Sunday. So, we'll both be here soon. Is there anything going on around here that you're doing?" Rachel hoped that her mother would be busy with something. She could also tell Don about any activities.

"I'll probably be seeing some movies. There will also be a concert on Friday. I don't know, just different things here and there. I'll be able to keep myself occupied until you and Leah come here."

"I'm glad. You might as well take advantage of what's offered here. Have some fun, right?" Delores nodded her approval.

They gave each other hugs and Rachel left to go home. It seemed that things had improved between the two of them since that intense day in her mother's apartment. Maybe life would be even better when Leah came to town.

Rachel arrived home with about fifteen minutes to spare. She freshened up a bit, and the doorbell rang promptly at 12:30. She was impressed. *The man was certainly punctual!* Rachel opened the front door, and Don was already smiling at her. She wondered if he ever frowned. Rachel hoped not. He seemed like a happy fellow with a kind heart.

"Hello!" Don was excited to see her.

"Come in. I assume you didn't have any trouble finding my home?"

"No, not one bit. I did just as you suggested and looked up your address in the phone book." He looked at her with an amused sly expression.

"I hope you didn't mind me putting you through that. It's just that… well…I don't know." Rachel shrugged. She didn't want to verbalize what she was thinking. She knew WHAT she was thinking, but she didn't want Don to know.

"Well, whatever the reason, it was more than okay with me. No worries." He really didn't know why she was so coy in front of their parents. Better to leave that as a mystery. She didn't want to embarrass herself by telling him that she didn't want Delores and Ben to think that she and Don were going out together. He probably didn't look at this lunch as anything at all, so she didn't want him to think it would be important to her mother.

"Thanks. Shall we go?"

"Sure. I'll let you guide the way to the café. Needless to say, I have no idea as to where it is." Don opened the passenger side door of the front seat, and Rachel got in. He slid into the driver's seat of his Lexus and they drove off.

Rachel directed him along the way, and they conversed a bit. Within ten minutes, they arrived at the café. Don stopped the car, and Rachel was about to open her door.

"Hold on just a moment." Don bolted out of the car, and went around to her side. He opened the passenger side door, and helped Rachel out. Don really was quite a gentleman. She didn't think there were any more out there. Rachel thanked him, and they went to the entrance of the restaurant. Naturally, Don opened the door for Rachel.

The café was a charming little place that looked like one was sitting outside instead of inside. The tables were wrought iron, and could have been placed just as easily on a patio as inside a restaurant. There was greenery all around, even overflowing from pots hanging from the ceiling. She and Steve used to come here a lot. The food was always good, and it reminded her of a place where she and her ex had eaten on a trip to Paris early on in their marriage. It wasn't painful for her to be here, especially not with Don. She did know the staff quite well, and when she saw the hostess, Melanie, the young lady looked at her, and then she looked at Don. She smiled at Rachel, and seemed very happy for her. Melanie hadn't seen Rachel for a while now, and she certainly had not seen her with this handsome man. Rachel found herself blushing slightly, and the hostess led them to a table. Don pulled out her chair and she sat down. Melanie was clearly impressed, and Rachel understood by observing Melanie's interested gaze that she approved of Rachel's companion. She handed them both menus, and left their table.

"So many things look good. Do you have any favorites?" Don seemed very pleased as he perused the menu. He was impressed by the restaurant choice that Rachel had made for them.

"I've never had a bad meal here. It just depends on what you're in the mood to eat."

The waitress came over, and took their drink orders first. Don ordered a bottle of white wine for both of them to enjoy. Then they decided on the meal. Rachel ordered a seafood salad, and Don ordered the tuna nicoise. They made small talk as they waited for their food. Rachel had to admit that she was intrigued by Don. He was always polite and friendly. He really did seem like a stand-up guy. Good looking too. What she couldn't understand was why he had remained single for so long. She realized that she should probably ask him some personal questions. She wasn't interested in him per se, just curious.

"So, Don, do you ever miss New York?" Rachel thought that was an easy enough question to start with.

Don shrugged a little. "Maybe a little sometimes. It's an interesting place to experience. I liked living there, but I also like living here. It's nice to be closer to my dad, especially because there's no other family around. Have you ever been to New York?"

"I have, many years ago with my ex. It's an incredible city, and it would be fun to go back at some point. I think my kids would like it too."

They chatted a little more about New York, their food was served, and they continued talking.

"Do you have any siblings?"

"Nope."

71

"Really?" Rachel was a little shocked by this revelation. Don had put a forkful of tuna in his mouth, so he just nodded. "Wow!" She never imagined that he was an only child. "How long has it been since your mom passed away?"

Don looked alarmingly at her. Then his expression changed to absolute understanding.

"She's still alive." Don paused and then spoke again. "My parents have been divorced for a long time."

Rachel nearly choked on a piece of seafood. "I am SO sorry! I didn't realize." She was mortified by her assumption.

"That's okay. You had no way of knowing. It's not a big deal."

Rachel couldn't understand this scenario. *What could have happened?* "Well, still. I apologize for making an assumption like that." Don waved his hand as if to indicate that she could sweep away her concerns. Rachel leaned forward a bit when asking her next question. She hoped she wasn't being too nosey. "Are you close to your mom?"

Don now did appear to be somewhat troubled as he leaned back a bit away from her. His eyes almost seemed to darken like a cloud ready to drop buckets of rain in a thunderstorm. "No, I'm not close to her." He said it very coldly, which was completely unlike him.

Rachel felt horrible now. She realized that she had opened a wound, and she was sorry that she had said anything. The last thing that she wanted to do was upset Don in any way. But, she couldn't seem to let this go. "May I ask why? I mean, if it's none of my business, or you don't want to talk about it, I'll understand completely. I'm just curious."

Don pushed his food around on his plate. His ever-present smiling face completely disappeared, and his eyes were downcast. "No, I don't mind telling you." He still wasn't looking at Rachel, but he put his fork down and put his elbows on the table leaning his chin against his folded hands. "My mother was unfaithful to my father." It felt like Don had dropped a two-hundred-pound weight on the table. Rachel jerked back as though she had been shocked by an electric prod. Her breath was momentarily taken away. She couldn't speak, and she knew that she must have quite a surprised expression on her face. In her silence, Don continued.

"Yeah. So, needless to say, I haven't been thrilled with her since that happened." Don looked directly at Rachel now.

"Oh, Don, I can't believe it. I'm so sorry. How long ago did this happen?" Rachel's mouth was gaping.

Don looked up at the ceiling as though calculating the years. "Let's see. I guess it's been about thirty-five years now."

"So, you were a teenager." Rachel shook her head in disbelief. She was stunned that he had gone through what her own kids had dealt with.

"Yes."

"Did your parents' divorce immediately after your dad found out?" That's what Rachel and Steve had done, but she wasn't divulging that piece of information quite yet.

"Oh, yes. My dad was devastated, but he saw the writing on the wall. My mom wanted the divorce. She was ready to run off with her new man."

"So, I guess that's what she did, right?" Rachel sat there like a deer caught in the headlights.

"She did indeed." Don said this with disgust. He took a swig of his wine as though he was cleansing away the bitterness.

Rachel tried to put a positive spin on the situation. "Your dad is lucky to have you here now. It's nice that you're close and you have each other." Her comments sounded lame, but she meant what she said.

Don gave a weak smile. "Those early days after the divorce were challenging, but we got through it as best we could. What choice does anyone have when confronted with a bad situation? You've got to move forward."

Rachel reflected on what he said, remembering exactly how she had felt when the stuff hit the fan for her. She felt like falling apart, but she couldn't. She had to look out for her children and for herself.

Don perked up and shifted everything back to Rachel. "You're divorced. What caused your break up? If you don't mind me asking?"

Rachel decided she just had to go for it and let it out. After his confession, he had a right to know about her situation. She took a deep breath. "Oh, you're gonna love this. Same thing that happened to your dad, as a matter-of-fact."

Don's eyes opened wide. He was obviously stunned. "No! No way! I can't believe it! YOUR husband cheated on YOU?" He said it too loudly because he was taken by surprise. A few diners turned to look at their table.

"Yes he did. Lucky me, huh? I guess that's one of the reasons I was so shocked that it happened in your family. Your dad is such a good man. It just didn't seem like that could have happened to him."

"It doesn't seem possible that it happened to you either. I mean, you're a lovely woman. Not only that, you're a really terrific lady. *What was he thinking?* Don realized what he had just said to her, and he suddenly seemed embarrassed by his confession of feelings towards her. He looked at Rachel and colored a bit. Then, he swallowed hard. He continued, trying to lessen the impact of what he had already said. "I just don't know what some people are thinking. The spouse has it good, and yet they need something else. Go figure."

Rachel was flattered, but she quickly let that feeling pass. "I don't get it either. I can tell you that I didn't see it coming. Maybe I wasn't paying enough attention." She seemed disappointed in herself.

Don looked at her cautiously. "Did he marry the girl?"

Rachel nodded. "Oh, yeah. He didn't wait long either."

Don cringed at what he was about to say. "Was she pregnant?"

Rachel laughed. "Oh, no. That wouldn't have worked for Linda at all. She definitely doesn't want kids. She hates it when mine visit their dad."

"So, you sort of know what I went through all those years ago. The hurt, the feeling of abandonment. Your kids must have dealt with a lot of issues."

"They did and they still do. I guess anyone impacted by infidelity is going to have problems."

"I know that I still do." Don said this in a way that begged Rachel to question him further.

"Really? How so?" Rachel didn't ask the question merely to allow Don to purge a bit. She wanted to know as well to satisfy her own curiosity.

Her queries were left unanswered because at that moment, the waitress came over to clear their plates. *What timing!* "Would you like to see a dessert menu?" She smiled at them with a questioning look.

"I don't want anything, do you?" Rachel didn't want to speak for both of them, but she really wanted to continue this conversation, maybe at her house. The subject was very personal, so a quiet place without eavesdroppers might be better for both of them.

"No, I'm pretty full. Thanks." The waitress left their table to get the bill.

"I thought that maybe we could talk at my house over a cup of coffee. If you'd like?" Rachel couldn't believe she was so interested in Don.

"I'd love to, but I do have to get back to my house and do some work."

Rachel was crestfallen, but she didn't let on. She backed off immediately. "Oh, okay."

Don looked at her feeling a little ashamed by his rejection of her kind offer. But for now, that's how it had to be.

The waitress brought the check, and Don grabbed it.

"Here, let me take care of my part at least." Rachel didn't want him to feel that he had to pay for her meal, so she reached for her purse to take out her wallet.

"No, no. I asked you to lunch, and I'm happy to pick up the tab."

"Well, thank you. That's very kind. Maybe I could make my world famous brisket for you one night?" Rachel felt it would be the right thing to do to reciprocate.

"That would be great. I'd like that a lot." Don looked at her very appreciatively.

Don paid the bill, and then he and Rachel got up to leave. They drove home, talking about various things including the weather and about the appeal of the retirement home. The conversation was just long enough to get them to Rachel's home. Don pulled into her driveway, got out of the car, and walked to the passenger door. She got out, and he walked her to the front door.

"Don thanks so much for the lovely lunch. That was fun." Rachel really meant it, and it showed in her smile.

Don had his hands shyly in his khaki pockets and he nodded agreeably with her. "I had a great time too, Rachel. Thanks for joining me."

"I'll call you to set up the time for you to come here for the brisket. Is that okay? I want to arrange it for when my kids are at their dad's house. That way, you won't have to contend with the commotion that normally ensues."

75

"Sounds perfect to me. I'm looking forward to it."

"It should be soon. My sister will be coming in town this weekend, so maybe the following weekend will work."

"Will you both be coming together to the home?" Don wanted to see Rachel again soon, hopefully before he came over to her house for dinner.

"Yes, we will. Maybe once. Otherwise, Leah will go by herself. You know, to spend time alone with our mom. They won't need me hovering over them."

"Maybe I'll see you both there."

"I think we'll be coming this Sunday."

"I'll probably be there."

"Well, thanks again, Don, and enjoy the rest of your day."

Don gave Rachel a "you're welcome" nod, and he went back to his car.

Rachel went inside, and sighed contentedly to herself. She had enjoyed her time with Don. He was easy to talk to, and he was a real gentleman. On the other hand, she told herself that she wasn't interested in any serious relationship, so she wouldn't allow herself to get head over heels with Don. However, he didn't seem to want that anyway. She had really thought that he would want to come in for a cup of coffee and to talk a little more with her. Just as well, though. She couldn't allow herself to get involved with any man. She had to keep her head on straight, and her children came first.

Chapter Eight

The week had come to an end, and Rachel and the kids were very excited about seeing Leah. The girls would be joining Rachel to go to the airport. David was going to a friend's house for a party. Just as well, because there was only so much room in the car for passengers. Rachel had contacted Steve about having the children at his house the following weekend. Although they had a specific agreement about weekends and holidays, they were flexible about the visitations. Rachel and Steve were on relatively friendly terms, in spite of the pain that he had caused Rachel. She wanted what was best for her children, and that meant being civil to their father.

Rachel decided to tell Don that next weekend would be fine for him to come over for dinner if he wanted to do so. She didn't want to push. She felt that she should reciprocate for the lunch that he had treated her to the other day. If he wanted to come, that would be great, if not, that was fine as well.

She called his number, and the answering machine came on. She waited through his short message and then spoke.

"Hi, Don, it's Rachel. Thanks again so much for lunch the other day. I really enjoyed the afternoon. Anyway, I want to let you know that I can have dinner here next Saturday if you want to come for brisket. How does 6:30 sound? Let me know if that's good for you. Have a great day! Bye."

He had her number, so she'd wait to hear from him. She'd LIKE him to come, but whatever. She told herself that it didn't matter one way or another. Talking with him had been fun, but she didn't need a boyfriend. As she was contemplating their situation, Rebecca and Sarah came downstairs.

"Mom!" Are we ready to pick up Aunt Leah or WHAT?" Sarah was constantly annoyed with her mother. Rachel always tried to keep in mind how she felt as a teenager.

Rachel stood up. "Yes, we are. Let's go."

She and the girls got into the car and drove off for the airport.

Rebecca and Sarah were chattering away, elated that they would soon see their beloved aunt. Leah was "cool" as far as they were concerned. Rachel had to agree. Leah was easygoing and fun. Of course she didn't LIVE with them, and she wasn't the one who had to lecture them or make demands of them. Leah wasn't the mean one. Rachel was looking forward to seeing her as well, so they'd make a wonderful welcoming committee.

The traffic had been a bit intense, but they arrived at the airport with time to spare and parked the car. The three got out and walked the short distance to the front of the building. People were quickly unloading vehicles and taxis were lining up. There was a flurry of activity. They made their way through the slight chaos and went inside. They weaved their way to the baggage claim area, and waited. The girls glanced at the arrival screen, their eyes wide open scanning it to check the information regarding their aunt's flight. They saw what they were looking for at the same time, and clapped excitedly. They practically ran over to Rachel.

"Her plane has arrived!" Rebecca was giddy. "She'll be here soon!" She and Sarah had moved away from their mother, and they were jumping up and down with each other and clasping their hands together. *Wow, I wish they felt as strongly about seeing me.* Rachel wanted to laugh at her own thought, but she didn't want to have anyone wonder why she was laughing when she was merely standing by herself.

Rebecca and Sarah were craning their necks, awaiting Leah's grand entrance. Rachel's heart skipped a bit. She couldn't help but be excited as well. She saw her daughters point and they began walking rapidly. *That must be the sign*, thought Rachel. She also moved forward, a little more cautiously, to give the girls a chance to greet their aunt. There was Leah, being hugged by two happy teenagers. Leah had a contented smile on her pretty face. It had been months since Rachel had seen her sister, but if anything, she noticed that her sister looked even more beautiful than she had before. Leah was a bit taller than Rachel. For the longest time, she had been sporting shoulder length hair. It was a soft light brown color that graced her oval shaped face. She had a very fit medium build, and her eyes were a lovely shade of brown. Rachel had more of her father's countenance, a slightly rounder face; although she always wished that she looked more like her mother. Leah seemed to get the best of both of their parents. Their mother's very attractive features and their father's vivacious more open personality. Fortunately, Rachel shared the personality trait, so that was something good.

Leah looked up as her arms were awkwardly holding her black leather tote bag, red purse and nieces. She gave a special smile to Rachel. Leah dropped her arms away from the girls as she and her sister approached each other.

"Hi, there, sis! How's it going?" Leah gave Rachel a warm embrace.

"I'm fine. How are you and how was your flight?"

"I'm doing well and the flight was so-so. Everything went well. It's just a pain in the you-know-what dealing with planes these days. Stuck in there like sardines. How much fun can I stand? But, seeing all of you makes the journey worthwhile. Where's my sweet nephew?"

"He's at a friend's house, but he'll be back for dinner. I figured we'd eat in tonight and gab, gab, gab. Does that sound okay to you?"

"Perfect! I just want to collapse, eat and talk."

They all went to the luggage carrousel and waited for Leah's suitcase. Leah pointed to it to let them know that her bag was there, and Sarah reached out to grab it. Rachel was stunned. Her daughter actually wanted to help. Rachel would have to convince her sister to move in with them.

The four of them walked out of the area and strolled to the parking lot. They were all talking and laughing. It felt good to have Leah with them. She added sunshine to their lives. They arrived at Rachel's car, and Rachel popped the trunk open to put her sister's belongings in the space. The trunk was shut, everyone was situated, and off they went to have a fun visit.

Leah was telling them about her home life and the things that were going on with everyone. The girls were riveted to everything she said. It was nice to see Sarah and Rebecca so cheerful. They'd seen their share of unhappiness, more than Rachel wanted to think about. Still, it wasn't easy having them look at her with annoyance and, at times, accusation. She wondered if they believed that their father did what he did because of her. She didn't want to start going down that horrible mental road, so she refused to allow herself one more moment of dwelling on anything sad. Rachel wanted to enjoy her sister's visit. Pure and simple.

The carload of family arrived at the house. Everyone got out, Sarah taking her aunt's belongings, and then the car doors were slammed shut. Rebecca and Sarah raced into the house ahead of Leah and Rachel.

Leah was led upstairs by her excited nieces. She put her personal items in her designated room, and the three of them came back downstairs. The girls were talking and Leah was listening. It made Rachel think how wonderful it would be to have backup as a mom. If she had a little assistance, life could be a lot more pleasant in the house. Rachel looked at the picture of the three of them and felt content. It was nice to witness this joy. Her family was happy right now.

Rachel went to her phone to find out if there were any messages. She picked it up, pressed talk and heard the beeping sound indicating someone had left a message. She pressed buttons to get the Caller ID information and realized that Don had been sole caller. She listened for his message.

"Hi, Rachel! It's Don. I got your message, and I would be very happy to come to your house for your famous brisket. Six-thirty is fine. Thanks for the invite! Have a nice day! Bye." Rachel smiled. It was a pleasure to hear his deep and kind voice. She was glad that he wanted to come over.

"You look like you're very happy! That must have been some phone call!" Leah smiled like a Cheshire cat. Rachel didn't even realize she was still holding the phone. She put it back in its cradle. Rachel wasn't ready to talk about any of this right know. Besides, there wasn't anything TO talk about. Don would be coming over for dinner next weekend. That was it. Their parents reside at the retirement home, and she and Don happened to share a few nice moments together. This was NO BIG DEAL. She got up from her chair.

"So, you're all settled in I presume?" Rachel was trying to be nonchalant about everything.

"Uh, huh." Leah clearly knew something was up with her sister. "Everything is very nice and I'm very happy here. So what gives?" She was still grinning at Rachel.

"Nothing. Really, it's nothing." Rachel was being very secretive.

Leah leaned in and put her arm around Rachel's shoulder. She whispered in her ear. "You can't hide anything from me you know. We'll talk about whatever it is later, when the kids aren't around. Okay?"

"Okay, but honestly, I don't have much of anything to tell you."

Leah looked at her skeptically. "Suuuure you don't. We'll see." Leah winked at her.

"So, do you want a snack before dinner? You must be hungry. I know that you couldn't have eaten much since you left your house."

"I could go for something." The subject was officially changed.

Rebecca and Sarah joined them in the kitchen. Rachel grabbed some homemade pasta salad, cheese, and some chips and dip. She poured iced tea for the group, and they enjoyed the feast as they chatted. It was such a pleasant change to experience the laughter and the fun.

They all heard David come in the front door. His friend's mom had kindly volunteered to bring him home when Rachel told her that she was driving Leah home from the airport. Her friends knew everything about Leah, and they knew how much it meant for Rachel to get a visit from her.

"David, Aunt Leah is here." Rachel shouted at him from the kitchen. He came running in and hugged his aunt.

"Hey, Davy, how's it going, Bud?" Rachel loved how casual and friendly Leah was with her kids. No wonder they loved her so much.

"Hey, Aunt Leah! It's great to have you here!" David showed a lot of love to everyone. He was just that kind of kid.

"Thanks, sweetie. It's great to be here and spend some time with all of you."

They all talked non-stop, and then later they enjoyed the chicken scaloppini that Rachel had lovingly prepared. Her daughters had even helped put together the salad and rolls for the dinner. The kitchen hadn't been filled with this kind of party atmosphere in a very long time. By the end of the meal, the family was a bit sluggish from the excitement of the entire day.

The kids watched some television while Rachel and Leah stayed in the kitchen relaxing with cups of coffee. They talked about nothing in particular until Leah could no longer contain her curiosity.

"Okay, girl, you've got to tell me about the phone call you

81

received. It must have been one amazing message!"

"I swear the message really wasn't anything exciting. I've had a conversation here and there with that son of mom's friend from the home. We went out for a nice lunch, and I left a message inviting him here for dinner next weekend. He was merely calling to say that he could come. That's ALL!" Rachel swung her arms out indicating that there was nothing else to say about this. And there wasn't.

"Wait a minute! Is this the guy that you DIDN'T want Mom pushing to ask you out?" Leah seemed confused.

"Well, yes and no."

"What? Please explain. Either he IS the one or he ISN'T the one." Leah wasn't going to give up.

"YES, he IS the same man, but we're NOT going out." Rachel thought that was a satisfactory answer. She was wrong.

Leah looked at her incredulously. "Well, apparently you ARE. In what world is it that inviting him over for dinner isn't going out? At least HE'S going out."

"I'm merely reciprocating for a lunch." Rachel looked a bit indignant as she answered the question. She felt that she had explained herself very clearly.

Leah slapped her hand on her leg and laughed heartily. "This is great! So, you DID go out with him! Rachel, my dear sister, you ARE seeing him."

Rachel wasn't accepting this theory at all. "No, I'm not. Don wanted to get out a bit because he's new here. I agreed to go with him so that he wouldn't have to eat alone at a restaurant. Really, that's all. I was helping him by joining him, he kindly paid the bill, and I am making dinner for him. We're being polite. Case closed." Rachel folded her arms across her chest in defiance.

Leah wasn't buying this at all. "Rachel, I don't think you're looking at this clearly at all. Are you *sure* that he didn't ask you to lunch, as in a *date*? And you think that you're not *seeing* him as in a *date*? Are the kids going to be around when he comes here? I mean, will they be joining you?" Leah would get to the heart of this no matter what it took and how long it took.

"Leah, the lunch was a lunch. That's all it was. And, no, the kids won't be here next weekend. They'll be with their dad. Still, I believe that I made it clear in my phone message that I appreciated him buying me lunch and I'd like to reciprocate. I don't know why you're making this into *way* more than it is!" Rachel was actually getting a bit peeved at her sister.

"I'm just trying to get you to see this for what it is. And really, sis, it's FINE. There isn't anything wrong with dating a man."

Rachel had just about enough. "Well, I'm not interested in dating, so that's not what this is. And I really don't think Don is interested either."

Leah didn't understand that comment. "Why wouldn't he be interested?"

"I just don't think he is. He hasn't given me any indication that he's interested."

Leah rolled her eyes at Rachel. "Oh, you've got to be KIDDING me, right? Come on! Are you blind, girl? He asked you out to lunch. He picked up the check. He accepted your dinner invitation. What more do you need?"

"You just don't understand. But that's okay, you don't have to understand. I KNOW what's what." Rachel looked very confident in her own understanding.

Leah looked at Rachel with kindness. "Rachel, do you like Don?" She spoke the words so gently that it made Rachel confused.

"Well, yeah, he's a nice guy and everything."

"No, I mean do you LIKE him? As more than a friend." Leah still had a very soft voice when asking.

Rachel paused, but only for a moment. "Of course not. He's just a pleasant person and that's it."

Leah gave her a coy look. "Is he handsome?"

Rachel shifted a bit in her seat at that question. "Yes, he's nice looking."

"I wonder if I'll get a chance to meet him."

"You probably will because he frequently visits his dad at the home."

"That's sweet. So, they get along pretty well?"

"Seems like it. Ben, his dad, appears to be a nice man."

"Oh, speaking of visiting, should I call Mom? I guess we'll go over there tomorrow?"

"Yes, I told her we would. You should call her now. Let her know you're in town and all is well."

Leah went to the phone and called her mother. Delores answered her phone.

"Hello?"

"Hi, Mom, it's Leah."

"Leah! How are you? How was your flight in? Tell me everything." Delores was very happy to hear from her daughter.

"I'm doing very well, Mom, happily situated in my wonderful sister's house." Leah and Rachel looked at each other. Leah was smiling while Rachel rolled her eyes in amusement.

"I'm glad. So, what's new?"

"I don't know, not much. Rachel and I will be coming over tomorrow. When would be a good time for us to visit?"

"Oh, whatever is best for you, dear."

"Okay, does one o'clock sound good?" Leah glanced at Rachel realizing that she had forgotten to ask her what time she normally went there. Rachel just shrugged like it didn't really matter.

"Unless you'd like to come at noon and we could have lunch together in the dining room?" Delores seemed to like having her family dine with her every now and then.

"Oh, lunch together at noon in the dining room?" Leah looked at Rachel again, questioning with her eyes if that was a good idea. Rachel nodded indicating that she was fine with that. Then she pointed questioningly at Leah, wondering if she was okay with the idea.

"Yes, I thought you might like that. We could talk and eat. Only if you want to. I'm fine with whatever you decide."

"It sounds like a great plan. Rachel and I will be there at noon, maybe a little before. I assume things are going well with you?"

"Yes, everything is fine. You get some good rest. I'm sure you must be tired after your long flight. We'll catch up tomorrow."

"Okay, Mom. Sounds great. See you then!" Leah clicked off the phone.

"So, you're okay with having lunch with Mom tomorrow?" Leah looked at Rachel with a concerned expression.

"Of course I am. I had lunch with her the other day."

"I'm sure that must have been fun for you."

"It went well."

"Was Mr. Nice Guy there?"

"Funny, funny, funny! My sister is SOOO funny!"

Leah grinned at her. "So WAS he?"

"Yes. As I told you, he sees his dad a lot."

"So the two of you sat next to each other and talked."

"No, I gave him the silent treatment and refused to even look at him. Of course we talked. Leah, you're making way too big a deal of my encounters with Mr. Nice Guy. You know, men and women do speak with each other even when they don't have a relationship."

"Yes, they do. However, you are two single people. He's a nice person, you're a nice person. It just seems like there might be more to it than you're willing to admit."

"Well, there isn't. Maybe you'll understand that more when you do meet him. I'm telling you that even if I had any interest in him, I don't believe he feels anything for me."

"What, is he gay?"

"Oh, come on! No, he's not gay. That's not what I mean."

"Well, you just indicated that even if you were interested, he doesn't feel the same way. YOU made it sound like there was a particular reason. I was just thinking that could be the only reason. Which would be fine. No big deal."

"No, that's not it. You know, sometimes people just aren't interested. I think one of the reasons is because his mother cheated on his dad. Maybe he has some issue with that."

"Wow! Isn't that weird? That may very well have something to do with it. He's shy of marriage because of his mother's infidelity, and you're shy of dating because your husband did the same thing to you. It's awful. I feel for both of you. However, you can move forward. Both you and Don. You don't need to let other people's bad behavior ruin your lives." Leah was almost imploring Rachel to understand this concept.

"Ah, yes! Spoken from the lips of someone who has not gone through that kind of crap. And, believe me; I am thankful that you haven't. I would never wish that on you, Leah. It's just that you can't imagine what it's like to experience such a betrayal. It does things to you. So, yes, I understand how Don feels. I sure know how I feel." Rachel looked forlorn as she stated that.

"I'm sorry, Rachel." Leah reached out her hand and patted her sister's arm. "I know what you went through. I just don't want you to close the door on future relationships. And, trust me; I will do my best to make sure that you don't get into trouble again. No more awful men. Not that we can control that completely, but I'm on your side."

"So, what are you saying? You think you could have prevented

85

me from marrying Steve?" No matter how much Rachel and Leah loved each other, Rachel didn't believe that her sister could have done anything about what happened in the past.

"No. Not really. It's just that you and I are older now, and we're more clued into things. I realize that none of us would have guessed how things would turn out. It's just that sometimes, we can tell if a guy is a jerk."

Their intense conversation was interrupted.

"Hey, Mom, can we have something to eat? Maybe some dessert?" David was calling from the family room.

"Sure, come into the kitchen." Rachel and Leah stood up as the kids came dashing in. They decided to change places with the kids, and they went into the family room. They curled up on to the couch and continued talking.

"I do appreciate your concern for me." Rachel wanted to make sure Leah knew how much her support meant.

"I know you do, and I'm not trying to force you into anything. I just don't want you to turn away from doing something that might be great for you. You certainly should always proceed with caution, but do proceed."

"I'm really quite happy if I just have a friendship with Don. That would be fine with me." Rachel seemed to be trying to convince herself that she could be content with friendship, but Leah had said all she was going to say. For now.

Leah called her family to let them know that she had arrived safely and to see how everything was going in her absence. She spoke with her kids and with Bob. Rachel couldn't help overhearing her sister talk on the phone. At certain points Leah was laughing, at others she was offering advice, and at the end of her conversation, she was talking with her husband. Rachel felt a slight twinge of jealousy when she heard her sister say that she missed Bob and she knew he missed her. They exchanged their "I love you" sentiments and she hung up the phone. Rachel pretended not to be paying attention, and Leah had no idea that she had heard anything.

"So, how are they doing now that you're here having fun? Are they coping?" Rachel was being amusing with Leah. She knew perfectly well that her family would be fine.

"I'd say they're all managing quite well. I wonder if they'll even care if I come back." Now it was Leah's turn to be funny.

"They're doing well, aren't they? Life is good?"

"Oh, yes, they're all doing well. Busy and happy." She looked at her sister with a lot of love. "Believe me, sis, I know how lucky I am. And it is luck. One can never know how things are going to work out, but life has been very good to me, and I'm grateful."

"Well, I for one am very happy that life has been good for you. I wouldn't have wanted it to be any other way. And really, I'm okay, so don't you worry about me. The kids can make life interesting for me here and there, but all in all, things are good."

Rachel and Leah decided to call it a night. Leah had already experienced quite a long day, and they both had to get up and get moving in the morning to get to the home. The kids stayed up for a little longer because they didn't have to get up early on Sunday. Everyone said goodnight to each other, and the evening drew to a comfortable close.

Chapter Nine

Leah was still sleeping, as were the kids, when Rachel woke up the next morning. She figured she'd let her sister sleep in until she really needed to get moving. Rachel showered and dressed, and made her way downstairs to brew the coffee and make breakfast.

Within fifteen minutes, she heard a shower running upstairs. Within the hour, Leah appeared in the kitchen. She was fresh from a good night's sleep and she had on white and navy thin-striped pants with a white collared shirt, and a bold silver necklace. She looked very chic. Leah didn't wear much makeup, but what she applied was perfect and natural. Delores would be pleased by her younger daughter's appearance.

"Hey, how'd you sleep?" Rachel got up to get a mug for her sister's coffee. She placed scrambled eggs, pancakes and fruit on a plate. Leah sat down, and took a sip of the luscious hot, black steaming liquid. No cream and sugar for her coffee. She drank it straight.

"Mmm, that's good! I slept very well, thank you! It felt like pure luxury. Normally, I don't get much rest at home. You know how it is. With kids, you're up and running. I feel like I'm on vacation now!"

"That's great! You should feel like you're on vacation. You will be pampered, my sweet sister, I promise you that." Rachel was happy to make Leah feel so special.

The two chatted for a while, and then David came into the kitchen. His face lit up when he saw his aunt.

"Good morning, David! How are you?" David came over and gave her a big hug.

"I'm fine." He looked at Leah and then he looked at his mother. He furrowed his brow in confusion. "You both talk all the time. What do you talk about so much?"

Rachel and Leah looked at each other and laughed. David scowled, placing his arms angrily across his chest, wondering what he said that made them laugh. Rachel realized that they might have offended her son just a bit. "David, we're sorry. We're not laughing at you, sweetie. We just know that we talk a lot and about everything. Sometimes females do this. We like to gab." He didn't seem to really get it, so he just shrugged and asked for some breakfast. Rachel and Leah gave each other a knowing look. They always had plenty to discuss, but most of the conversations were for their ears only.

Rachel prepared a breakfast plate for David, poured a glass of milk and a little glass of juice. She set it down in front of him, and he dug in.

"Aunt Leah, what will you do while you're with us?"

"Your mom and I are going to visit Grandma for lunch today. I'll be visiting Grandma by myself on one of the days. Otherwise, I'm just hanging around with all of you." Leah affectionately ruffled his hair. David smiled.

"You two may talk while I go upstairs and finish getting ready." Rachel thought she'd give David some time with his aunt, so she took some time for herself. Rebecca and Sarah were still sleeping and probably would do so until after Rachel and Leah left for the home.

Later that morning, Leah and Rachel drove to their mother's residence. It was a lovely Sunday with clear skies and comfortable temperatures. Rachel was glad that it was so pleasant, especially considering that Leah was used to perfect weather. They made their way to the expansive property and noticed people taking their leisure outside. The fountains were spouting and the flowers, as always, looked beautiful. Rachel parked her car, and she and Leah got out. They made their way to the lobby door and went inside. Leah took in the beauty of the area. Although she had been there before, she was always pleased to see that such a lovely place was chosen for her mother.

Leah looked at Rachel. "I hope Mom realizes how fortunate she is to reside here."

"Who knows? You know that Mom takes a lot of things for granted."

"Rachel?" Rachel looked to the side and saw Don standing there. Her heart pounded for a moment.

"Hi, Don, how are you?"

Leah turned very quickly to see him. She smiled broadly.

"I'm fine! It's great to see you!" He looked hesitantly at Leah, wondering if the lady was Rachel's sister.

"Don, I'd like to introduce you to Leah, my sister. Leah this is Don Levy." Don shook Leah's hand.

"It's nice to meet you, Leah."

"Thanks. It's nice to meet you too." At that moment, Leah knew that she had to encourage Rachel to think of Don as more than just a friend. She had heard what Rachel said about him, noticed his polite manners and his good looks. Leah believed that Rachel should take a chance.

Don looked at Rachel. "I'm sure you must be very happy to have your sister in town."

Rachel looked lovingly at Leah. "You bet I am. We've been talking non-stop since she arrived." The three of them laughed at Rachel's statement.

Don pointed to Delores, who was walking towards them. Her face lit up with joy at seeing the three standing together. Leah approached her mother, and the two embraced warmly. Rachel watched them as Don stood by her side and then Delores and Leah walked towards them. Delores leaned into Rachel to give her a small peck on the cheek.

"Hello, Mother. How are you today?"

"I'm doing well. It's so nice to see all of you, and that means you too, Don."

"Thank you, Delores. It's always nice to see you."

"So, should we head to the dining room, Mom?" Rachel wasn't sure if it was time to eat or if they should wait.

"Oh, you're here for lunch as well?" Don didn't realize that they too would be eating in the dining room.

"Yes, Mom thought that would be nice." Rachel now assumed that Don and Ben were doing the same thing.

"Don, if you and your dad will be eating there also, would you like to join us at a table?" Delores was hoping that he would say yes. She always enjoyed his company. Leah looked at Rachel wondering if this would work for her as well. Rachel gave no indication as to how she felt about it. Don did glance at Rachel, and then she smiled.

"Well, I guess if it's okay with all of you, my dad and I would like that. I'm sure he'll be here within a few minutes. If you want to go ahead, we'll meet you in there."

Delores, Rachel and Leah headed for the dining room and found a table near the entrance. There would only be room for one extra person to sit when Don and Ben joined them, so it was possible that the table would belong only to their group. The three ladies sat and talked for a few minutes. Leah was next to her mother, and she was telling her about some of the things going on in her life. Delores was giving Leah her full attention.

Don and Ben came in and saw them immediately. They came over to the table. Ben was introduced to Leah, and Rachel got up and moved to a seat next to Don so Ben could sit next to Delores. It was a cozy group.

"I'm looking forward to our dinner on Saturday." Don whispered this as he grinned at Rachel. He seemed very pleased by the fact that they were getting together.

"I am also." She whispered it as well. There was no way that she wanted her mother to hear any of this. She wished that Don hadn't said anything, but he had, so she went with it. He leaned in a little closer, she assumed to make sure that no one at the table heard their conversation.

"Is there anything I can bring?"

"Nope, just yourself." Rachel prayed that her mother didn't notice any of this interaction.

No one else came to eat at their table, so the group enjoyed good conversation by themselves. Leah was asked a number of questions, mostly by Ben. Don listened attentively, but he also enjoyed a glance or two at Rachel. She wanted to know what he was thinking, but she let that go. She was listening to Leah. The meal ended, and Ben and Don excused themselves. Ben said that he wanted to leave them to talk with each other, which wasn't necessary, but it showed how thoughtful he was. Leah and Rachel stood up to say goodbye, and Don nodded at Rachel, but he didn't say anything. She knew that his gesture meant that it was nice to see her, and that he would see her on Saturday. She thought for a moment how funny it was that she knew what he was thinking without him saying a word.

Delores, Rachel and Leah got up to leave a few minutes after the men left. They went back to the lobby and took seats there.

"It was so nice having lunch with my girls." Delores beamed a nice smile at both of them.

"I'm glad that we were able to do this. It's nice to be in town

91

for a little while." Leah smiled at both Rachel and Delores.

"So, Rachel, you appeared to be in quite a conversation with Don." Delores's eyes were piercing. Rachel almost flinched.

"No. Not really. Mostly, we were enjoying listening to Leah." She wanted to get the spotlight off of herself right now.

"No, Don was leaning pretty close to you. I couldn't help but notice that." Delores didn't take her eyes off of Rachel. Leah didn't say a word. Rachel wasn't happy that Delores had caught Don and herself talking somewhat more intimately than usual with each other.

"Really, it was nothing. He was just saying something about Leah and me. I can't even remember what it was now." Rachel sounded as nonchalant as she could.

Delores looked at Leah who gave nothing away. Rachel was feeling uneasy, but she knew she had to be cool. There was no way that she wanted her mother to know anything that had or would be transpiring between Don and herself. Not that anything major was happening, but she believed that Delores would blow everything out of proportion. She'd think that the lunch and the upcoming dinner were special events.

"Hmm. You're not going to tell me anything, are you? Well, that's fine. I suppose it's none of my business anyway." Delores looked hurt, but Rachel didn't care.

"Mom, there's NOTHING to tell you. Sorry!" Rachel looked at Leah with pleading eyes. Leah needed to break this tension.

"Mom, I do want to spend time with you before I have go back home." Leah felt this would be a good way to distract her mother.

Delores agreed and they discussed the schedule. After they talked for a while longer, the sisters decided it was time to get back to the house. They both hugged their mother and Leah told Delores she'd see her soon.

Rachel and Leah didn't speak until they were in the car and safely out of hearing distance from anyone at the home.

"Boy, Rachel, I thought that Mom was going to sniff out your relationship with Don. That was one close call."

"Well, as I've stated before, there is no relationship, but I certainly don't want her thinking there is one. That's the only thing I was worried about."

"Rachel, I'm telling you that there's something between you and Don, whether you want to admit it or not. I can tell by the

92

way he looks at you. There's a spark."

"Oh, come on, Leah. You could tell he's just a friendly guy. That's ALL!" Rachel was getting tired of explaining this.

"Okay, okay. I'll let it go. But, I know things. I can see what's right in front of me. I just don't know why you're fighting it." Leah was exasperated with Rachel at this point.

"Let's drop it, at least for now." Rachel started the car, and they drove back home. They made small talk, which worked for both of them. They had always had an easy relationship, so they were never angry with each other.

They arrived home, and went inside. Rebecca and Sarah were sitting in front of the television eating junk food. They looked away from the television for a moment.

"Hey, Aunt Leah." The sisters spoke in unison.

"Hi, girls. Whatcha' doing?"

"Just eating and relaxing. How's Grandma?" Rebecca chomped away on chips.

"She's fine. Aunt Leah and I had a nice visit with her. Where's David?"

"He's upstairs." Sarah was watching the television again so she didn't even look at her mother when she answered the question.

Rachel left Leah with the girls went upstairs to see her son. David's door was open, and he was on his bed reading a comic magazine. He seemed very content.

"Hi, David. Everything okay in here?"

David looked up with his sweet smile. "Hi, Mom. Yeah, I'm fine. Just reading my magazine."

Rachel came into his room. He always had everything organized. There was a wall of shelves built for his books and knick-knacks. He liked anything to do with action heroes and trains, so there were collectibles of anything pertaining to those interests. He was very happy to spend time by himself in his room.

"So, are you ready for school tomorrow? I assume you've done all of your projects."

"Sure have."

"You and your sisters are going to get another weekend with your dad. Maybe you and your dad can do some stuff together, just the two of you. Would you like that?" Rachel always felt horrible that David never had enough time with Steve. David was such a good kid, and he needed and deserved a male role model.

93

"Yeah, that would be great. Whatever Dad wants to do is fine with me."

David was so easy to please. Rachel just hoped that Steve would make time for his only son. David continued looking at his magazine, so Rachel left his room, allowing him some quiet time. She decided that she would, maybe after Leah left town, call Steve and calmly suggest that he do something special with David. Steve had been so caught up in his own world, which included his new life with Linda, that he seemed to be losing connection with his children. He didn't mind seeing his kids, but he wasn't "into" it. She wanted her children to have an involved father, although she knew she couldn't force him to feel or act a certain way. Rachel went back downstairs to be with Leah, Sarah and Rebecca.

"Everything okay with David?" Leah loved her nephew and nieces, so she was always showing concern for their well-being.

"He's fine. He's reading his comic magazine. Now, let's concentrate on you. Is there anything in particular that you'd like to do tomorrow?

"I can't think of anything specific. Maybe we can take a nice walk, go out for lunch. Just hang out wherever. I don't think I want to DO anything. I like having some down time."

"Okay. That's the plan then."

The following day, Rachel and Leah spent their time together talking, eating and enjoying each other's company. Leah didn't mention anything about Don, although she was hopeful that, in time, she would hear some good news regarding a more serious relationship between Rachel and Don. She desperately wanted to see her sister be truly happy. Leah was disgusted by what Steve had done to Rachel, and she feared that her sister would never trust herself to have a solid relationship again. Once Steve betrayed Rachel, she put up her defensive walls, and they hadn't come down yet. She felt unworthy of being loved, and she simply didn't trust men at all.

The next day, Leah had breakfast and went to the home to visit with Delores. She decided that she would probably stay there until it was time to come back to Rachel's for dinner.

"Are you *sure* you want to stay that long with Mom?" Rachel was concerned that it would be too much for Leah to be there all day.

"Yes, I think that would be best. You spend so much time with her, the least I can do is spend one day with her. I feel like you've been burdened with all of the responsibility because you live here. That's not fair to you, so maybe I can do my share. I'll even tell her that you won't be able to see her until next week. Would you like that?"

"That's not a bad idea. I really don't want to bother going back over there until maybe Monday. I want to be under the radar until after the weekend. NOT because there's anything going on, but because I don't want Mom to think there is something happening. And please don't feel guilty. You live out of town, and there's nothing you can do about that. I'm okay with visiting her. Maybe we even have a new understanding with each other now. Do me a favor; don't say anything about Don or about him coming to my home for dinner."

"Sure. No problem. That's up to you."

Leah borrowed the car that Sarah drove, and she left to visit Delores. Rachel put a grocery list together because she needed to do her regular weekly shopping. She drove to the nearby store, parked her car, and went inside. After grabbing a cart, she checked her list and started in the produce aisle. Rachel picked up a bag of carrots, and a female voice rang out right near her.

"Hi, Rachel?" Rachel turned to see who was talking to her

"It's Melanie from the restaurant?" Melanie looked at Rachel questioning if she remembered the hostess. Rachel registered that she knew her. She had just never seen Melanie outside of the restaurant, so she was momentarily confused.

"Well, hello! Yes. Melanie. Of course. How are you?"

Melanie smiled brightly at Rachel. "I'm fine. I thought I recognized you. It was so nice seeing you at the restaurant the other day."

"It was nice seeing you also. Love the food there!" Rachel was trying to be cool about the whole thing, knowing full well that Melanie was probably wondering about the tall, handsome man who was dining with Rachel.

"I'm so glad! So, you had a nice time?" Melanie was starting to dig. Hopefully not too deeply.

"Yes, yes I did! The food was amazing!" Rachel wasn't completely comfortable having this conversation because she feared it would lead into a little discussion about Don. She was

95

hanging on for dear life.

"It's nice working at a restaurant where the food is so terrific. I feel like I'm associated with a class act."

"I agree. That's the way it should be." Rachel nodded her head in agreement. She was holding her own as best she could. Rachel really wanted to just move on, but she wasn't about to be rude.

"So, I was wondering who the gentleman was with you that day? He seemed to be quite the guy." Melanie had her hand up at her chin in a questioning gaze. She was intrigued.

"Oh, he's the son of a man who lives at the same retirement home as my mother. He's new in town, and I was just showing him a nice place to eat." Rachel tried to indicate that it was no big deal, barely worth mentioning.

"So, you're not dating him?" Melanie seemed surprised and disheartened.

"No, no, we're just friends." Rachel smiled shyly at Melanie.

"I'd think you'd want to be more than just friends with HIM. I mean, he seemed like a pleasant and attractive man. And now that you're free..." Melanie stopped herself suddenly, looking mortified that she had said anything. "I'm so sorry. I didn't mean it like that." She was clearly embarrassed by what she had said to Rachel, but Rachel took it all with ease, brushing the comments off as if they were nothing.

"Oh, please Melanie. Don't worry about it. You didn't say anything wrong." Rachel put her hand on Melanie's shoulder, trying to reassure her that everything was fine.

"It's just...well... I know it's none of my business what you do. Every now and then I see your ex-husband in the restaurant." She rolled her eyes at that. "I think YOU should be having fun!"

Rachel had to wonder how much Melanie knew. She never wanted the details of their problems aired out in public, but it seemed that Melanie might be very aware of the issue that caused the divorce.

"So, I guess you've seen Steve with his new wife?" Rachel was probing now.

"Yes. She seems like she's a piece!" Melanie had quite an attitude about this.

Rachel laughed at her comment. "Melanie, you are very observant! But, really, I'M fine, so don't worry about any of it."

"You're so sweet! I just want you to have someone as special as you are!" Melanie looked at her with kindness, and Rachel felt very modest about the compliment.

"Thanks. I really do appreciate that. Well, I guess I have to get some shopping done. I hope that things are going well for you?" Rachel felt that it would be polite to ask about Melanie.

"Oh, I'm fine. I only wish I could find a big hunk of a man like you have as your *friend*." Melanie smiled at her when she said *friend* as though she wasn't quite buying that term.

Rachel laughed. "I know you'll find just the right person. I'm sure there's a big hunk of a man coming your way."

They said goodbye to each other and parted ways. Rachel went through the store as quickly as she could, and she found everything she needed. She checked out, emptied the bags of groceries from her cart into the trunk of the car and returned home.

Rachel enjoyed some quiet time before she had to pick up the children from after school activities. She hoped that Leah was having a nice experience with their mother, and Rachel looked forward to hearing the details of the day. For a moment, she wondered about the things that Leah and Melanie were saying about Don. Rachel realized that neither knew him. *She* didn't know him very well for that matter. Melanie didn't have any details, yet she seemed to sense something was happening. Rachel had extreme doubts that Don was interested in her in any other way than friendship. Well, she didn't WANT to be interested in him. She knew she was not ready for another relationship, and might never be again. Rachel was hurt very badly, and didn't know if she could risk having that kind of pain again. Even if it wasn't the heartache of infidelity, there were many other problems that could exist.

Rachel was forced out of her thought process when she looked at her watch and realized it was time to bring the children home. She picked up Sarah from a sewing class, Rebecca from her art club and David from soccer practice. During the ride home, she let them decompress from their hours away. When they returned home, she figured she would talk with them a bit more about their lives.

"Did you all have a good day?" Ah, yes, her typical question. Maybe she'd get an answer, and maybe she wouldn't.

"It was fine. It's school." David always responded, but she doubted that her daughters would say much, if anything.

97

"So?" She glanced quickly at Rebecca and then at Sarah.

"Everything's fine." Rebecca had nothing more to say as she went to get a snack from the kitchen.

"And?" Rachel looked again at her oldest child.

"Fine." Sarah looked at Rachel as if to say, what more do you want from me?

"Fine, fine and fine. I guess everything is fine. I'd love more details." Rachel pleaded for more information.

"Where's Aunt Leah?" The question was put forth by Sarah, but all three looked questioningly at Rachel. Rachel looked back at them and started to laugh hysterically. They looked at each other, wondering why their mother had suddenly lost her mind.

"Mom, what IS your problem?" Sarah was not happy with her mother's amused outburst.

Rachel attempted to contain herself. Then her bad attitude started to rear its ugly head. "Oh, I don't know. I ask a simple question. I don't get much out of any of you, and then you want to know something from me. Hmm. Let's see. Oh, yes. Aunt Leah's out." She amused herself by giving the nothing answers that she always received.

Sarah, Rebecca and David looked at each other with very confused expressions. They turned to look back at their insane mother, and then Rebecca became the spokesperson.

"Out where?"

"I don't know. Out." Rachel thought this game was quite entertaining.

"So, you don't know WHERE she is?" Sarah was frustrated.

"What do YOU care?" Rachel was lobbing the comments like tennis balls, right back at her daughter.

Sarah sighed impatiently. "We want to know. Just tell us!" Sarah stood with her hands on her hips, waiting for an acceptable answer. Rachel wasn't sure that her daughters even cared at this point where Leah was, but they wanted to win the battle. She wasn't quite ready to surrender. So, Rachel stomped off into the family room and didn't say anything.

"Mom!" Rebecca was now sharing her sister's discontent.

Rachel decided to give in. She spoke in a very soft, conciliatory tone. "She's with your grandmother. Okay?"

The girls looked at each other with their typical eye rolls. David giggled.

98

The kids went about their business, and Rachel started to prepare dinner. She heard the garage door open, and she smiled. Leah was home! Funny how having her sister staying with her had brought such joy into her life. She was excited knowing they would have so much to discuss. Rachel heard the car door shut, and the door into the house opened.

"Hello!" Rachel was so pleased to see Leah.

"Hello, and how are you?" Leah gave her a big hug.

"I'm fine! So, how was YOUR day?" Rachel raised her eyebrows in questioning manner, hoping there would be lots of juicy details.

"Everything went well." Leah was acting all casual and sneaky.

"Tell, tell. Your sister wants to know everything." Rachel rubbed her hands together wanting the dirt.

Leah got something to drink and sat down. Food was cooking away on the stove, so Rachel could at least find out a thing or two before the kids came downstairs for dinner.

"Where to begin? Mom is doing fine. She talked a bit about the home and the people living there. She wanted to know everything that was going on with my family." Rachel gave a little smirk when she heard that. Delores was never quite as interested in her family.

"Was anything of significance said? I mean any good gossip?"

"Not really. She did say that it's been nice of you to come and see her so much. I thought it was good that she was appreciative. She worries about you being alone, but that's probably not news to you. She mentioned Don very briefly, but I steered her towards other topics. I did tell her that you wouldn't be able to see her until next week sometime. She seemed fine with that."

"I'm sure she did. I sometimes wonder if she does really want me to visit her. I need to have to have an alibi as to what will have kept me away from her for a longer time." Rachel tried to think about something, but decided to wait until she was closer to her next visit with Delores. This was Leah's time, and she didn't want to waste it with unimportant thoughts. "Did you have fun?" Rachel hoped that it had been a good day for her sister.

"Oh, I managed perfectly well. I took her out for lunch. We went to a place near the home. Really, sis, I wish I could be here more to take the burden off of you. I know that it's not easy for you to deal with Mom on a regular basis." Leah looked at her with sad eyes.

"Please don't even think about it. I manage to deal with her. You have a family in California, and that's okay. I'm glad that we can speak on the phone about everything. That always helps." Rachel gave Leah a reassuring smile. Leah patted Rachel's hand, indicating her gratitude for Rachel's endless understanding.

The kids came downstairs, and the family ate dinner while talking and laughing. Rachel cherished these special moments, knowing they would be over too soon.

Chapter Ten

The next day, the children went to school, and Leah and Rachel had their day together. They took a walk in the neighborhood and enjoyed lunch at a nearby restaurant. Leah and Rachel spent the day talking. Their relationship had always been special, but they found that it grew stronger over time. Rachel enjoyed hearing every detail of Leah's busy life and that of her kids and her husband. She was glad that things had turned out well for her sister.

Leah spent the next day with her mother. She drove to the retirement home, and went inside. Delores was sitting in the lobby talking with Ben and Don. The three were as thick as thieves. It was amusing to see them chattering away. Leah made her way over to them, and Delores spotted her.

"Hello, Leah! How are you today?"

Don and Ben rose to greet Leah.

"Hello all! I'm fine. How's everybody doing?"

"We're great! Having fun talking here, aren't we?" Delores looked very happy as the men smiled in agreement.

Ben looked at Delores and spoke. "Delores, I wanted to show you that bulletin of events. We won't be long, Leah. I know you're here to visit with your mom, and you don't have much time." Leah wasn't concerned about her mother being away for a moment or two. She indicated that her mother's temporary absence was perfectly acceptable. "Don, wait here with Leah. We'll be right back." Ben and Delores took off, leaving Leah and Don alone. They sat down and started talking.

"So, I assume that you're happy with your dad being here?" Leah wasn't sure what else to say. She didn't want to get too deep into a conversation, or to end up saying something that could make Rachel uncomfortable when dealing with Don. Leah was convinced that chemistry existed between Don and her sister, but she'd never let him know that.

"I'm happy that he's here, and he's happy too. This is a great place. Your mom seems to like the facility too."

"I think she does. Of course, who wouldn't like it?" They both laughed. Anyone looking at the retirement home would realize that this place was a grand way to spend one's later years.

"When do you have to leave town?"

"Tomorrow, unfortunately. Well, not unfortunately. That's a bad way to put it. I'll be happy to see my husband and kids again. I love being with Rachel, though. And Mom too. It's not easy living so far away them."

Don nodded his understanding. "Your sister is really good to your mom. She visits her frequently. Of course, I visit my dad quite often, so that's how I know. It's got to be a lot for her considering that she's a divorced mom."

"Rachel's a good daughter. She's also a good sister and mother. I think it probably is a lot for her, but she always keeps her chin up. She manages everything very well." Don could clearly hear Leah's admiration for her sister. He thought that was very sweet.

There was a space of silence, and then Don spoke again. "Your sister has kindly invited me to her home this weekend. I get to eat her famous brisket." He smiled at the thought of the upcoming event.

Leah smiled as well. "That will be nice. She makes a killer brisket. Rachel is the good cook in the family. I wish I had her talents for putting together a great meal. I cook, but not as well as she does, and I don't enjoy it as much as she does. My husband is our family's resident chef."

Ben and Delores made their way back to Leah and Don. Leah was very glad that their conversation had ended before Delores had a chance to hear about Don coming over to Rachel's for dinner. That would have been very awkward, and Rachel would not have been pleased to have the parents know about the weekend event.

Delores and Leah said their goodbyes to father and son, and Leah suggested that it might be nice to take a walk outside. Delores concurred, so they went outside and walked on a path. The weather was perfect with blue skies, billowy clouds and a light breeze. This was Leah's kind of weather, and she wanted to get Delores out into nature for a little while.

They ambled along the path, past statues and fountains. Leah still couldn't get over how nice a life her mom had and yet how her mother didn't always seem to appreciate it as much as she should. Leah and Rachel's father had worked hard, and his wife had reaped the benefits. Leah was glad about this, because the home really did help take good care of Delores. Living in California, she found that she didn't have to worry as much knowing that her mother was in a caring, pleasant environment. Not that Rachel didn't do her part. She did and then some. Leah just felt that this place clearly provided peace of mind for the families.

They walked in silence for a short time, and then Delores began to talk. "So, I assume you've had a nice visit with us?"

"Yes I have. It's been wonderful."

"Have you and Rachel been gabbing day and night?" Delores eyed her with amusement.

"Well, maybe not 24/7, but quite a bit. It's been fun, and I'll be sad to leave. Rachel's the best. She takes such good care of the kids and the house. Considering everything the poor girl has been through, she's pretty impressive." Leah never failed to express her admiration for her sister.

"That's a very nice thing to say. I guess Rachel has seen her fair share of challenges. You've been lucky, though. Maybe not just lucky. It always seemed to me that you purposely made good choices. You took your education seriously, you worked, and then you married well. None of this head in the clouds stuff." Delores was very emphatic about how she believed Leah had led her life.

"I suppose that's true, but one never knows what will happen. I feel like I have been lucky. YOU'VE been lucky. Rachel's been lucky here and there, but I think she's stronger than the two of us put together." Leah wanted to make sure that her mother didn't have some nasty take on Rachel's life. She wanted to make it perfectly clear that Rachel was amazing and quite a survivor.

"I'VE been lucky? How so?" Delores furrowed her brow, obviously not seeing things in the same light as her younger daughter.

Leah was taken aback. "How so? Are you serious?"

"Well, yes, I'm serious. Would you consider yourself to be lucky if you lost your husband too soon? That's far from lucky, Leah." Delores wanted to set Leah straight on this topic.

"Okay, yes, that was awful. No question about it. But your life HAS been pretty good. Look at how you're living now. Do you know how many people, older people, might love to live like this? You never had struggles. Daddy loved you, and he took good care of you. I'm sorry but I'm not going to throw a pity party for you." Leah's face became stony. She had always known that Rachel had many difficult moments with Delores, and now she really began to understand the depth of the challenges.

"So, you think it's easy to be alone and then to leave your house forever? Well, I hope that you're luckier than I am." Delores was taking a stand.

"Mom, you're missing the point. I'm not saying that anyone's life is perfect. But your life, considering everything, has been pretty good. Look at what Rachel has dealt with. Her husband cheated on her, she's raising three children, virtually on her own, and she's had to sacrifice a lot of her own happiness to make sure those kids are okay."

"I'm not saying that Rachel's life has been a walk in the park. Had she made better choices...?" Delores put her hands up, indicating that Rachel made too many mistakes, and there was nothing that could be done.

Leah stopped on the path and looked at her mother. "I cannot believe you! Rachel made choices that were right at the time. Steve was the one who screwed up, not Rachel. She was a good wife from the beginning."

"She shouldn't have married him. Clearly. I'm not saying it was HER fault, but she was too young and inexperienced to know what she was doing. She was always like that. She didn't think things through."

"Okay, I think I'm done discussing this with you. We need to change the subject because this is no way for us to leave things."

"Oh, Leah, come on. I'm just being honest. I can't help that you don't like what you're hearing." Delores set her chin in defiance.

"No, as a matter of fact I DON'T like what I'm hearing. I love my sister with all of my heart, and I don't like how cruel you're being about her. This conversation isn't working for me."

"Fine. I don't mean to be cruel. I love her too. She IS my daughter! I'm just stating my opinions."

Leah and her mother continued their walk, fortunately only seeing a few people out and about. No one heard their heated discussion. They approached the front entrance and walked back inside. Leah had a much better understanding of Delores. This had been an educational although not always pleasant visit. However, she saw more of her mother's true colors. Leah glanced at her watch and decided that they should have lunch together and then she needed to get going.

They ate at a table with two ladies and a man. There was light conversation, and that was fine with Leah. She didn't feel like talking much more. The lunch was over, and she told her mother that she had to leave. Leah wanted to spend her last bit of time with Rachel.

"Well, it's been wonderful seeing you, Leah. Maybe you can bring your family with you sometime."

"I'd like that, Mom. I know they'd love to spend some time here as well. I'll see what can be worked out."

They hugged each other, and Leah went through the lobby and walked through the doors. She was grateful to be away and heading back to her sister. Leah wasn't sure what she should tell Rachel. She didn't want to hurt her, so she decided to be supportive about everything Rachel was handling. She wasn't about to tell her what Delores had said.

Leah returned to the house, happy to be spending time with her sister before the kids arrived home from school. She came in the house, and went into the family room. Rachel was sitting in a chair, drinking some flavored iced tea and reading a book. It was so nice and quiet! Rachel smiled at Leah and rose from her chair.

"So, want any iced tea?" Rachel furrowed her brow in concern. "Or something stronger? By the look on your face, I think the latter of the two would be better."

"I'm fine, and an iced tea would be great." Leah plopped down on the couch, took off her shoes, and put her feet up on the couch. Rachel brought in an iced tea and a plate of chocolate chip cookies.

"Ah, yes, just what the doctor ordered." Leah sniffed in the chocolaty scent of the cookie, and proceeded to stuff the cookie in her mouth.

"Wow, you must have had quite a day with Mother Dear, hmm?" Rachel analyzed her sister's face wondering what had made her so tense.

"Oh, just the usual. I lectured her a bit about how she should be a little more grateful about her nice life."

"Oh, ho, ho! I'm sure that went over REALLY well. Are you crazy? You were taking your life in your hands with that admonition."

"Well, she needed to hear it. She needs to cop a clue." Leah took another cookie, put it in her mouth and defiantly ripped off a piece.

"Better you than me telling her what she needed to hear. Of course, now that I think about it, coming from you it probably went over okay."

Leah chewed her cookie and responded. "Guess again."

Rachel laughed at Leah, and held her hand to her chest in shock. "Do you mean that you, Leah, beloved daughter of Delores, actually said something that made your mother angry?" Rachel was having fun mocking the entire situation.

"What can I tell you? I'm an imperfect daughter." Leah responded with mock hurt.

"Join the club." With that, they both started laughing uncontrollably.

After regaining their composure, they talked about other subjects. It was such a relaxing time for the two sisters, enjoying each other's company. The time for just the two of them was gone before they knew it because suddenly the front door flew open. Sarah, Rebecca and David came in, saw their mom and aunt sitting with a plate of cookies, and they ran right over.

"Hello all." This setting reminded Leah of her own house. Kids running, wanting snacks.

"Hey." David chomped down on his cookie.

"So, how's everybody doing?" Rachel wanted to get something more out of her kids than just a grunt.

"Fine" was once again the only response that was uttered. Rachel looked at Leah and rolled her eyes, just like her daughters always did to her. That made Leah laugh, and then the sisters started their giggling fit again. The kids looked at each other, questioning their mom's and aunt's sanity.

"What?" Sarah never liked to think that her mother was laughing at HER. It was okay for her to roll her eyes at Rachel, and be annoyed with her, but the tables being turned didn't work one bit for Rachel's older daughter.

"I'm just sick of you all saying 'fine.' It's annoying." Rachel felt empowered by Leah's presence. She knew she could let it rip because she had support for a change. It felt great!

"Whatever!" Sarah couldn't think of anything else to say.

Rachel decided to bait her a bit. Perhaps this wasn't the most mature move, but she really didn't care. She was a human being

106

with feelings, even if she was a mom. "Yes, like, whatever!" Rachel rolled her eyes at Sarah. Rebecca and David started laughing. Sarah looked angrily at the two of them, and folded her arms in disgust. Then she looked in frustration back at her mother.

"Just stop. You're not funny and you're not cool."

Leah didn't like her niece's tone. She was tired of Delores being judgmental of Rachel, and she wasn't about to accept Sarah talking back to her mother. "Hey! That's not cool. Who are you to talk to your mother like that?" Rachel looked at Leah like she was a deer caught in the headlights.

Sarah looked like she'd just been slapped. "Excuse me? Mom was making fun of ME! How is it okay for her to do that?"

"Because your mom was trying to explain how you're behaving. She was being kind enough to use humor instead of wanting to throttle you. You need to show a little more respect." Leah was in a lecturing mood today.

"She wasn't funny. And I'm sick of her always wanting to know everything. I don't have to talk if I don't want to." Sarah looked at Leah and stood her ground.

That didn't quite work for Leah. She got up off the couch went over to Sarah, and got in her face. "Oh, yeah? Well, you need to appreciate everything that your mom has done for you. Be grateful that she gives a damn what you do. She doesn't need your crap. If she asks you a question, answer her politely. Otherwise you should go and live with your father. See if he'll treat you any better."

The room went silent. Rachel was too shocked to say anything. Leah wasn't sure if she had crossed the line, but she couldn't take it anymore. She knew that Sarah and Rebecca had not always made life easy for Rachel. It tore at her, and she felt that someone needed to give the girls a reality check, although Rebecca wasn't quite as difficult as her sister.

Sarah's face went red, and she stormed off, stomping up the stairs. David and Rebecca slithered out of the room and went into the kitchen. Leah looked at Rachel. She needed confirmation that she hadn't done anything wrong, hadn't over-stepped her bounds. In an instant, she knew that her sister was overwhelmed with gratitude. Rachel went to Leah and gave her a big hug.

"Oh, Leah! Thank you for sticking up for me! I needed that."

Leah breathed a sigh of relief. "I'm happy to be of assistance. There's just no excuse for Sarah to behave like that towards you."

"I don't know. She is a teenager and she has been through so much." Rachel gave a guilty look.

"Hey, don't go down that road. I understand the teenage issue, but that doesn't give any child the right to act in such an unkind manner. Also, realize that many teens experience the same things that Sarah has dealt with. Divorce is ever so common these days."

"I know, but that doesn't make it any easier. I'm sure she blames me for everything that transpired. What happened wasn't my fault, but Sarah thinks her father is the be all and end all. I'M the reason that we're all not together. She's going to be angry with me."

"How about counseling? I know she had some right after the divorce, but she may need professional help again. You can't do it all."

"Yes, she did have some therapy. Probably not enough. And anyone who has counseling has to WANT to have counseling. She wasn't all that keen on listening. Surprise, surprise."

"I think you need to talk with Steve about this. I mean, he's not dealing with this as much as you are. Maybe he's not aware of the problem because she doesn't show the anger with him as much as she does with you."

"You have a point there. I'll see what I can do." Realizing how helpful and understanding Leah was being, Rachel had an amusing thought. "Are you SURE that you don't want to move back here and help your older sister?"

"Believe me; I'd do it in a heartbeat if I could. Yes, maybe I'll see if Bob can find a job here. I'm sure that would go over really well with him." Leah laughed and Rachel did as well.

Rachel began preparations for dinner. She made a first course of summer rolls with peanut dipping sauce. For the main course, she put together marinated Asian chicken with vegetables. The kitchen had an intoxicating scent, and it must have permeated upstairs because before too long the children came downstairs.

Sarah seemed to be in a better mood, and the evening went smoothly. They ate in the dining room, where Rachel had set the mahogany table with her finest china, crystal and silverware. Leah felt quite honored to be part of the family, enjoying the delectable meal. The kids talked, and it became a truly festive evening. Rachel looked around the table and felt contentment.

Leah and Rachel spent the rest of the evening talking, while the kids went upstairs to complete their homework. When bedtime rolled around, they came downstairs to say goodnight. Leah and Rachel hugged them and wished them pleasant dreams. After the kids went back to their rooms, Leah and Rachel finished talking.

"I've been having the best time here, you know. It's been a real treat talking with you face to face. I really hope that you and the kids come to California soon. You can stay with us and just have a nice vacation."

"That would be great. I'll see what I can arrange. You'd need to check your schedule to make sure that you have time to be with us. YOU'RE the busy one."

"We'll work around my stuff. You could come this summer or wait until winter."

"The kids and I could definitely come in the summer, but Steve will be with the kids for quite a bit during the winter holidays."

"Oops, I forgot about that. Hey! How 'bout you and the kids come during the summer, and then YOU can come back during the winter holiday? That way, you and I can have some sister time together." Leah loved her sudden inspirational thought.

"Ooh, I like THAT idea!" Rachel was getting excited already.

Leah looked at her hesitantly, wondering how much she should say about Don. "I guess we'll know soon enough what your relationship is with Don."

Rachel looked startled. "What? No, no, let's not go down that path. There won't be any relationship. Well, maybe a little friendship, but don't assume anything more than that, okay?"

"Okay. I won't say another word right now. But you will share your life with me? You will tell me everything that's happening?"

"I always do. And you will do the same with me?" Rachel didn't want to be the only one discussing her life.

"Absolutely. My life may not be quite as exciting as your life may become." Leah smiled wickedly.

"Oh, you stop!" Rachel smiled at Leah. They talked more and then the night allowed for a quiet house.

Chapter Eleven

The next morning brought sunshine and activity. Rachel prepared breakfast for everyone, and Leah said a mournful goodbye to her nieces and nephew. The children's faces sagged with sadness as they hugged their aunt and told her how much they'd miss her. The three departed for the school bus, and Leah and Rachel discussed their mother and other matters. They looked at each other with wistful expressions.

"Hey, we'll see each other really soon. And, I will call you when I get home. So don't think this visit is the end of us talking." Leah hugged Rachel tightly.

"I know. I shouldn't feel too sad. It's just that I AM going to miss you!"

"And I will miss you. But, I think that we should start planning your trip to California. I'll get home, check things out, and we'll get something done. Before you know it, you and the kids will have plane tickets in hand."

Rachel loved Leah's eternal optimism. And Leah was right. It would be good to focus on a trip to California. Leah went upstairs to get her suitcase, came back down and then they both headed for Rachel's car, chatting as they drove to the airport. They arrived at the airport, and Rachel pulled up to the curb. They both got out and Leah grabbed her luggage.

"Thanks again, sis. I've had the best time with all of you. I can't wait to tell Bob and the kids about everything."

"Thank you for coming, and please tell them we all say hello. Maybe let them know that we'll be there for a visit very soon."

"You got it!" Rachel and Leah gave a last hug and then they said goodbye. Leah waved back at Rachel as she went into the building. Rachel sighed heavily as she got back into her car and drove off.

Rachel wasn't quite ready to go back home, so she decided to pick up the brisket for Saturday night's dinner. She arrived at the store, went in and bought the meat and various other items. She paid for her groceries and went back home. As Rachel pulled into the driveway, she glanced at her garden. She thought that later in the day it might be a good idea to look at the flowers, plants and herbs and find out what would need tending.

Rachel unloaded her groceries and put them away. She stood for a moment in the kitchen and thought about the fun times she and her sister had these last several days. Leah had really made time for her, even though she had precious little of it to spare. Rachel decided that she'd call Steve about taking the children with her to California. She would talk with Leah about the timing as well, and if everyone was on the same page, Rachel would make plane reservations. The thought of the trip put a smile on Rachel's face.

Rachel prepared the brisket and put it in the oven to cook for dinner the next evening. After she did that, she fixed a simple sandwich for lunch. When she finished eating, Rachel picked up the phone to call Steve about his weekend with the kids as well as the trip to California. Within a couple of rings, he answered.

"Hello?"

"Hi, Steve, how are you?"

"I'm fine! How are you?" Steve sounded very happy to hear Rachel's voice.

"Doing well, thanks. Listen, I wanted to confirm everything about you seeing the kids tonight. They'll be ready to leave when they get off of the bus this afternoon, so I'll bring them over. Okay?"

There was a slight pause. "Oh. I kind of forgot." Steve sounded guilty.

Rachel's heart thumped wildly. She needed her Saturday. "Oh, no! What do you mean you forgot? Is there a problem with you taking the kids?" Rachel felt like she was ready to panic.

"No, there's not a problem. The only thing is that I can only be with them on Saturday and Sunday. I can't take them tonight. Will that work?"

Rachel breathed a sigh of relief. "Oh, sure, that's fine. What's going on tonight?" Rachel was curious as to what he was doing.

Steve cleared his throat. "Uh, well, Linda wants to have a dinner party at the house. I guess I wasn't thinking about the kids being here this weekend." He sounded contrite, realizing he was abandoning his parental responsibilities.

Rachel wasn't quite ready to let him off the hook, however grateful she was that he could take the kids on Saturday. "You weren't thinking? Okay, that's interesting." Rachel decided this would be a great time to mention California. "Steve, Leah suggested that the kids and I should come for a visit sometime this summer. You don't care when we go, right? Anytime is acceptable to you?" Rachel sounded all concerned about what would work for him, not really giving a hoot as to how he really felt.

"Yeah, I'm sure that would be fine. You and I are flexible about visitation. You and the kids can go whenever you want for however long you want. I understand your desire to see her and her family. By the way, how is Leah? I'm sure you two had a great time together." Steve was sounding much more at ease now.

"Leah's doing very well. We all had fun together. I miss her already, but I'll let her know that we'll be seeing her whenever it's convenient for her."

"Okay. So, do you want me to pick up the kids on Saturday?"

"That would be great. Say, nine o'clock?" If Rachel didn't have to take them to the house, that was even better. She didn't want to see Linda.

"That works." Steve paused for another moment. "You seem to need me to take the kids this weekend. Something must be up with you." Rachel didn't respond at all, but she was holding her breath. Steve realized that she wasn't going to say anything. "I guess I'll see you tomorrow."

"Okay, bye."

Rachel clicked off the phone, grateful not to have had to tell Steve anything. She didn't need him knowing about her upcoming dinner with Don. The phone rang, and she jumped, thinking it could be her ex really wanting to know what was keeping her occupied on Saturday. Thankfully it was her friend, Grace, calling to see if Rachel wanted to stop by for a cup of coffee. Grace and Rachel became good friends when Rachel and her family moved into the neighborhood. Grace was sitting on a park bench watching her children and Rachel was there with her kids. They struck up a conversation, and their personalities clicked. Grace had been a good friend to Rachel. She stuck by her and supported her through the trauma of Rachel's divorce. Rachel had been there for Grace when her beloved mother died.

It had been too long since they had seen each other, and Rachel was happy to be able to spend some time with her friend. Grace's company would be a perfect salve to Rachel now that Leah had left town.

Grace lived a couple of streets away, so Rachel enjoyed the short walk to her house. Her home was a lovely beige brick with gorgeous gardens surrounding the entire two-story home. Grace had quite a green thumb, and she inspired Rachel to work on her own flower beds. Rachel strolled up the stone walkway, and made her way to the covered porch. Grace enjoyed reading outdoors in her antique wooden rocking chair. The chair, a distressed wooden table and an outdoor rug adorned the brick paved porch. Rachel rang the doorbell, and Grace opened the door, giving Rachel a warm smile and a huge hug. Grace was of average height and very fit. She had brown hair with a slight hint of red, which was most often in a ponytail. Her skin was merely touched by the sun, because she was always very careful to use sunscreen. However, with all of her outdoor activities, she always sported a healthy glow.

"It is so good to see you! Come in! We'll make our way to the back and sit on the patio."

"Sounds wonderful to me. I'm so glad that you called. I've missed you, and I want to hear everything you're up to."

The two walked through the house. Grace took incredible care with her domicile. The kitchen, although large, had a cozy feel to it. She had chosen an updated old fashioned range done in red enamel which was strikingly beautiful. The counter tops weren't the typical granite found in current homes. This one was a stained off white concrete with a huge butcher's-block island. The family room consisted of a vaulted ceiling, and the room was appointed with cream and green cotton upholstered chairs along with a light brown suede sofa. There was a wooden coffee table with vases of flowers and decorating magazines. The room was simply charming.

Grace and Rachel walked through the French doors that led to the patio. Situated on the flagstone was a black wrought iron table surrounded by four matching chairs, each adorned with a pale yellow cushion. The area was covered with an arbor of multi-colored roses. The fragrance the roses emitted was as intoxicating as the beauty of the blooms. There were hanging plants, and an herb garden surrounded by a rock garden. Grace had meticulously managed everything, and she was always working on some outdoor project. A while back, Rachel told her that she should teach gardening classes. Grace laughed that off, saying that she only knew what she wanted to do in her own garden.

The table was set in preparation for Rachel's arrival. There were green woven cloth placemats accompanied by white dishes, coffee cups and saucers. The silverware rested upon green cloth napkins. Grace had a server with a silver coffee pot. The cream and sugar were contained in white porcelain vessels and there was one white china platter with banana and cinnamon muffins and a glass bowl with strawberries (from Grace's garden), pineapple and cantaloupe. Rachel felt like she was a queen sitting in an enchanted garden. That was true except for the queen part, although her friend made her feel like royalty. Grace served the coffee, and they both put some food on their plates.

Rachel took a bite of the freshly made muffin. "Mmm, this is delicious! Thanks so much for putting this all together!" Rachel was beyond happy right now.

"It's my pleasure, and I'm thrilled that you were able to come over. It's been too long since we've seen each other. I missed you!" Grace touched Rachel's arm affectionately.

"I've missed you too. So what's new with you? I hope things are going well." Rachel used a napkin to wipe muffin crumbs off her hands.

"Everything is fine. Just busy with the kids, as I know you must be. They're so ready for summer!"

"My kids too. So, you have summer plans, right?

"Yes, indeed. Ashley is going to be babysitting quite a bit. She's very happy about that. She likes kids, and she loves that she'll be earning money. Andrew will be at summer camp for a few weeks. Overnight. Yippee!"

Rachel and Grace laughed. Andrew was a wonderful boy, but he was full of energy and needed an outlet.

"I think we're also going to try to get away somewhere as a family. Mike will figure all of that out." Mike was a wonderful husband and father. He worked hard at a computer consulting company, but he was also an involved family man. "What about you and your kids? I hope you have some fun things planned." Grace took a sip of coffee.

114

"The kids and I will be visiting my sister soon. She just left from her short visit, and she suggested that we come to California and spend some time with her family."

"That sounds like a perfect plan! I love how close the two of you are. It's a shame that you don't live near each other."

"Oh, how I wish that she lived here. But that's not going to happen."

"I assume she spent a lot of time with your mother?" Grace looked warily at Rachel. She knew everything about Delores and how challenging it was for her friend to be with her mother on a regular basis.

"Yes, she did. Now, it will be back to me seeing her. At least it's a nice place to visit. Mom doesn't realize how lucky she is, but she seems okay there."

They ate a bit more, enjoyed some more coffee, and conversed about all kinds of things.

"So, what are you up to this weekend?" Grace asked a very innocent question, although Rachel wasn't quite sure how to answer her.

"I've invited someone to dinner tomorrow night. The kids will be with their dad." She poured herself more coffee, hoping she sounded casual enough. By the happily surprised look on Grace's face, Rachel knew she had failed to make the upcoming dinner sound relatively unimportant.

"Really? Do tell!"

"Oh, no, no, it's nothing like that." Rachel swept away the unwarranted excitement.

"Okay, then. You need to explain." Grace was on the edge of her seat, coffee cup in hand.

"He's just the son of a man who lives at the home where my mom is. He's new in town, and he treated me to lunch one day. I'm just reciprocating. Giving him a little home cooked meal. No big deal." Rachel sipped some coffee.

"No big deal? It sounds like it is a little more than that. So, obviously he's single?"

"Yes, that's right."

"And? You have to give me more than that, Rachel." Grace's eyes were dancing with interest.

"Honestly, there's really nothing more to tell." Rachel sounded very calm.

115

Grace was prepared to coax the information out of Rachel. "Okay, I can see I'll be pulling teeth here." She held up her thumb indicating she was starting to count. "He's nice, right?"

"Yes."

Grace kept up her thumb and then used her forefinger indicating there would be another good characteristic. "Good looking?" Grace was willing to play twenty questions if necessary.

"Yes."

"Okay, are you at all interested in this nice, good looking man?"

"Oh, I don't know. Not really. Grace, I'm just not ready for any relationship. I'm really not sure that I ever will be. I was burned, as you well know. Very badly. My life is fine as it is, and I don't want any complications."

Grace looked sympathetically at her friend. "Oh, Rachel. I understand. I'm sorry. I know you had a rough time of it, but it wasn't your fault, and not all men behave so poorly. Don't punish yourself for the sins of your ex-husband." Grace was so compassionate that she brought a mist to Rachel's eyes.

"I know you're right. And I appreciate what you're saying. It's just not easy for me to trust right now. Besides, I don't even think that Don is interested in me. At least not in having a relationship. Maybe just a friendship. And, truly, that would be fine. It's more than enough."

"Well, you will let me know how your dinner goes, won't you? Relationship or not, I'm interested in everything that happens in your life."

"Thanks. I will let you know. What would I do without you, Grace?" Rachel really appreciated Grace's kindness and understanding.

"Hey, what would I do without YOU?"

The two chatted for a little while longer, and then Rachel thanked Grace for her always wonderful hospitality. It was time to get back home and work in her garden. Rachel and Grace agreed to meet again the following week.

Rachel walked back slowly from Grace's. In the short distance to her house, she replayed the words that her friend said to her. Grace was correct. Rachel did have a right to enjoy life and to spend time with a nice man. But, as Rachel kept telling herself, Don might very well not be interested. So, she decided to play it close to the vest and not rush anything. That would be the best thing to do.

She unlocked the door to her house and walked in. Rachel checked her answering service, and was happy to find out that there were no messages waiting for her. Rachel made the decision, after having had such a relaxing time at Grace's house, that she and the kids would have dinner at a restaurant. It was Friday, the brisket was still cooking for dinner the following evening, and there was no need to whip up anything for tonight. Rachel retrieved her sun hat, clippers and gloves. Then she went outside and began to work in her garden. Time ebbed away, and as Rachel was bent over in the mulch, she heard the motorized sound of the school bus. It screeched to a halt, and Rachel stood up. She watched as a number of children stepped off the bus, and then she saw her own going down the steps and onto the sidewalk.

She could see the three talking, hands in motion, as they gossiped about their day. As the children approached the house, they noticed their mother standing with her gloved hands holding a clipper. Rachel waved at them. Rebecca and David waved back, and then David raced in front of his sisters. He was panting slightly when he stopped in front of Rachel.

"Hi, Mom! Whatcha doin'?"

"Working in the garden. It's such a nice day, and I couldn't resist being outside. Figured my flowers could use a little TLC. How was your day?"

"It was okay. Nothing amazing. I'm going to get a snack." David slid his backpack off his back and went in the house.

Sarah and Rebecca had arrived and were standing on the lawn.

"Hi, girls. How is everything going?" Rachel attempted to sound cheery.

"School's school. I'm ready for summer break." Rebecca was a good student, but she was weary from the school year and wanted to have some fun.

"Okay. And how about you, Sarah? Everything okay?" Rachel hoped to get some kind of response. A pleasant one if at all possible.

Sarah looked a bit sullen. "Everything is fine. So, Aunt Leah left." It wasn't a question. She sounded downhearted.

"I'm afraid so. However, she wants us to come for a visit this summer. How does that sound?" Rachel looked hopefully at her

117

daughters. Their faced erupted into big smiles.

"That would be fun! It's been so long since we've been to California." Rebecca was gleeful and turned to see Sarah's reaction to the idea.

"Yeah. I think it would be great to go there. Did you talk with Daddy about it yet?" At least Sarah was interested.

"Yes, I did. I want to talk with your aunt and see what her schedule looks like. When she gives me the acceptable date, I'll book the trip."

Rachel went inside with her daughters. All three kids were now talking up a storm, very excited that the weekend had arrived. Rachel removed the brisket from the oven and then she told the children that she wanted to go out for dinner. They were happy about the prospect of eating out. There was a great Italian restaurant in their area, so she called ahead and made reservations for six o'clock. Rachel freshened up, and the children relaxed for a bit. Later, Rachel put the brisket in the refrigerator and then they all got into the car and went to dinner.

They arrived to find a crowd, but they were escorted to their table for four. Rachel ordered a number of dishes for all of them to share. It felt like a little party, and the joy that existed when Leah had been in town was able to linger for a while. This was one happy table!

When they came home, the kids did their homework. They wouldn't have any other time during the weekend, so they all buckled down and did what they had to do. As Rachel was reading a book, the phone rang. It was Leah. Rachel eagerly clicked the talk button.

"Hello there, Mrs. California! How's it going?"

"I'm doing well. The flight was smooth, and I actually think my family missed me." Leah laughed at her own humor.

"Well, I miss you already. I want you to know that I did talk with Steve today. He can't take the kids until Saturday, which is fine. I was a little concerned thinking that he couldn't take them at all this weekend, but we're set. Anyway, I decided that it was the perfect time to mention about wanting to visit you and your family over the summer."

"And?" Leah was on pins and needles waiting to be told that their trip was on.

"And, we'll be there whenever you want us for however long

118

you want us!" Rachel was practically jumping out of her chair.

"Fabulous! This is great news! I'll get right on it. You'll be able to book your airline tickets within days. I'll call you soon with the details. Does that sound good?"

"Sounds fantastic! I'm so glad that you suggested this. The kids are already excited, and as you would expect, so is their mother." Leah and Rachel laughed.

"Okay, I'll be in touch. By the way, good luck on Saturday. I hope that you have fun. FUN! Plain and simple fun."

"Thanks, Leah. I hope I do too. I'll probably talk to you Sunday."

Rachel let the kids know that their Aunt Leah had called and she was thrilled that they would be visiting. Rachel told them that she'd most likely be able to get the airplane tickets next week. The children clapped with joy. So, in spite of the sadness of Leah's departure, there was the happiness that came with knowing they would all be with her again very soon.

While she was talking with the kids, Rachel's mother phoned. Rachel hadn't really wanted to speak with her until the following week, but now she didn't have a choice.

"Hello?" Rachel knew who it was, but she didn't say "Mom."

"Hello, Rachel. How are you?"

"I'm doing well, Mom, how about you?"

"I'm fine. I heard from Leah. She mentioned that you might be going to California with your children."

"Yes, she kindly invited us to visit. We're looking forward to seeing the family."

"That's nice. It will be fun, I'm sure. So, you're not coming here until next week, right?"

"Yeah. I hope that's okay?" Rachel really didn't want to see Don at the home the night right after their dinner. She assumed he'd be going to visit his dad on Sunday. Rachel intended to see Delores on Monday.

"Of course it's okay. There are some activities going on around here over the weekend, so I'll be busy."

"It sounds like you'll be having some fun. What is the home doing?" Rachel was very happy that her mother was getting involved.

"They're showing some old movies. There will also be card games. There are singers and dancers coming here. Just lots of

119

different things."

"Sounds great. You'll have to let me know all about it when I come there. Probably Monday if that works for you."

"Sure, that would be wonderful. Maybe you'll come for lunch?"

"Yes, that would be nice."

"Okay, then. You enjoy the weekend."

"You too, Mom. Bye."

Rachel was tired so she said goodnight to the children and made her way to her bedroom. Rachel had changed things in her home since the divorce. The master bedroom was the first part of the house to be redecorated. The room was large with tan walls and a sitting area that had a comfortable soft white leather chair and a round glass table for books, a vase of flowers and whatever else Rachel wanted to put there from time to time. It was a very bright and cheerful room, which overlooked the front lawn. She still had the king size bed that she had shared with Steve, but the linens were all new. All white and a very high thread count. The room was an oasis for her, a kind of sanctuary. She was proud to have many pieces of Rebecca's framed artwork on the walls.

Rachel went into the master bathroom and got ready for bed. She took off her makeup and looked in the mirror. *I don't look like I'm nearing fifty*, she thought as she reflected on her looks. She took good care of her skin, just like her mother had always done. Her complexion was clear and without wrinkles. She believed that she still had a lot of her youth left. Not that fifty should be considered old!

Rachel went back into her bedroom. As she sank into her bed, she realized how good things were right now. She seemed to be getting along better with her mother. Rachel and the kids would be going to California soon. She had a wonderful friend just a few- minutes-walk from her house. And tomorrow, she would be having a pleasant dinner with a male friend. Not bad. Not bad at all. Rachel closed her eyes and slept soundly.

Chapter Twelve

The next morning, Rachel and the kids were up by seven. Steve was picking them up in a couple of hours, so she wanted to make sure that they were ready. She prepared a nice breakfast for them, and then they all sat together in the family room. At 9:07, the doorbell rang. Sarah dashed to the door to let her father in the house.

Rachel politely greeted him. "Hi, Steve, how are you this morning?" Rachel was always pleasant with him, if only for the sake of their children.

"I'm fine, how's everybody?" Steve always seemed a bit reticent around Rachel, and as far as she was concerned, he should be uncomfortable about what he had done to her and put their family through. Although he still had his looks, he had aged a bit. He seemed a little wearier these days.

"We're fine, right kids? You guys ready to go with your dad?"

They all picked up their overnight bags, and she gave them quick hugs. David was still the one who totally allowed the affection. Sarah and Rebecca tolerated the contact, but barely. They stiffened every time their mother went to hug them.

Steve led the way out the door. The kids then went ahead of him towards his black BMW. He turned to speak to Rachel. "Thanks for understanding about last night. I would have taken the kids otherwise. I hope you know that."

"Oh, sure, it's okay. How was the party?" Rachel really didn't care one bit about it, but she continued to be gracious.

"It was fine. You know how much Linda loves a party." He seemed a bit sarcastic about that, and Rachel thought his tone seemed odd.

"Did you enjoy it?" Rachel now assumed that the party was Linda's idea and Steve might not have had a say in the matter at all.

"Sure. It was okay, I guess. The guests didn't leave until two in the morning. So, I'm a little tired."

121

"I guess you would be tired on such little sleep." Steve's life was so different than the one Rachel was living. He was more interested in Linda and his own happiness. Rachel's life was mostly about the kids.

"What time do you want me to bring the kids back?"

"You can bring them back after dinner. Seven or eight. Whatever time seems good to you. I could use a bit of time for myself this weekend." *I deserve it*, thought Rachel. *You and Linda are party animals, but this weekend, you can be the parents.*

"Okay. That's fine. Well, I guess we had better get going. Have a nice weekend, Rache." Steve smiled, but he didn't convey happiness.

"Thanks. You too."

Rachel gladly closed the front door. She sensed something different about Steve. Something was off about him, although she suspected he was just worn out from hosting a party that went way too late. That wasn't her problem. She was going to have a fun day and evening. Today was about her.

Rachel made some cinnamon and raisin rugelach for the dessert. After baking those, she put together a salad without the dressing. She'd mix the dressing with the greens before she served it with the brisket. Rachel prepared some stuffed mushroom as an appetizer. Then she set the dining room table with her favorite pink, yellow and violet colored floral china along with crystal stemware. These were wedding gifts which she decided to keep even after the divorce. Rachel did a little more gardening, and then came inside to take a short nap. After that luxury, she showered and dressed. She put on charcoal gray silk slacks and a short sleeve V-neck pink colored silk shirt. With some silver jewelry, she was appropriately adorned.

Rachel was puttering around the house, making sure that everything was in its place. Her nature was one of being neat and organized, so she didn't have to do much fiddling. The living room, which harbored a lovely more formal seating area with a pale blush and cream marble cocktail table, also housed her prized collectibles. Rachel was very fond of nature, so she had various shapes, sizes and colors of crystal sea life, flowers and other pretty items all meticulously housed in a big glass cabinet that, when lit, made the objects come to life.

She checked the brisket, which was warming nicely, and

122

realized that she was ready to enjoy her evening. At least that's what she hoped. Suddenly, she felt a bit nervous. In all the years since the divorce, she hadn't dated. Rachel wasn't interested and that was that. NOT that she wanted to consider this a date. *No, no, it's just a dinner to say thanks for the nice lunch. He's a friend, and this is all very casual.* Still, she couldn't fight the butterflies. There was an open bottle of red wine from its slight use in the brisket. She decided to pour a little glass for herself, just to take the edge off. Seconds after she took a sip of the wine, she put the glass on the counter, and the doorbell rang. Rachel's nerves were on end, so her body jerked slightly. She noticed the time on the kitchen range displayed 6:30, so Don was prompt.

Rachel walked calmly to the front door, slid her fingers through her hair, and collected herself and her emotions. She opened the door, and there was Don, looking quite handsome. He was wearing navy pants with a white dress shirt and a matching navy sport coat. He was also holding a gorgeous bouquet of daisies, tulips and other spring flowers. Rachel smiled brightly, and he returned the expression.

"Please, come in! It's so great to see you!"

Don entered the house, and he gallantly handed her the bouquet. "For you. I hope that you like these. I thought they were so pretty." He looked at her in a very admiring way, as though he thought she was even lovelier than the bouquet.

"Thank you! The flowers are lovely. I'll put them in some water."

Rachel grabbed a Baccarat crystal vase from a cabinet in the dining room, filled it with water, and placed the flowers in the vase. She put the display in the middle of the dining room table. It was as though they were meant to be in that spot with her china. She glanced at the stunning arrangement, and then made her way back into the kitchen.

Don was tentatively standing just outside of the kitchen, so Rachel gestured that he should enter.

"I have stuffed mushrooms in the oven. Let me get those out." Rachel grabbed her oven mitts, opened the oven door, and pulled out the casserole dish in which the mushrooms were resting. She placed that on the countertop and closed the oven door.

"Wow, those look so good, and your kitchen smells wonderful!

123

If the brisket tastes as good as it smells, I'm very glad to be dining here!"

Rachel laughed. "I hope so. If I do say so myself, I think you will like it." She was feeling very secure right now. Rachel was surprised at how comfortable she felt with him, even though it was only the two of them alone in her house.

"I'm sure that I will like it. I can't thank you enough for inviting me to dinner. Being here means a lot to me." Don bent his head down a bit, rather shyly.

"It's my pleasure. You were so kind to treat me to a nice lunch, and I enjoyed your company. I'm glad that you wanted to come here to try my brisket. And the mushrooms. This is another favorite of mine."

He grabbed a napkin from the counter and picked up a mushroom. And then another, and then another. Rachel couldn't have been more pleased by his enthusiasm over her cooking efforts. She offered him a drink, and he chose the red wine. They chatted amiably in the kitchen, talking about their parents, the home and some activities to do in town. When there was only a brief pause, Rachel took the brisket out of the cooker, and plated the steaming meat onto a china platter. Egg noodles had been boiling on the stove, so she drained them, buttered them lightly, and scooped the pasta into a matching china bowl. The gravy made from the brisket juices was ladled into a crystal boat, and Rachel then poured the vinaigrette for the salad over the varied leaves, carrots, tomatoes and radishes.

Don looked on, captivated by Rachel's motions. Her efforts were flawless and smooth, but he knew that this dinner took hours to prepare. She was facing the countertop, so he was able to respectfully admire her without his attentive gaze being discovered. He appreciated her movements and hard work, all as she was dressed most attractively. He felt that he knew her well enough to assume that she wasn't vain. That made her even more appealing.

As Rachel turned around to begin taking the serving dishes in the dining room, Don left his moment of reverie, and assisted her in carrying them into the room. As he placed the platter of brisket onto the finely set table, he took in the surroundings. The room was so comfortable and yet so elegant. From his point of view, the setting fit Rachel's personality. She was humble and easy going, and yet she was so pulled together.

Once everything was placed on the table, Don pulled out a chair for Rachel. He made her feel like quite the lady. She thanked him, and he took his seat. Their wine glasses were full, and Don raised his glass to her.

"To you, Rachel. Thank you for making this incredible meal and for welcoming me into your home. I am a lucky man for having met you."

They clicked their glasses together. Rachel was stunned by his kindness and appreciation, so she was rendered speechless for a moment. Then she raised her glass to Don.

"Don, I thank you for your sweet comments. I am honored to have you in my home and in my life." She meant the last statement to sound a lot less serious than it came out. Don reacted to it with obvious pleasure. He smiled with his mouth and his eyes, and nodded once in appreciation. Rachel hoped that he didn't think too much of what she had said, but she couldn't take it back now.

Don reached for the silver serving fork that was resting on the china platter, and he picked up some slices of the thinly cut, tender brisket and placed it on Rachel's plate. Then he served himself. They each took a spoonful of the wide egg noodles, and poured a little gravy on everything. Rachel picked up the salad tongs, and put the green leaves on their salad plates. Don took a bite of the brisket. He looked very pleased.

"Rachel, this is fantastic! As I've told you, my mom used to make brisket, but not like this. Honestly, yours is the best brisket that I've ever eaten. It should be on a menu at a nice restaurant."

"Gosh, thanks. That means a lot to me. I love making it, and it's really simple."

"Well, simple though it may be, this has flavor and it's *so* tender."

"Thanks. I'm glad that you're enjoying it." Rachel appreciated that Don was being so complimentary. Don took a bite of the salad, and told her how great that was as well. He looked at her very seriously, and she was suddenly alarmed, although she didn't know why.

"Rachel, have you ever thought of being a chef in a restaurant?" Don was dead serious.

Rachel chuckled lightly. "No, Don, I haven't. I don't mean to laugh at your question; it's just that I would never be able to do that. I'm really not THAT good. I know I cook well for anyone who sits at my table, but a restaurant? I don't think so." She waved his comment away as though he shouldn't even think it.

"I don't know, Rachel. I don't think you realize how good you are. I guess maybe that job wouldn't necessarily be fun for you, but any food establishment would be lucky to have your talents." Don WAS serious.

Rachel raised her eyebrows with surprise. "Thank you for saying all of this. But, no, I don't think I would like that kind of a job. Besides, my job is taking care of the house and the kids."

"Oh, I didn't mean to make it sound like you don't have anything else to do. I know how busy you are." Don was almost ashamed for having insinuated that Rachel had plenty of free time, but Rachel didn't want him to think she was offended.

"No, no, I know that. Please don't think that I am upset by what you said. Not at all. I didn't mean to make it sound like I was defending myself. I'm more than pleased by what you said." Rachel smiled reassuringly at him, and Don eased. Rachel wanted to focus more on Don's life. "So, how is your work going?"

"It's fine. I'm very glad that I can do everything from here. It's amazing how this works nowadays. A person can live almost anywhere, and be employed using a computer. It's really worked for me. I didn't feel comfortable being a plane ride away from my dad. I like knowing that I'm here if he should need me."

"Of course. I understand completely. It's difficult if a parent doesn't have any family around."

"Is it any easier on you knowing you have a sister to help, even if she lives in California?"

Rachel took a sip of her wine and then answered. "Yes, I guess. I am the one who has to deal with almost everything, but I'm fine with it. Leah is very supportive, and I know how she feels about not being able to do more. Not that I want her to feel bad about any of it. I don't know what we would do if I lived somewhere else. Maybe I would have been able to be more flexible, as you are."

Don paused for a moment, although Rachel could tell that he was ready to say something. It was clear that he was trying to think how he was going to state his thoughts.

"Is it more difficult for you because you're a single mom? I mean, you have to be everything to everybody. A great mom to three kids, a supportive daughter to your mom. All without much assistance. How *do* you deal with it?" Don looked at her with keen interest.

"I just do it. I don't have a choice. I'm very lucky in many ways. I don't have to work, so I have time to do what needs to be done. My ex takes the kids every now and then, hence our quiet evening here." Rachel gave devilish smile. "Things could be far worse."

"Maybe it's none of my business, and please tell me if you don't want to talk about this, but how do you and your ex get along?"

"I'd say pretty well for the sake of the kids. I wouldn't deal with him at all if not for our children. Trust me; I don't like what he did to me." Rachel gave a look that indicated her displeasure over Steve's unconscionable behavior.

"I can understand that. Does he feel any guilt for what he did?"

"I have no idea. He went from having the affair, to us divorcing. Soon after that, he married Linda. I never had a conversation with him about it."

"Really! You never wanted to know why he did what he did? You never wanted him to know the pain he caused you?" Don looked at her in disbelief.

"No, I didn't. He told me about the affair, and I remember being in shock. I didn't want to hear anything about it. I was devastated, so he certainly knew that. But to have allowed him to explain himself or to give me any details? That would have been too much for me to take. I knew that I had to accept what had happened and move on. For my own sake and for the sake of my kids. I wasn't going to exonerate him for his bad behavior, and it wouldn't have made me feel any better knowing how, when and why."

"Did he *want* to tell you? Did he try?"

"I don't know if he wanted to tell me, and I didn't care. I never gave him the opportunity to say anything."

Don had a distant look as his eyes were fixated on the wall behind Rachel. He made a rhetorical comment. "I wonder if he feels any remorse?" Don focused on Rachel again. "I'm sorry. I don't know why I'm bothering you with these questions. Here, we have the most wonderful dinner, I'm sitting with an incredible woman, and I'm on a topic that must be painful for you. Truly,

127

I apologize for my rudeness." Don was ashamed of himself, but Rachel let him off the hook completely.

"Don, I don't mind you asking me these questions. You are the kindest man I've ever met, and I like that you're interested. At least you want to discuss something important. And I also understand why it's this subject. You were hurt when it happened to your dad." Rachel looked at him with sympathetic eyes.

Don sighed. "Yes. I was hurt. I don't think my mom ever cared what impact her actions had on me."

"I'm sorry to say that she probably didn't. It's cruel, but that's reality sometimes. I wish that my ex had thought about his behavior and the consequences that came from his selfishness."

"Do you think that your children will have a hard time getting into good relationships? Will they be able to trust and feel happy about being with someone?"

"I don't know. I hope that I can help them with this, but only time will tell. I'm here for them, in whatever capacity they need me. The problem is that I can't say that this could never happen to them. I can't possibly guarantee that." At this point, Rachel was just picking at her food. She had eaten most of the food on her plate.

"That's right. There are no guarantees. Would you ever remarry?"

Rachel didn't know what to say. She was surprised that Don asked this question. "I can't answer that. I have no idea. I doubt it, though." Rachel decided to toss the question back to Don. "You've never been married. Would you ever take the plunge?"

Don looked as if he was going to say something big, but instead he responded in a pithy manner. "Sure. I'm just very cautious. As you can imagine."

The phone rang, and Rachel debated answering it, as the call could be something to do with the kids. Don could tell that she wasn't sure about interrupting their time, so he told her to please feel free to take the call.

Rachel ran into the kitchen, and looked at the Caller ID. It wasn't the children, but the call was coming from the home. Not her mother's phone but the name of the retirement home was displayed. Rachel was confused, but she answered the call.

"Hello?"

"Hello. Mrs. Blum?"

"Yes, this is Rachel." She hated being called Mrs. Blum.

"This is Ellen Roth. I'm the Resident Advocate at your mother's home. Everything is okay, but we want to let you know that your mother took a little fall. She's at the hospital right now, and they'll keep her overnight, just for observation."

Rachel's heart was pounding. "How did she fall? Did she break anything? You said she's okay?"

"Your mother lost her footing on the walking path outside. I believe she'll only be a bit bruised."

"Walking on the path? Was she with anyone?" Rachel couldn't imagine her mother choosing to walk by herself.

"Yes. Her friend, Mr. Levy, was with her. He had her wait on the path while he got help. He was quite alarmed, but he knows she's not seriously injured. It was just a fluke kind of accident."

Don was now standing in the kitchen with Rachel, concerned about what he couldn't help overhear.

"Okay, well, thank you so much for calling. I'll probably try to get to the hospital to see her. I assume that's okay?"

"Of course it is. And if you need to talk with me, please feel free to call me. I'll give you my phone number."

Rachel, hand shaking, wrote down the number, thanked Ms. Roth, and hung up the phone. Rachel had turned slightly pale, and she was bracing her arm against the cool granite countertop.

Don approached her. "Are you okay? What happened?" He was very concerned.

Rachel collected herself. "Yes, I think I'm okay. That was the home. My mom was on the walking path, actually with your dad, and she took a wrong step and fell. She's probably okay, but she's being kept in the hospital overnight for observation."

"I'm so sorry, Rachel. I'm glad she's okay, though. That's good news. Should we go to the hospital?"

Rachel wasn't sure how to answer Don. She wanted to go by herself, mostly because she didn't want her mother to know that Don was with her this evening.

"I think I'll just go. The thing is… well… how should I put this?" Rachel started babbling. "I don't want my mom to know that you and I are together tonight. Not because of you, but because of me. You see, she'll start jumping to conclusions and pushing me. I can't deal with that right now. Do you know what I mean? This is nothing against you, please believe me." Rachel

129

prayed that Don would understand and not feel like he didn't matter or that she was shoving him aside. It became clear that he totally comprehended what she was saying.

"Rachel, I completely understand. Please, don't worry. I won't even mention anything to my dad. He'll probably tell me what happened, but I will feign surprise. But, believe me, if there's anything that I can do for you or for your mother, please let me know. You're not alone, Rachel." Don looked at her in a way that made her feel like he would want to help her if she needed him.

"Don, I can't thank you enough for coming tonight, not only for dinner, but for talking with me about important things. Just thanks for being such a nice guy. I so appreciate your desire to help me."

"It's been my pleasure. And thank YOU for everything. You're great Rachel. You've been nothing but kind and understanding to me. And, maybe when the dust settles, we could go out? Perhaps see a movie and have some dinner?"

'I'd like that. I'm so sorry that we have to cut this evening short. However, please let me give you some of the rugelach that I made for our dessert tonight." Rachel hurried to get the rugelach into a plastic bag, which she handed to Don. "Thanks also for the lovely flowers."

"You're more than welcome. May I help you clear the table?"

"Oh, no. No, you don't need to think about that. I'll take care of it, but thanks for offering. I guess I'll just have to say goodbye." Her expression indicated that she regretted that their evening had to be cut short. Rachel knew that her mother would have preferred Rachel stayed with Don and not concern herself with going to the hospital. Still, Rachel wanted to make sure that Delores was truly okay.

"Will you call me to let me know how your mom is doing? I don't care what time either. Honestly, even if it's late, I'd like to know."

Rachel couldn't ever quite believe how thoughtful and caring Don was. "Sure, I'll call you."

"I also want to be sure that you get home okay. And seriously. If you need anything, let me know. Even if it's a ride home from the hospital. I can always get you back there to get your car."

Rachel led the way to the foyer and opened the front door. "Thanks again for coming. I will call you when I get home. And

I hope I'll see you soon." Rachel meant every word.

"Okay. And I promise I won't let your mom or my dad know about our evening. My lips are sealed." Don pretended to zip his mouth, and that made Rachel laugh. He looked sweetly at Rachel, and gave her a kiss on the cheek. It was an appropriate and romantic gesture, perfect considering they had just started seeing each other.

Don went outside, and waved goodbye to Rachel. He held up the bag of cookies. "Thanks for the rugelach. I know I'm going to like these also!"

"Enjoy! See you soon!" Rachel waved goodbye to Don.

She closed the front door, and touched her cheek where he had kissed her. Then she went into the dining room. Rachel quickly cleared the table, and put the leftover brisket in the refrigerator, along with the remaining salad. That might not last for too long, considering that there was dressing soaking into the delicate leaves. Rachel figured she'd leave the rest of the cleaning until she returned from the hospital. She debated giving Leah a call, but decided to wait until she came back home. She'd know more by then.

Rachel grabbed her purse, went into the garage, and stepped into the car. Fortunately, the hospital was located just a few miles away. So, within minutes, she had arrived at the parking lot. The hospital was a huge white edifice, which gave it a rather sterile appearance. There was a parking lot and a parking garage, but Rachel found a space in the lot, so she got out of her car and walked right into the building.

Rachel walked swiftly through the automatic front doors, and went to the reception area. There was one person in front of her, asking for a room number. The older volunteer, dressed in black slacks and a white shirt with a light blue jacket, clicked buttons on the computer keyboard, and read through the lower part of the lenses on her glasses. She gave the room number to the lady, who thanked her for her help.

Rachel said hello to the volunteer, and asked for her mother's information. The lady went through the same process she had just gone through seconds earlier.

"Oh, yes, here we are. Delores Weinstein is in Room 2002." She pointed in the direction Rachel needed to go. "You just take the elevator to the right, and go to the second floor."

131

"Thank you so much." Rachel smiled at the woman, who told her she was welcome.

Rachel went across the taupe colored carpeted floor to the elevator. She pressed the up button, the door opened, and no one was in it. She pressed the number two button, and in seconds, the door opened again. Rachel walked out, looking to see whether she should turn left or right. She saw the numbers, and turned to the left. Her mother was two doors down. Rachel glanced in, to make sure it was her mother's room. She saw Delores lying in the hospital bed with her eyes closed.

Rachel walked in quietly, but her mother must have merely been dozing because she woke up. She smiled gently at Rachel. Delores was in a hospital gown with fluids hooked up to her arm. There was a light above her bed, which glowed softly.

"Hello, Rachel." Delores did sound a bit groggy. Rachel assumed she was on some pain medication.

Rachel whispered, even though there wasn't anyone else in the room. "Hi, Mom. How are you feeling?"

"I'm okay. I guess the home called you to tattle on me." Delores smiled at her own humor.

Rachel nodded her head in agreement. "Yes, they did, and that's exactly what they should do. So, Mom, tell me what you can. What happened?"

"It was just stupid. Ben and I were enjoying a pleasant walk on the path, and I was looking at him, not totally paying attention to my footing. I tripped and fell. Not a fierce fall. It wasn't that hard of a landing. But I fell forward and grazed my arm. There's no break. I'll probably have a bruise, but I'm fine. I don't even think I need to be here."

Rachel was relieved to know that things were okay. The nurse peered in, and saw Rachel talking with Delores.

"Hello. How are you both doing?" She looked at Rachel.

"I guess we're fine. I'm Rachel, her daughter." Rachel unnecessarily pointed to her mother.

"I'm Beth, your mom's nurse." Beth looked like she was somewhere around mid-thirties. She had short brown hair and was pale with no makeup. She wasn't heavy, but she wasn't thin either. She did have a very sweet and professional way about her, which was all that mattered.

"Hello, Beth. It's nice to meet you. Mom says she's fine. I

132

assume all is well?" She wanted to make sure her mother had her facts right.

"Oh, yes, she's doing great. She'll be able to return to the home tomorrow. We just keep older people overnight as a precaution. The home wanted to make certain that she was fine."

"I'm glad to know everything is okay. I felt I should see her."

"I understand. No need to worry, although she really does need her sleep. We have her on mild pain meds, so rest is in order."

"Of course. Should I come by tomorrow morning to take her back to the home?"

"Sure, if you'd like. We can let the home know that you'll be driving her back."

"Okay. Well, I'll be back around nine. Will that be all right?"

"Yes, sounds perfect. I'll write that down, so that everyone knows when you'll be here to get her."

"Thanks for your help. I really appreciate it." Rachel was grateful for the nurse's information.

"You're very welcome. We appreciate you being here. Your mom is lucky to have you come for a visit." The nurse smiled at Delores.

Rachel smiled at the nurse, and then looked back at Delores. Her mother was falling asleep.

"I'll head out now." Rachel whispered to the nurse. They walked out of the room together.

"Enjoy the rest of your evening." The nurse was very sweet. Rachel wished her well also.

Rachel made her way back down to the first floor and left the hospital. She had an easy drive home, and came back inside the quiet house. She put her purse down on the family room sofa, and stood for a moment. It was hard to believe that, just a little while ago, she was having a nice time with Don. Now, nothing. She realized that she should probably give him a call before calling Leah. Leah would be awake for a while considering the time difference.

Rachel punched the numbers on the phone and the phone rang. Don answered immediately.

"Hello?"

"Hi, Don. It's Rachel."

"Rachel! How are you? How's your mom?"

"I'm fine, and she seems to be doing okay as well. No broken bones, so that's good. She was a bit groggy and was falling asleep as I was discussing her condition with the nurse. I'll be bringing her back to the home tomorrow morning."

"Well, that is a relief. I'm sure she was glad to see you."

"I guess. Like I say, she was a bit out of it, but she was able to tell me what happened. I think she's a little embarrassed that she fell, but the important thing is that she didn't injure herself."

"Rachel, I really appreciate you letting me know. And I also want to thank you again for the delicious dinner and your wonderful company. By the way, the rugelach is amazing."

Rachel smiled even though Don couldn't see her pleased expression. "Thanks. I'm glad you liked everything. I'm just sorry that I had to end the evening so abruptly. We were having a good time." Rachel sounded a bit wistful.

"Yes, indeed. I'd like to go out sometime soon. Dinner. Dinner and a movie. Whatever you'd like. I know that you and I just want to have some fun."

"That sounds great. Yes. Fun. That would be nice!" Rachel was feeling excited about seeing Don again. "You can let me know when you find out what works well with your schedule."

"I'll do that. I'll see if my ex can take the kids next weekend. If he can, I'll let you know

"They're old enough to be home alone, right? We could meet somewhere other than your house if that would work better."

"Well, that might be good, but let me see if I can make arrangements first. I don't want anyone questioning what I'm doing."

"Understood. Well, I'm sure I'll see you at the home sometime this week."

"I'll be there tomorrow. Thanks again, Don. For everything."

"You bet. Talk to you soon."

They said their goodbyes, and Rachel clicked off. Now it was time to call Leah. She clicked her numbers as she had done so many times before, and listened to the ringing.

"Rachel? Is everything okay? What's up, and why are you calling me? Aren't you supposed to be with Don this evening?" Leah seemed frantic that something had to be wrong.

"Hello, Leah. I'm fine, so don't worry. Yes, Don and I had a nice dinner tonight, but the evening was cut short by the retirement home calling. Mom fell, so they took her to the hospital for observation. She's okay, no broken bones, and I'll be taking her back tomorrow morning."

"Oh, boy. Unbelievable. I'm sorry you had to deal with this, although I'm glad Mom is okay. Talk about a mood crusher for your evening. Tell me about your dinner."

"Everything was great. The food was terrific, and we had a good time together. I called him before I called you because he wanted to know how Mom was doing. Don and I will be getting together again sometime soon. Maybe next weekend. Dinner. A movie. Something."

"Oh, sounds good! So, you ARE in a relationship!"

"Not the kind that you're thinking. We are friends. And that's great."

"Friends. Well, maybe that's how YOU see it, but I wonder if he's on the same page. Well, whatever. It's no big deal. You'll let me know how things are as you go along. I just want you to be happy."

"Thanks. I appreciate that. How are things in California?"

"Good. We're all home tonight, relaxing. I was thinking. Are you SURE that you want to come here soon? I mean, what about going out with Don?"

"Yes, we do want to come for a visit. If I'm away for a while, it's not going to be a problem. Don will be more than okay with this. Honestly, Leah! My life isn't about Don right now. I mean, I LIKE him, but there's nothing else going on right now. He's not my boyfriend. And even if he was, I'd still want to come for a visit. Got it?" Rachel was razzing her sister a bit.

"Got it. Just giving you an option, that's all. So, I'll know soon when you and the kids should get your plane tickets. Please give Mom my best."

"I sure will. I'll be in touch."

Rachel ended the call, and placed the phone back in its cradle. She put her head back on the chair and closed her eyes. What an evening! She had planned to enjoy Don's company for hours. Accidents happen, and she had to accept that. Rachel was so tired now. She drifted off into a deep sleep. She woke up suddenly with a slightly stiff neck. As she rubbed it, she looked with bleary eyes at the clock on the cable box. It was 2:32. She got up slowly, turned off the lights, and forced herself to go to her bedroom.

Rachel didn't have the energy or the desire to brush her teeth, wash her face or change into her night wear. She threw off her shoes and all of her clothes, and dropped onto the comfortable bed.

Chapter Thirteen

Rachel woke up at 8:10. She needed to take a quick shower and get her act together if she was going to pick Delores up by nine. She flew out of bed, showered and was ready to leave at 8:45. As she made her way in the car, she was glad that traffic was light. It was a Sunday morning, so there wouldn't be any commuters going to work. She arrived at the hospital, and went straight to her mother's room. Delores was sitting in a chair, dressed and ready to go.

"Hi, Mom. How are you feeling this morning?" Rachel tried to muster up some cheer.

"I'm feeling fine. I think the pain killers still have my brain a bit muddled, but I am more awake now."

"Is your arm bruised?" Delores had her arms covered with the long sleeve shirt she had been wearing when she went for her walk.

"It's not too bad. There's some discoloration and a scrape, but it's not horrible. I'm just ready to go back to the home. I hate hospitals."

"I understand. Let me check with the nurse and find out if I need to sign any papers. I'll be right back."

Rachel went to the nurse's station, and said that she was Rachel Blum, Delores Weinstein's daughter. "My mom seems very ready to go, so I wondered what I needed to do to take her back."

"Yes, she is ready to go. You need to sign a few papers, and we can discharge her."

Rachel took the papers, and signed her name. The nurse retrieved a wheelchair, and she and Rachel went into Delores's room.

"Okay, Mrs. Weinstein. Your transportation back to the home is here. Let's get you into the wheelchair."

"I really think I can walk. I'm okay."

"Oh, I have no doubt that you can, but hospital protocol states that you have to leave in a wheelchair. You know, rules are rules."

137

It seemed that the nurse had heard previous patient requests to walk instead of ride. She had the pat answer that was always required. The nurse flipped the levers on the chair to lock it, and then she helped Delores get into the seat. Then, she flipped the levers back so she could push the chair.

"Okay, Ms. Blum, if you'd like to go ahead of us and pull your car around to the front, we'll be waiting for you." The nurse was cordial, but she seemed worn out.

"Yes, I'll do that. Mom, I'll get there as fast as I can."

Rachel sped past them, took the elevator down, and ran out into the parking lot. She got in the car and drove to the front to find Delores and the nurse patiently waiting for her. Rachel got out of the car and assisted the nurse in getting Delores into the front seat.

"Thank you so much for your help." Rachel wanted the nurse to know that her efforts were appreciated.

The nurse gave a weak smile. "You're welcome. Have a nice day, and take care of yourself, Mrs. Weinstein."

"I will. Thank you."

Rachel got into the car, and drove Delores back to the home. They didn't talk much, just a little remark here and there about the weather and the lack of cars on the road. They arrived at the home not long after their departure from the hospital.

"Mom, I'm going to park the car. Do you want to walk with me into the lobby or would you feel more comfortable if I drop you off and you wait for me inside?"

"I can walk with you. I'm okay." Delores wanted to make sure that Rachel understood that everything was fine now.

Rachel found a space close to the front, so she parked there. She turned the car off, got out and proceeded to assist Delores. Her mother did seem like herself, and she walked with ease into the lobby of the home. Rachel had been concentrating on watching her mother, and she continued to do so until she heard Ben's voice.

"Delores! How are you? Gosh it's good to see you! And Rachel. So nice to see you too."

"Hello. How are you?" Rachel was happy to see him.

"I'm doing fine. I've been so concerned about your mother."

"Now, now, Ben, I was okay last night, and I'm doing well now too. I don't want you worrying about me." Delores seemed to enjoy admonishing him, in a sweet way.

"She is okay." Rachel wanted to reassure him.

The three went to sit in one of the areas that had a couch and some chairs. Ben and Delores sat on the couch, and Rachel sat down in a chair. Ben had asked Delores about the hospital experience, so she was telling him all about that. Rachel listened half-heartedly. She was still a little tired herself, so she zoned out for a bit.

A few minutes into Delores's monologue, the sliding doors whizzed open. Rachel did a double take when she saw that it was Don coming through. He surveyed the three sitting together, and approached the group. He smiled at Rachel. She had to admit that it was so nice to see him. She had actually missed him. Rachel assured herself that it was only because their evening had been cut short by the home's phone call.

"Hello! How's everybody doing?"

Rachel was so grateful to him. He didn't let on that he knew about her mother. He was so smooth, merely asking about them as a group. Perfect!

"Oh, son, I can't believe I forgot to tell you. I guess I was shaken up. Delores and I were walking outside last night, and she fell, so she stayed overnight at the hospital."

Don was convincingly concerned, furrowing his dark brows. "Mrs. Weinstein. Are you okay? It doesn't look like you broke anything."

"I'm fine. I'm really fine. Your father is overly distressed, that's all. It's a shame, though. We were having such a nice walk. I was disappointed to have it interrupted by my mishap." Delores shook her head, disgusted with herself.

Rachel kept her eyes glued on Delores. She KNEW that Don heard the irony in her mother's comment that she and Ben were interrupted. Rachel almost wanted to laugh at their inside joke. When she did look at Don she noticed that his lips quivered a bit, as though he too wanted to react but knew that he couldn't.

"That's okay, Delores. We'll walk again very soon. I promise." Ben was so sweet to her.

Rachel thought that was pretty amusing as well because she and Don fully expected to have some fun together soon also.

Don sat down in the chair next to Rachel. They didn't look at each other, but both could sense what the other was thinking.

They were both recalling last evening and a future date.

Some residents came by to say hello and to find out how Delores was feeling. News of any resident's problems spread like wildfire. Delores seemed to perk up with all of the attention she was receiving. She and Ben were talking and laughing with their visitors.

"So, Rachel, how are you this morning?" Don figured that he should talk to her.

"I'm fine Don, how are you?" They both had the same tone, as though they were reciting lines in a stage production.

"Not too bad. Just glad that your mom is okay. That must have been scary for her, taking a fall and spending a night in the hospital." He looked very serious. Such a good actor.

"She wanted out of the hospital this morning. I think she should take it easy, but she was walking perfectly well. I guess she's resilient."

"Must run in the family." Don smiled at her, and Rachel blushed slightly.

Delores cut in to speak to Don. "So, Don, what have you been up to these days?" Delores wanted the scoop on his life.

"Oh, uh, working hard. And visiting Dad." Don wasn't sure there was much that he could tell her.

"Is that still ALL you're doing? You need to get out and enjoy yourself. You're in your prime, Don. You should be having fun and seeing people. Maybe younger people than you see here." Delores had a sneaky look on her face.

"I'll get to all of that soon I'm sure." How badly he wanted to say, "I'm enjoying your daughter's company." But he knew that he couldn't say that. Not only because Rachel didn't want her mother to know anything, but because he didn't want to frighten Rachel into realizing that he did think of the two of them as more than friends.

"I hope that's true. I'm sure there are ladies out there who would love to spend some time with you." Delores looked at Rachel and grinned.

Rachel wanted to slink away. She hoped that Delores was still doped up, and that was why she was saying these things. Don didn't say anymore on the subject, but he smiled kindly at Delores.

Rachel leaned forward in her chair, looking like she was ready

140

to rise. "Mom, you should take it easy today. I'm going to head on out now."

"So soon? Well, if you must." Delores said this more a practical idea than anything snotty.

"I think it would be best for you. And I have things I have to do before the kids come home."

"Were they with Steve this weekend?"

"Uh, yes. Yes, they were."

"So, what's kept you occupied while they've been gone? Other than your dealings with me, of course."

"Just this and that. I don't know." Rachel was feeling flustered, and Don chimed in to assist her.

"Mrs. Weinstein? I meant to ask if you and Rachel would like to come to my condo for a Sunday lunch? I'm settled in now, and I'd love to have you both over to my place. Of course, my father will be there as well." He grinned at his dad and winked.

Rachel looked at him, and then realized that he had saved her from further questioning. It was a good save too. This was a very easy invitation. He was inviting both she and her mother to his home.

Delores stared at him with obvious pleasure. "Oh, Don, I'd love that! Rachel, you'd like that as well, wouldn't you?" She was clearly telling Rachel that she had better take part in this lunch.

"Of course. I'd be happy to join you and your father for lunch. It's very kind of you to extend an invitation to us." Rachel smiled demurely.

"Great. You and Delores can let me know what Sunday would be good."

"Sure. And I can pick up my mom and your dad, and bring them to your home. I'll need your phone number and address." Both Don and Rachel were well aware of the fact the Rachel already knew Don's phone number. She didn't know his address though, so it was just one little fib.

"Thanks. That's very nice of you to be willing to pick them up." Don seemed genuinely touched by her offer.

"That's good. Don, give Rachel your information. Rachel, do you have paper and pen?" Delores was eager to have something happen here.

"Yes I do." Rachel dug into her purse and pulled out a pad

of paper and a pen. "Here, Don. You can write the information for me."

Don took the paper and pen and wrote down his phone number and address. When he handed the paper and pen back to Rachel, he lightly touched her hand. The slight brush made her heart beat a bit faster. She didn't look at him. Rachel concentrated on placing the paper and pen back into her purse, appearing as though she wanted to make sure that the items were securely in there.

Rachel looked up and smiled at her mother. Delores could not have been happier. She sat in her chair with an air of certainty and a smile to match. It was as though she had arranged a marriage for Rachel, and she knew it was the smartest thing she could have done.

Ben started talking about how great the lunch would be. He was happy that his son had offered to do this for their nice group. Don said that he was looking forward to having everyone over and that he hoped they would be able to come soon.

Rachel said her goodbyes, and Don and Ben both stood to say goodbye to her. Rachel let Don know that she would call him soon to set up the lunch date. Delores told her to have a nice day and Rachel made her way out the door.

It had been a pleasing day so far. Rachel felt fortunate to have the day ahead of her, free and clear. As she was walking towards her car, she was glad that the kids wouldn't be back until after dinner. She'd have plenty of time to do anything that she wanted. *But do what?* Now that she really thought about it, Rachel wished that she had made plans with Don today because she had plenty of time. They hadn't had the chance for a lingering dinner the previous night. Now, she was feeling a little pang of regret at having left them all behind. Don was still there, with his dad and maybe her mother. She stopped for a moment before reaching her car. *Should she go back, making some excuse as to why she had returned?* That would seem foolish. Rachel didn't want to be obvious. Besides, Don was there to spend time with his dad not with her.

Rachel shook her head, not believing that she had actually been thinking about a way to see Don again. That was ridiculous. She knew she was making way too much of everything. *Okay, so she liked him. So what? He's a good guy, fun to be with, quite attractive. No big deal.* She had convinced herself of her foolishness when she heard his voice.

"Rachel?" He was right behind her.

Rachel swung around, startled that he was there as she had been thinking about him.

"What? Oh, yes. Don. Uh, hi. What's going on?" Rachel was flustered. All out flustered and she was convinced that he had to know.

"Hi. Sorry, I didn't mean to scare you. I made an excuse to come out here and catch you before you left."

He made an excuse? Interesting. She had to find out how he did that. "What on earth did you tell them?" Rachel was intrigued.

"I said that I needed to mention something about the directions to my house. It seemed to work for them because they were busy talking with each other."

"Very good." Rachel was impressed by his desire to see her. "So, what can I do for you?" Rachel wanted to sound very casual. She wasn't feeling like that at all, but she didn't want to let on that she was so pleased to see him.

"I was hoping that you might want to go out for an ice cream or something this afternoon? I'm having lunch with my dad, but I can come by after that, if you're not too busy. Your kids aren't coming back until later, right?"

Rachel was elated, although she dared not let on. *He wanted to see her! Not that it was that big of a deal. Just two friends getting together. Still, this was really great.* "Sure, that would be fine. I'd like that." How she could speak so casually when her heart was pounding rapidly?

"Terrific! So I'll come by your house around two or so. Is that okay?"

"Yes. Yes, it is. That would be great. Thanks!"

"Okay, then. I guess I had better get back in there. I'll give you the directions when I see you today. We might as well make my comments to our parents as legit as possible." He grinned mischievously at Rachel.

"Yes, that's a good idea. I'll see you later. Enjoy your lunch."

"Thanks. I will. I'm looking forward to seeing you." He smiled broadly at her, and Rachel's heart did a little flip again.

Don left to go back into the building, and Rachel almost felt like skipping to her car. She couldn't believe that he made a special trip to come outside and ask her to go out in the afternoon.

There she had been thinking that she wanted to see him, and he was thinking the same thing. Still, she wasn't willing to believe this was any more than a lonely guy who had found a friend. A friend who happened to be a woman.

Rachel concentrated as best she could on the ride home. So much had been happening so quickly. She needed to focus on reality. As she parked her car in the garage and went into the house, Rachel allowed herself a moment to reflect upon her relationship with Don. *Okay, so she did like him. She was attracted to him. That's okay. I'm allowed to be attracted to a man.* Still, there was a huge part of her that refused to consider that this could or should go any further. She had no idea if he felt anything for her, and she wasn't sure it mattered. Trust was still a huge issue for her and getting back into the dating game wasn't necessarily an idea she relished.

Okay, so she would just have fun with her friend, her male friend. She checked her answering service, and listened to a message from Leah. She wanted to know how everything was going and if their mom was still feeling okay. She also said that if Rachel and the kids wanted to come to California right after the kids were out of school Rachel should go ahead and arrange the trip.

Rachel had time, so she picked up the phone to call her sister.

"Hello?" It was Amy's voice.

"Hi, Amy! It's Aunt Rachel. How are you?"

"I'm fine. How are you?"

"I'm great, thanks. So, what's going on with you? How's your play?"

"It's so much fun! I'm the best Eliza Doolittle ever!"

"That's wonderful! I bet you are perfect in this role. Is everything else going well?"

"Yeah, everything is fine. Mom says that you and my cousins are coming here for a visit. Is that really going to happen?"

"Yes, it is. Your mom left a message about that. We're so happy that we are going to be seeing all of you."

"We're happy about it too. I think you're going to have a great time with us. There will be plenty to do."

"Well, we're happy to be able to visit with all of you. The activities are just the icing on the cake for us."

"Do you want me to get Mom for you?"

"Yes. Thanks Amy. It was great chatting with you, and I'll see you soon."

"It was nice talking with you too, Aunt Rachel. Tell my cousins that I'm looking forward to hanging out with them."

"Will do."

"Mom!!!" Rachel laughed as she heard Amy yell for Leah. "It's Aunt Rachel!"

Leah picked up the phone. "Hi, Aunt Rachel!" Leah laughed.

"Hi, Mom!" They both laughed.

"So, how's life? You got my message?"

"I did, and I'll make the plane reservations. How long do you want us to stay?"

"How does forever sound?"

"Sounds like a plan."

"I realize that won't actually work. However, I'd be happy to have you stay as long as you can. Truly, I'm going to let you figure that out."

"I probably should check with Steve, although he did tell me that I could do whatever I want. I mostly have to work the trip around the kids. They all have activities, but David won't start camp immediately. Sarah is working, and Rebecca has her art classes. So my guess is that we might come for a week or so."

"Well, we'll take you for whatever amount of time we can get you. And remember, you'll return during the holidays."

"Oh, I won't forget that!"

"So, how's Mom?"

"She's fine. I brought her back home, and she's happy. So, all is well with the world."

"And?"

"And what?"

"Anything more to tell me about Don? Only if you want to tell me."

Rachel laughed. "It's okay. I don't mind telling you the facts. I saw him at the home this morning. He's invited Mom and me to his place for lunch. His dad as well, of course. Don and I are going to get ice cream today."

"Oh? Did he say this in front of Mom?"

"No, no he didn't. I was heading outside, and he came out into the parking lot. That's when he mentioned the idea."

"Interesting. Well, I hope that you enjoy your ice cream."

145

"Thank you very much. I do like ice cream."

"I know that you do. I'm sure that won't be the ONLY thing that you'll enjoy. I suspect Don's company will be in equal standing with the frozen treat."

"Perhaps."

"Well, you have fun, and let me know everything if you want."

"Will do. Have a good day, and I'll be in touch soon."

They said their goodbyes, and Rachel just sat for a moment. Life really was looking up. Delores was okay, and Rachel would be having some fun. Before she knew it, she and the kids would be in California. The phone rang and the sound startled her. She saw that the Caller ID displayed Steve's home. She knew she had to answer it.

"Hello?"

"Hello, Rachel. It's Linda. Can Steve bring the kids back now? We have other plans today." She was very cold in delivering her request.

Rachel was not amused. Steve, not Linda, should be calling her. Rachel decided she wasn't going to hold back.

"Linda, first of all, it's up to Steve to be calling me, not you. And no, he can't bring the kids back yet. I, too, have plans, and Steve is their parent also. He'll have to deal with it. If he has any thoughts of his own, he can call me. I'm in a rush. Bye."

Rachel was seething as she hung up the phone. *That little stinker. Okay, so she doesn't want to deal with the children. That's her problem, not mine.* Rachel decided that she wasn't going to wait around to find out if Steve would be calling her back. She suspected that, at this very moment, Linda was reading him the riot act. That was HIS problem. Rachel had over an hour before Don would be coming by. She wanted to go sit out at the park for a little while. Just to get away and collect her thoughts. She grabbed her purse, and started walking.

When she arrived home thirty-five minutes later, she checked her answering service. Unfortunately, there was a message from Steve.

"Rachel? Hi, it's Steve. I'm sure you know why I'm calling. I am terribly sorry about what happened with Linda. She told me everything. Well, she screamed everything, but that's neither here nor there. I didn't tell her to call you. Please believe me. I'm more than happy to have the kids with me." He paused for just a moment, and Rachel waited to hear the rest. "I hope that you are having a great weekend. Don't worry about anything here. I'll deal with Linda, and the kids are fine. Honestly, I'm so sorry. I don't know why this happened. Bye."

Rachel held the phone for a moment, even though she had clicked the end button. She actually felt sorry for Steve. He sounded so down, and she couldn't say she blamed him. Linda had crossed the line, and Steve didn't have any control over her actions. Rachel wasn't about to call him back now. She intended to have her mind free and clear to enjoy Don's company. That was what mattered right now. She put the phone down and went upstairs to freshen up.

She came back downstairs and picked up a book. She was engrossed in the story when the doorbell rang. She looked at her watch, and it was two o'clock on the dot. She loved that Don was so punctual. Rachel put the book down, rose from the chair and went to the foyer to open the door. There he was with his ever present smile, which made her smile.

"Hello again, Rachel."

"Well, hello to you too! Come in."

Don came into the house, and Rachel invited him to sit down in the infrequently used living room. He waited for Rachel to sit down before he took his seat.

"So, how was lunch with your dad?"

"It's always a pleasure to be with him. We talk a lot. He's a great father."

"I should have stayed with my mother, but I really think she needs her rest. Did she eat with you and your dad?"

"No. She went to her apartment, and I know that she was going to have lunch there and take it easy. She is fine, though, so no worries." Don didn't want Rachel thinking that her mom wasn't feeling well.

"That's good. Thanks for letting me know. Do you want to go out? Your suggestion of getting ice cream sounded great to me, but we can go wherever you'd like."

"Ice cream always works for me. Is there a particular place where you normally go?" Don wasn't familiar yet with all of the places in the area.

"Yes, there's a great ice cream parlor nearby, all retro and very good ice cream. I think you'll like it." Rachel was practically

147

salivating just thinking about it.

"I know I'll like it." He looked at her very sweetly.

They went out to the car, and Don opened the passenger side door. Rachel slipped into the seat, buckled herself in, and Don slid into the driver's seat. He started the car as she told him where to drive. Nothing was far away in the community, and they arrived at the parlor in less than ten minutes.

Don quickly got out of the car, once again opening Rachel's door. She had to force herself to let him do this. Her normal inclination was always to unbuckle and hop right out, completely unassisted. She liked Don's old-fashioned manners.

They went into the parlor, and found a table. The place was crowded. It was a lovely day, so everyone was out and about. After the waitress came over with menus, Rachel and Don looked over the selections and decided what they wanted. The waitress returned with water, and took their orders. Rachel was in the mood for butter pecan with chocolate sauce, and Don chose a chocolate soda with peach ice cream.

They chatted comfortably while they indulged in their frozen delights. When they finished, Don paid the bill, and they left. Rachel asked him if he'd like to go to the park. Even though she had already been there today, going back with him seemed like a nice idea. He was in complete agreement that they should enjoy being outside.

He drove the car into the lot at the park. They got out and started walking. It was so wonderful to be strolling along with Don on a picture perfect day. There were other walkers, and every now and then women would pass them in the other direction, giving a quick glance of admiration at Don. After walking along the path for a while, Rachel suggested that they return to her house and have a cold drink on the patio. Don liked that idea, so they left the park.

Upon entering the house, Rachel quickly checked for messages, but fortunately there weren't any. She grabbed a pitcher of iced tea, a couple of glasses and some napkins, and placed them on a tray to take outside. Don took the tray from her. She opened the back door, and they went to the table.

As they sat drinking their teas, Don said, "Rachel, I am having the best time with you! This has been so much fun for me, so I want to thank you for your wonderful company."

Rachel cocked her head shyly to the side. "Thanks, Don. That's very sweet of you. I appreciate your company as well." Rachel looked at him, and a burning question ripped through her. She was prepared to open up the conversation, and she hoped he didn't mind. As she looked at him curiously, he looked at her, wondering what she was thinking. "Don, there's something that I've been wondering about. And, if you don't want to talk about it, that's fine. Just say the word, and the question gets dropped."

"Okay. Shoot." Don looked a bit wary as he drank his tea, but he was open to hearing about whatever Rachel wanted to know.

"I'm trying to figure out something." She took a sip of her tea, hoping that she would find the right words to use. "I'm laying it on the line, so hang in there with me. You're a nice guy. You're interesting, funny and attractive." Rachel felt a little odd being so directly honest about how she viewed him, but Don seemed flattered. He smiled shyly. "You seem to like my company very much." Not that Rachel wanted to toot her own horn, but he had said as much to her.

"I do like your company, and I appreciate your kind words about me." Don took another drink of his iced tea.

Rachel asked the question, point blank. "You've never been married, and I'm wondering why that hasn't happened yet." She wanted to make sure that he understood that whatever had prevented him from making the marriage leap was perfectly fine. "Not that it's a big deal. Some people don't want to get married. Like I said, maybe it's none of my business, and you certainly don't owe me an explanation. It's just that I don't get it." Rachel's mouth was suddenly dry, so she took a swig of iced tea and braced herself for whatever answer was coming.

Don appeared reflective, and his usual smile dissipated. He didn't seem sad, so Rachel was happy about that. The last thing she wanted to do was cause him pain. "It's perfectly fine that you're asking me this question. It's one that I've asked myself over the years. I mean, here I am, a fifty-year old bachelor." Don sighed deeply, shaking his head with uncertainty. "One reason is that I've been very cautious. I was affected by my mom's infidelity towards my dad. She trounced on our emotions and never looked back. My mom was a strong, beautiful woman. Trusting women has never come easily to me. I like being around women, but I've never felt confident about having a happy, solid long-term relationship"

149

"Have you ever come close to being in love and wanting to get married?" Rachel now felt comfortable pursuing this topic.

Don looked at her, a serious expression blanketing his face as he contemplated his response. It was clear to Rachel that he seemed ready to divulge something. "I've thought that I have, but I always backed off before I would allow myself to feel that way about a woman. However, there was one time when I came close to proposing." Don looked away for a moment, seemingly recalling what had happened. His expression became sad, and Rachel hoped she hadn't opened a painful wound.

"Many years ago, when I was in New York, I was seeing someone for quite a while. She indicated, on more than one occasion, that she wouldn't mind settling down and having a family. I was cautious, and I somehow kept putting her off. I felt things were fine as they were, but very early one morning she called me and practically gave me an ultimatum. It was clear she had been thinking about our relationship almost all night. She said she wanted to meet after work, and we were going to have to have a serious discussion about marriage. We did have deep feelings for each other; it was my fear of commitment that was preventing me from moving forward with her. It's crazy, I know."

Rachel was very understanding. "No. No, it's not. You've just been protecting yourself. Who could blame you? You've had to look out for yourself."

Don looked at her with total understanding. "So, you DO get what I'm saying, what I'm feeling?"

"Of course I do. Maybe it's because I've been burned. But please continue with your story."

"Maybe she caught me off guard so early in the morning, but I wasn't thrilled with the idea of having a huge discussion about marriage. I told her that I'd call her during the day, and maybe we'd figure out where to meet for dinner. We didn't leave the conversation on the best note, and you'll soon understand why I have regretted it to this day." Don looked pointedly at a now confused Rachel.

"I arrived at work very early. I had thought about what she said as I was heading to work. I was thinking that I was ready for marriage and would surprise her by proposing with an engagement ring which I was going to buy that day. I knew where I wanted to buy it because she had hinted about the jewelry store

150

she liked. Anyway, I had a television in my office, and it was on mostly as background noise. After I was working for a bit, on September 11, 2001, I suddenly saw the reports about the planes flying into the Twin Towers." Rachel gasped when Don said this. "Yeah. As you may now realize, my girlfriend worked in the first tower that was hit."

Don looked down, closing his eyes momentarily. Rachel almost wanted to cry for his loss. "I have always regretted that I wasn't more pleasant with her during our last conversation. I suspect we could have been very happy together. Although I guess, after my girlfriend's death, I still wasn't 100% emotionally in a good place because I couldn't forget what my mom did to my dad. So, I haven't had a long-term relationship since. I came so close with her, but tragedy intervened." Don looked forlorn, and he became very quiet.

Rachel wasn't sure what to say. She felt horrible for everything he had been through. The death of his girlfriend, the pain his mother had caused. "I'm so sorry for your loss, Don. I'm sorry about everything. Have you talked with your dad about your feelings? About what you have dealt with because of your mother's behavior?"

"No. I don't want to open old wounds for him. This isn't his fault, and it shouldn't be his problem. I'm a big boy, and I need to cope with this myself." Don seemed very certain about this decision.

"I think he would understand your feelings, but I get what you're saying. I don't confide all that much in my mother either." Rachel gave a look that there was no way that was going to happen.

"That's interesting. I always thought that women discussed everything with each other." Don gave her a quizzical look.

"You're correct in the sense that girlfriends chat with girlfriends and sisters talk with sisters. But mothers and daughters? That can be a whole other ball game, trust me." Rachel gave a look that indicated that she knew the ins and outs of the whole thing.

"I didn't know that. So, when you went through your divorce, did you talk with Leah and your friends about everything?"

"Yes. I don't know what I would have done without them. They were my support, my life line." Rachel recalled that with gratitude.

151

"But not your mom?" Don looked at Rachel, trying to figure out how these situations worked.

"Not so much. Certainly, there weren't any deep conversations. I've really never been able to do that with her. Well, maybe a little bit more recently, but I'd confide in Leah and my friends long before I ever would with my mom."

Don nodded his head, understand things more clearly now. "So, it seems that you and I have mother issues." Don smiled at Rachel.

"On different levels, yes, I guess that's true. And now neither of us can imagine having a good stable relationship with a member of the opposite sex." Rachel thought that was an amusing conclusion until she really thought about how it came out. She held up her hand in defense. "Not that I'm looking for that." Rachel wanted to correct any misunderstanding before she made a complete fool of herself.

Don chuckled. "Well, I'm not discounting that for myself. I think it's possible to have that. I'd like to think that I could be in a healthy relationship with an incredible woman. It's just that I've got to get over the fear."

"Yes, fear, trust. Those are mountains to climb."

Don and Rachel both took swigs of their drinks and sat in silence for a moment. Don looked at Rachel very seriously, as though he had just thought of something very monumental. "Rachel, why don't we give it a shot?"

"Give what a shot?"

"Us."

Rachel had taken a sip of her iced tea, and she started coughing as she swallowed it wrong. She waved her hands away, indicating that she was fine. "I'm sorry. The tea went down wrong."

"What do you think? I mean, we like each other. We have fun together. I find you very attractive, and you seem to like me enough. I think that we have a certain bond. Looking at each other as more than just friends could be fun."

Rachel didn't know what to say. She agreed, but like Don, she was afraid. Rachel looked at him for a moment, just to see how serious he really was. She cleared her throat. "So, you really think this is a good idea? I have three kids and an ex-husband. You can deal with that?" Rachel wanted her situation to be crystal clear to Don.

152

"Yes, I think this is a very good idea. I know what your life is like, at least somewhat. I'm not trying to push you into anything ultra-serious, but I think it would be nice to go out on a regular basis. Not to have to tiptoe around each other. Really know that this matters." Don pointed at Rachel and back to himself.

"What you're saying makes sense. I know that this would be nice. I just don't want either of us to get hurt." Rachel looked at Don, her eyes pleading for this all to be okay.

"I don't want either of us to get hurt either. I don't know why, but I don't see that happening. I'm not a bad guy. I respect you. I appreciate the way that you live." He leaned forward and looked at her intensely. "And I would never betray you."

Rachel looked at Don, wanting to believe him with all of her heart. *It had been too long since any man had shown an interest in her. Who was she kidding? No man had shown that since Steve.* "That's a very thoughtful thing to say. Considering what we've both been through, neither one of us could deal with infidelity." Rachel paused for a moment to consider the idea. Then she knew. "Okay. I'd be happy to try this."

Don beamed with pleasure. Rachel returned his expression with her own grin.

"So, we can be open about this? Our parents can know?" Don looked cautiously at Rachel.

Rachel frowned with the idea. "Oh. I hadn't thought about that. I don't know. I mean, your dad probably would be fine with this. He wouldn't make a big deal out of it. I confess that my mother might not be so relaxed about this."

"What do you mean? I assumed that she liked me. She's always been very nice to me." Don looked a bit surprised, and Rachel realized that she had not said that correctly.

"Oh, no. That's not what I mean at all. She does like you. She's liked you since before you and I met." Rachel hung her head down a bit. "Truth be told she's wanted THIS since she met you."

"What? I don't understand." Don was rightly confused.

"She wanted me to ask YOU out." Rachel felt funny telling him the secret.

Don started laughing, more so than she had ever seen him. She looked at him, not sure what to make of his amused outburst.

"Wow! That would have been something. Ha! I would have loved that!" Don was enjoying the concept.

"Are you serious? Why?" Rachel was now the confused one.

"Why not? A pretty lady wants to go out with me? I liked you from the first time that we met. I would have been flattered."

"And you would have accepted my invitation? Really? It wouldn't have scared you to go out with me?"

"No. Not at all. I didn't realize that your mother had been talking to you about me, very interesting." He looked at her like the cat that swallowed the canary.

"So, you would have liked to be asked out." Rachel said that as a statement, not as a question. She was just very surprised by his enthusiasm.

"Well, there you go. I'm glad that I've suggested this arrangement. Maybe it's time we both admit to having some feelings, and we just go with it."

"Yes, we can do that. But I'm still not sure if I want my mom to know. Not yet."

"That's fine. We can take this slowly, and we have no obligation to let on about anything."

"I guess we can go out whenever we want. Weekends are okay, as long as I can get Steve to take the kids. That may not happen every weekend. I don't want the children in on this either. Lunches, if that works in your schedule?"

"Absolutely. We'll have plenty of time to get together. Oh, and what about lunch at my home? When should we do that?"

"Next Sunday should be fine. It wouldn't matter if my kids are around or not. My mom and your dad are included. So, I'd tell them that, and they'd be fine here during the day."

"Would you like them to join us?"

"No. That's not necessary. Besides, you don't need to deal with them right now." She looked at him making it clear that he was jumping the gun if he thought he could handle a relationship with her children at this point in time.

"Whatever you think is best." Don looked at his watch and realized that he probably should get going. "I've got to get some work done before the end of the day. But Rachel, this has been an exceptional day for me. Thanks for listening to me talk about my past. And I'm really am happy about our decision to date."

"Same here. I think we'll have good times together."

They walked back into the house with Don carrying the tray to the kitchen.

"Do you want to have lunch with me this week?" Don was already making plans, and that made Rachel feel good. It was nice to know that he wanted to see her soon.

"Sure. That would be great. I'd be happy to have lunch here as well at some point."

"That would be fine. I love your cooking. But keep in mind that I'd also like to take you out. So, we'll do that sometimes. Okay?" He looked at her, questioning how she felt about that.

"Of course it's okay. I'd like that. I'm just happy to have us here in quiet and privacy. Lunch out is fine, though. I'm very up for it."

"Sounds good. How 'bout Tuesday? Does that work well for you?"

"Yes. That's perfect. Around noon?"

Don liked the idea, and he headed to the front door. He stood looking at Rachel for a moment, but he didn't say anything. She felt a little uncomfortable, but she enjoyed his soft gaze. As if he was taking her in and appreciating her.

"This is good! This is really good!" Don made it clear that things would be fine. "So, I will see you on Tuesday? And let your mom know about Sunday. I'll let my dad know that you'll be picking him up when you get your mom?"

"Yes. That would be great."

Don looked at her again, as though not believing his own luck in being with Rachel. He bent down to lightly kiss her lips. Rachel blushed a little, but was quite happy with his romantic gesture. It had been a LONG time since she experienced that feeling.

"Thanks, Don. I've had a great time with you today. So, I'll see you Tuesday."

"Yes, Rachel. You will indeed!"

And with that, Don walked out of the house and to his car. He waved goodbye, got in, and drove off. Rachel hadn't been this happy in years.

Chapter Fourteen

Rachel spent the rest of the day doing laundry and paying bills. It was nice to have some quiet time. As the evening drew near, she made a simple dinner for herself. She ate her meal and went over the events of the day. She felt confident that Don really was interested in her. He had said as much, and she believed him. Still, she wanted to keep up her emotional defenses. *I'm mature now, and I can really think with my head as well as with my heart.* She kept telling herself that, making sure that she didn't lose her grip on reality. Rachel definitely liked Don. She was attracted to him. But she had learned the hard way that one really needed to exercise caution with any relationship. She took some time to relax in front of the television. At eight o'clock, the front door burst open, startling her.

The kids flowed in and Steve followed. She was surprised to see him. He didn't normally bother bringing them into the house. Rachel went over to the foyer to say hello to everybody.

"Good evening all. How's everybody?"

There was a chorus of "fine" and that was that. Nothing had changed in the day or so since they had visited with their father. They went on their merry ways. Steve looked drained. Was it the time he spent with his children or something else?

"And how are you Steve?"

"I'm okay. How about you? You look good. Happy."

"I am, thanks. So what's up? I'm surprised to see you here."

Steve cleared his throat. Rachel offered him a glass of tea and to sit in the kitchen. Steve sat down, although he looked uncomfortable. She felt that he had aged since being married to Linda. Rachel could believe that living with that woman would send anyone closer to the grave. However, she kept that feeling to herself.

Steve thanked Rachel for the drink and he shifted in his seat a bit. "Rachel, I cannot apologize enough for the phone call you received from Linda." Steve clearly felt horrible about what had happened, so Rachel let him off the hook.

"Forget about it. It wasn't your fault. It's okay."

Steve looked disturbed. "She was just so wrong in calling. I couldn't believe it when she came to me, angry and screaming. SHE was the one who did something wrong." Steve shook his head, as though trying to rid himself of that horrible moment with his wife.

"Thank you for saying that. I happen to agree. I don't know what her problem is, but I'll hold my own with her. Don't worry about me." She nodded assuredly.

Steve looked at her, amazed by the conviction that she felt. He was impressed by her stronger character. "I guess I won't worry. And I do know what her problem is. She's selfish and spoiled. I told her that I want to be with my kids whether she likes it or not. She's angry with me for not supporting her about having the kids leave earlier. She'll get over it."

"She'll have to. They are part of your life, and she was well aware of that when…" Rachel stopped what she was going to say.

Steve looked at her, knowing full well what she wanted to say. He bent his head in shame, afraid to even look at her. "I hope she never bothers you like that again. You'll let me know if she does?" Steve looked hopeful that Rachel would communicate anything that bothered her.

"Yes I will. Believe me." Rachel steadied her gaze on Steve, not sure what he was feeling. "Steve, is something wrong? You don't seem like your old self."

"I'm okay. I…well…things have been a bit strained at home. I guess it's worn me out a little."

"I see. Well, hopefully things will get better soon." *What else could she say?* It was hard to feel too sorry for him considering everything that had happened. He had a good life with Rachel and the kids, and he blew it. It was up to him to live with the consequences. Rachel wanted to talk about the trip to California. "Steve, I want a week or so to take the kids to California. You said that was okay, right?"

"Whatever you want to do. I know you want to see your sister, and the kids haven't seen their cousins in quite a while." He wasn't about to fight her on anything.

Rachel smiled at his generosity. She also told him that she alone would be planning another California trip during the winter

157

holiday. Steve said that he'd take the kids for as long as Rachel needed. She appreciated his cooperation.

Steve stood up, getting ready to depart for home. He placed his hands in the pockets of his jeans and looked around at the kitchen and the family room, taking it all in. Then they walked towards the front of the house and Rachel opened the front door for him.

"You've kept this house running very smoothly and the kids seem to be flourishing. I'm impressed by how well you've handled everything. Life seems to be agreeing with you." He smiled warmly at her.

Rachel wasn't sure what to make of all of this flattery, but she politely accepted it. "Thank you. Things are going well. I'm keeping my chin up!"

"Good for you! That's how you've got to do it. I'll talk with you soon." He shouted goodbye to the kids, but they were too busy upstairs to even hear him.

As he left, Rachel knew that he was feeling very melancholy. Well, he had made his choice when he gave up his family and his home. Maybe he was having a mid-life crisis. It wasn't her problem now. As long as he cared for his children, that was all that mattered to her. Rachel went back inside to spend time with the three of them.

The next morning, after the kids left for school, she began the process of booking the airline tickets for California. Sarah said that she would be fine with taking a week before starting the job. The store didn't need her until a couple of weeks after school let out, so she had some time. Rebecca's art classes started three weeks after school was over, and David's schedule was also clear for those first few weeks, so Rachel decided that they would leave the Sunday after school ended. They would spend a week there, which would work out for everyone. She knew that her sister didn't mind if they stayed longer, but it was a lot for any family to have Rachel and three children descend on them all at once. After arranging their flights, both to and from, Rachel called Steve at the office to inform him of the schedule.

"Hello?"

"Hey, Steve. It's Rachel."

"Hi, Rache! How are you?" Steve sounded much more upbeat today.

"I'm fine. How's life with you?

"Not bad. It's nice hearing from you. What's up?"

"I want to let you know that I booked the trip to California."

Steve sounded fine with all of the information. He wrote it down on his calendar. The call was brief but pleasant. Time had made dealing with each other more tolerable. Rachel didn't feel the painful sting anymore when talking with Steve.

After speaking with her ex, Rachel called her friend, Grace, and wondered if she'd like to have lunch and walk in the park. Grace said she'd love to, and she'd come get Rachel at noon. Then Rachel called Leah to let her in on everything.

"Hi, sis! How are you?" Leah always sounded peppy, even in the early morning hours.

"I'm doing very well. I assume life is good for you?"

"Yep. Especially if you're calling to let me know when you'll be here."

Rachel laughed at her sister's enthusiasm. "Yes, I am calling to let you know every detail."

She gave Leah the dates that they'd be there and the times of arrival and departure. They talked about their families for a few minutes, and then Rachel let her in on some of her fun news. "Okay, I guess I need to tell you some other stuff."

"Really? Am I going to love this or what?"

"I suspect you'll be happy with my news." Rachel was very coy with her sister.

"Okay. So tell, tell!"

"Weellll, Don and I are kind of seeing each other. As in sort of dating."

Leah let out a squeal. Rachel removed the phone from her ear for a few seconds. "Kind of. Sort of. Come on, sis. You're DATING. This is terrific! I couldn't be happier for you!" Even over the phone, Rachel could imagine Leah's face right now, a little red with excitement and a smile that showed her dazzling white teeth.

"I don't want to over-state this in any way. I have no grand expectations. We're just friends hanging around with each other. This is really not that big of a deal." Rachel was still trying to convince herself that she wasn't in a romantic relationship.

"Uh, huh. You keep telling yourself that, if it makes you feel better. It sounds to me like you two are going to be more than just friends. By the way, who brought this up? I assume it was Don because I can't imagine you taking the leap."

"You're right about that. I don't know. We were just chatting about stuff, and the subject came up. We discussed the topic of dating, and we're taking a chance here. We like each other, so why not try? Right?"

"Absolutely right. Are you going to mention this to Mom?"

"No. Not yet. I told Don that I wasn't ready to have our parents know anything. It sounds so *teenagery* doesn't it?" Rachel felt a little foolish for her clandestine ways.

"It's okay. This isn't about her anyway. You two do what you want."

"We're having lunch at Don's on Sunday. That should be interesting."

"Will you see him before then?"

"Yes, on Tuesday for lunch. We seem to see each other around food." Rachel laughed self-consciously at that.

"Nothing wrong with that. And you're not telling the kids either?"

"No. Not yet. I'll see how this goes for now. I'm not rushing anything."

Rachel and Leah wrapped up the conversation and Rachel got ready for her afternoon with Grace. Her friend came by and they went to lunch at soup and sandwich place located near the park. They chatted easily about their kids and events while they ate, and then they talked more at the park. Rachel mentioned the situation with Don, letting Grace know that things had progressed a little. Grace was thrilled to hear about this news. She insisted on being updated and told her friend that she would always be there if Rachel needed advice or to just to talk.

Rachel arrived back home by three, and the kids arrived shortly thereafter. They all came in, talking and ready for snacks as usual. Sarah approached Rachel and actually started to talk with her.

"Mom, can I talk with you about some stuff?" Sarah seemed uncertain and uncomfortable, and Rachel felt her heart skip. This was a new occurrence, and she hoped everything was okay.

"Of course you can. Do you want to sit outside and chat?" Rachel wanted her daughter to be free to open up without fear of being overheard by her siblings.

"Yeah. Sure. That would be great." Sarah sounded tentative.

They went outside, both carrying drinks and Rachel holding

a plate of cookies. Rebecca and David had already gone upstairs to start their homework. The two sat down, and Rachel looked at her daughter with an open expression. Sarah twisted her hands together insecurely.

"Mom?"

"Yes, Sarah? Rachel was holding her breath.

"I have a question about boys." Sarah's right leg was bouncing up and down. This was not the most comfortable situation for her, but she needed her mother's advice.

"Okay. Sure. What can I do for you?" Rachel looked at Sarah with a smile that showed that she was merely waiting to assist.

"Well, there's a boy I like, and he seems to like me. He's cute and funny, but, well, is all of this worth bothering with right now?" She seemed unsure of herself.

Rachel was a bit puzzled. "I'm not sure what you mean. Why wouldn't you want to bother with him right now?"

"I don't think that I want to go through stuff. I mean, I don't want to end up hurt. You know? I look at everything you've gone through, and it just seems too painful." Sarah looked down, unable to meet Rachel's gaze.

Rachel felt her stomach lurch. Guilt was flowing through her entire body, and she felt worse than she had when Steve confessed his sin to her. Her daughter had already witnessed too much heartache. Rachel felt disgusted with herself and with Steve for bringing on such doubt to their child. However, she knew that this was not the time for recriminations against herself for her failings. It was time to step up and help her angst-ridden daughter.

"Oh, honey, please don't feel that way." Rachel instantly realized that it was not an appropriate thing to say this. Her daughter had every right to feel how she wanted. She quickly changed her statement. "What I mean is that you are a teenager with every right to have some fun. My situation shouldn't influence you. We all make mistakes in all kinds of ways. But we have to live. We have to allow for errors of judgment. I hate to tell you this, but pain is part of the process. But it's worth it. The joys can reach so much higher than the challenges." She reached her hand out and put it on her daughter's arm. "Sarah, you're a lovely, smart, fun young woman. It's okay to go out with boys and explore life a little. I can't tell you what will happen. I suspect that he won't be your one and only, but he'll be a first step

161

towards other relationships." Rachel remained strong for Sarah, although she felt like breaking in two.

Sarah nodded as though she did understand. Still, she had a curious look in her eyes. "Why did you make such a mistake with your choice? Clearly, Daddy wasn't right for you? You'd never want to go through that again, right?" Sarah looked for affirmation about her thoughts.

Rachel tried to lighten up the topic a little, so she laughed gently. "I don't really think I made a mistake. Things went wrong, but your daddy was right for me at the time. And, my dear daughter, I feel so blessed to have three wonderful children. No, I wouldn't want to go through the pain again, and I am cautious. But life continues. I've learned a lot, as you will over time." Rachel couldn't help but think about Don.

"So, you're saying that I have to take chances. That if I like this boy and he likes me, it's okay to see what happens." Sarah stated these comments as facts, reassuring herself that this was all okay. Rachel seemed to have answered the question fairly well.

"That's exactly what I'm saying. By the way, is this young man in your class? Would you tell me a little about him?" Rachel was softly prodding her daughter, and it felt good to have a real conversation with her.

Sarah proceeded to tell Rachel everything. They laughed about some things and were serious about others. Rachel was in the moment, enjoying this one-on-one time with Sarah. They got up to go back inside and Sarah spoke once more.

"Thanks, Mom. This really helped. I've talked with friends, and they're all like, go out with him. Not that I didn't want to go along with what they said, but I knew that they couldn't possibly understand what I was thinking. My concerns about all of this." She waved her hands around.

Rachel was very touched by Sarah's comments. She was being so kind and open that Rachel wanted to cry. Happy tears, but tears nonetheless. However, she knew she couldn't do that.

"You're welcome. I'm glad that you wanted to talk with me. You know, you can always come to me. I'm not saying that I'm an expert on anything, but sometimes talking it out can help. I know THAT from personal experience."

Sarah looked a little bewildered. "Mom, have you talked with Grandma about stuff?"

Sarah's question caught Rachel off guard. "Probably not as much as I should have. Grandma is of a different generation. I'm not sure that she would have understood what I went through. Not that infidelity didn't exist in her era, but it just wasn't as acknowledged back then." Rachel knew that she was offering excuses, but it was the best she could do at the moment.

"You know, Mom, maybe you should have given her a chance to help you. We're all unsure of going to our parents, but look how this turned out." Sarah was feeling rather proud of her new found information.

Rachel had to agree. Maybe her daughter had taught her mother something. "I think you're right, Sarah. We never know what help we'll get unless we tell people what we're going through."

They went back inside, and Rachel and Sarah got the dinner together. Rebecca came downstairs, and looked at the two of them. She was quite confused seeing them talking and laughing in the same room. This was highly unusual. She shrugged it off and went into the kitchen to join them. Eventually David came down, and they all sat down to enjoy a nice dinner. As a happy family.

Chapter Fifteen

The next morning, after the children went off to school, Rachel decided to see her mother. She had no intention of letting on about anything to do with Don. She'd steer the conversation in safe directions.

This was another gorgeous day, so as Rachel drove through the grounds of the retirement complex she saw a number of people walking as well as sitting on the benches near the fountains. She hadn't called Delores before coming, but she hoped that she would find her there somewhere. Rachel parked her car, and walked inside the building. She was putting her car keys in her purse, when she heard familiar voices.

"Well, look who's here! Rachel! Over here!" She turned to the left to see Ben Levy waving her over in his direction. Delores wasn't there, but Don was. Ben and Don stood waiting for her. They both had broad grins across their faces.

"Hello. How are you?" Don spoke in a slightly secretive way to Rachel, as though he knew exactly how she was.

"I'm fine. How are you two doing?" She looked from Don to Ben.

"We're great. Getting caught up on life." Ben put his arm around Don. He was always so upbeat and friendly.

"I stopped by here for a half an hour. I have to be going, but I told Dad that you would be bringing him to my home on Sunday. About noon?"

"Yes, that's fine. I'll tell my mom that as well. I'll get you at 11:45?" She looked at Ben making sure he was okay with the timing.

"That would be terrific. Thank you Rachel."

"My pleasure. It's nice that your son is doing this for all of us." She looked at Don admiringly. "I guess that I had better get going. See you later."

Rachel went to her mother's apartment, and knocked on the door. Delores opened the door within seconds.

"Rachel! How are you?"

Delores opened the door widely, and Rachel entered.

"How are you doing Mom?"

"I'm doing well. Would you like something to eat or drink?"

"No, I'm fine, thanks. You want to just sit and talk for a while?" They both sat and readied themselves for conversation.

"Mom, Don will be having lunch at his house this Sunday. I'll come by here and get you and Ben at 11:45. I spoke with them as I was coming to see you, and I told Ben that I'd be here at that time. Does that sound okay?"

"Sure. It sounds wonderful. It's so sweet of Don to be doing this. A nice bachelor having a pleasant lunch for you and two old people." Delores laughed at the thought.

"It is very nice of him to do this. So, what are you up to this week? Anything fun going on around here?" Rachel didn't want to keep the conversation on Don. The less of the "D" word, the better.

Delores looked up with a furrowed brow, trying to think if there was anything going on. Then, she smiled, her eyes wide. "Yes! There's going to be a big dance here on Thursday night. A band is being brought in, and there will be cocktails and gourmet food. We're all dressing up for the occasion. I think it will be wonderful!" Delores looked very happy about this. Rachel was pleased. She remembered when her mom and dad went dancing. Those were fun times for them, so this could be a fun event for Delores.

"So, all the residents are participating?"

"Oh, yes, I think that everyone will be joining in. I can't wait to dance! I haven't done that in ages!" Delores hadn't looked this excited in, well, a long time.

"I think it will be fun for you. You'll dance the night away!"

"What are you and the kids up to these days?"

Rachel was surprised by the interest, but she was happy to comply with an answer. "The kids are busy finishing up with their school work, and we will definitely be visiting with Leah and her family this summer. Only for a week because of David's camp, Sarah's work and Rebecca's art classes, but we're looking forward to going. The cousins will have a chance to spend time together. It's been a while."

"That should be very nice. I'm sure you'll all have a great time

165

together. I've always been so pleased that you and your sister have such a nice relationship. That can be unusual, so you're very lucky."

Delores and Rachel continued to chat about family and the retirement home. Rachel told her mother that she had a busy week, but obviously she'd see her on Sunday. They said their goodbyes, and Rachel headed back towards the lobby.

Ben was sitting down speaking with someone. He saw Rachel and beamed his nice smile. "Rachel! Hello again! How's your mother doing?" Ben got up to talk with her.

"She's doing well, thanks. I told her about the Sunday plan, so we're all set."

Ben introduced her to the man with whom he had been conversing. The gentleman excused himself, and Ben started talking with Rachel again. "Rachel, I'm delighted that you and Don are so friendly. You give both of us your time, and that's very sweet."

"I'm very happy to spend time with you two. You're both wonderful men, and I like talking with you. We have a nice little clique here with mother as well. Quite the team, aren't we?" Rachel just wanted to be cute and casual about everything. She assumed that Don had not divulged anything about their relationship to his father.

"We sure are a good team. And Don and I are looking forward to spending time with you and your mother on Sunday."

"Well, thank you. So are we. See you Sunday!"

Rachel ran errands and then returned home shortly before the kids were due back from school. The phone rang, and she saw that it was Don calling. A little smiled crossed her face. "Hello?" Rachel spoke very softly.

"Hello, Rachel, it's Don."

Rachel was pleasantly aware of that fact. "How are you?"

"I'm great. Just wanted to touch base with you. It was a nice surprise seeing you today by the way." Rachel could hear the joy in his voice.

"Thanks. I was happy to see you as well. I saw your dad again as I was leaving the home. He's such a sweetheart."

"Yeah, he's a great guy for sure. So, I assume that everything is all set for Sunday? Your mom is fine with the timing?"

"Absolutely. She's very excited about this lunch. Really, it's nice of you to do this for all of us. What can I bring? I'm happy to assist."

"You don't have to bring anything. It's just nice of you to bring your mom and my dad here. You're all my guests. You're not to lift a finger."

Rachel chuckled at that comment. "I have no problem helping, believe me. But if I am to feel like a pampered princess, that's fine with me."

"So, pampered princess, are we still on for tomorrow's lunch?"

Rachel laughed at his comment. "Of course we are! Noon, right?"

"Yes."

"I'm looking forward to seeing you."

"Same here. So I'll see you tomorrow. Have a nice evening."

"Thanks. You too." Rachel was very content.

The kids came home from school and ran to the kitchen to get their snacks. Their chatter was almost deafening. Rachel noticed that they were always like this when the school year was drawing to a close. They had work to do, but they could see the light at the end of the tunnel. After about fifteen minutes, they all went upstairs to do their homework. That was Rachel's chance to start dinner preparations.

As Rachel stirred sauce for spaghetti, she thought about herself and how proud she was that she maintained such an organized home. Her children had their routines, and life wasn't too chaotic. She knew some mothers, many of whom were still married, who didn't have much control over their family lives. Many teens were running wild, and there was plenty of trouble to be found. Rachel was amazed that, so far, life in her house was relatively stable.

The children came downstairs to eat, and they all talked to each other and to Rachel. They helped her clean the dishes and then she and the children all went into the family room to watch television. As they sat for a while, Rebecca piped up with a question.

"Mom, what do you do while we're at school? I mean, you don't go to work, so what's your day like?"

Rachel was surprised by the question. She shifted in her seat a bit because she was caught off guard. "I'm happy to tell you, but where's this coming from?" Rachel wasn't annoyed, just very curious.

Rebecca didn't think her inquiry was so strange. "My friends and I were talking at lunch about our moms. Ellie's mom works at a law firm, and Patty's mom spends a big part of her day working out. I just didn't know what to tell them."

Rachel chuckled at that. *So, I don't do a darn thing?* No, she didn't want her daughter to think that. And, at this moment, she had six eyes staring at her. "I do lots of things. I run errands, take care of the house, and visit with your grandmother. I cook and sometimes I see friends. The day is pretty full when you're doing these things."

Sarah looked at her, wanting to know more. "Do you ever get lonely? Like, when we're not around? On weekends when we're with Dad?"

"No. Not really." Rachel didn't know what else to say.

The three looked at her, somewhat perplexed, and then they started to watch television again as though there hadn't even been a conversation.

Rachel found her mind drifting, and the television became background noise. She wasn't going to mention Don at all. There was no reason to say anything. They barely had a relationship, even if they had been out a little and had spoken frequently at the home. She was protecting herself as well as her children. Keeping this to herself was the only thing she could do.

The children went to their bedrooms, as did Rachel. She sat on her bed and read a book. As she held the book, she realized that she hadn't been concentrating. She put the book on her nightstand and thought again about the questions that her daughters had asked. Rachel didn't feel lonely. She had plenty to keep herself busy, and her friends were also a great part of her life. There hadn't been any man since Steve, and Rachel suspected that her daughters wanted to know if she was lonely for male companionship. She hadn't been because she didn't want the stress of a relationship. Being wary of any potential problems seemed like too much to bother with, so Rachel didn't even want to attempt to have a man in her life.

However, Rachel did like Don. He was polite and easy to talk to. *Did she want a more serious relationship?* Rachel simply didn't know the answer to that question. Sensibly, she knew it was simply too soon to even contemplate the idea. She had reached her decision. There was no reason to even think anything of this at all, and she felt the burden leap off of her. Just have fun. That's all she wanted to do. She turned her bedside light off, and went to sleep.

Chapter Sixteen

The next morning, Rachel went downstairs and prepared breakfast for the children. They were up and raring to go, so the day had started off very successfully. After the kids went to the bus, Rachel took a walk in the neighborhood. Others were out bright and early as well, so she found herself waving and saying hello to familiar faces along the way. She came home and showered. There were still a couple of hours to go before Don would be there. She had to admit that she was excited about seeing him. Now that they had decided to have a go at a relationship, whatever that meant, she felt that seeing Don took on a whole new dimension. She was like a giddy teenager. As she was sitting on the couch in her own little world, the phone rang.

Rachel looked at the mini screen on the phone and saw that the caller was Steve. She felt her happy bubble burst a little. "Hello?"

"Hi, Rachel. It's Steve."

"Yes, hi. How are you?" Rachel didn't really care how he was, but she was being polite.

"I'm fine. How are you?"

Rachel knew by his tone that he didn't really care how she was doing either. *Oh, these stupid formalities*! "I'm fine. What's up?" Rachel needed to cut to the chase.

"I wondered if you wanted to have lunch some afternoon and we could discuss the summer plans for the kids. I know that you're all going to California, and I know what they're doing during the summer, but I want to figure out more details. You know, like visitation and maybe other things they'd like to do."

Rachel was stumped. She and Steve had not had lunch together since his confession about his affair. Any discussions about the children were handled over the phone or when she was at home while the kids were right there. There was never any private face-to-face discussion. She wasn't about to start that now.

"Uh, actually, I don't think that's necessary. I'd be happy to go over anything with you right now. Also, you're welcome to

170

talk with the kids about everything. They'd love to let you know what they want to do. I'm sure lots of visitation could be in order. Really, it's no big deal to talk with them."

There was a slight pause, and Rachel wasn't sure what was happening. She was ready to ask if he was still on the phone.

"So, I guess there's no need to get together? I should just call the kids, right?" Steve sounded a bit terse, and Rachel didn't understand why.

"Well, yeah. I guess I don't know what the problem is. Why would we need to get together for lunch when we normally discuss everything over the phone? And, like I said, you really should talk with the kids about their plans. That's easy enough. Am I missing something here?" Rachel was confused and a bit annoyed at this point.

Steve let out a big sigh. "No, you're not missing anything. I don't know, I just thought it would be a nice change of pace to sit down and have a quiet lunch while we discuss our children. We do have them in common, you know." He still sounded angry.

"Yes, I know. Why all of the sudden do you want to get together? Besides, I don't think that Linda would be too thrilled knowing that we had lunch out, just the two of us."

"Oh, she'd get over it. I don't care how she would feel. It's none of her business anyway." Steve was practically spewing venom.

"Really? Boy, Steve, you just cut into her. Is something wrong?" Rachel was actually feeling a bit concerned for Steve. Why, she didn't know. This wasn't her problem.

"Oh, I don't know. She's…kind of a pain sometimes."

Sometimes thought Rachel. *Try every moment of her life.* But she wasn't going to jump in and play this game. If Steve had issues with his wife, then he'd have to work them out.

"I'm sorry if you're having difficulties with her." Rachel really wasn't sorry, but she thought it was the appropriate response. "Maybe she's going through something right now." Not that Rachel cared.

"Who knows? She's been nagging at me a lot recently, wanting everything her way. I'm working hard, supporting her in good style, and she's being snippy."

"This really isn't any of my business. Maybe you'd be better off discussing this with one of your friends."

171

"I'm sorry Rachel. I wasn't even thinking. I know that I shouldn't put you in this position. You're right. I'm going to talk with the kids and figure things out from there. But if YOU ever want to have lunch, let me know. I'd be happy to get together with you. I honestly don't think there'd be any harm to an innocent lunch."

"Whatever. Just talk with the kids." Rachel wanted out of this conversation right now.

"Will do. Thanks."

"Sure. Bye."

Rachel clicked off the phone, and sat in disbelief for a moment. Steve had a lot of nerve talking with her about his problems with Linda. He wanted the "B" and he got her. Deal with it. Rachel was trying to have a relationship with a decent man. She wasn't about to blow her chances at happiness. She didn't want to get anywhere near Steve.

Noon rolled around, and the doorbell rang. Rachel went to the front door and opened it to find a smiling Don. He was wearing tan slacks and a white dress shirt.

"Hello! How are you today?"

"I'm fine. Come in."

Don remained on the porch. "Actually, I have a reservation for us at 12:15. I hope that's okay. I wanted to give us plenty of time to have lunch before I need to get back to work."

"Sure, that's perfect." Rachel grabbed her purse and her keys, locked the front door, and went to Don's car.

Don drove them to a restaurant overlooking a pond. Rachel had never been to this place. Even though the drive only took fifteen minutes, it was in a different direction than Rachel normally went. The restaurant was situated in a more country-like setting. It was lovely and very serene. As they got out of the car Rachel asked Don how he knew about this establishment.

"I've been doing business with a guy in town, and he said that he and his wife eat here frequently. I mentioned that I'm trying to get more familiar with the area, and he suggested that I check this place out."

"It looks lovely."

Don and Rachel went inside. It had a woodsy feel to it, with huge picture windows, and the lighting was soft. Don gave his name, and they were taken to their seats. The tables were covered with a white linen table cloth. The diners had a perfect view of the pond, and swans were gliding along in the water. So far it looked like Don had made a very good choice.

The waitress handed them menus, told them the specials, and left them to peruse the choices. Don and Rachel chatted about the different entrees that were offered. The descriptions of the dishes sounded delicious. When the waitress returned, Rachel selected a turkey and brie sandwich and Don chose a steak sandwich. They both ordered glasses of white wine. This was a celebration!

Don looked at Rachel with an intensity that made Rachel lean back in her seat. She looked at him wondering what he was thinking.

"Sorry, I don't mean to make it seem like I'm searing into your soul. I was wondering what you like to do. What things make you happy?" Don was being very serious.

"I don't know. I do what I can for my kids."

Don brushed away her comment. "No. You don't understand. I mean, what do YOU like to do? What do you do for yourself? Hobbies. That sort of thing."

"Oh. As you already know, I like to cook. Um, I like reading, going to movies, theater, a little gardening. I hang out with my friends. I used to travel when I was…well, I used to like to travel." Rachel lowered her eyes feeling the pang of leaving that part of her former life behind.

Don picked up on her sudden change of demeanor. "There's no reason that you can't still travel."

"The kids and I will be visiting my sister soon. And I'll see Leah by myself during the winter break. But I really miss seeing the world. There's no way that I'd want to do that alone."

"I'm sure you'll do more traveling before too long. I like the idea of going to different places also. Europe, Hawaii, almost anywhere. Maybe we can go somewhere. At some point." Don didn't want to push Rachel on this. He knew that she wasn't in a completely trusting mode as far as male/female relationships were concerned.

"So what about you? What do you like to do?"

"I'm kind of like you. Everything you mentioned works for me as well. I'm pretty game for anything. I like to get out and have fun when I can. I'm willing to see almost any movie.

Rachel was impressed. Don was not only a nice man, but

173

he had a desire to enjoy life. Although she and Steve had fun before the kids came along, in the years after the births of their children, he wasn't interested in doing much of anything other than working. Well, Rachel knew that he did find time for Linda. She didn't know that then, but she certainly found out. It was just a pleasure to be with someone who wanted to have fun and be with her.

Rachel had a plan. "I think this means that we should go to a movie sometime. Or wherever."

"I can go along with that idea. If your ex has your children during the weekend, we can do something."

"That will work fine. Steve will probably have them more often over the summer break anyway."

"Rachel, I do think that we will need to be more open about us." He looked at her point blank. "This isn't the biggest town in the country, and someone you know may see us when we go out. Truthfully, It's okay with me if your family and my dad know about us. What do you think?"

Rachel put her fingers through her hair. She did that when she was insecure sometimes. She bit her lower lip as she thought about what Don said.

"I know you're right. We shouldn't have to hide. The only thing stopping me is my mother. I don't want her getting too excited about us. I mean, I'm happy that we're seeing each other, please believe me." She paused briefly. "I don't know what to do." Rachel did feel a little defeated.

"Okay, that's all right." Don reached out his hand to her. "There's no reason to rush anything. We can keep this to ourselves. As long as we're happy, that's all that counts. I was just thinking that word could get around *if* someone sees us. How would you feel if someone in your family finds out that we are seeing each other and you didn't say anything?" Don was being very clear-headed. Rachel appreciated that.

"You have a point. I guess I should go for it, and not worry. This really is *our* relationship, and everyone else can just deal with it and not get involved."

"Very true. So, do we mention our relationship on Sunday? To your mom and to my dad? Tell them everything?"

Rachel bobbed her head side to side, weighing the thought. Then she concluded the inevitable decision. "Yes. Yes, we

174

should. Let's go ahead and tell them. BUT, we only need to say that we're hanging out together. This doesn't have to be some dramatic confession. Don't you agree?" Rachel looked at Don, hoping he saw this the same way that she did.

"Sure. That sounds like a good plan. I think that telling them something is better than trying to hide everything. I mean, we're not teenagers."

Don and Rachel both laughed at that. The waitress came over with their food, and the two talked easily throughout the meal. It was nice to have so much in common and to discuss things so freely. Don wanted their time together to last a bit longer, so he suggested that they order dessert. Rachel agreed but asked if sharing was an option. After indulging in a piece of decadent chocolate cake, she was pleasantly full. Don paid the bill, they left the restaurant and drove to Rachel's house. He had to get back to work, but he came inside for a few minutes.

"Don, I've enjoyed every minute with you, and I thank you for the wonderful lunch." Rachel and he were sitting in her living room, relaxing and enjoying the quiet of her home.

"I can tell you that this has been the happiest time for me. I'm so glad that we decided to make a go of this." He pointed back and forth between the two of them. "So, other than Sunday, when will I see you again?" Don didn't want to waste any time.

"Should we try for Friday or Saturday?"

"What about both? I'd be happy to go to a movie. Have dinner out. Go for a walk. I just want to be with you." Don sat forward in his chair, emphasizing his desire to be near her.

"Let me see what I can do. I'll find out if Steve can take the kids."

"Is that even necessary? I mean, if we fess up about us, shouldn't your children be made aware of everything as well?" Rachel was alarmed. She hadn't considered the idea of her children knowing about the two of them. Don could tell by the look on Rachel's face that she didn't count on this. "Only if that's what you're comfortable doing. I don't want to pressure you into telling your kids. I just thought that might be part of the plan. You know, to tell everyone that we are seeing each other."

"I get what you're saying...yes... I suppose that my children should know what is going on...yes... I think so...I'm sure you're right... I hadn't thought about it." Rachel realized that she was

175

babbling, but she was trying to sort out everything in her mind.

"We're not doing anything wrong. They should be okay with this. It's not like the situation that you faced with your ex. I can't even imagine how you told your children about that."

"Yeah, well, that wasn't easy. I made him tell them, although I was in the room at the time. Needless to say, I had three very unhappy children. There's no easy way to break the news that their father had been unfaithful, their mother was divorcing him, and he was going to remarry shortly thereafter. That was a dark moment. For all of us. As I'm sure you, of all people, understand."

"I'm sorry. I didn't mean to dredge up that part of your life. I only wanted to make it clear that I know this should be an easier thing to say to them. Your kids *will* be okay with this, won't they?" Don was momentarily concerned that there could be a problem. What if they didn't want their mother to see any man?

"I think they'll be fine. Really, they don't have a say in any of this. It's MY life. I want to be with you, and that's THAT!" Rachel felt certain about her statement.

Upon her making the passionate declaration, they looked at each other with a new desire. They leaned into each other, and began to kiss. Rachel's heart started to pound fiercely, and their kissing took on a fervor. They clung to each other as though their very lives depended on the embrace. Don's hand slipped to the front of Rachel's shirt, and he adeptly began to unbutton Rachel's silk blouse. Rachel, nuzzling his neck, drank in his manly scent, but then, as though a hammer went down, her brain took over her needy body. Rachel knew that this had to stop. She hadn't felt this wonderful sensation in a long time, but she wasn't ready to go to this next level. So, gently, she pulled away. Don appeared somewhat surprised by her pull back, but he wasn't angry. After taking deep breaths, they smiled at each other with understanding, that this was only the beginning of wonderful moments with each other. Rachel started to button her blouse.

Don gazed at Rachel with fondness and understanding. He loved being in her presence, talking with her about everything, and he was impressed by the way she lived her life. She had been through so much, and yet it gave her a wisdom that he appreciated. He knew that both of them had emotional barriers that needed to be torn down, but they were taking steps in the right direction. His eyes showed all of his thoughts, and Rachel was pleased.

They talked and decided to go to a movie on Friday night. Rachel told Don that she'd call Steve to find out if he would to take the kids for the weekend. Even if he couldn't, the two of them would still spend time together. She would let the kids know that she was going out. Don seemed pleased with either scenario. They would deal with everything as it was happening. If Steve was with the kids, then nothing needed to be mentioned yet. If the kids were going to be at home, Rachel would explain the situation.

As their heart rates slowly decreased, they chatted comfortably for a few more minutes, and Don told Rachel he would call her to make arrangements for Friday night. He left, and Rachel couldn't believe how wonderful everything was right now. She almost wanted to do a little dance in her house, but she didn't. She needed to believe that what she and Don had was real and honest. She *did* believe that, but she couldn't escape the instinct to be cautious. The first few months of any relationship Rachel had ever had was almost always incredible. From high school on, she had always felt the initial giddiness that accompanied dating and companionship. The main problem was that there had never been any relationship that had worked well. Here, she stood in her house, alone. There was no amazing man who would be coming home to stay with her. There was no wedding band on her finger indicating sworn and undying love. Rachel sank down into her leather couch and accepted that there were no guarantees. Just as she had told Sarah. She knew she had to take her own advice and go for it. At least she was more mature now and hopefully life's experiences had taught her something. She would protect her fragile emotional core, but she would also open herself up to all of the possibilities that this new relationship was offering. She decided to call Steve before the kids came home.

"Hello?"

"Hi, Steve. It's Rachel."

"Well, hello! How are you?" Rachel could almost tell that Steve was smiling.

"I'm doing well. How 'bout yourself?"

"Great. Now that I'm talking to you."

Rachel took her phone away from her ear and gave it a perplexing look. Why on earth was he so excited to talk with her?

"I called to see if you could take the kids from Friday through Sunday?"

There was a pause. "Sure, I guess I can. What's up? You seem to be asking me to take the kids more than usual. Not that I mind. I'm more than happy to spend extra time with them. I'm just wondering what is occupying your time so much these days." Steve was questioning her more than Rachel thought he had a right to do.

Rachel chose to be vague. "Just doing this and that. Besides, I really want you to have as much time with them as possible. They're going to be so busy, and we're all taking that trip to California soon."

Steve seemed skeptical. "Okay. I'm not sure that I completely understand. You're just doing this and that? You can't be more specific?" He actually sounded annoyed. As though he had every right to know exactly what his ex-wife was doing that was occupying so much of her time.

Rachel wasn't happy with this interrogation. "Steve, whatever I'm doing can't possibly be of any concern to you. I do have a life of my own you know!"

There was another pause. "I'm sorry, Rache. I didn't mean to press. I'm just a bit curious, that's all." There was another pause. "Rachel, are you seeing someone?"

Rachel's heart thumped heavily. Here was the moment of truth. She might as well confess. "Kind of. It's no big deal." Rachel had no idea as to how much she should say. She wasn't sure why she was being so secretive with Steve. She wasn't cheating on him.

"I see." Steve sounded a little dejected. "So, what's the lucky guy's name?" He said that with a bit of contempt.

Rachel didn't care for his tone. "His name is Don. He's a very nice guy who seems to have a great deal of respect for me. He's smart, kind, good-looking, and he's got the best manners that I've ever witnessed. I'm very happy that we're seeing each other." Rachel hoped her direct description felt like a slap in Steve's face.

Steve didn't say anything for a moment, and then he cleared his throat. "He sounds like a nice fellow. I'll be happy to take the kids after school on Friday. I'll come by and pick them up. Is that okay?" Steve sounded much more conciliatory right now.

Rachel took a deep breath to release her tension. "That would be great. I'll let the kids know that they'll be seeing you."

"Just wondering what you and Don will be up to this weekend. Anything in particular?" Steve seemed a little too interested in her social life.

Rachel wanted the conversation to end. She was weary from talking with him. She had such a nice day with Don, and now Steve was sucking the life out of her. "I don't know. Probably a bunch of different things. Should I send you an e-mail of the play by play of my dating habits?" Rachel oozed sarcasm

"Okay. I get it. I'm probing too far into your lovely new world. Sorry!" Now Steve was a bit sarcastic.

Rachel was exasperated. "Well, come on, Steve. Why do you need to know anything? Why is my social life any of YOUR business?"

"I was just curious. Gosh, Rache, it's not that big of a deal. By the way, shouldn't I know where you are in case something happens while the kids are with me?"

"We all have cell phones. Isn't that sufficient? I hope nothing bad happens. If Heaven forbid it does, you can handle everything until I find out about whatever it is that transpired. Okay? I'm tired of being grilled. I haven't even had a relationship since we split up. You couldn't possibly understand that, I know, but let me have my fun. If that wouldn't be too much trouble." Rachel was irritated.

"Let's have a cease fire here. I honestly didn't mean to upset you. I really do want you to be happy. Please believe me. In spite of everything that I did, I still care about you."

Rachel didn't know what to say. She was obviously still angry with her ex. He had cut her to her core when he was unfaithful, and she felt like she was just now starting to recover from the gaping hole that he left. Still, she needed to calm herself down and think of her children. "Okay. Fine. Whatever. By the way, I haven't told the kids about Don. I will be saying something to my mom on Sunday, but I'm not ready to let the kids in on this. Please don't say anything. Okay?"

"Okay. I'll let you tell them when you're ready. So, I'll see you Friday. I'll come by around five."

With that, they hung up their phones. Rachel didn't understand why Steve was so interested in her dating ways right now. It disturbed her, but she didn't want to think about that right now. The truth was that she really didn't want to think about it at all.

179

Rachel left a message on Don's answering machine that she was all set for the weekend. She told him that she looked forward to seeing him soon. After a couple of hours of doing chores around the house, Rachel's phone rang. It was Don She happily answered.

"Hello?"

"Hello! Rachel, it was great being with you today. I'm so glad that we can spend a lot of time together this weekend. I guess your ex is taking the kids?"

"Yes, he is. He did ask what I've been up to that I want him to take the kids more often. He guessed that I was dating."

"Oh? So, how did that conversation go?" Don sounded apprehensive.

"Interesting." Don and Rachel laughed.

"I assume everything is okay?"

"Yes, I think so. Steve will be picking up the kids from here after school on Friday.

"So movie and a dinner it is!"

"That sounds great. I haven't been to a movie in ages. Is that really okay with you?"

"Sure. I haven't been to a movie in a while either. What time will your kids be leaving the house?"

"Steve is coming at five."

"Okay, I can be there at 5:30 if that works for you. Then we'll go to a movie. Anything in particular that you want to see?"

"I haven't even checked to see what's playing. I'll let you decide. I'm just very happy that we'll be able to go out." Rachel's smile came right through the phone.

Don chuckled. "I feel the same way. I'll look into what's in the theatres, but no matter what, I will be at your house at 5:30."

"Perfect! I'll see you Friday."

Rachel was feeling very good right now. She had plans this weekend. A real date! Nothing like going out with a wonderful man to help the old self-esteem issues. The kids were due home soon. She finished up her household chores and waited for them.

The three came bursting through the front door, laughing and talking a mile a minute. They all yelled, "Hey, Mom!" Then they put their backpacks on the floor and went into the kitchen. Rachel decided to let them do what they wanted. They could take their school things upstairs when they were done snacking. She went into the kitchen and joined them.

"So, how's life at school? Everything go okay today?"

They nodded as they chomped down on cookies and chips. Rachel brought out some fruit, just on the off chance that they might eat something nutritious as well as devouring the junk food.

Rachel sat down putting her elbow on the table and her hand under her chin. She watched the kids for a moment before speaking. "I want to let you know that you'll be with your dad from Friday through Sunday. Sounds good, huh?"

The three looked at each other with expressions of uncertainty and slight unhappiness. Rachel was confused. She thought they'd be happy spending more time with their father.

Rachel sat up very straight. "What's wrong? You don't want to be with your dad?" Rachel felt a sense of panic. What was the problem here?

David spoke up for the other two. "Why do we have to go there this weekend? We've been with dad a lot." He seemed a bit whiney.

"I know you have. Why wouldn't you want to spend more time with him?" Rachel wondered what was going on.

David seemed uncomfortable talking about this. So, Rebecca piped in with her thoughts.

"Mom, we can't stand Linda. She's so nasty." Rebecca wriggled her nose in disgust and the other two nodded affirmatively.

"What do you mean by nasty? What does she do?" This was the first Rachel had heard that there was a problem.

Sarah spoke this time. "She clearly doesn't want us around, Mom. She's always snotty with us and she hangs all over Dad. It's not comfortable being over there. And Daddy doesn't stand up to her either. We do some stuff with him, but mostly we just hang out with each other in our rooms."

Rachel was shocked. "Why didn't you tell me this before? I would have dealt with this immediately. I don't want you to have a miserable time at your dad's house."

Rebecca spoke up quickly. "No, Mom, that's exactly what we DON'T want to have happen. We don't want you to say anything to Dad."

Rachel was perplexed. "Why wouldn't you want me to say anything? He's your father. You should have good times with him."

The kids looked at each other again, wondering if they should say more. Sarah dove in this time.

"Dad seems sad. He doesn't talk much, and it's obvious who rules the house." She rolled her eyes as she looked at Rachel. Clearly, Linda was a dictator. "We don't want to cause him more pain."

Rachel put her hand on her forehead, not knowing what to do. "I don't want you all worrying about this. I will discuss the problem with him. Maybe we can figure out what's going on and what we'll do about it. I still think it will be fine for you to visit with your dad. This can all be resolved by Friday." Rachel smiled at them praying that she knew what she was talking about.

The kids looked at her and shrugged. Rachel wasn't sure if that meant that they knew she'd handle it or if they weren't sure about anything. She went upstairs and called Steve at his office.

"Hello?"

"Hi, Steve. I need to talk with you about something." Rachel couldn't deal with any pleasantries.

"Sure. What's up?"

"When I told the kids they would be spending Friday through Sunday with you, they didn't seem all that…how shall I put this? They weren't totally comfortable with the idea." Rachel physically cringed when she stated that. She didn't want to hurt Steve in regards to the children, but she had to be honest.

"Really? What's the problem?" Steve was taken aback.

"They tell me that Linda isn't very nice to them, and that you don't seem to do anything about this. They also said that you seem a bit sad." Once again, it disturbed Rachel to tell him any of these things.

There was a bit of a pause, and Rachel knew that Steve needed a moment to group his thoughts together. She was prepared to give him all the time he needed.

"I am really sorry about this. I guess I haven't been paying enough attention to how Linda is treating the kids. I know she doesn't want the kids around. Still that's no excuse for her to be difficult. As for me being sad…well…I don't know what to tell you Rachel. I'm just going to have to be more aware of my emotions and my actions when I'm with the children."

"Are you sad, Steve?" Rachel found herself being very concerned for him. Her compassion was clearly audible.

182

"Rachel, don't worry about my feelings. I know that you don't want to have to deal with my problems." He stated it factually.

"Steve, you are the father of my children. If something is wrong, I should probably know about it."

Steve let out a huge sigh. "Rachel, Rachel, Rachel. I have no intention of unburdening myself on you. Besides, I don't think Don would want you to get too involved with me." He said that with a bit of an attitude.

"I don't plan on getting involved with you at all." Rachel was a bit miffed by Steve's comments. "As I said, you're the father of my children. For THEIR sake, I need to know what's happening."

"It would take too much time and effort to go over this with you on the phone. If you're really interested, I could meet with you and talk about everything. But that's completely up to you." He left the ball in her court.

Rachel didn't know what to do. She didn't want to spend any one-on-one time with her ex. And yet, she did need to know what was happening so that she could help her kids. She wanted to protect them. But she wouldn't see him. "If you promise that you won't act like you're having a problem when the kids are around, we can leave it at that. I won't delve into your personal business as long as the children don't witness your sadness." Rachel knew this sounded cold, but she couldn't worry about that now.

Steve laughed uncomfortably. "Well, Rachel, I'll try to not show my emotional weaknesses around my children. I wouldn't want to scar their psyches."

Rachel was more than a bit put off by him. "If you're having some problems, why don't you talk with your wife?" Rachel said this and it was like having a door slammed in his face.

"Because, my dear Rachel, she's the reason that I'm unhappy. Okay? Does that satisfy you?" He practically spit the words at her.

Rachel refused to get sucked into his drama. "Okay, well, I guess that's that. I suppose you should discuss this with Linda, but that's up to you. My only concern is for our children. I'll let them know that things should be better for them this weekend. That's the truth, isn't it?" Rachel prayed that would be the case.

"Yes, that's the truth. I will make sure that they have a happy environment. Maybe I can get Linda to go out of town or something."

"Whatever you do is up to you. I just want the kids to have a good time with you. That's what's important."

"Okay. So that's all settled. I hope that you and Don have a nice time together. I guess you're ready for a fun weekend." Steve didn't seem happy or excited for her.

"Thank you. Yes, I am looking forward to having some fun. See you Friday."

Rachel abruptly clicked off the phone. She didn't know what to think at this point. She felt for Steve because she was a caring person. However, as always, she believed that he controlled his own life. He chose Linda, and he'd have to make the best of things. Rachel had finally found someone to spend time with, and she didn't want to get caught up in Steve's marital issues. She went back downstairs to chat with the kids.

"Okay guys. Everything is set for Friday with your dad, and it's all going to be fine."

Sarah looked incredulously at Rachel. "Mom! Did you actually tell dad what we said?"

"Yes. I felt that everything needed to be dealt with. And it was. Don't worry about it." Rachel laid it on the line as simply as she could.

Sarah rolled her eyes, not believing that her mother did this. "Mom, I don't think you needed to say anything. I hope that dad wasn't upset." Sarah looked very concerned.

"No, no. Please don't think that. He's fine. And he very much wants to see all of you." She looked at them almost imploring them to understand what she was saying.

The kids seemed uncertain. However, it was clear to them that they were spending the weekend with their father.

Rebecca looked curiously at Rachel. "Mom? Why is it so important to you that we stay with Dad this weekend? You seem a bit desperate. Not that it's bad if we spend time with him, but if we wouldn't want to right now, would that really be a problem?" Rebecca squinted at her like she was suspicious about something. She could smell a rat.

Rachel had no intention of letting them know about Don and that he was the reason behind her desire to have them stay with their dad over the weekend. "No, it wouldn't be a problem. I just think it's important for your dad to spend time with you. I get you all week long, and we'll be going to California soon. I thought it

184

would be nice for all of you to be with him. I also think that, if there's ever a concern about anything, it needs to be discussed."

Sarah had a question for Rachel. "What DID you and Dad talk about? Is he okay?"

"We didn't talk for very long, but from what I can gather, I think he's going to be okay. Sometimes even adults have things that bother them or preoccupy them." Rachel didn't want to let on that their dad was having issues with Linda. It wasn't her place to divulge that kind of information.

"So, he's okay, right?" David wanted everything to go well for everyone all the time. He was always a caring child.

"He's okay. So, now that everything is settled, I have a dinner to make." Rachel sincerely hoped that there would be smooth sailing ahead.

Chapter Seventeen

The next couple of days went by uneventfully. Rachel was grateful for the calm and normal routine. She ran errands, did work around the house, and chatted with friends.

When Friday rolled around, she was up and ready to start her weekend. The kids went to school, and she packed for all of them. Rachel told the children that she would have everything ready for them to take to their dad's house by the time they got home. Rachel hoped that things went well this weekend so that she could totally focus on her new relationship with Don.

The children came home from school, and they appeared to be in good moods. Rachel had their bags sitting in the living room, waiting for Steve's arrival. At 5:05, the doorbell rang, and Rachel opened the door. She was surprised to see Linda standing there, arms crossed, looking annoyed.

"Linda? Hi. Where's Steve?" Rachel was taken by surprise and not at all happy to see Linda instead of Steve. He hadn't mentioned anything to Rachel about his wife coming to get the children.

Linda sighed deeply, and there was not a trace of a smile on her face. "Steve called me to say that he was running late, and could I pick up your kids." Interesting that she said "your" kids. She looked at Rachel as if to say, "Are they ready to go?"

Rachel gave an annoyed look of her own. "Come in for a moment, and I'll get them." Her voice indicated irritation.

"I'll wait in the car. I'm sure you'll have them out here in minute." She started to turn around and head to her car.

Rachel didn't like her attitude, so she bristled a bit in her response. "Linda, would it KILL you to just wait a frickin' moment? They'll be right with you!"

Linda looked shocked. Rachel had never spoken to her like that, and Linda wasn't sure how to react. She must have figured it out quickly enough because she scowled at Rachel. "How dare you? I can do anything I damn well please! If I want to wait in the car, then I will. Got it?"

"No, I don't." Rachel wanted to keep her voice down so the kids wouldn't hear any of this. "Steve didn't bother to call me to let me know you were coming here. I would have brought them to you if he had let me know. Since he didn't pick up the phone, you can come into my home and wait for them."

"Fine!" She looked at Rachel with a nasty grin. "I can see why Steve had a problem with you."

Rachel was now over the edge. She decided to give it right back to Linda, no matter the consequences. It seemed that a verbal cat fight was happening. "He certainly has one with you right now." Rachel gave her a smug smile, like she knew something that Linda didn't.

Linda's expression went from amusement to shock. Her complexion reddened and her eyes were open wide. "What does THAT mean? What the hell do you think you know?"

"Figure it out for yourself." Rachel decided that she would not have her kids drive with Linda. She would bring them to Steve's office, and he could drive them to his house. "I think you should leave. I'll take the kids to their father." Rachel said this coldly.

Linda didn't speak. She turned and walked directly to her car. Rachel shut the front door, and was paralyzed for a moment. She knew she had to get in touch with Don and let him know that she was now running late, and that she would call him when she returned after dropping off the kids. She wasn't even sure if she felt comfortable with her children being in Linda's presence right now. Even though Rachel felt very flustered, she needed to phone Don immediately.

Rachel listened to his phone ring, and within three rings, Don picked up.

"Hello?"

"Hi, Don, it's Rachel." She spoke very softly into the phone.

"Rachel? Is everything okay?" He sounded wary.

"Yes, everything is fine. I have a slight glitch in our plan. I need to drive the kids to Steve. It's a long story, and I'll explain it when I see you. Is it okay if I call you when I return home? We won't be too far off with our timing."

"Yes. No problem. You're sure you're okay?"

"Absolutely. I'm just sorry that I'm changing our timing a bit."

"Please, don't worry about that. I'm just glad that you're okay." She could hear how relieved he was that she was all right.

187

"Okay. Well, I hope to call you soon. I'm certainly looking forward to seeing you."

"I know how you feel. I can't wait either."

They hung up, and she called Steve at his office.

"Hello?"

"Steve. It's Rachel."

"Oh. Hi, Rachel."

"I assume you know why I'm calling?" Rachel knew she sounded pissed.

"Well...maybe. I'm sorry that I couldn't pick up the kids myself. I hope you don't mind that I sent Linda in my place." Steve sounded guilty.

"Guess again. I told Linda to go home. We kind of had a little...how shall I put it? Confrontation. I told her I would bring the kids to your office and you can take them home from there."

"What? What happened?" Steve sounded panicked.

"She was nasty with me, and I returned the favor. I decided after the riff we had that I didn't want her driving the kids. Honestly, I don't really want her near them at this point. So please do me a favor and stay with them at all times. You're on duty from now until you bring them home on Sunday. Got it?" Rachel wasn't accepting anything other than his full cooperation.

"Okay. So, you're bringing them here? To my office?"

"Yes. And I'm leaving right now. I don't have time to waste." Rachel was determined to start her weekend with Don and she was ready to have the kids quickly join their father.

"All right. I'll see you soon." He paused for a moment, considering another alternative to make Rachel happier. "Are you sure you don't want me to pick them up at your house?"

Rachel thought for just a moment. "Only if you promise to leave right now. I mean RIGHT NOW."

"I can do that. I know I screwed up. I should have left and been at your house like we said. Sorry, Rache."

"Just get over here. Please." Rachel was desperate and at her wits end at this point.

The kids came downstairs, wondering what was going on. "Mom, didn't the doorbell ring?" David was curious.

"Yes, it did. Linda was here, but she left, so your dad will be here soon. Just a little confusion. That's all." Rachel tried to make light of it all. *Why did everything have to be so challenging?*

David still needed answers. "Why didn't we just go with Linda? She must have come here to get us." He couldn't figure out what happened, and Rachel knew she had to be careful.

"I figured that your dad might as well come pick you up. It just made more sense to me." Rachel knew her answer wasn't logical at all. *Why don't we just pick up the shovel and start digging now?* Rachel hated being deceptive, but she was stuck in this mess. And she didn't want to put her children in the middle of the muck.

"Okay. I guess." David wasn't buying her answer, and by the look on Sarah and Rebecca's faces, neither were they.

So be it, thought Rachel. *They don't have to understand everything. Besides, this was her battle. If for one moment her kids didn't understand what she was saying, she didn't care.* She was on edge, praying that her ex would keep his word and show up soon.

Nothing more was said, and fortunately fifteen minutes later, the doorbell rang. Rachel opened the door, and Steve was standing there with an uncertain smile on his face. She could tell that he didn't know if she was ready to bite his head off, but he was hoping for the best. His tie was loosened and he was ready to be a dad for the weekend. Rachel didn't say a word, but merely motioned him to walk into the house. This time, the kids were right there waiting.

Steve whispered to Rachel. "Honestly, Rache. I'm very sorry about what happened. My delay couldn't be helped, and I just thought that, instead of bothering you, I'd ask Linda to pick up the kids. I didn't think it would be a problem."

Rachel whispered back. "Well, it wouldn't have been a problem if your wife could learn how to be civil. She was oozing nastiness, and I couldn't take it. I hate to think of the kids being in her presence. Please, try to do something about this." She looked at him practically begging him to help.

Steve nodded his head in agreement, perfectly understanding the situation. He held up his hands as if to surrender. "I'll do what I can. It's just not so easy right now."

Rachel didn't care if it was easy or not. However, the kids were waiting, and she wanted to get everyone out of the house. She gave quick kisses and hugs to the children, and sent them off with their father. Rachel sprinted to the phone and called Don.

It was about 5:30 now, so they wouldn't be too far off of their planned timing.

"Hello?"

"Hello. Guess who?"

"Rachel! That was quick."

"Steve came here immediately to get the kids. As I said before, it's a long story. But I'm ready to go if you're ready to come over."

"I'm leaving now." Rachel was thrilled that Don seemed to be in such a hurry to get to her. It was nice to have a man anxious to be with her.

Rachel made sure that she looked presentable, collecting herself after having had all of the challenges. She was elated to hear the doorbell ring this time, and she opened the door to see Don standing there looking very handsome. He was wearing navy blue slacks and a crisp white dress shirt. He was also holding a pretty box of chocolates. Coupled with his broad smile, Rachel wanted to melt. He handed the box to her, and gave her a long kiss. Rachel couldn't have been more delighted.

"I figured that for our first real date, chocolates might be in order."

Rachel ushered him into the house, and she gratefully took her favorite sinful food. "Thank you so much." She knew by the box that these were very special candies. "We will share these, I promise."

"You don't have to share them. I just want you to know how much our first date means to me." He was so wonderfully charming. There was never anything phony about him. His sincerity was always evident.

Rachel looked at him shyly. "It means a lot to me as well." She put the candy on the table in the living room.

Don looked at his watch. "If it's okay with you, I decided to make a reservation for dinner, and then we can go to a movie after that."

"Sure. That sounds perfect. What movie are we seeing?"

"There's a 'chick flick' playing." He made quotation marks with his fingers as he said that. "I'm one of those guys who will see just about any movie, so I thought this one might work. You'll see my sensitive side." Don said that with humor.

"I personally think that you are a very sensitive man." Rachel fluttered her eye lashes and looked sweetly at him. She and Don laughed.

"Okay, schweetheart, let's go to dinner."

"Oh, so that's your Humphrey Bogart imitation, huh?" Rachel was cringing.

"Uh, oh, was it that bad?"

"No. It was endearing." She smiled to let him know she appreciated his charming ways.

Don drove them to a little Italian restaurant near the movie theatre. They talked throughout the dinner, and Rachel told him about the fiasco with Linda. He was very sympathetic towards Rachel upon hearing what she went through. After their dinners were happily consumed, they headed to the theatre. They had plenty of time, so they talked more in their seats before the show started. Entertainment now seemed to be their favorite topic. They both loved comedies and music and, occasionally, going to museums. The movie started, and it proved to be very entertaining. Don suggested that they grab coffee and dessert. Rachel was all for the idea.

After spending more time laughing, discussing the movie, and chattering away, Don drove Rachel back to her house. Neither could remember a happier time. He walked her to her porch.

"Would you like to come in? We can share some of the chocolates?" Rachel wanted to spend even more time with Don.

"I'm pretty full after that decadent dessert, but I'd love to come in."

They went inside, and Rachel made the mistake of checking her messages. There was one from Steve's home. She debated listening to it, but knew that she had to. She'd only dwell on it, wondering what was happening, so she figured she should find out what was going on.

"Don, I'll just be a moment. There's a message that I have to check. May I get you something to drink?"

"Nope. I'm fine. You go ahead and check your message. I'll wait in the living room."

Rachel always appreciated his understanding ways. She began listening to the messages on her voice mail.

Sarah's voice boomed her message. "Mom, we don't want to be at dad's house this weekend. Linda is being a pain and Dad doesn't seem to know how to deal with her. She's yelling at us and telling us that if we have a problem with her we should go home. Like this isn't our home too! I don't know what else to do. Dad keeps trying to calm her down, telling her we have every right to be here. But she's making it very clear that she doesn't want us in the house. And then she said something about Dad not being happy with her. That she didn't know that, but she found out. We're all confused. Would you at least call here? Let us know what we can do? Call whenever. We don't care how late it is." Sarah hung up clearly desperate. There was another message, and Rachel closed her eyes, trying to wish the calls away.

This time it was Steve. "Rachel, I know Sarah called you. I'm so sorry. We are having some issues, although I'm trying my best to resolve them. I don't know. Give me a call if you can. I know you have a big weekend. I hate like hell to interrupt your plans. Well, just do whatever you can do." He hung up seeming confused. Rachel didn't know what to do. Her first step was to talk with Don.

Rachel went into the living room where Don was patiently sitting reading one of her magazines. He must have been doing his best to pass the time because the reading material was a gardening magazine. She seriously doubted he was interested in that subject. She sheepishly came towards him, and he looked up at her. "Don, I'm so sorry to keep you waiting. I have a problem on my hands, and I need your advice as to how I should handle it."

Don dropped the magazine on the table, and looked at her very thoughtfully. "What's up?"

Rachel sat down in a chair next to him, took a deep breath and plunged in. "I received two messages, the first one from Sarah, and the second one from Steve. Sarah and Steve both indicated problems at home. Naturally, Linda is the culprit." Rachel gave a look that implied that no one would be surprised that Steve's wife was causing trouble. Considering that Rachel had told him what had happened, Don knew the entire story.

"Oh, boy. Sounds a bit tense."

"To say the least. Anyway, what should I do? Do I call them and ruin our weekend, do I call them and tell them to deal with it, or should I ignore this and not call them? I've looked so forward to our time together. I don't want to throw away our fun." Rachel was feeling desperate.

192

Don looked at her so sweetly she could have cried. He had the most understanding expression on his face. Rachel couldn't help feeling that everything would be okay.

"You have to call them, Rachel. You don't have a choice. Your kids need you. I'm only telling you what you already know. But what is it that you really feel most comfortable doing? I understand that you want this weekend for us. But, do you think you should tell the kids to come home?"

Rachel was torn. "That's what I don't know. I mean, why can't Steve deal with this? I've had my life on hold for a while now. He never did. I don't want to get dragged into their mess and lose… well, not have this." Rachel bent her head down, not wanting to confront her fear that Don would want to walk away.

Don, ever so gently, put his hand on her hand. "Rachel, I'm not going anywhere. I would never expect you to choose between dealing with your children and their problems and having me in your life. Remember, *I'm* the one who suggested we go for a relationship. I knew about your kids. I knew about your ex. I came into this with eyes wide open. For me, this relationship isn't about skipping out on life's challenges. It's about being with you."

Rachel couldn't speak for a moment. Her throat had constricted with emotion. She honestly didn't feel like bawling her eyes out right now so she pulled herself together. His compassion had overwhelmed her. She had never realized that she was this worth it to anybody. She looked at him with misty eyes. "I really appreciate that. You have no idea how much your words mean to me. I guess I do need to at least make a phone call."

"Would it be easier if I left right now? I only want to do what's best for you." He looked at her with complete compassion.

"I'd rather you stay. Just in case I'm lucky enough to have this actually work out in my favor." She looked at him with a goofy grin.

"Okay. Take all the time you need. I'm perfectly content to sit and wait. I'm just happy being here with you."

How did she get this lucky? Could Don really be this incredible? Apparently, yes. Rachel felt it was still way too soon to tell, but she had to go on faith that he really was a true gentleman.

She left Don in the living room, went to the phone, and braced herself for whatever was coming. It was late already, but she

193

didn't care. If her daughter needed to talk, Don was right. Rachel had to make the call.

The phone rang twice, and Sarah answered. "Mom! Where have you been? I called, Dad called. Can you believe what we're dealing with here?" Sarah was practically raging with irritation.

Rachel's heart sank. "Obviously I received your messages. I was out, and I didn't think I'd need my cell phone considering that you're with your dad. So, what's going on over there?" Her voice was calm.

Sarah wasn't happy. "You were OUT? Out where? Gosh, mom, we leave, and you act like you aren't a mother anymore. We're not happy here!"

Rachel snapped. She refused to have her daughter take this tone. Rachel never forgot, not for one moment, that she was a mother. If she wanted to go out, that was her business. Now she wondered why she did bother making the call. "I'm sorry you're not happy, Sarah. I'm calling to find out what the problem is and why it can't be resolved. Would it be better if I spoke with your dad?" Rachel couldn't help sounding snippy.

Sarah sounded somewhat mollified as her mother was showing due concern. "No. There's probably no point in talking with Dad. It's just Linda. She's toxic to be around." Rachel thought it was amusing that her daughter used the term "toxic." She wasn't sure where she came up with that one. It sounded very dramatic.

"You're going to have to try to talk with your dad about this. Linda is his wife, and you're going to be with your dad. It's not like you won't want to see him."

"Maybe we should just go out somewhere with him when we see him. Not stay over at his house."

That thought made Rachel wince. Her children were entitled to be at their father's house. "Sarah, let me speak with your dad."

Sarah paused for a moment, and Rachel could tell that her daughter was considering the suggestion. "Okay. I guess it can't hurt. Hang on."

Rachel could hear that Sarah still had the phone in her hand. She heard her movements, and then Sarah spoke with her father. It was slightly muffled, but Rachel could gather most of the conversation.

"Dad, mom wants to talk to you. I told her we're not happy. That Linda is a problem. Will you talk with Mom?"

"Sure, honey. Let's see what we can do here." Rachel thought he sounded ever so sweet with his daughter. He was placating her.

"Rachel?"

She made sure to convey her irritation. "Yes. I'm here. Steve, what is going on there?"

"You know. It's Linda. She wasn't thrilled by your exchange today, so she's been taking her anger out on the kids since she got back from your house. She's not happy because she believes I told you I'm having a problem with her. She doesn't want me talking to you about her or anything pertaining to her life. So, she's not in a good mood."

"And you're telling me you don't know how to deal with this? You'd better figure out a way because our children are with you this weekend, and I don't want them to be miserable." Rachel was laying down an ultimatum.

Steve cleared his throat, as was his habit when he was uncomfortable or unsure of something. "Rachel, I'm sorry but I think the kids should be with you this weekend. I need to work this out with Linda, but I can't do that with them around. I know this isn't ideal for you, but we have to put the kids first."

Rachel was beyond miffed at this point. She *always* put the kids first. She wasn't going to hold back her thoughts. Her ex needed to step up and manage his life. "Steve, this isn't about putting the kids first. I think you want to put yourself first. Well, guess what? You're going to have to figure out how to juggle everything. Just like I always do. Even if I didn't have plans this weekend, I would still think that the kids should spend time with you. You'll have all week to work things out with your wife."

"Rachel, she's not going to make things easier just because the kids are here. You know how she is. When she's angry, everyone knows it."

"Then it's time for her to grow up. You married her. You figure out how to make this work for the kids."

Steve sounded defeated. "I'll try. No guarantees though. You want to talk with Sarah again?"

Rachel didn't know. She thought for a moment and decided to let Steve handle everything. "Steve, you assure the children that things will be fine and that they'll have a wonderful time with you. Concentrate on them. If you have to put Linda on the back burner, then that's what you have to do. As you said, the kids come first." Rachel decided that she had dealt with this enough. She pressed "end" on the phone without even saying goodbye.

Rachel was wiped out by the drama. Her life was such a mix of calm and hysteria, but she supposed most people experienced that combination of emotions in their own lives. She hurried back into the living room, hoping Don wasn't completely fed up with her by now. He had assured her that he understood. Still, this was a lot to deal with for anyone.

She gave him a little wave as if to suggest that she was back with him and things were okay. Don stood up and looked at her. Obviously he wanted to know if everything was settled.

He looked tentative. "You okay?"

"I think I'm still standing, although I may be a little wobbly." She laughed uncomfortably at her own joke.

Don came over to her and wrapped his arms around Rachel, wanting to comfort her. She was pleasantly surprised. He let her go after a moment, and then he looked at her with intensity. "So, what did happen?"

"Steve's wife is being a pain in the you-know-what, and she's making life awful for everyone around her. I spoke with Sarah and then with Steve. I simply told him to deal with it. I don't want our kids to be unhappy, but I also don't want to give up my fun. Steve's a big boy. He's got to be mature enough to deal with the bumps in the road."

Don looked unsure. "Is he really prepared to do that? I mean, will he make things okay so your kids will have a nice weekend with him?"

Rachel looked at Don with massive uncertainty and hope. "He's got to."

The two talked for a little longer, kissing and cuddling, and then decided it was time to call it a night. They both enjoyed their hours together, in spite of the family drama interruption. Don felt Rachel deserved a romantic and elegant night out, so he suggested an upscale restaurant for the next evening. A place where they could sit, relax and enjoy each other's company with delicious food. It sounded wonderful to Rachel.

Don and Rachel stood at the door and shared a long kiss. It was comforting and stirring at the time. It was just what Rachel needed. They parted, and Rachel went upstairs to sink into bed. She prayed that everything would work out and that she would have a peaceful night of sleep.

Chapter Eighteen

On Saturday, Rachel woke up feeling much better about life. There were no frantic calls from any of her children to jar her from her slumber, and the sun was shining. After lingering as long as she could, Rachel got out of bed, exercised and showered. As she was sitting in her kitchen eating breakfast, she decided she would make a call to her salon and find out if she could get a manicure. Today was about pampering herself, and she wanted to look her best for her dinner date with Don.

Because it was a Saturday, there was only one appointment available, so it was now or never. Rachel immediately made her way to the salon. She arrived to find the ample sized parking lot jammed with cars, but she found a couple of open spaces, and she pulled into a spot. Rachel walked into the lobby.

The salon had been built two years earlier, so it was new and beautiful. Every woman Rachel knew, who lived in the area, came here. The place attracted the best employees, and they constantly went through training. The owner was a woman who was divorced and had received a lofty settlement. She loved every aspect of beauty, and wanted to make this an oasis for women and for men, a place where, upon entering, they knew they would be able to indulge themselves. Rachel had her hair done every six weeks, but this was the first manicure she would be experiencing at the spa.

The floors throughout the building were a gleaming white marble, and there were soft, frosted white lights everywhere. The desk in the lobby was clear Lucite, and it was shaped like a sliver of the moon. There was plenty of space for a number of receptionists, which was good because they were always busy. Each one answered the constantly ringing phones, made appointments, checked clients in, and settled their bills. Though there was always a flurry of activity, everything went seamlessly. There was nothing chaotic about the setting.

Rachel walked to the reception area, and was immediately

waited on by a perfectly coiffed thirty-something elegant woman wearing the name-tag "Diane." The lady was of medium height, thin and dressed in the women's required attire of a white blouse and black skirt with a light pink lab jacket. The men working there wore white dress shirts, black slacks and a white lab jacket. The receptionist was wearing very tasteful makeup, and looked professional. She smiled at Rachel and stood up to greet her.

"May I help you?"

"Yes. I'm Rachel Blum." One did not need to say when his or her appointment was or with whom. Once a person gave a name, the rest was up to the receptionist to handle.

The woman clicked away on the computer, and found the appointment. "Ms. Blum, please follow me. I will take you to see Beverly. She'll be your nail technician."

Rachel followed her past a large room filled with every beauty product that was used in the salon. The owner wanted a special area just for those items, so the client felt as though it was more of a shopping experience to go into a room and be able to leisurely browse for what he or she wanted.

Diane guided her into an elegant, serene room decorated with scenic ocean paintings and framed tropical photos on white walls. It was wonderfully tranquil. There were numerous cozy sections, and each had a Lucite table with comfortable black, white and pink striped cushioned chairs. There was a flat screen television on the wall in each partitioned area, as well as flowers, plants and all of the manicure products anyone could imagine. There was another larger area with light tan leather seats and magazines. After having one's nails done, this was where one could wait for them to dry. The back wall had a bar area. All drinks were complimentary, even the only alcoholic beverage of champagne, Dom Perignon. No expense was spared.

Diane invited Rachel to sit in one of the chairs, and asked her if she would like something to drink. She didn't, so she was told Beverly would be with her momentarily. And Diane wasn't kidding. Beverly appeared, seemingly out of nowhere. That was one of the many reasons people came here. Not only could they be pampered from head to toe, but there was absolutely no waiting. Ever. The operation was as smooth as anyone could ever imagine. The owner was particular, knew what she expected for herself, and gave no less to those who frequented her upscale establishment.

"Hi! How are you Ms. Blum?" Beverly was bubbly with a generous smile. She was short and had medium length wavy auburn hair. She also wore the prerequisite uniform. And, no, she didn't know Rachel. She had already been told the name of her client.

"Hello. I'm doing very well, thank you. How are you?" Rachel responded with her own smile.

Beverly took a seat on the opposite side of the table. "I'm fine, thank you! Would you like me to turn on the television or would you prefer it remain off?"

"I don't need it on. Thank you."

Beverly nodded her understanding and was ready to begin. "If at any point you'd like to have the television on, just ask. Or if you want anything to drink, please let me know."

The televisions were new, and Rachel was curious as to why those were necessary. So, she asked.

Beverly chuckled a bit, and explained. "There was a request made for this. Sometimes clients who come here during the weekdays want to keep up with the stock market and everything going on in the financial world. So, you'll find that CNBC can be very popular here. Of course, having the televisions has promoted a lot of other program viewing as well, but that's what got the ball rolling.

Rachel realized that the media age had now invaded salons. At least the owner knew how to keep people happy.

Beverly placed Rachel's hands in a crystal bowl containing a silky solution. "So, what color would you like? Did you have a specific choice in mind, or would you like some help deciding?

Rachel gazed at the colorful bottles of nail polish nestled on a mirrored tray. It was like looking at gems in a jewelry store. She really hadn't thought about the color, so she asked for the woman's advice.

"Is this manicure being done for a special occasion? Do you favor any particular colors?"

Rachel did consider this evening to be a special occasion, but she didn't want to go into all of that. "I like plums, pinks and reds."

For a split second, Beverly looked spooked. Rachel realized why when she took another look at the polishes, and it dawned on her that ninety percent of them contained a variation of one of

199

those three shades.

She flushed slightly with embarrassment at her own comment. "I guess most women like those shades." Rachel laughed insecurely. "I am going to be dressy tonight." She hoped that piece of information, letting Beverly know something about what she might need, would negate any doubts that Beverly might have had about how this session would go with Rachel.

Beverly looked more confident now. "Okay. What color is your outfit?"

Rachel hadn't thought about that at all. "Uh, well, I don't know yet. I hadn't thought about it." *So much for sounding smart and savvy.*

"That's okay." Beverly patted her soaking hand reassuringly. "Let's see. What colors are in most of your wardrobe? If you have black, any shade would be fine, but do you feel like a certain color today? Are you in a pink mood, or red? You're wearing a lavender blouse right now. Is that what you're thinking?"

Rachel felt a bit sorry for this woman. She was trying to help, and Rachel needed to assist her with some idea. "I don't think I'll be wearing any lavender or purple. Maybe red? I think that's what I'm going to wear. I have a red beaded dress."

Beverly sighed almost imperceptibly. "That sounds lovely, but I have to ask you another question then, because reds can be tricky." Rachel felt very insecure for one moment. "Is the dress a blue red or an orange red?" Beverly looked hopefully at Rachel as though she was begging her to come up with the right answer.

Rachel looked at Beverly, praying she was going to give the correct response. "It's probably considered a blue red. It's very red. Like a Valentine's Day red."

Beverly looked more comfortable with that remark. It was as though she had struck gold. She smiled at Rachel as though to say "Job well done. You answered correctly and passed the test."

Beverly looked at the colors of polish, and instantly found the shade that she wanted to use for Rachel. She looked very satisfied as she reached for the bottle. She showed it to Rachel holding it, as it if it was a premium bottle of wine that she was ready to pour. "Does this appeal to you?"

Rachel looked at the red polish contained in the sleek bottle. Normally bottles were not shaped like the ones on this tray. These glass vessels were flared at the bottom and came up to a narrower top. The bottles and their shades were made specifically for the owner for her salon. They couldn't be found anywhere else. The same thing applied to every product in the building. The owner worked with specialists in Europe to create everything. One could understand why this was a sought-after salon.

"I think it will be perfect."

Beverly got to work on Rachel's hands and nails. They made small talk. Otherwise, Beverly worked silently and thoughtfully. Rachel felt very relaxed.

There were other clients in the area, and Rachel could hear just a murmur of conversation taking place between the partitions. No one could be seen, which allowed for privacy. About fifteen minutes into her luxurious manicure, Rachel heard a somewhat louder voice interfere with the calm and quiet of the area.

"She's just a bitch. I don't know what my husband EVER saw in her." The voice sounded familiar to Rachel, although she couldn't place it just yet. She strained to hear.

"And their kids are pieces as well. I can't stand any of them, but my husband is stuck with them. Well, I'm NOT. I don't have to be nice to them."

Rachel's stomach dropped and she flinched. She realized it was Steve's wife.

Beverly stopped her work suddenly. "Are you okay?" She looked alarmed, thinking she might have hurt Rachel.

Flustered, Rachel responded. "Oh, yes, I'm fine. Sorry." Rachel smiled to reassure her that everything was okay.

Beverly took a cotton swab and dipped it gently in nail polish remover. Because Rachel had flinched, Beverly brushed some color on Rachel's skin and not on her nail. She easily removed the spot, and began the polishing process again.

Rachel wondered if Linda's nail technician had any thoughts about her rude client. She's the one who sounded like a bitch, not Rachel. *Who tells someone she doesn't have to be nice to her husband's children?* Rachel continued to try to hear something, although if she did, she doubted that she would feel any better about what was being divulged.

"Well, yes, I did know about my husband's kids." The nail technician must have asked her a question about choosing a man with children. "Still, we certainly weren't thinking about them when we were together." Rachel heard a dirty laugh.

Sadly, Rachel just wanted to get out of the salon. She had been enjoying every moment of the experience until she heard Linda. Now, she felt uncomfortable. She secretly prayed that Beverly would finish as fast as possible. This wasn't the type of place where any client could possibly feel the need or the desire to rush out, but Rachel did, not through any fault of Beverly's or the salon. This was all Linda's evil doing.

Beverly must have sensed something because Rachel could tell that she seemed to be working a little faster. Any technician could work quickly, but that request was probably never stated here. This was an expensive pampering experience to be savored. However not today for Rachel. Maybe some other day.

Rachel wondered how she would deal with drying her nails. She didn't want to see Linda, so sitting in the waiting area was out of the question. And she couldn't sit in the chair. Beverly or someone else would have a client coming in right after Rachel. She thought she might just go in the store.

Beverly sprayed Rachel's lacquered finger nails. She told Rachel that it would help dry her nails faster. That was something at least. She looked at Rachel.

"Are you *sure* you're okay? I feel like something is wrong. Did I do something to upset you?" Beverly appeared to be very worried, her eyebrows knitting together.

Rachel was horrified to have this sweet, professional woman think anything of the kind. "Absolutely not. Please don't think that. You have been so kind and you've done such a wonderful job." Rachel realized that she should whisper. She didn't want Linda to hear her, not that she'd be paying attention to anyone but herself.

"I appreciate that. Still, something is bothering you." Beverly didn't want to let this go.

"I was thinking about something, and I tensed a little. That's all." Beverly didn't need to know the truth. Rachel was not about to go into the details of her personal life with this woman. She had always heard that people bared their souls to bartenders, but she wasn't in a bar, and she wasn't that type of person.

"Okay." Rachel could tell that Beverly wasn't buying her excuse, but she let it go. It wasn't her place to question a client. "Can I get you anything while you're waiting for your nails to dry completely?"

"No, I think I should be fine. I'll go browse in the store."

"Okay, but be careful with your nails. They could get smudged." Beverly looked at her with some admonishment. She didn't want her expert work ruined because Rachel was in a hurry.

"I promise I'll be careful. Thank you again. She put her hands in front of her, praising their appearance. "They're gorgeous!"

Beverly softened a little and smiled. "I'm glad that you're happy with them. I hope I'll see you again soon."

"You will." Rachel wanted to make sure Beverly knew that she was very happy with the job she had performed.

Rachel darted out of the nail area, head down. She went right into the store, holding her breath, hoping she would not run into Linda. When she thought about it for a moment, she realized it was good that Linda was not with Steve and the kids. Maybe Steve and Linda decided she should stay away for a while. Still, why did Linda have to come here? Of all places!

Rachel browsed for a short time. The nail polish was high quality, so her nails were dry and looking fabulous. She quickly went to the front desk to pay for her manicure. She gave a twenty percent tip, was handed her receipt and practically ran out the door.

Rachel was a little shaky as she drove home, but she managed to get there safely. She felt very relieved as she walked through the door into her kitchen. She heated water for a cup of tea, and checked for messages. Fortunately, there weren't any.

As Rachel sipped her tea, she admired her nails. They were very pretty, and she would be happy to have Beverly give her another manicure in the future. Rachel made the mistake of thinking about what Linda had said in the salon. The problem was that Linda really hated the kids. Rachel didn't want her children being with someone who didn't like them. Children could dislike each other. That was part of life. But adults had to behave differently, especially if they were the step-parents. Rachel debated telling Steve about the incident.

After contemplating this for longer than she wanted, Rachel decided to soak in a bubble bath. She wanted to feel completely relaxed for the fun evening ahead, so she went upstairs to run a hot bath, pouring fragrant bath salts and bath gel in the steaming water. After becoming a prune in the tub, Rachel got out, put on her plush bathrobe, set her alarm, and took a nap. She felt very refreshed when her alarm went off. Rachel gave herself plenty of time to dress for her date and to put on her makeup. She accessorized with diamond stud earrings and a simple pearl bracelet. She rarely wore pumps, but this time she put on ones that had four inch heels. Don was tall, so she knew that wouldn't be a problem. Rachel thought she looked magnificent. She realized she hadn't eaten lunch, but that was okay. She wasn't too hungry. She and Don would have a nice lingering dinner, and she'd enjoy every bite of the gourmet meal.

Rachel and Don had agreed that he'd pick her up at eight. At precisely that hour, the doorbell rang. She was always impressed that he was so timely. She opened the door, and they both gasped. He looked beyond handsome, and it was obvious that he admired her appearance as well. He wore a charcoal gray suit with a white shirt and a solid red tie. Even though they hadn't coordinated their looks at all, the red of his tie was the perfect choice to match her red dress. They looked like they would be walking on the Red Carpet tonight.

She invited him in, they kissed, and then they just stared at each other for a moment. Each always found the other to be attractive, but tonight they had both pulled out all the stops.

"Hello, my dear Rachel. How are you?" Don even sounded gallant.

"Right now, I'm doing great! How are you?" Rachel was happy. In spite of the day's events, tonight was going to be wonderful. She felt it to her core.

"Seeing you, I can tell you that I've never been better." They talked for a few minutes before they departed for the restaurant. Don told Rachel about his day. She didn't want to say anything about her challenging moments. Tonight was all about fun and forgetting problems.

It was a wonderfully clear night, and Rachel noticed that the stars were shining brightly. They arrived at the restaurant, and there were cars everywhere. Valet parking was provided, so Don chose to have his car parked by the staff. Rachel stepped out of the vehicle and realized that she must really look good. The young man who opened her door observed her politely from head to toe and smiled. There was nothing vulgar in his gaze, only admiration. Rachel never thought of herself as attractive, but she always tried to rise to the occasion when she was doing something special.

Don lightly touched her back and they walked into the restaurant. There were people both standing and sitting in the waiting area, and there was a murmur of sound. This was not a place to be loud and boisterous. The elegance of the place was obvious. Rich wood paneling lined the walls, and the lighting was dim. The reception desk consisted of a huge slab of tan marble sitting on top of a block of mahogany. There were roses and plants placed smartly around the entryway. Don and Rachel found their way past others waiting for a seat, all dressed to the nines. A woman in her fifties with short hair framing her jaw was checking people in. She was wearing a black dress and a strand of pearls around her neck. Rachel caught a brief whiff of some floral perfume.

"May I help you?" The woman had a dignified and pleasing voice.

"Yes, thank you. I'm Don Levy. I have a reservation for two at 8:30."

The lady glanced at her computer screen and nodded affirmatively. "Yes, we have you down here." She spoke to another woman, younger but attired in exactly the same manner, and asked her to take them to their table. "Carol will show you to your table. Enjoy your evening."

Rachel and Don thanked her, and followed Carol through the dining area. All tables were draped in white linen, and little lamps on the tables illuminated the customers. There was quiet conversation, but no one could hear anyone else other than the people with whom they were dining. Waiters and Sommeliers glided through the restaurant as though they were in a choreographed production. Everything was flawless.

As they arrived at their table, Don pulled out a chair for Rachel. Then he took a seat and the lady told them she hoped they would enjoy their dining experience. Rachel was thrilled already. She had never been to this restaurant so she asked Don how he knew about it.

"I ask people through work as well as my neighbors. I figure that's the best way to find out about places. If there are restaurants you'd like to try, please let me know."

"I'm sure I'm going to love this restaurant. It's funny but I've never been here. I have never even heard about it. I've stuck to all of the places near my house, and I don't get to too many nicer ones because of the kids. I guess I'm still just in mommy mode."

"Just because you're a mom doesn't mean you shouldn't go to nice restaurants. I'm going to see to it that you do just that." He looked at Rachel with conviction.

"You're right of course. It's just that, well, I haven't had the opportunity to go out like this. Anyway, I'm glad to be here and to be with you." Don and Rachel briefly clasped hands and smiled at each other.

A waiter in tails and white gloves came to their table and gave them menus. He asked if they would like wine, and they both decided that they would have a glass. He told them that the Sommelier would come by as they ordered their food, and he would let them know his suggestions. They both knew what they wanted for their appetizer and entrees, so the correct wine was ordered, and shortly thereafter they were presented with an amuse bouche of a thin piece of round lightly toasted bread with smoked salmon mousse, a dollop of crème fraiche and caviar. It was delicious.

Don and Rachel talked, ate and enjoyed every moment of their time together. The servers were never intrusive, and Don and Rachel were made to feel like royalty. As they were eating dessert (they decided each should get one and they could try both) and having coffee, they sighed contentedly at the same time. Rachel felt as though she had been transported to another time and place. Even though it wasn't her birthday, it felt like it was. She was with someone wonderful and she was getting everything that she could possibly want.

The restaurant had started clearing out as they were finishing coffee and dessert. It was almost eleven, but they hadn't even noticed the time. The waiter brought the check, and Don gave him his credit card. Don looked at Rachel. He was very happy. After a moment Don spoke.

"This has been an incredible evening. It seems I keep thinking the same words every time I'm with you. Incredible, amazing, wonderful. You name the good adjective, that's how I feel. I can honestly say that I have never felt all of these emotions at once."

Rachel was beyond flattered and she smiled demurely. She had never had anyone express himself like that to her. Steve had, at one point, cared about her and enjoyed being with her. But he never said anything like this to her. She didn't think he ever felt that deeply about her.

"All I can tell you is that I understand. I feel the same way when I'm with you. I never thought I could feel like this." The waiter brought back the credit card, and Don handed him the receipt to get his car. Then Don asked a pointed question.

"Are you still feeling cautious? About us? About being in a relationship?"

Rachel wasn't sure how to express her thoughts. She gave herself a moment to think before speaking. "Yes and no. How's that for answering a question?" She smiled, and Don gave a little laugh. "I can't help but be cautious. However, I am feeling okay about everything. My defenses have been up for so long that I'm not sure I can tear them all down in one fell swoop. The need to protect myself is huge. Still...you're making me feel like this really *is* good. That I can attempt to trust again and be happy."

"I hope so. But, believe me, I know how you feel. Trust takes time. Probably more time than we've known each other. You were hurt. I can relate because I know what my dad went through. I've got plenty of time to prove to you that you can trust me and that what we have might be pretty wonderful."

"I know it might be pretty wonderful. It already is. Do you feel like you can trust?" Rachel hoped that Don felt okay about everything at this point.

"I feel like I can trust YOU. Other women, not necessarily. But you? Yes. I have no doubt." Don was unwavering on his certainty.

Rachel felt very good about Don's certainty. She knew she was loyal, and that anyone getting involved with her need not feel she would betray him. "So, there's nothing about me that bothers you?" Rachel smiled and batted her eyelashes.

Don smiled. "Not at the moment." He leaned forward in a secretive manner. "What? Is there some deep dark thing I should know about you?" His smiled was devious.

"I wish I was that exciting." Don laughed. "Nope. Nothing at all. What you see is what you get." Don gave an intrigued smile at her comment, and Rachel realized what she had said. "You know what mean." He nodded.

They both stood, ready to leave, and the restaurant staff began to thank them as they were walking outside. Don's car had been brought around, the valet opened the passenger side door and Rachel stepped into the car. They continued talking as Don drove towards Rachel's house. That was one of the many aspects of Don that Rachel adored. From the first time that they met, they were always able to carry a conversation.

He pulled into her driveway and got out of the car. As always, he assisted Rachel out of the vehicle. After closing and locking the car doors, they went inside the house. Rachel had to admit to herself that she enjoyed coming into a quiet home. She told Don that she should check to make sure no one left a message. Fortunately, her children had not called and nor had Steve. Maybe that was a good sign. Her mother had called. She was excited that they were all going to lunch at Don's tomorrow, so she was verifying the time that Rachel would pick her up. "And Ben as well." Rachel had to laugh. Her mother liked Ben very much and tomorrow would be fun. Delores wondered where Rachel was because she was "concerned because it's already ten and I feel like I'm even calling too late right now." Oh, if her mother only knew. Well, Rachel had decided that she would know tomorrow. Oh, yes, this should be something! She went into the living room where Don was patiently waiting.

"Everything okay I hope?" He knew that there could be trouble based on yesterday's phone message.

"Yes. Thankfully, everything seems fine. My mother called to make sure that I know to pick her up. And your dad as well. I assume you're prepared for this lunch?" She was hoping that he knew what he was setting himself up for.

"Oh, sure. I have lots of food."

Rachel laughed. "No, silly, I mean *prepared*. For my mother. For us telling our parents everything."

"Oh, that." His expression indicated that it was no big deal at all. "I'm more than okay with all of it. I like your mom very much, and I think it will be nice to get our relationship out in the open."

Rachel was very satisfied with his answer. "I'm impressed. You have a good head on those broad shoulders. I know I've told you this already, but my mom has wanted this for me since she met you. She could be really pushy." Rachel gave him a look that said she hoped he could handle that.

"No problem. She can be as pushy as she likes. She means well. I think she just wants you to be happy."

Rachel stood there, surprised. It was like he knew her mom better than she did. Don seemed to see more than Rachel could. Maybe Delores did just want Rachel to be happy. It could be as simple as that. That's what any mother should want for her child.

Don and Rachel looked at each other, and the desire that they felt the other day washed over both of them. Don and Rachel kissed passionately. They were nearly breathless when they pulled slightly apart. Looking at each other, they expressed a non-verbal agreement. This would be their night. Rachel took Don's hand, and quickly led him upstairs to her bedroom. Rachel turned on the light, and they kissed again. In a frantic and loving motion, they started removing each other's clothing. Her shoes flew off her feet, and her dress fell in a heap on the floor. She laughingly struggled to undo Don's buttoned shirt, but finally that slid off of his muscular torso. Within seconds, every piece was on the floor, and they stood, looking at each other in the naked silence of the room that was Rachel's sanctuary. Rachel reached over to turn off the light switch, and a peaceful darkness enveloped them. They kissed again, and Don fluidly placed Rachel on the soft mattress. There was enough light from the moon flowing into the room so they could look at each other and fully appreciate what was about to happen. Don and Rachel kissed with fervor, and then his teeth playfully bit her chin. He continued kissing her all over her body, and as he started to suck her nipples, Rachel arched her back with pleasure. As she did that Don knew that all barriers were discarded and they happily and passionately became one.

Chapter Nineteen

The next morning, Rachel woke up feeling happy, relaxed and nervous all at the same time. Don and she had enjoyed a night of abundant pleasure, and they had fallen asleep, exhausted and content, in the early hours of the morning. It was comforting to see Don sleeping beside her so peacefully. He was a considerate and amazing lover, and she had finally allowed herself to feel joy again. But this was the day they were going to tell their parents everything. It all seemed so juvenile. They didn't need permission or approval of any sort. Rachel just hoped that her mother wouldn't make a big deal out of any of it. She thought she might be in for a *See? Didn't I tell you this would be good for you?* Rachel would just have to accept whatever happened. At least she'd have Don by her side.

Don woke up soon after Rachel. They kissed and caressed each other. After a bit, Rachel used the bathroom, and then went downstairs to prepare some fruit, bagels with cream cheese and some coffee. Soon after, Don came downstairs to join her. They couldn't stop kissing each other! But they ravenously ate breakfast, and Don said that he needed to return to the condo to prepare for the upcoming party.

Not long after Don left, Rachel drove to the retirement home to pick up her mother and Ben. As she entered the property, she noticed a lot of people enjoying the day. The residents were sitting on benches with loved ones, grandchildren ran around the fountains, and others were taking advantage of the walking paths. This was fairly typical for a lovely Sunday. Rachel was ready to park her car when she noticed that Ben and Delores were sitting outside waiting for her. They looked happy and were chatting away. As Rachel pulled her car into the circle, Delores saw her, and actually leapt up from her seat and waved. *Wow, she must be very excited about going to Don's*, thought Rachel.

Rachel stopped, put the car in park, and got out to assist them into the car. "Hello you two! How are you on this fine Sunday?"

Rachel, Delores and Ben were all smiles.

Ben gave Rachel a hug, and then Delores did as well. In unison, they said, "We're great!"

Rachel opened the back doors as Ben got in on one side of the car and Delores went to the other side. Rachel was to be their chauffeur, which was fine with her. She closed the doors as they buckled in, and drove off as another car was waiting to pull up from behind her car.

Delores was a chatterbox, and Rachel found that amusing. There was nothing stoic about her mother today. One would have thought they were going on an exciting excursion somewhere. Rachel guessed that, in a sense, they were.

"Oh, isn't this so fun!" Delores was almost childlike in her enthusiasm. Delores leaned in towards Rachel, as far as her seatbelt would allow. "So, you know how to get to Don's, right Rachel?"

Rachel laughed lightly. "Yes, Mom, I do. However, I suspect that Ben also knows the way to his son's house." Ben and Delores laughed heartily at the obvious thought.

"Rachel, it seems that you and Delores are happy to be doing this today. I can tell you I am as well, and I'm sure Don is too." Ben was always affable.

"We are excited, aren't we Rachel?"

"Yes, Mom. It's very nice of Don to host a lunch today."

Delores turned to Ben. "Don is such a wonderful young man." She said it as though Ben should be very proud of his son.

"Mother, we're *all* looking forward to seeing him. Let's just enjoy the drive, shall we?" Delores was making Rachel a bit nutty by her overly enthusiastic attitude.

Fortunately, Rachel was able to drive the car with only a little more chatter from her mother. All she could think about was the surprise her mother would feel when she heard the news that Rachel and Don were seeing each other. Ben might be surprised as well, but he wouldn't overreact the same way that her mother possibly would.

Don's condo was just a short drive from the home. The complex had been developed about five years earlier, and it was quite a popular place for younger executives as well as empty-nesters. Don didn't fall into either category because he wasn't considered to be a younger person and he'd never married and had kids. Still, he didn't want to have to take care of a lawn or any outside maintenance. The other added benefit of the complex was that he lived close to his father.

Ben pointed to the condo area as they were driving near it as if to say, *here it is. We've arrived.* Delores was craning her neck to see how amazing this place must be. Rachel drove in and veered to the left. Don had told her how to meander and find his place, but Ben also guided her through. The condos were situated on nicely kept grounds that were being lovingly tended even at this moment. It seemed everyone was choosing to be outside today.

Rachel parked the car in the covered area designated for visitors. There were a number of vehicles there already, but she had no trouble finding a spot. The three got out of the car, and walked towards Don's condo. Delores stayed close to Rachel as Ben led the way up the front steps. He rang the doorbell, and Don opened the door within seconds. Rachel and he took each other in for a second, and then he welcomed them into his home.

Don was dressed casually and neatly as always. He and Rachel were both wearing light gray slacks. Don was wearing a white and gray horizontally striped polo shirt, while Rachel wore a cotton raspberry-colored shirt.

Rachel and Delores deposited their purses at the entry, and Don offered to give them a tour of his condo. Delores was beaming, and Ben followed happily along with the group. The living room was just off the foyer, and Don had decorated it in a very neutral and comfortable manner. The walls were painted light mocha and there was a cream colored leather couch flanked by glass tables with brass lamps and a glass coffee table. There were a couple of brown suede chairs, which looked like a person could even nap in them. A large flat screen television dominated the opposite wall. The tall windows allowed sunshine to filter in on the few plants that were placed throughout the room.

On the opposite side of the foyer was a small dining room, painted off white with a simple wooden table, and wooden chairs with dark brown leather padding. Don had the table set for their lunch with white china plates, beige napkins and simple silverware. The kitchen was directly behind the dining room, and though small, it had all of the upscale amenities. Stainless steel refrigerator, stainless steel four burner stove, and cherry cabinets with glass fronts. There was a dinette by a bay window as well, and the floor was the same gleaming hardwood found throughout the entire lower level.

The upstairs had one guest bedroom which was used as Don's office, a guest bathroom and the master suite. The master bedroom was average in size, and it contained Don's king-sized bed, as well as an antique dresser which was ornately carved. Rachel wondered if this was a family heirloom. The master bathroom had a walk-in closet and the standard whirlpool tub, vanity and separate shower, all done in tan marble and accented with brushed nickel fixtures. The entire upstairs had cream colored carpeting.

After Delores finished complimenting everything she saw, they headed back downstairs, and Don began to take things out of the refrigerator to place on the table. Rachel assisted him while Ben and Delores waited in the living room. Rachel nervously looked at Don. Don looked at her wondering what was wrong.

"Rachel? Is everything okay?"

"Oh, yes, of course. Everything is great and you have a lovely home. It's a real treat to be here." Rachel forced a smile.

"But…?"

"But nothing." Rachel said this with a pitched voice.

Don looked at her and realized the problem. "Okay, do you want to bite the bullet and get it over with?" He smiled knowingly.

"What?"

"You know. Do we confess now or after lunch?"

"Oh. I…well…um."

"How 'bout now? I think you might enjoy lunch more if we just spill the beans right now. I really think everything will go perfectly well." He gave her a very reassuring look.

Rachel heaved a big sigh. "Okay. If you say so."

After placing everything on the table, they went into the living room where Ben and Delores were sitting and talking. They smiled as they saw Don and Rachel.

"So, young man, are you ready to host this lunch?" Ben had a glint in his eyes.

"Yes, in a moment Dad. Um…Rachel and I have something to say to you and to her mother." Rachel looked like a frightened animal. She glanced at Don, figuring she'd let him break the news.

Ben looked somewhat perplexed and Delores looked like she

213

couldn't wait to know what was going to be said. "Is everything okay, Son?"

"Yes. Everything is great, Dad. We want to let you both know that we're seeing each other. We're dating. Rachel and I." Don looked at Rachel hoping he had said everything in the right way. Rachel stood frozen.

As the parents stood, Ben's eyes danced with joy, and Delores looked like she had been given a gift of diamonds. They looked at each other with pure happiness.

Delores clasped her hands together. "Oh, this is WONDERFUL! I couldn't be happier! I had no idea. When did this happen?"

Rachel looked down and then looked up again preparing herself for a grilling. "Well, it just happened. We got to talking and things progressed from there." She tried to sound as calm as possible.

Delores looked at her admonishingly. "But you said you weren't interested. You were so angry with me, accusing me of pushing you. I don't understand." It was amazing how her mother could go from being boundlessly joyful to being pissed off within seconds.

"Mom, there's nothing to understand. Just be happy for us." Rachel looked at her pleadingly.

"Well, I think it's fantastic!" Ben was positively beaming. "Rachel, you're a fine woman and my son is lucky to spend time with you."

Rachel blushed. "Thank you Ben. I'm lucky too." She looked at Don with a contented smile.

"What do you say we celebrate with some lunch?" Don led the way into the dining room. They ate the various salads and sandwiches that Don served. Had anyone else been looking, the person would have observed four people talking and laughing and having a joyous time together.

Don served a cake that he had purchased at a nearby bakery. The entire meal was delicious and the company made it even better. They had coffee, and then it was decided that Ben and Delores should get back to the home. There were some activities they were participating in later in the day, and Rachel's kids would be coming back in the evening.

Don was thanked profusely for his efforts, and Delores gave him a big hug. He looked at Rachel with an amused smile as this was happening. Rachel also hugged him goodbye, and Don said he would call her to make arrangements for another date. Delores had apparently heard this because she was grinning from ear-to-ear when Rachel turned around to head for the door.

More words of appreciation were spoken as they made their way out of the condo. The three were leaving happy and full. Don waved goodbye and thanked them for coming. He winked at Rachel as she turned one last time to wave goodbye to him. They both knew that things had gone well and that life was very good.

On the drive back to the home, Delores couldn't contain her excitement at the news of her daughter and Don dating. She chattered on and on that she knew this was going to happen and that everything would be wonderful. Every now and then Ben added a chuckle or a word of agreement. He was so mild-mannered. Rachel was pleased that her mother wasn't making him insane.

Rachel arrived at the home, and pulled into the circular driveway. She got out of the car and assisted her mother and Ben out and into the building. After hugging them both and wishing them a fun afternoon, she stepped back into her car and drove home. She was happy to find a message from Don waiting for her on her answering service.

"Hi, Rachel. We all certainly had a great time! I'd like to see you again as soon as you're available. Give me a call when you have a chance. Bye!"

Rachel was overjoyed. She had to believe that this was all good, that some other shoe wasn't about to drop and ruin everything. Rachel called Don immediately.

They spoke for a few minutes and made a date to have lunch during the week. Rachel realized it was time to tell her children about Don so that plans could be made more easily on the weekends. Or on a weeknight. How daring! Rachel thanked Don again for the lunch and they ended the conversation.

Rachel wanted to tell her sister know about everything before the kids came home, so she made the call. The answering machine clicked on. Leah's cheerful voice came through clearly.

"You've reached the Stern residence. Please leave a message, and we'll get back to you ASAP." Then the beep sounded.

"Hello. It's Rachel. Like I needed to say that. Anyway, I just want Leah to know that all is well. Leah, you know what I mean.

I'll talk with you soon. Bye."

Rachel hated leaving messages on any machines. She never knew what to say, and without a response from the person she was calling, she felt like an idiot just talking away on a recorder. She knew she needed to say something because everyone had Caller ID now, so they'd know she called and would wonder what was going on.

Rachel had a little time before the kids would be home. She did a bit of laundry and took care of some paperwork. After relaxing for a while, she made dinner and watched some television. At 6:30 on the nose, the front door swung open. Then three kids came bounding in as though they were being chased. Steve followed. There was a chorus of, "Hey, Mom," and then they were off in various directions. Rachel stood up to see Steve. He looked very tired, with slightly dark circles under his eyes. His hands were in his pockets and he seemed very ill-at-ease.

"Hey, Rache. How's life?" He didn't sound very cheerful.

"I'm fine." Rachel answered very cautiously. "What's up?"

Steve looked exasperated. "Why do you always have to say it like that? You're so suspicious of me, like you think there's always something going on, and you're not so sure that you like it!"

Rachel was shocked and angered by his outburst. "Excuse me? How dare you yell at me!" Rachel lowered her voice so the children wouldn't hear their parents arguing. Sometimes she felt like she was the only parent who treaded carefully where their children were concerned. "You know I have every reason to be suspicious. EVERY reason. However, your past horrible behavior is not the cause of my questioning you. You come in here, and I can sense that something isn't right. I worry for the children."

Steve's expression changed to a more apologetic appearance. "Okay, okay. You're right. I'm sorry. It has been a long weekend, and I'm just feeling a bit off these days."

"*Are* you okay? I know Linda hasn't been making life easy for you, but are you physically okay? You don't look so great." She eyed him with concerned suspicion.

Steve ran his hand through his graying hair in a tired fashion. "Yeah, I'm fine. My personal life must be taking a toll on my appearance." He looked pointedly at Rachel clearly begging for more concern from her so that she should ask him more about his problems.

Rachel sighed and folded her arms. "Do you want a cup of coffee? I have a moment or two if you want to let me know what's going on. I should know about your life if the kids are going to be involved with you." She wanted to make it perfectly clear to Steve that her concern wasn't for him but for her children.

Steve smiled. "I'd like that very much."

Rachel and Steve went into the kitchen, and he sat down as Rachel poured them both mugs of coffee. She put milk and sugar on the table, and then she sat down. There was only the sound of their spoons clinking against the porcelain mugs as they were stirring the ingredients into their coffee. Steve began to speak.

"Oh, Rachel. I don't even know where to begin." He was shaking his head in disbelief. "Things haven't been going well for a while now. Linda has been very difficult, almost since we were first married. Just so demanding and manipulative. I began to realize that she wasn't interested in me so much as what she could get from me." Steve looked at Rachel expecting her to comment. She didn't. Rachel kept sipping her coffee, preparing to hear more. Her silence prompted him to continue.

"I guess sometimes we make mistakes. Looking back, I don't know what I was thinking. I mean, I threw everything away. Everything that really mattered." Steve looked intensely at Rachel.

"Well, you have to keep moving forward. Just like everyone else does." Rachel sounded very practical. She didn't want to put forth any emotion. This was Steve's problem, and as far as she was concerned, she was only the kind listener.

Steve's eyes pierced through her. "Have you? Moved forward?"

Rachel nodded. "Yes I have. I didn't have a choice. Life simply has to go on."

Steve looked at his mug of coffee, and tapped his fingers against the warm porcelain. "Is Don a part of your moving forward?" Steve didn't look at her.

Rachel's mug was at her lips as she spoke into the coffee. "Perhaps."

Steve pursed his lips. "Perhaps? You're really not going to tell me more than that, are you." It wasn't a question. He knew that Rachel was playing it all very close to the vest.

They both heard the children coming towards the kitchen. Steve and Rachel's conversation had to stop abruptly. Steve put on a fake smile for the kids.

"Hey Dad, what are you still doing here?" David looked at him with a confused expression.

"I'm just discussing things with your mom. I'm heading out soon."

Rachel stood, ready for Steve to go. "Yeah, your dad is ready to leave."

Steve took the cue, and got up as well. He put his arm around David. "I'll see you and your sisters very soon. I hope that you had a good time this weekend." He winked at David, but David didn't respond. That concerned Rachel.

Steve hugged the kids, and went to the door. "Rachel, thanks for the coffee. I hope we can chat again soon."

"You're welcome. Take care." Rachel wasn't going to encourage him. Steve looked a little disappointed that she hadn't responded to his desire to see her again. He waved goodbye, got into his car and zoomed away.

The children went to their rooms to finish up their last bit of homework. The phone rang just as Rachel sat down to read in the family room. Her sister was calling.

"Hello!"

"Hello to you! So, everything went well? It sounds like life is very nice right now. How's our main man?"

Rachel laughed. "*Our* main man is fine. We told Mom and his dad about our relationship. The brunch was great, and Don and I will be seeing each other for lunch this week."

"YES! I'm thrilled for you! Little Miss 'there's nothing going on and nothing to tell you.' Uh, huh. *That* tune has changed. So, do the kids know?"

Rachel spoke quietly. "Well, not exactly. Not at all, actually. And before you say anything, I KNOW I need to tell them. And I will. I'm just not sure when."

"What are you waiting for? It's not like you're telling them you've committed a crime, and you're going to prison. Their mother is dating a wonderful man. This is good news!"

"Yes, and maybe under normal circumstances I would think you're right. It's just that… well…things are a little challenging for their dad right now. I'm afraid to rock the boat any more than necessary."

"Okay, what does that mean? What's going on?" Leah sounded worried.

"Steve is having problems. With Linda. It's disrupting his time with the kids. When he dropped them off, he wanted to talk about it. He looks awful, so this is obviously taking a toll on him."

"No, no, no. This isn't happening." Leah was very adamant in her displeasure.

"What do you mean? You're shocked that Linda would be causing a problem for him? Come on, you know how she is." Rachel didn't know why her sister would be so surprised.

"That's NOT what I mean. I know she's a piece of work. Who cares? That's HIS problem, not yours. Don't fall for his crap."

"Huh?"

"He doesn't need to burden you with his garbage. Your only connection with him is the kids. That's it. Don't get sucked in."

"I'm not getting sucked in."

"Sis, he's always been a sweet talkin' guy. You have a wonderful thing going with Don. Now is not the time to start talking with your ex about his problems. I don't want you falling for him."

"WHAT? I'm not going to go back to him! Not a chance! I don't have any feelings for him now. Geez, Leah!" Rachel couldn't believe that Leah would think for even one moment that she was going to get involved with Steve again.

"Okay, sorry. I just don't like that Steve is talking with you about his life. I'm wondering if he might want you back."

Rachel answered emphatically. "Uh, well, that is NOT going to happen, so don't worry." Rachel wanted to make sure her sister knew that there was no way that she would even consider going back to Steve.

"Good. You can never forget what he did. Also, Don is a wonderful man, so it's best if you just continue to focus on him. And you need to tell the kids about your relationship. Right away. You don't have to say that he's going to be their step-father, but let them know what's happening."

"I know. You're right. I guess it's best if I just take the plunge. I don't know if they'll be happy about this." Rachel was doubtful as to how this would turn out.

"Maybe. Maybe not. That's not the point. The point is that you should be completely honest with them. I'm sure when they meet him, they'll realize he's not like their wicked step-mother."

Rachel enjoyed a good laugh over that one. "Okay, you've convinced me. I think I'll even mention it all tonight. Thanks for

219

your always good advice. I appreciate everything you've said."

"No problem. I want my big sister to do what's right. If you need to, call me after you've talked with the kids. Even though I'm not there with you, I'm always here for you."

The warmth and sincere love brought tears to Rachel's eyes. Leah was the best sister in the world, and Rachel knew she could always count on her. "Thanks. You mean the world to me, you know that."

"Yep, I know that. Right back at you. I wish you all the best. I hope everything works out."

"Same here. I'm sure I'll talk with you soon."

After hanging up, Rachel took a deep breath and figured it was time to talk with her children. She wasn't exactly sure what she was going to say, but she knew if she put it off much longer, it would be more difficult to discuss her situation. And she wanted to have the freedom of seeing Don at all times. Rachel didn't want to have to sneak around.

She went upstairs, and called out to the kids to come downstairs. She went back down to the family room and braced herself. The three came into the room, and gave her an odd look. They knew something was up.

"Hey, kids. I want to let you in on something. Something that is going well for me, and I thought you should be made aware of it."

They continued to stare at her, wondering what they were in for. After Rachel had paused to collect her thoughts, Rebecca chimed in. "So? What is it? What's the big announcement?" She seemed to be in a hurry for her mother to speak and get it over with.

"Okay. I want you to know that I'm seeing someone. A man I met at the home where Grandma lives." She stopped and looked at the three faces. David didn't have a reaction. He seemed fine. Not happy, not horrified. Sarah looked suspicious and Rebecca looked annoyed.

"You're dating?" That was all Rebecca could say.

"Yes. I met this nice man, and we started to form a friendship. His father lives at the home." Rachel wasn't sure what else she should say. There wasn't much to tell.

Sarah spoke up next. "So, Grandma knows this man?"

"Yes, she does, and she really likes him. She actually wanted me to go out with him before I was even ready. Kind of funny, isn't it?" Rachel laughed uncomfortably. She wasn't quite sure any of this was so amusing.

Rebecca was biting her lip, contemplating the whole idea of her mother seeing someone. "You do realize that we don't like Linda." She was understandably concerned that her mother could possibly have chosen a bad man.

Rachel looked at her with sympathy. "I know, honey. I'm sorry Linda has been causing so much trouble. Your dad is trying to figure things out on that front. I can assure you that Don is not at all like Linda. You have to know that I'm a wary person. I'm not leaping into anything, but Don is very kind and interesting. He's a good man. But even so, I promise you, I'm taking this very slowly." She looked at them hoping her words were reassuring.

Her comments seemed to appease her children. She could see them physically relax. Rachel was very pleased.

"So, when will we meet Mr. Wonderful?" Sarah gave a devilish look, and Rachel was able to breathe easier knowing that she was okay with the newfound relationship.

"When would you like to meet him? I'm sure he would be happy to see all of you as soon as you want."

"How about right now?" Rebecca wasn't going to waste any time. Rachel suspected that her children needed reassurance that Don was really the way their mother described him.

Rachel looked at her watch. It wasn't too late, so if Don was able to come by, even for a short time, she thought that would be fine. "I'll give him a call."

The children stayed in the room while Rachel placed the call to Don. He answered immediately.

"Hi, Don, it's Rachel." Rachel looked happily at the children who appeared to be hanging on her every word.

"Hi, Rachel. How are you?"

"I'm doing well. Don, I told the children about our relationship, and they'd like to meet you."

"Oh, Rachel, that's great news! I couldn't be happier. I'd like to meet them as well."

"How does right now sound to you?" Rachel prayed that he wouldn't be thrown by this sudden request. If he was okay with it, the kids would probably respect him more for being willing to come over right away.

221

"Oh. Well, sure. Now would be fine. I guess they're anxious to meet me."

"Yes, they are. I'm so glad you can come now. So, we'll see you soon." Rachel gave a satisfied look to the kids like she had just achieved something very special.

"Yep. I'll be there soon."

Rachel hung up the phone. "So, there you have it. He's coming over now. He doesn't live far from here. I don't intend to have him stay very long." Rachel wanted to make sure that the children understood that this meeting would not be a lengthy questioning and grilling session.

The three seemed excited and anxious. This meeting would be far different than the one they had experienced with Linda. That had more tawdry overtones. Their father had already been secretly seeing Linda, and he was preparing to marry her by the time they were introduced to her. There had been no chance to get to know her, and from the beginning, they hadn't liked her. Not only for the bad things that had happened, but because she was not a nice person, at least not to them. This time, things would be different. Don wasn't being sprung on them in some awful manner. Hopefully they would like him and he would return their feelings.

Rachel was a bit nervous. In her wildest imagination, she would never have expected to have to introduce her children to another man. They all chatted excitedly until the doorbell rang. Rachel's heart practically leapt in her chest. She even stumbled slightly when she went to answer the door. She opened the door to a smiling Don. He greeted her with a kiss on the cheek and a hug. Sarah, David and Rebecca were a slight distance behind her checking him out. He came forward, and Rachel introduced her family to him.

David came forth from behind his sisters, and proudly held out his hand to Don. "I'm David. It's nice to meet you." David sounded so paternal.

Don shook David's hand. "I'm Don, and it's very nice to meet you too." He looked at the girls. "And your sisters as well. I'm so glad that you want to meet me."

Rachel introduced Don to her daughters and guided them all into the family room. "Shall we sit down?" She thought she sounded way too formal.

They all sat down with the girls eyeing Don like they wanted to really see who their mom was dating. They were curious but also polite.

"Don, would you like something to drink?" Rachel wanted this to be a casual gathering, and she figured Don should be as comfortable as possible.

"No thanks. I'm fine. I'm just happy to be sitting here with your family." As always, Don's comments and smile were genuine.

Rebecca didn't beat around the bush. "So, how long have you and my mom been seeing each other?" Rachel's middle child was ready for all the details.

"Not long. We had seen each other a bit here and there at the retirement home where your grandmother lives, as does my father. I moved here rather recently to be closer to my dad. Your mom and I got to talking, and we decided to hang out together."

Rachel loved how calmly and easily Don spoke about everything. He wasn't the least bit intimidated by her investigative children.

"What do you do here? What do you do for a living?" Rebecca was now in the midst of an interview. The only thing missing was a pen and a clipboard.

"I do advertising computer graphics for companies. So, I can work anywhere. It's a good setup for me." Rebecca nodded her head in understanding. So far, so good.

Sarah decided it was her turn to let Don know the score. She continued to look upon him with great suspicion. "You know our mom has been through a lot, right? She doesn't need any more problems. My dad is married to a horrible woman, so we're done with difficult people." Well, her older daughter certainly knew how to cut to the chase. Rachel shifted uncomfortably on the couch, but she was willing to let the kids say whatever they needed to say without any interference. As long as they were respectful to Don, she would keep quiet.

Don looked very serious. "I know your mom has dealt with a lot of garbage. I even somewhat understand what you've all gone through because my dad raised me by himself when my mom took off with another man." All of the kids gasped lightly and gawked at Don. Their jaws could have hit the floor. They were surprised by his candor. "Believe me; I would never want to hurt your mom or anyone else. I happen to think your mom is an amazing woman. I like spending time with her. I'd also like to spend some time with all of you. You could get to know me better and I could get to know more about you."

Rachel was so touched by his comments. She still couldn't quite believe she was lucky enough to be with someone who was so decent and thought so highly of her. Her children had to see him the way she did.

David looked at Don with huge round eyes. "How did you feel not having a mom around?"

Don smiled at David, "It wasn't easy. My dad was great, though. He's always been a good parent. I learned that we have to deal with things in life, some good, and some bad. It also taught me that no one is perfect. People make mistakes, and we have to find a way not to be hurt by their actions."

"Our mom was very hurt. Dad did an awful thing." Sarah looked at Don almost challenging him to understand their family dynamic.

Don nodded his head in agreement with what Sarah was saying. "I know. There's no easy way around problems. I suspect even your dad has learned a lesson from the mess he created. However, look at your mom now. I don't know how she was when everything hit the fan, although I'm sure it was a very difficult time. Still, she survived, she's stronger, and thankfully she's willing to take a chance with me. I'm not about to let her down." His eyes were piercing as he looked at Rachel.

Those last statements seemed to have impacted the kids. They were looking at Don and at each other very happily. Then they glanced at Rachel, and they all smiled as if they had come to some mutually satisfactory answer. They had given Don a chance to explain himself as well as to have him understand what they were feeling. It was a very positive moment. He seemed to pass their test.

"Okay, kids. I think that's it." Rachel stood up and then so did Don. "Why don't you all say thank you and goodbye to Don and head upstairs." It wasn't a request. It was a gentle command.

The children did as she asked, and that left Don and Rachel alone in the family room.

"Don, I can't thank you enough for what you just did."

"I'm happy I could come here and talk with them. Your kids seem terrific. I'd say you've done a great job raising them in a very difficult situation."

"Everything you said was just...well...incredible. I feel so much better. I'm glad things are out in the open." Rachel looked relieved.

"That's the only way to live. Well, I suppose I should be on my way. Would you like to get together for lunch tomorrow? I can pick you up at noon if that's okay with you?"

"That would be perfect. And guess what? We can go out whenever we want. If the kids are home, it's okay. Now that they know, I don't have to work around schedules." Rachel felt like a curfew had been lifted.

"Then you may have a problem keeping me away." He kissed Rachel goodbye, and returned home.

Later that night, Rachel went to bed and slept very peacefully.

Chapter Twenty

The next morning was a typical Monday. Rachel and the kids were up and moving. She got them off to the bus, and thought about her plans for the day. Although she enjoyed the down time during the day while her children were in school, she was also looking forward to the start of their summer break. Things would slow down at least a little bit, and of course she and the kids were looking forward to the trip to California.

Rachel had housecleaning to do, and then it would be time for her lunch with Don. She smiled when her mind wandered, thinking about the excitement she always experienced when she knew Don would be with her soon. She felt like a teenager in that sense, although fortunately maturity had made her wiser. Rachel would never again sit by the phone waiting for it to ring, nor would she wonder what a man was thinking and if she was good enough for him. Those days were long over. She cared, but not to the point of near insanity. If Rachel wasn't happy or feeling comfortable about something, then that was that. She would be done with the whole mess. However, so far that wasn't the case. There was a little piece of her that was still waiting for the possibility of something to go wrong, but she tried not to be plagued by those doubts. She just wanted to have fun. That was how Rachel would continue to live her life.

At eleven, she was done with the cleaning, and she took a quick shower and got dressed. Rachel was feeling rather playful, and she attired herself appropriately. It was a lovely mild day, so she chose coral colored Capri pants with a lighter tone of coral blouse. She threw on strands of white and peach pearls and a mother of pearl bangle. A neutral pair of sandals completed the picture. She looked like she was ready for an excursion in the Bahamas, but she didn't care. Rachel was feeling light and happy. She applied her makeup and was ready to go.

Don, ever prompt, rang the doorbell at the designated time. Rachel opened the door, and upon seeing her, Don raised his eyebrows.

"Wow, you look amazing! As had now become a tradition, he kissed Rachel. You always look terrific, but you look a bit different today."

"Thanks! I wanted to change my look a little. I feel free. So, where are we off to for lunch?" Rachel grabbed her tan leather purse.

Don couldn't take his eyes off of her. "Uh…oh yeah… lunch. Well, I was thinking of the place that has gourmet sandwiches and soups. How does that sound?"

"Sounds perfect! I'm just so happy to see you!" She kissed him.

Don smiled. He took her by the hand and helped her into the car. The drive was short, and they chatted the entire time. He told her how grateful he was to have met her children and how he hoped they felt happy about Rachel and his relationship.

They arrived at the restaurant and felt fortunate to find a parking space. This was a popular lunch place because it was convenient for business people as well as housewives, and the food was incredible. Rachel had been here with friends over the years, and she was happy to return.

They walked in and had a five-minute wait. Rachel and Don continued talking and then were seated and given menus. They quickly looked over the selections. Rachel decided to have a chicken salad sandwich and mushroom bisque, while Don's choice was a tuna sandwich and tomato soup. After placing their orders and chatting, they were suddenly interrupted. Steve was looming over them, dressed smartly in a black suit and gray tie.

"Hi, Rache! How are you?"

Rachel's heart thumped heavily in her chest. "Steve! Uh, I'm fine. Um, Steve this is Don. Don this is Steve, my ex-husband." Rachel fixated her gaze on Don as though to prepare him for whatever might be said.

Being the gentleman that he always was, Don stood to greet Steve and shake his hand. "Hello, Steve." Don's voice was steady and polite.

"Don." Steve nodded once at him as an introduction.

Rachel wasn't sure what to say. She was caught completely off guard. "So, are you here on a business lunch?"

"Yes I am. What kind of lunch is this?" He knew the answer, but he was getting in his digs as quickly as possible.

"We're eating before Don gets back to work." *What kind of lunch did he think this was?*

"That's nice. Very nice." Steve clapped his hands together once. "Well, I guess I'll leave you two to your lunches. Don, it was a pleasure meeting you. Rachel, always good to see you." He smiled slyly at her. Rachel gave a pursed smile back and was grateful that Steve was leaving.

Rachel looked down at the table, briefly unable to look at Don's eyes. "Sorry about that. If I had known he'd be here, I would have suggested any other place."

Don reached out for her hand. "Rachel, there's no need to apologize or feel uncomfortable about what just happened. We're allowed to have a meal out anywhere we want and so is Steve. We're bound to bump into him every now and then. It's really no big deal. At least not for me. He's going to be a part of your life because of your kids, so I know we're going to see him sometimes."

Rachel felt very reassured. Don had such a logical, easy way of looking at everything. Normally, she was more rational about life, but now that she was with Don, she didn't want anything to shake their world. She was relieved he didn't mind dealing with Steve. "Thanks for understanding. It is nice to know you are okay with my odd little life."

Don laughed. "It's not that odd, Rachel. We both know this is actually very common." Don paused briefly. "What I find a bit interesting is that it's obvious to me that Steve seems to still have some fondness for you. I can understand that. I have more than some fondness for you." He smiled at Rachel. "However I wonder how he's feeling about you these days?" Don looked uncertain.

Rachel's eyes widened in horror. "Oh, I don't think he's feeling much of anything for me. We're over. He's knows that." She wanted to make sure Don felt totally secure about his own relationship with her. She didn't want him to think for one moment that Steve could intrude on what Don and she had together. She leaned in towards Don and spoke in a whisper. "He's actually having some problems with Linda. You know? His wife."

"That is interesting. He seems to be creating a lot of trouble for himself. It's a shame."

Rachel nodded in agreement. "Well, Linda is a very challenging person. Even so, I doubt that Steve is a gem of a husband."

Don had an uncomfortable look on his face. "You don't think he's been unfaithful to HER, do you?"

Rachel looked confused and doubtful. "Oh, no, I don't think so. I mean…well… I don't THINK so. Gosh, I honestly don't know."

"It doesn't matter. Fortunately, that's not your problem."

Don and Rachel smiled at each other, realizing they had their happiness and that was what counted. Their meals were brought to the table, and they ate and enjoyed talking about some activities that they'd like to do together. After they finished eating, the server brought the check. Don immediately grabbed it, making sure that Rachel wasn't going to pay for anything. After he signed his name on the credit card slip, they both stood up, ready to leave. Steve showed up again.

"Ah, you two leaving so soon? I hope you enjoyed your meals." Rachel didn't like Steve's ultra-cool tone.

"Yes, we did." Don answered for himself and for Rachel. There was no emotion in his voice. If anything, his tone indicated that he wasn't interested in continuing any conversation with Steve.

Steve looked around. "Yes, indeed, this is one terrific restaurant." He looked at Don. "It's nice that you can take the time to get out and have lunch." Steve then looked at Rachel. "And with such a lovely lady."

Don didn't flinch. He looked lovingly at Rachel. "I couldn't agree more. It's always a pleasure to spend time with her." Rachel blushed.

Rachel decided to end the conversation. "Okay then. I guess it's time for all of us to leave. Hope the rest of your day goes well, Steve." She didn't wait for Steve to say anything else. She took Don's hand, and they left the restaurant.

On the drive back to Rachel's, she and Don agreed to have dinner out on Friday night. Just a relaxing, casual dinner. There was a movie coming out they that wanted to see on Saturday, so that date was also set. Don suggested going to lunch after visiting their parents on Sunday. Rachel's weekends were becoming busier than ever.

After Don brought Rachel home, she called her sister.

"Hello! How's life with Don?"

"Hello to you too. I wish you didn't have Caller ID. You ought to watch yourself. At some point it could be one of my kids calling you instead of me." Rachel had a playful tone with her comments.

"So sorry, my dear sister. And how are you today? So nice of you to call."

"Ha, ha. Very funny. How are YOU?"

"I'm fine. Life is going well. Busy as usual. I'm counting the days until you get here."

"We're looking forward to that as well. It's hard to believe school is almost over."

"Okay, enough of the small talk. I enjoy it, but I do want to know how life with Don is going."

"Yes, I know you do. Everything is going well. Really well. We just had lunch together. Unbelievably, Steve was there. He stopped by our table."

"Oh, lucky you. How did that go?"

"Without a hitch. Don knows how to handle these situations. He's so cool about everything. I give him credit for going with the flow. It isn't easy with this family."

"I hope Steve isn't bothering you."

"No, he's not. We just happened to be at the same restaurant, and he stopped by to say hello."

"Let me ask you this. If Steve and Linda were somewhere together, and you were in the same place, would you stop by to say hello?"

Rachel thought about that for a split second. "No, I probably wouldn't. I don't like her, and I'd rather not have to talk with either one of them."

"See! You wouldn't stop by their table if you could avoid them. So, why is Steve coming to your table?"

Rachel responded with humor. "Probably because he's more polite than I am. I don't know. Honestly, let's not make a big deal out of this."

"I hope it isn't made into a big deal. I truly think that Steve doesn't like the fact that you are seeing Don. He'll get in the way if he can."

"Well, he can't. I don't care how he feels about anything. I'm enjoying Don's company. Steve will have to deal with it."

"Okay. I hope so. Just be aware of everything."

"Trust me. I'm a lot more clued in than I used to be. Steve isn't going to dictate my life. He won't get the opportunity. I've lived and I've learned. It's my life, and he has no say in it."

"I feel better about this if you're being serious. Stick to your guns, Sis. You've got a good thing going here."

"I know that I do. However, I still want to make this clear. Don and I are seeing each other, but I have no intention of going too deeply into this relationship. I'm not looking for a commitment. I only want to have some fun and spend time with a nice man. Nothing more." Rachel was trying to convince her sister as well as herself.

"Nothing more? Nothing? You just want this to be all casual?"

"Yes, exactly. It's easier that way. No strings, no problems." Rachel sounded emphatic.

"Okay. So what about how Don sees this? What if he's looking for more?"

"Geez, Leah. I don't know. That's not my problem. He's an adult. He can deal with whatever this is." Rachel was tired of discussing all of this.

"I just want to make sure you understand that you are in a relationship. Don may look at this more seriously. Not that you have to, but perhaps at some point, you might want to have a discussion with him."

Rachel really was getting peeved with Leah's commentary. "Okay, okay. I know you're the one who has the perfect marriage. You know all about happy, healthy relationships. But I'm not an idiot. I think I'm mature enough now to have a man in my life without it being a catastrophe for him or for me."

"Oh, sweetie, I don't want to make you angry. I know you're not an idiot. I only want you to be happy. I'm not an expert on anything, and I've been lucky to have had such a happy marriage. Please don't think I'm trying to make you feel like you're clueless."

"I know you're not. It's just that I don't want to make a big deal out of this. After everything that I've been through, I want to enjoy my life."

"You've got it. Just enjoy. I totally understand, and I want that for you too. So, anything else fun going on I should know about?"

"Not really. Everything else is life as usual. Is there anything I should know?"

"Just the usual here as well. Amy is enjoying her role as Eliza.

231

She's my drama queen after all."

Rachel agreed. She was glad Amy was having so much fun. She and Leah talked a little longer. Then it was time for Leah to head out the door so they said their goodbyes.

Rachel felt like she was in a fog. She loved talking with her sister, but all this discussion about relationships was a bit much for her. She didn't want anything to be complicated. Sure she liked Don. She liked him very much. But that didn't mean whatever they might have would need to turn into a lifetime together. Rachel was far away from that idea.

She blew out tense air. *I didn't even WANT to see Don, and now everyone is expecting me to be falling head over heels and ready to marry him. How did this happen? Okay, now I'm talking to myself. That can't be good.*

Rachel decided to run some errands. It was a nice day for a drive, and the weather reports indicated that rain would be coming in the next couple of days. She went to the bank and decided to go to one of the clothing stores in her neighborhood. *Why not treat herself to a pretty new outfit?* She had some anxious energy to burn, and a little shopping spree was just the answer.

She pulled into the parking lot of the upscale store. There were some cars there, mostly luxury, but not that many so she suspected the store wouldn't be too busy. She happily walked in and made a beeline for the dressy-casual clothing area. That was Rachel's favorite section. She was looking through the racks when, just as luck would have it, Linda was at another rack across the way. Rachel had hoped to avoid her, but Linda sensed that someone was there, so she turned and spotted Rachel. First the salon, now here? They weren't so much alike that they would see each other at the same places. Still, this was a smaller community, and familiar faces existed.

Rachel gave a little smile of acknowledgment, why she didn't know. Linda didn't smile back. She actually looked tired and sad. She didn't have her typical smirk, so Rachel had to wonder what was up. She figured she'd bite the bullet. She walked over to her.

"Hi, Linda."

"Hey." Linda sounded as bad as she looked. Rachel was actually a little worried.

"Are you okay?" Rachel sounded sincerely concerned, and that seemed to ease Linda's expression.

232

Linda looked at her, wondering if she should even talk with Rachel. She decided to take a chance. "Not really. I mean, I'm not sick or anything. I'm just dealing with a lot right now." Linda truly appeared forlorn.

Rachel nodded in understanding. She knew some of the problems only because Steve told her certain things. Still, this seemed beyond all of that. She looked at Linda uncertainly. "Do you want to talk about it? Is there anything I can do?" Rachel hoped that she wasn't making a mistake in trying to help.

Linda's eyes widened in surprise. She seemed genuinely amazed that Rachel was showing any concern. Of course, her surprise was understandable considering their history. "Oh. Uh… no, there's nothing you can do. It's very kind of you to offer. Really, I appreciate that. The truth is that…well…" Linda looked away for a moment, clearly uncertain as to how to proceed. She turned her face to look directly at Rachel. "I just found out that I'm pregnant."

Rachel could have fallen over. This was not the response that she would ever have expected. She was speechless and obviously gave a shocked appearance. Then, she realized that she needed to collect herself. "Wow. Well…um... congratulations?" She wasn't sure how she should have responded. She knew she couldn't sound excited because Linda clearly wasn't.

"Thanks. You're right about how you said that." Linda looked dejected.

"I'm sorry, Linda. I didn't mean it that way. Really, congratulations." Rachel attempted a weak smile.

"No, don't apologize. This isn't good news."

"Oh. Does Steve know?"

Linda looked away, this time appearing rather pale. Rachel was concerned thinking that Linda was unwell, and she reached out to touch Linda's arm. Linda didn't pull away. "No, he doesn't. I'm not quite sure how I'm going to handle this."

"What do you mean? I think he'll be okay with it. Maybe he'll even be more than okay." Rachel doubted her own words, but she wanted to be as positive as possible.

Linda looked grave. "No, Rachel, he won't be happy. And I wouldn't blame him. I'm not thrilled about this, but he'll definitely have a reason to be upset."

Rachel was confused. "I don't understand. He is a dad. He's

233

not anti-children."

"True. But he would be anti another man's child." Linda looked pointedly at Rachel wondering if she understood. She couldn't believe she was telling Rachel this. Her weakened state had left her vulnerable.

"I don't understand." Rachel's expression was one of confusion. Linda looked at her as if willing her to understand the message. Suddenly it hit Rachel. This baby was not Steve's. She swallowed hard, trying to get her bearings.

Linda could tell that she got it. "Yes, you do understand."

"Oh, Linda. I can't believe this. How…why?" Rachel couldn't form a sentence.

"I know, I know. What I did was awful. Steve and I have been having problems, and I guess I was looking for trouble. Now, I'm in BIG trouble. I never even wanted kids." Linda looked pathetic and sad.

"I know. I suspected that." Rachel contemplated this for a moment, realizing that Steve was going to have to deal with his wife's infidelity. What goes around comes around. Not that this made her feel any sense of elation. She wasn't feeling any joy at the moment.

Another shopper came towards them. The lady had silver hair and was older. She appeared to be very focused on her shopping mission. Linda and Rachel walked further away to continue talking. Neither wanted this conversation to be overheard.

"So," continued Linda, "I don't know what I'm going to do." She looked imploringly at Rachel, hoping for advice.

Rachel cocked her head in certainty. "Well, you really only have one choice. You have to tell Steve."

Linda shook her head in disagreement. "I can't do that. I just can't. He won't forgive me. I wouldn't forgive him if he got some other woman pregnant." Even though Linda wasn't pregnant when Rachel found out about Steve's affair, Linda's expression revealed that she realized what she had said. She knew Rachel couldn't forgive Steve back then, and their marriage was over.

"He might or he might not. But you have to tell him. You don't want to try to pass this child off as his. That wouldn't be the right thing to do. For anybody." Rachel paused for a moment and then thought of something else. "Do you love the father of this baby?"

"No, I don't." Linda looked down, ashamed. "This was a one-night stand. I don't even know the guy's name."

Rachel felt a little sick. Not physically, but emotionally. "Maybe Steve will understand?" Rachel didn't even believe that, but she had to try to sound upbeat.

Linda's head jerked up in disbelief. "I don't think so. You think he'd care that I didn't actually love this man?"

"I don't know. But what I do know is that Steve is obviously familiar with infidelity." Linda gave her a sudden disapproving look, indicating that she felt she was being judged. Rachel immediately changed the tone. "All I'm saying is that he's not one to be able to stand in judgment. Remember, the relationship you and Steve had was an affair, not a one-night stand."

Linda softened as she understood that Rachel was putting this on Steve and not solely on her. "I still don't quite know how I'm going to handle this. We're already having so many problems. This might be the nail in the coffin. And then what will happen to me?" Linda looked alarmed.

"I don't know. Steve may try to accept the situation. Honestly, though, you're a survivor. You will get through this."

For the first time since seeing her at the clothing rack, perhaps since forever, Linda gave Rachel a warm smile. "That's the nicest thing you could have said to me. I have always thought that I was tough. I just don't want to lose what I have. The problem is that I'm gaining something that I don't want." Linda patted her stomach.

"You know, if Steve can deal with this, you might actually find that you like being a mom."

Linda scoffed at that comment. "Nope, I don't think so. It's too much work and I like to enjoy my life."

"Well, yes, it is a lot of work, but that doesn't mean all the fun stops. It only means you're adding a different kind of fun."

Linda raised her eyebrows in skepticism. "Sure. If that's how you want to look at it. Good for you."

Rachel wasn't sure what else she could say. Her compassionate nature is what started the conversation, but she didn't want to make this problem her problem. She only hoped everything would work out okay.

"I do wish you the best of luck with everything. I'm sorry you're having difficulties, but try to work it all out." This sounded lame to Rachel's ears.

Linda gave a little smile. "Thanks. I guess I'm going to have to do something." Suddenly her expression changed to excitement. "Hey! I have an idea! Would you be willing to tell Steve that I bumped into you and told you about the baby? You could be honest and tell him how horrified I am by what I have done, but that you know, because I told you, how much I love him, and that I'm sorry. That I don't know how to bring up the subject, but that I hope he'll understand? Maybe he'll be able to have it sink in, and he won't be so mad at me. You could buffer the blow?" Linda looked at her with hope.

Rachel was seeing the old Linda. The manipulator. She was no longer feeling so giving and understanding. "No, I'm sorry. I can't."

Linda was crestfallen. "Why not? You seem to be able to understand this. I don't know why you can't just be casual about it."

Rachel sighed loudly. "Because it's not up to me, Linda. This is between you and Steve. If he comes to me, after you tell him about this, and he asks me for advice, I might be able to tell him to deal with this. That he should try to be understanding and work things out. But that's about it."

Linda seemed to understand and her tone began to change. "Yeah, I guess you're right. I'm sure he *will* want to talk with *you* about this." She frowned as she considered that scenario. Then, her claws came out, as was customary. She was upset that Rachel wouldn't help her and she wanted to be cruel. "You know, it's funny. Considering all of the fooling around we did when you two were married, it's amazing that this never happened then. She smirked at Rachel, and that was it.

"Oh, sure. I guess you were bound to get into trouble at some point. Looks like you're in it now." Rachel smirked back at Linda. Rachel had spewed her own venom, which didn't happen often.

Linda looked like she had been smacked. It appeared that she was trying to think of something to say, to have some witty comeback. Nothing came, so she gave Rachel a dirty look and took off.

Rachel was a bit shaken by the encounter. She had no idea as to how this would pan out, but she suspected she was going to be precariously placed in the drama one way or another. She needed to relieve the tension that was creeping up her spine, so she thought it would be a wonderful idea to continue the search for a nice outfit. She went back to her favorite section, and slapped through the racks, clinking hangers together along the metal bar. Finally, she found a pantsuit that would be perfect for a nice outing. It was a pretty shade of rose with some tonal beading on the jacket collar. She dashed into the dressing room and was grateful that the ensemble fit as though it was made for her. She made her way to the cashier, paid for her purchase, and dashed out to her car. She drove directly home.

Rachel arrived just moments before the kids came home from school. They came running in just as she came downstairs after depositing her new clothing in her closet. Rachel needed to mentally block out the tense moments she had with Linda. It was time to focus on her children and on preparing dinner.

"Mom, I need some new clothes before we go to California. When can we go shopping?" Rebecca eyed Rachel expecting a quick answer.

"What can you possibly need? Your closet is over-flowing right now."

Rebecca rolled her eyes as if it was going to be a burden to have to explain herself to her mother. "I need *newer* things than what I have." Like, duh, you couldn't figure that out?

Rachel gave her younger daughter an admonishing look. She didn't like her attitude, and she also wasn't sure Rebecca needed any new clothes. "Like what?"

"Like shorts, tops, shoes. You know. Clothes for summer."

"And you don't have any right now?" Rachel looked at her not believing what her daughter was saying.

"Mom! I've grown since last summer. Don't you think?" Rebecca placed her hands on her hips, modeling her maturing figure.

"Yes, I suppose you have. We'll get to the mall before we go to California. I promise that you will be clothed by the time we get on the plane."

Rachel thought her own comment was amusing, but Rebecca just rolled her eyes again. *Was I ever this difficult*, Rachel wondered?

The kids finally situated themselves in the family room. They did some homework before eating dinner. Rachel was stirring sauce for a chicken dish when the phone rang.

"I'll get it!" Sarah yelled into the kitchen. Rachel was happy to have her help.

Seconds later Sarah came into the kitchen with the cordless phone. She held the phone to her body so that the caller couldn't hear her talk to her mother. Then she whispered "It's your boyfriend." Sarah gave Rachel a look of exasperation as though she couldn't believe that she had answered this call for her mother. She then handed the phone to Rachel.

"Thank you, my sweet daughter." Rachel fluttered her eye lashes at Sarah, and her daughter turned around and walked out of the kitchen.

"Hello?"

"Hi, Rachel. It's Don. How are you?"

"I'm fine, and I want you to know that I had a great time with you today."

"Thanks! I had a great time also, as usual. I have a question for you. Would it be possible for you to come with me to a business dinner this week? I just decided that I was going to attend this function. I know a week night might not be so easy for you, but I thought I'd ask. I'll try not to have us stay too long. I belong to an organization that helps with business contacts in my area of expertise, and I thought this would be a good event to attend. I'd like you to be there with me. Do you think you would be able to go?"

Rachel didn't hesitate. There was no reason why she shouldn't be able to go with Don. Her kids could manage for a few hours without her. "Absolutely! I'd be thrilled to go with you. I even have a new outfit that I can wear. What day and what time?"

"This is great!" Rachel could imagine him smiling broadly. "It's Wednesday, and I'll pick you up at six. How does that sound?"

"Perfect. And, Don, I'm so glad that you want me to come with you." Rachel had her own sweet smile that perhaps Don could imagine.

"You bet I want you to come with me. I guess I should let you go. But I'll see you Wednesday night."

"Sounds wonderful. I'm looking forward to seeing you."

Rachel felt the problems of the day slide off of her. It was always so nice to hear Don's voice, and she was feeling giddy that he wanted her by his side at his business event. She felt special. Rachel went into the family room to let her kids know about her plans.

"Hey, gang. I need to let you know something."

The children stopped what they were doing, and they stared at her.

"As you know I was talking with Don. He's invited me to a business dinner on Wednesday, and I agreed to go with him. Is that okay?" Rachel looked hopefully at her children. She hated to think she needed their approval, but she respected them and wanted to be sure this wasn't a problem.

The children looked at each other, seemingly not sure what to say. David piped up. "Sure, Mom, that's great. We'll be fine. Don't worry." The girls didn't speak.

"I'm so glad!" Rachel went over to David and hugged him. "Thanks, sweetie." She looked apprehensively at her daughters. "You are okay with this? I mean, it shouldn't be a big deal. I'll be leaving at six, and I'm sure I'll be home before your bedtime." She didn't want to start sounding insecure about her decision to leave them for a while.

Sarah looked at her without smiling. "It's fine, Mom. Do what you want to do."

Rachel knew that wasn't a ringing endorsement for her decision to go with Don. However, she didn't care. Going out wouldn't harm her children. She spoke confidently with her response. "Thank you. I agree with everything you said." With that, she got up off of the couch and let her children continue with their homework.

She went into the kitchen to finish dinner. The phone rang again, but this time there was no offer to answer it. So, she went to the phone and saw that it was her ex-husband's home phone number. Rachel didn't want to answer it, but she knew that she had to.

"Hello?"

Rachel heard crying on the other end. "Rachel? Oh, God, Rachel! He walked out the door telling me to pack my bags and go and not to be here when he gets back! I don't know what to do!" More sobbing.

Rachel whispered into the phone, hoping that her children wouldn't overhear anything. "So, you told him." It wasn't a question, just a statement of fact.

239

Linda gulped her sobs before she spoke. "Yes, I told him. I thought I should be honest and tell him what happened. I said I was sorry, but he didn't care." She started wailing.

"Linda. You did the right thing. Of course he's going to be upset. That's understandable. You just need to give him time to deal with everything."

Shakily, Linda spoke again. "He said he wants a divorce. That's how HE'S going to deal with it. I wish I hadn't said anything. This is awful." She was in full lament mode.

"Well, yes, it is awful. Just don't think about it right now. Steve will come around." Rachel wasn't so sure, but she didn't want to further upset Linda. Why she didn't know.

Linda gave a grunt. "Just like you came around when you found out about us."

Rachel couldn't argue with that. She wouldn't have cared if Linda was pregnant or not at the time. She wanted out of the marriage. Of course, Steve did as well. He was "in love" with Linda.

"I don't know what to tell you. I assume you have friends and family who can help you deal with this. I don't think that I'm the right one to..." The doorbell rang as Rachel was speaking. "Linda. I've got to go. Someone's at the door."

"But what should I do?" Linda wasn't ready to let Rachel hang up the phone.

Rachel yelled into the family room. "Sarah, would you please find out who is at the door? Linda, I honestly don't know right now. Call your best friend or your mother. I have to go."

"Fine! Don't help! You're the one who told me to tell him!" Linda clicked off her phone.

Rachel gratefully hung up, and went into the family room. Steve was standing there, practically seething. She didn't want him to make any kind of a scene. *Why did he come to her?*

With fists clenched at his sides, he spoke to Rachel. "Rachel. May I speak with you in private?" He had a dark sound to his voice.

"Uh, sure, I guess. Kids, could you go upstairs for a while? I'll get you when it's time for dinner. Okay?" She looked at them with a tense smile.

The siblings looked at each other with uncertainty, but they slowly made their way upstairs. Steve and Rachel went into the living room. Rachel sat down, but Steve started pacing.

"I assume you know. Well, I know that you know. Linda told me she saw you today, and you suggested she tell me the truth."

"Yes, that's correct." Rachel was sitting calmly with her hands folded together.

"I cannot believe she did this! I mean, I know we have our problems, but THIS!"

Rachel was annoyed by Steve's thoughts. "You, of all people, YOU cannot believe this?"

He ran is hands through his hair. "I know, I know. That doesn't make sense to you. Maybe it doesn't make sense to me either. Still. I never saw this coming."

"Welcome to the club." Rachel was being very sarcastic now.

"Come on, Rachel! Help me here!"

Rachel leapt out of her seat like a cat that just saw a mouse. "YOU come on! Steve, how is this MY problem? You come over here, without even calling, and then you expect ME to help you figure out your problem about your wife being pregnant with another man's child? I don't think so. You must have someone else to confide in. Remember, I'm your EX-wife."

Steve sat down with a thud. He knew she was right. It was unfair to drag her into his mess. But he couldn't help it. "Rachel, I know this isn't fair to you. I'm sorry. I guess I've always felt comfortable talking with you. We've been through a lot together."

Rachel shook her head in disgust. She couldn't believe what she was hearing. You've GOT to be kidding me. I don't think you have always felt comfortable talking with me. You never communicated anything to me when you felt we were having problems. You went straight to Linda. Well, you need to head right back to her. I'm no fan of hers, as you well know, but she seems to want you in her life. Why, I don't know. She made a mistake, just as you did. Find a way to forgive her." Rachel was now in lecture mode.

Steve looked at Rachel point blank. "You didn't forgive me."

"No, I didn't. But you probably didn't want me to forgive you because you already had Linda in your life. At this point, you should have a full understanding as to what she's dealing with. You're no better than she is. You're both the same."

Steve looked wounded, but he knew what she said was true. He and Linda deserved each other. But his feelings for Rachel had never fully died. He hadn't told her that, but perhaps he should now. He looked at her, wanting to speak, wanting to say it right. Rachel eyed him suspiciously. She could tell he was thinking about something, but she didn't know what.

Steve let out a big sigh. "Oh, Rachel. My dear Rachel. I know you're not going to want to hear this, but I have to say it anyway."

Rachel tensed immediately. She didn't like the sound of this at all. "No, you really don't have to say anything. I think you should just go back to your wife."

"No. I can't walk out of this house without confessing." He paused, but only briefly. "Rachel. I never stopped loving you." His eyes were tired, but he actually seemed sincere.

Rachel wasn't sure what to say. She was horrified. Then, she found the strength to speak. She sat stoically, needing to make her thoughts crystal clear to him. "Steve, I really don't care at this point. I have moved on. I don't have feelings for you anymore." She wasn't trying to be hurtful. She just wanted to be honest.

Steve was stunned. His mouth was gaping and his eyebrows shot up. "I don't believe you! You were so upset when you found out about Linda and me. You still loved me then. That couldn't have changed."

For Rachel, a steel wall slammed down. "Yes, it did change. Time will do that sometimes. Distance from you made me see things more clearly. We have the kids in common, but that's all." Rachel felt a sense of calm in expressing her thoughts.

Steve nodded looking like he suddenly understood something. "I know what this is really about."

Rachel looked perplexed. She thought she had made everything quite clear. "I don't understand."

"Sure, you don't understand. Does the name *Don* mean anything to you?" He continued nodding as if he was sure he had figured out the big secret.

Rachel was still confused. "What does Don have to do with this?"

"I think that you might be giving me a second chance if it wasn't for Mr. Perfect."

Rachel was pissed. "Guess again."

"Oh, really? So, he has nothing to do with your not wanting me in your life anymore?"

Rachel answered in a pithy manner. "No, he doesn't."

242

Steve wasn't buying her answer. "Well, whatever. If you don't want to admit that I still mean something to you, then so be it. The next question is where do I go from here?" Steve stretched out his legs and crossed his arms in back of his head. Rachel thought he was a bit too relaxed. She didn't want him settling in for the evening.

"Where do you go from here? How about back to YOUR house? We're done here. Work things out with your current wife." Rachel had had enough of him. For a lifetime.

Steve seemed surprised that he was being ousted. "What's the problem? I just got here!"

Rachel placed her hands on her hips. "The problem is that you're not my husband, and I don't want you to stay. Go home!"

The children must have heard them because Rebecca and David came downstairs. Sarah probably didn't want any part of the drama. Smart girl.

"Hi, Daddy!" Rebecca came over to him and gave him a big hug. He lapped up the attention.

Steve then went to David. "Hey, buddy! How ya doin'? Steve was pouring it on very thick, trying to be all loving and close to his children. David didn't say anything, but he looked curiously at his father. "Hey kids, how would you like it if your dear old dad stayed for dinner? Wouldn't that be great?" Rachel was stunned by his audacity.

Rebecca looked like she had won the lottery, but David still didn't say anything. He was perceptive. He knew something was up. Rachel, however, could have killed her ex at that moment. *How dare he invite himself over!* He knew she wanted him out, but he was playing daddy right now. He never worried about what Rachel wanted.

Rachel gritted her teeth. "I thought you had to go home? I thought you were having dinner with Linda."

Steve had no intention of letting Rachel get her way. "No. Not tonight. She's busy. I'd be happy to stay. Hey kids, go get Sarah. Let's have a family meal."

Rachel went into the kitchen and Steve followed her. Was there no way for her to get rid of him? She turned to face him. "Steve, just go deal with the kids. You're in father mode right now, so that's what your role will be tonight. Hang out with them,

243

have dinner with them, and then go." She would plead with him if necessary.

He put up his hands to surrender. "Okay. Okay. I won't bother you. I'll leave you to finish cooking." He made a show of bowing as he left the room.

Steve went into the family room to be with the children. The kids had to wonder what was going on. Their dad never ate with all of them at the house. She hated that he was so selfish. He had no problem disrupting their lives when it suited him. Rachel couldn't believe how dense she must have been during their college years. Not to see how self-centered he was. All she knew back then was that he was intelligent, charming, out-going and witty. Those traits appealed to her youthful dreams. If they had been tempered with caring, honesty and decency, then everything would have been fine. Perhaps her mother saw through him and knew that this was not the man she would have chosen for her young daughter. Well, those days seemed like a whole other lifetime. Rachel certainly appreciated what she had now.

When she finished preparing the dinner, she called the kids and Steve into the kitchen. They seated themselves as she plated the chicken with the sauce. She placed a dish of asparagus on the table and a bowl of jasmine rice. Then the feast began. She ate and stayed out of the conversation that was taking place between Steve and the children. Rachel had lost her appetite. They were all laughing and talking loudly, and all she wanted to do was go upstairs and lie down in her quiet bedroom. She didn't want Steve around, but she missed the complete family picture. She had become so used to her new life that she had forgotten what it felt like to have their father at home to share the children's stories and their questions. They all seemed to be relishing the dinner and the togetherness. She didn't feel the same way as they did, but Rachel was happy that her children were smiling and chattering away.

The meal was finally over, and she told Steve that it was time for him to leave. He didn't argue about her decision, but Rebecca immediately wanted to know when he was coming again for dinner with them. Then, she had an idea of her own. "Dad, Mom is going out on Wednesday. Why don't you come over and we'll all have dinner together? Maybe we can order pizza or Chinese food!"

Steve looked at Rachel. His interest in her was piqued. "Oh? And where are *you* going Wednesday night?"

Rachel's response was curt as she folded her arms across her chest. "Out."

Steve chuckled, although Rachel suspected he didn't find anything funny about what she said.

Rebecca responded for her mother in a very sing-song voice. "Mom's going out with Don. On a weeknight." She felt proud of herself for letting the fact be known. Rachel gave Rebecca a look.

Steve put his hands in his pockets with authority. "Out with Don, hmm? Very interesting. Where to?"

Rachel smiled sweetly. "None of your business. Rebecca, honey, why don't you and your siblings head back upstairs to finish your homework. Say goodbye to your dad."

"Dad, will you come over for dinner?" Rebecca wasn't giving up on her original plan.

Steve winked at his younger daughter. "Of course I will. I'd be happy to come here and spend time with you. When should I be here?"

Rachel answered quickly for her daughter. "Six-thirty should be perfect." She didn't want Steve around when Don came by.

"Six-thirty it is."

Rebecca wrinkled her nose a bit. "It will be just you, Daddy? We only want you to come over." She was very much insinuating that Linda would not be a welcome member at their dinner.

"Of course. Only your daddy, sweetheart." Steve smiled lovingly at his daughter.

Rachel was truly ready for him to go. She didn't care where he went; she just wanted him out of her house. "Okay. So that's settled. Steve, say goodbye to the children."

"Okey dokey. Hey, kids. Daddy's got to go now, but I'll see you Wednesday night." He looked directly at Rachel. "At SIX-THIRTY." Then he smirked.

Rachel prayed that he wouldn't decide to show up early. Now that she thought about it, she was considering telling Don that she needed to leave early for the dinner. Maybe he could come by at five-thirty. Oh, how she hated playing games. This wasn't her style. Steve was making her insane.

He gave his hugs and kisses to his children, and he attempted to hug and kiss Rachel. She backed away as casually as she could.

245

He thanked her for the dinner and was on his way. Rachel had to wonder how Linda was holding up. *Would Steve return home? Would Linda still be there if he did come home?* Rachel hated the drama. She might not have as much of a problem with it if they'd all be kind enough to leave her out of it.

The kids were wound up. They had enjoyed the dinner with their father in their own home, and the promise that he would return on Wednesday for another dinner and time spent with them sent their spirits soaring. Rachel was happy for them. They needed their dad. She knew that. She just knew that she didn't need him. She was now worried that her sister's concerns about Steve trying to work his way back into Rachel's life were not unfounded. If Steve really wanted her back, he wouldn't stop trying. Not that it would matter. Rachel didn't want him back. Even if Don wasn't in her life. She didn't love Steve anymore.

Chapter Twenty-One

Tuesday brought a more normal day. Rachel visited her mother and ran some errands. She had coffee with a friend and did some work around the house. Rachel called Don to find out if he could come to the house earlier the next evening. She figured she'd just be honest with him and tell him that Steve would be arriving at six-thirty to have dinner with the kids and she wanted to be out of the house in case he arrived early.

Rachel picked up the phone and placed the call.

"Hello?"

"Hi, Don. It's Rachel. How's life?"

"Life is great. How about with you?"

"Everything's fine. I just had a little question to ask you." *Why did she feel the need to describe what kind of a question she had? Little implied that it almost wasn't a question.* However, Rachel knew she didn't want to make a big deal out of this.

"Sure. What can I do for you?"

"Would it be possible for you to pick me up at about five-thirty instead of six?"

"Of course. I'd be happy to see you sooner." Don paused. "Any particular reason?"

Rachel tried to sound light-hearted about it. "Oh, it's just that Steve is coming to the house at six-thirty to have dinner with the kids. As you can well imagine, I have no desire to be here when he comes."

Don completely understood. "I got ya. You don't want to take any chances that he'll come by sooner than expected."

"Yes. Especially because he knows I'm having dinner out with you that night."

"I think it's great that he's having dinner with his children. They might as well spend some time with him on their own turf."

"Yeah, I guess. And when I see you, I have some interesting news. It's quite something, so you'll have to brace yourself."

"Something about you?"

"No. Oh, no. Definitely NOT about me. Thankfully. I'll let you in on it tomorrow."

"Okay. I'm looking forward to seeing you."

"Me too. I mean about seeing YOU."

They both laughed and said their goodbyes. After Rachel hung up the phone, she gave a contented sigh. It was always so easy dealing with Don. He wasn't manipulating her or wanting everything to be about himself. She mattered.

Rachel went upstairs to say goodnight to the children. She knocked on Sarah's door, and Sarah opened it.

"Hi. Just wanted to say goodnight. Everything okay?"

"Yes." Sarah looked at Rachel as if she had something more to say. Rachel stood there for a moment, waiting for more words to come out. When Sarah didn't speak, Rachel took the lead.

"Sarah? What is it? Is there something on your mind?"

Sarah looked at Rachel with intensity. Her expression almost made Rachel want to step back. "Yes. There is something I've been wondering." Then she was silent again. *Did Rachel really need to drag it out of her?*

"So?" Rachel wasn't in the mood to pull teeth.

"I was wondering what the deal is with Daddy? Is there something going on with him? With both of you?"

Rachel wasn't sure how to respond. So, she asked Sarah a question. "What do you mean?"

Sarah stepped more into her bedroom, and Rachel eased her way in also. She was rarely permitted much entry into her daughter's room, unless her daughter wasn't home at the time. Sarah seemed to be trying to formulate her thoughts. When she had done so, she turned to look at her mother again.

"Okay. I guess I don't know why Dad was here tonight. I mean, he NEVER has dinner with us here. With all of us. He seemed so happy and it was almost like it was before. I mean, before he left. Are you two sort of back on? Why wasn't he home with Linda?" Sarah was looking very suspicious. She had folded her arms as if protecting herself from the answer that was coming.

Rachel looked at her reassuringly. "No, honey. We're not together. I think he has things going on, and he just wanted to spend some time with you guys. That's all." Rachel prayed that her answer was sufficient, but the skeptical look on Sarah's face indicated that she knew there had to be more.

248

"Mom. I'm not an idiot. SOMETHING is going on." Sarah was a bit defiant now.

"Nothing is going on between your father and me. I'M with Don right now. We're seeing each other. Your father and I are not getting back together. Ever." Rachel didn't want this conversation to continue, although she was afraid she had sounded too harsh. However, if Sarah wanted to know more, she should ask her father.

Sarah still wasn't buying all of this. She knew there was more to her father being away from his home and with them, even if it wasn't about her parents being together again. She had to ask one more question. "Is it about Linda?"

Rachel turned her head away from her daughter's searing eyes. She tried to be casual about her answer. "Ask your dad. I really don't know all of the details about his life."

Sarah looked a bit irritated, but she ceased her interrogation. "Okay. Well, goodnight then."

Rachel exited the room, and felt very tired. She said goodnight to Rebecca and David, and considered herself lucky that they didn't say anything other than "goodnight." She went into her room, brushed her teeth, washed her face and put on comfortable pajamas. Then she crawled into bed, and fell into a deep sleep.

Chapter Twenty-Two

Rachel's alarm blared at six o'clock with her favorite oldies music. Of course, some of the "oldies" music was now coming from the 1990's, so she was disturbed by that concept. However, this morning she awoke to Elvis Presley's "Blue Suede Shoes." That worked well for her, so she sprang out of bed. Her normal morning routine commenced. She brushed her teeth quickly, threw on an old cotton robe, and knocked on each child's door, opening it to say a bright, "Good morning!" She bounded down the stairs, ready to prepare their breakfasts. She was forever grateful that she only had to go to their rooms once. Rachel could already hear their sounds upstairs.

Rachel scrambled eggs, put bread in the toaster, and brought out butter and strawberry jam as well as some cut up fruit that was in the fridge. She filled one glass each with orange juice and another with milk. By 6:30, the children started trickling down into the kitchen. She liked the fact that they ate a leisurely breakfast. Rachel didn't want them gobbling down their food and drink and then running out the door to frantically catch the bus. They had all somehow taken on her characteristic of being more methodical and timely about everything. Organization was the key if three children were going to get ready and walk to the school bus without sheer panic taking place.

By 7:15 they were headed to the bus, and within five minutes or so, off they went to their daily adventure of learning and socializing. Rachel exercised and showered. She came out of the bathroom and checked for any phone messages. Steve had called saying that he would be there at six-thirty, Chinese food in hand. She wasn't going to bother calling him back.

Rachel stayed home for the day. She didn't want to run herself ragged with her big evening ahead. Closer to noon, she called Leah. She wanted to let her in on the news about Linda and to know how life was going in California.

"Hello, Sis!"

"Hello! How are things in California? Don't worry, I won't sing the song."

"Please don't. Just kidding of course. Things are fine here. What's up with you?"

"Hey, have I got some gossip for you!"

"Do tell!"

"I was out shopping the other day, getting a well-deserved new outfit. So, guess who I unfortunately ran into? Well, you'll never guess, so I'll tell you. Linda."

"Yikes! Not such a pleasant encounter. Did you have to talk to her?" Rachel could imagine the grimace on her sister's face right now.

"Yes I did. AND, I found out she's pregnant."

"You're kidding? Of course you're not kidding. I wonder how Steve feels about being a daddy again."

"Well, that's the interesting part of the whole story."

"Okay. What does THAT mean?"

"It means that Steve is not actually going to be a daddy again."

"Huh?"

"*He's* not the father."

"What?" Leah screamed into the phone.

"You heard me correctly. The baby is not Steve's."

"Linda TOLD you that? Why on earth would she fess up to you about something so personal?"

"She was distraught. I knew she didn't seem okay so, kind person that I am; I actually expressed concern about her. She must have felt the need to purge."

"So, just like Steve did to you, she was having an affair."

"No, not exactly. This was a one-time event."

"Oh, man, that's almost worse. If something like this can be anything but worse. So, what happens now?"

"I told her to tell Steve. Mr. Cheater himself should be more than understanding about something like this."

"And was he?"

"Not exactly. She called my house, crying salty tears that he was leaving her, and then *he* showed up at my house."

"Oh, no. I don't like that at all. Why did he come to *your* house?"

"I don't know. He was upset. And yes, I think he wouldn't mind getting back together with me, but I told him that we were done. No more."

"I can't believe this. I hope he doesn't try to push his way into your life. He and Linda are truly meant for each other. They're both pieces of work."

"He stayed for dinner that night. I'm going out tonight with Don, so Steve is coming here to have dinner with the kids. I plan on avoiding Steve and Linda like the plague."

"Yes, avoid Steve. You don't need to be dragged into his mess. Do you think he'll find a way to accept the situation, or will he really leave Linda?"

"I honestly don't know, and I don't care what he does. As long as he deals with the kids and supports them, that's all that concerns me. I've never liked Linda, so her future isn't something that's on my radar."

"Good point. However, it is interesting that he's made his feelings clear to you. Rachel, he could cause trouble." Leah sounded very worried.

"How could he cause trouble? He's got his own life, and I'm not about to turn mine upside down for him."

"So, you're never going to ditch Don for him?"

"Leah! If things went south for Don and me I can assure you that it wouldn't be because of Steve. I am not interested in resuming a relationship with him again. Trust me."

"Okay, I believe you. Now, let's stop talking about your ex and let's focus on your current wonderful man. What's happening with the two of you?"

"We're enjoying our time together and life is good. He's a very nice guy. I'm lucky to have him in my life."

"He's lucky to have you in his life too. Are there sparks, or do you just think of him as a nice guy?"

Rachel didn't feel the need to tell Leah *everything* that had transpired between Don and herself. "There are sparks. I promise you that I don't just think he's a nice guy. I really am happy with him. However, I'm not pushing anything. Slow. That's how it's going to be. Got it?"

"Hey, you don't have to tell me. As long as you are both on the same page, that's what counts. I'm just happy you're dating him. Whatever way this turns out."

"Thank you. That's how I feel. I'm looking so forward to seeing him tonight. I love that he wants me to join him at a business dinner. It's very exciting."

"How cute! He wants to have his little woman on his arm!"

Rachel laughed. "Oh, you stop it! There's nothing cute about this, and I'm not his little woman. You're so silly!" Rachel was enjoying being playful with her sister, even if it was by way of long-distance.

"Just have to razz you every now and then. You know that. Be sure to let me know the details."

"Will do. Have fun!"

"YOU have fun!"

The sisters hung up their phones, and Rachel prepared lunch for herself. She spent the rest of the day relaxing with a book, and then the kids came home. Rachel told them that their dad would be coming with Chinese food for dinner. They were already licking their chops just thinking about it. She let them do their own thing while she went upstairs to get ready for her evening. She put on her new outfit and appropriate accessories. After applying her cosmetics and doing a final brush of her hair, she eyed herself in the mirror. She smiled at her own reflection, then donned her shoes and grabbed a purse.

Rachel glided down the stairs, and David noticed her immediately.

"Wow, Mom! You look amazing!" His eyes were shining brightly.

"Thank you!"

The girls walked in from the kitchen to see their mother. They both looked at her with surprise. They never thought of their mother as all that lovely, but even they were amazed by how well she pulled herself together.

"Okaaay. You look very nice." Sarah was trying to figure out how she felt about her attractive mother.

"Thank you." Rachel was very pleased by her daughter's approval. Rachel looked at her gold watch. "Okay, guys. It's 5:15, so I think you might want to finish your homework before your dad gets here. That way you'll be able to spend the evening with him and not have to worry about getting everything done before tomorrow. Sound good?" She looked at them hoping they'd like the plan.

The children didn't give a verbal response but they did go upstairs to their rooms. That worked well for Rachel because she still had fifteen minutes before Don was due to arrive at the house. She didn't check the powder room mirror because the children's responses were enough to assure her that she looked fine. She sat down and watched television to pass the time. At 5:23, the doorbell rang.

Rachel jumped up to answer, hoping that it would be Don, even though he was seven minutes early. Don was always punctual, so the early timing threw her. She held her breath as she opened the door, praying Steve wasn't arriving this early.

She let out the pent up air when she saw Don standing there, handsome as ever, his usual smile lighting his face.

"Hello! I know I'm a tad early, but I wanted to make sure that your plan of avoiding your ex was air tight." He looked at Rachel, admiring her attractiveness. "You always look pretty, but may I just say, wow!"

"You may indeed, and I thank you. Come in." Rachel stood out of the way of the door to let him into the foyer. The kids came down, wondering if their dad might be very early.

Don said hello to them. They all politely responded with their own greetings.

"Do you think we should get going?" Don wanted everything to run smoothly for Rachel.

"Yeah, that would be fine." She looked at her children and smiled. "Okay, your dad will be here in about an hour. I'm sure you're all going to have a fun evening. I'll be home before you go to bed." She reached out to hug them all.

Rachel got her purse, and she and Don walked out to his car. It felt a little strange to be leaving her children on a weeknight. She was happy to be going out with Don, so she ignored her feelings and proceeded to have a nice time.

They chatted with ease as Don drove towards the restaurant where the business dinner was being held. The place was located about twenty minutes away, and Rachel was not familiar with the establishment. When they arrived at the restaurant, the parking lot was only about one third full. They were early, though, so they knew that many more cars would be there soon.

Don assisted Rachel out of the car, and they went inside. The entryway was roomy and had wooden floors and black leather chairs and sofas. The lighting was muted, and it was very cozy and inviting. There was a large sign indicating the dinner meeting.

Don approached the reception area, and he and Rachel were escorted to the designated room.

They were led to a large room with tables and chairs. It reminded them both a little of the dining area at the home where their parents lived. They thanked the hostess for her help and went to the large rectangular table where name tags were placed. Rachel wasn't a fan of wearing name tags. She never felt the need to announce who she was, but this was Don's event, so she complied. They took the paper off of the tags, and stuck them to their garments. Each tag had a little number placed at the bottom corner which informed them of their table number. They didn't take a seat yet because there was plenty of time to mingle. Don spotted a man he worked with at a local business, so they went over to chat with him. The man smiled broadly when he saw Don. It seemed Don had that effect on everyone. People were happy to see him. The older man shook Don's hand vigorously and placed his arm squarely on Don's shoulder. The man, about sixty-five or so was large and bold. He had thinning brown hair without a touch of gray. His black suit jacket buttons were barely holding in a rather large belly. He was wearing a gaudy huge gold watch, and Rachel suspected that fit his personality perfectly. His smile was as grand as Texas. The only thing missing was a big cigar.

"Hey! How are you? It's wonderful to see you here!" His voice was strong.

"It's nice to see you too, Hal."

A lovely lady in her early sixties was standing next to Hal. She was of average height with short white hair that looked as though it was maintained professionally. She was wearing a lilac-colored silk dress with designer shoes and a matching handbag. Her neck was adorned with a simple pearl necklace. Her wedding ring was a thin gold band that was stacked next to a simple round solitaire diamond.

"Don, this is my wife Clara. Clara, this is Don Levy. He has done amazing things for our business."

Clara smiled warmly at Don and gently shook his hand. "Such a pleasure to meet you Don."

"Likewise. Clara. Hal, this is my girlfriend Rachel." He looked proudly at Rachel.

Rachel acknowledged the couple warmly. "So nice to meet both of you."

Clara smiled demurely at Rachel and nodded. Hal was more boisterous.

"Ah, so you're Don's gal? Well, you've chosen a nice fellow, that's for sure."

Don smiled sheepishly and Rachel responded. "I think so too."

"Don? Can I talk with you for just a minute about business? I want to ask a couple of questions and maybe arrange a lunch date with you to go over a bunch of things. Clara, we'll be right back. Okay with you Rachel?"

Rachel nodded her acceptance, and Hal put his arm roughly around Don's shoulder and walked a few steps away from his wife and Rachel. That left the two ladies standing alone.

Clara spoke. "Hal loves to talk business wherever he is. Of course, this *is* a business dinner, so it's perfectly okay." It was obvious that Clara had experienced this occurrence for many years.

Rachel wasn't sure how to respond. It wasn't like she was being asked a question. Clara had merely made a statement.

"Yes, you're right. This is a good place for chatting about business." Rachel tried quickly to say something else. She was never comfortable with a void in the conversation. "So, what kind of business does Hal have?"

"He sells women's fashions online." Clara slightly flared out her arms indicating that she was advertising one of the dresses.

Rachel was impressed. "Oh! It's very lovely! You're a perfect model for him."

Clara smiled with a happily surprised expression, as though she never thought of herself that way. "Thank you! That's very kind!"

"Well, it's true. You have a nice figure, and that color is gorgeous on you."

Clara looked down at her outfit as though she hadn't seen it before. "You really think so?"

"Of course. I'm sure Hal must have told you the same thing." Rachel felt confident that Clara's husband would always compliment her.

Clara's expression went from utter joy to a little somber. "No, Hal didn't tell me that. He doesn't generally comment on me wearing the clothes. There are so many pretty girls in the office who wear the designs. He probably doesn't even notice the clothes once he leaves for the day."

Rachel felt sorry for Clara and wished she hadn't assumed anything. She tried to turn things around a bit. "Well, I'd say that business sometimes stays at the office. It's probably just as well. You wouldn't want Hal to be consumed by it when he gets home."

Clara seemed conciliatory with Rachel's comment. "I suppose that's true." She looked at Rachel's outfit. "That's very pretty."

"Thanks."

"Where did you buy it? If you don't mind me asking?"

"No, that's fine. I bought it at a little shop near my house. Penelope's. I don't know if you have heard of that one."

Clara's eyebrows went up indicating that she was impressed. "Oh, yes, I have heard of that shop. Very nice. Do you shop there often?" Clara was intrigued.

"Every now and then. It depends on what I need. Have you ever bought anything there?"

"Oh, no. I mostly get my clothing through the business."

Rachel nodded as though what Clara said should have been obvious. "Of course. That makes perfect sense. That must be great."

"It's fine. I like the clothes." Clara didn't seem overly enthusiastic about her wardrobe only coming from the company.

Rachel felt that the clothing conversation had gone on long enough. Just in time too, as Hal and Don made their way back to Rachel and Clara.

Hal put his arm roughly around his wife's thin shoulder. "So, did you miss me?" He laughed heartily.

Clara stood there, and smiled blandly without looking at Hal. Rachel was curious about their relationship. Hal was very outgoing, and Clara seemed a bit more reserved, almost as though this was the only way she could be because she was with Hal. As though her own personality had been squashed a bit over time. She seemed like an old-fashioned business man's wife. Hal was the shining one, and she was the supportive wife behind the man.

Hal's attention was diverted to another person he knew. He raised his arm to wave to the newcomer in the room. "Don, it was great talking with you, and I'll see you soon." He looked appreciatively at Rachel, his eyes dancing. "It was a pleasure to meet you."

"Thank you." She then looked warmly at his wife. "Clara, it

was nice chatting with you." Rachel wanted to acknowledge her.

Clara appreciated Rachel's comment. "Thank you Rachel. I enjoyed speaking with you also."

Hal looked at Don's name tag, noticing the table number for the first time. "We're not sitting together. So, have fun you two." With that, Hal and Clara were off in the direction of the man with whom Hal wanted to talk.

Don looked apprehensively at Rachel. "So? How did it go with Clara?"

"Fine."

"Fine? That's all you're going to tell me?"

"What else would you like to know?"

"What's *she* like? Hal is a nice man, but…well…he's Hal. You know what I mean?"

Rachel laughed as quietly as possible. "I think I do. She's very sweet, but I suspect he's like dealing with a bull in a china shop."

"Yes, that's how I'd describe him."

More people began making their way into the room, and the relatively quiet space they entered earlier had begun to crackle with voices as people were milling about. Don and Rachel continued to talk with other couples and some individuals who had come by themselves. For the next hour, some people introduced other people to Don. After a while, an announcement was made that it was time for people to take their seats. Everyone started to get situated, and soon the crowd was seated. Don knew the people sitting next to him at the table, and he introduced Rachel to them.

Waiters began to serve salads and more chatter took place. The evening continued to move along with ease, and the laughter and sometimes loud voices echoed throughout the room. The entrees consisted of chicken pieces with rice and a vegetable medley. The typical fare found at these kinds of events. After that, vanilla cake and coffee were served.

As everyone was finishing eating, the woman seated next to Rachel leaned towards her to speak. Rachel had been focused on Don and his part of the table, so she had only said hello to those on her side.

"Excuse me, but I noticed that your name tag says Rachel Blum."

Rachel looked down at her name tag as if to verify that's what it said. "Yes, that's right." *Obviously that's right,* thought Rachel.

She wondered why the woman, stylish and appearing to be in her early thirties, mentioned this.

The woman seemed a bit uncertain as to how to proceed. "I assume you're the Rachel Blum who was married to Steve Blum?"

Rachel felt her heart pound, although she tried to keep her expression calm. *Where was this conversation going?* "Ye-yes. That's right."

"I'm Linda's sister." She looked apprehensive as she made the statement.

Rachel had never met any of Linda's relatives, so she was a bit stunned by the revelation. "Oh, I see."

The woman looked a bit downcast. "Yeah." Then she looked directly at Rachel and pointed to her name tag. "My name is Lori Belker."

"Hi, Lori." Rachel wasn't sure what to say. Lori looked pleasant enough, but this was a very awkward situation.

Lori turned to her husband, tapping him on the shoulder to get his attention. "John. I want you to meet Rachel Blum. Rachel, this is my husband John."

John looked momentarily startled upon hearing Rachel's name, but he quickly regained his composure and smiled at her. "Hi Rachel. It's nice to meet you."

Lori looked with compassion at Rachel. "I know this is all very strange. I mean, you probably never expected to meet the enemy."

Rachel didn't think of Lori that way. Heck, she didn't even know her. "I don't think of you as the enemy. What happened was not your fault." Rachel meant what she said. She wasn't about to hold the sins of Linda against Lori.

Lori perked up a bit upon hearing that. "Thanks. I just want you to know that I am sorry for what happened. I mean, I know how my sister can be. We aren't anything alike, and believe me, my family was sick when we heard what she did. She's sort of the black sheep of the family." Lori leaned forward and looked across Rachel at Don who was chatting closely with the person beside him. "It looks like you're doing great right now." She smiled at Rachel.

Rachel grinned. "Yes, fortunately I am."

"That's good. I think you can do better than to be married to

Steve. Leave a guy like that to my sister." She made a motion as though swatting a fly out of the way.

"I certainly found out what he was all about."

"You have children, though. That means you still have to deal with him. And with Linda." Lori looked sympathetically at Rachel.

"True. And believe me; Linda isn't too happy about that."

"Linda has her own issues." Lori looked at Rachel as if to say, "You have no idea." However, Rachel *did* understand.

"Yes, she does. I've spoken with her about her biggest issue as of late."

Lori sat back in her chair looking shocked. "She told you? About the….you really know?"

"I ran into her at a store the other day. She poured everything out to me. It was quite a moment."

"I can imagine."

"I don't know what's happening now, though. Is Steve still with her?"

"I have no idea. When she told me about her being pregnant, I told her she had better get her act together. What she did with Steve was bad enough, but this is unbelievable. I haven't spoken to her since."

"She really has gotten herself into a mess. Still, I thought that Steve should try to be more understanding. Considering." Rachel gave Lori a knowing look.

"True. But he's probably feeling wounded. I almost think it would serve Linda right if he did walk out on her. Let her face what she's done."

"But there's a baby involved now. I'd hate to think of any innocent child having challenges because of this."

Lori sighed with uncertainty. "I just don't know. It's horrible. Fortunately it isn't your problem. You should just be enjoying life." Lori wanted to change the sad tone to a cheerful one.

"That's what I intend to do."

Don turned to Rachel to find out what deep conversation she was having. Rachel introduced him to Lori, explaining who she was.

"Small world, huh?" Don was amazed that, out of all people, Linda's sister would be here.

Lori smiled. "I know. We're here because John and I work for a couple who own a children's bookstore. It's a unique business, and they are always looking to advertise. The Internet is a huge venue for the company to put itself out there."

Rachel pointed to Don. "He's your man. Don knows all about this kind of thing."

Lori looked excited. "Really? Could you actually steer us through this? It would be great to have an expert assisting the company."

Don looked sure of himself. "Of course. I'd be happy to see what I can do for you." He put his hand into his pocket to retrieve his wallet and took out a business card. He reached across Rachel to give the card to Lori. "Feel free to contact me whenever you want."

Lori looked approvingly at the card. "Great! Thanks! We'll be in touch."

The event began to draw to a close. People were talking, saying their goodbyes and their *nice to meet you* pleasantries. There were handshakes and laughter, as well as promises to keep in touch. All in all, the evening had been a success.

Don and Rachel made their way outside. Along with the crowd, they walked in the parking lot. They approached Don's car, and after getting in, Rachel relaxed against the leather seat. It felt good to have some quiet time.

Don got in and started the car, looking pleased. He turned to Rachel and kissed her. "I can't thank you enough for coming here with me. It was wonderful to have your company."

Rachel was pleased to hear him say that. "I was happy to be with you. It was nice of you to want me to join you." She smiled lovingly at Don.

"It felt good to have your support. I like what I do, and it was nice to have you by my side. I can't describe how special you made this evening for me."

Rachel was very touched by his openness. "Well, you are easily able to stand on your own, but I'm glad I could even make this better for you."

They drove back to Rachel's home, chatting about the evening and the contacts Don had made. Rachel was very happy for him. Business was going well and Don was bound to have things go even better in the future.

He pulled the car into Rachel's driveway. No other car was

there, so Steve must have gone home. It was close to ten o'clock, and the children would probably be getting ready for bed. Don stopped the engine, and looked at Rachel.

"Well, I guess this is it. We'll see each other this weekend, right?"

"Yes. Definitely."

"Rachel, you're an incredible woman. I know I've said that before, but I never want you to think that I'm taking you for granted. I can't believe how happy I've been since I met you. I love my job, but I always look forward to seeing your sweet face. I've never met anyone like you."

Rachel was speechless for a moment. She was very flattered. Don had always been kind to her, and complimentary, but his tone tonight was different. More intense and more passionate.

"Don, you're so sweet! I really appreciate your kind thoughts about me. I always look forward to seeing you too. I know how lucky I am to have you in my life."

Don leaned into Rachel, and put his hands on the sides of her face. He kissed her with a combination of tenderness and eagerness. He gently pulled away from her and looked into her eyes. He cleared his throat. "I guess I really should let you go in the house."

"Unfortunately, that's true." They laughed as they both got out of the car.

Don led her to the front door and kissed her again. "So, I'll call you?"

"Please do." Rachel's voice sounded sultry.

Rachel fumbled for her keys, and found them. Don was standing close to her as she unlocked the front door. He lovingly caressed her arm.

"Goodnight Rachel."

"Goodnight Don. Thanks again for a wonderful evening."

"My pleasure." As he walked back to his car. Rachel waved at him, and in the dim glow of the outside lights, she could see him wave back to her.

Rachel went inside, and found the kids sitting on the family room couch. There were Chinese food cartons strewn on the table, along with plates and glasses. The children turned to look at her.

"Hi, Mom." David greeting her warmly.

"Hello. I guess you all had quite the time around here." Rachel tried not to sound too annoyed, but she did have expectations of coming home to a clean house. She couldn't understand why Steve didn't tell the kids to throw things away and put their dishes in the dishwasher. "So, how did everything go with your dad?"

"It was fine." Sarah didn't have much to say.

"What did you do together? Did you talk a lot?" Rachel wanted a bit more information, if she could get it.

"Uh, sure." Clearly Rebecca wasn't going to offer up much information either.

"So that's it? Nothing more to tell me?" Rachel was a bit exasperated.

"Mom? Did you have fun?" Once again, she could only count on David to show interest in her life.

"Yes, I did. Thank you for asking." Rachel waited for a moment to see if the children had anything else to say. Not a word was spoken, so she decided to close the evening. "I guess if you all have nothing else to say, I'd like you to clean up this mess and then get ready for bed."

The children slowly rose off the couch. They each carried the remains of their dinner into the kitchen. Rachel stood in the family room, listening to the noises taking place in the kitchen. Thump as cartons were being tossed into the garbage can. Clink, clink. Dishes and glasses being placed into the dishwasher. Upon hearing the dishwasher door close, the kids came out of the kitchen. They looked tired, so without being told, they went silently upstairs. Rachel sensed a major lack of enthusiasm from the moment she came home. *Were they angry with her for leaving them for the evening? She didn't think that would be the case. Was it that bad being with their father? She didn't want to believe that.* She'd give them time to get ready for bed and then she'd say goodnight to each of them, as was the usual routine.

Rachel turned off the lights downstairs, and climbed the staircase up to her room. The light shone under the door from the bathroom the children used. She heard water running and teeth being brushed. After quickly changing out of her clothes and into her pajamas, she threw on her robe, and made her way to Sarah's room knocking softly on her door.

"Yes?" Sarah's tone sounded slightly harsh. Rachel didn't like that, but she wasn't about to reproach her right now.

263

"May I come in please?" Rachel's tone was a bit tight, but she tried to sound pleasant.

"Yeah." Sarah was lying in bed, looking at her cell phone. She didn't bother to look up when Rachel came into her room.

Rachel folded her arms. "Did you have a nice time with your dad tonight?"

Sarah shrugged. "I guess."

"Well, either you did or you didn't. It can't be that complicated."

Sarah gave her a mean look. "What do you care whether or not I had a nice time with Daddy? You're out having fun. That should be all that matters, right?"

Rachel took a step back, surprised by her daughter's outrage. "Where is this coming from? What did I do that was so awful?"

Sarah looked away again and shrugged, she didn't say anything.

Rachel approached Sarah. "Oh, no. You don't put that out there and clam up. I haven't done anything wrong, and I don't appreciate your tone."

Sarah looked at her with contempt. "Okay. If that's how you feel." She was ready to lay it on the line with her mother. "You seem to be living it up while we're all on the back burner. I don't know what's going on with Daddy either. He was with us, but he didn't talk much. He ate and we all watched television together. It's like he was in his own little world."

Rachel was stunned. Her children did not have a very good evening. However, that didn't mean she couldn't have a life. "I'm sorry about that. I think your dad is going through some challenging times. BUT, that doesn't mean that I'M putting you all on the back burner. I'm here for you all the time. Pardon me if I'd like to do some other things every now and then."

"Right. With your boyfriend." Sarah's face contorted in disgust.

Rachel raised her eyebrows at the way her daughter said "boyfriend." Sarah was very snotty. "You have a problem with me having Don in my life? Is THAT it?"

"I don't know."

"Apparently you do. I'm sorry you feel that way, but at least for now, that's the way it is. We like each other, and we're going to continue to go out. Case closed."

"Fine. Do whatever you want."

"Gee, thanks. I've been granted permission from my

264

daughter." Rachel rolled her eyes. She knew that she was being a bit immature herself, but she couldn't help it.

Sarah looked at her cell phone, and she he didn't say anything else.

"Goodnight, Sarah." Rachel walked out of the room.

She went to David's room and then Rebecca's. There was a lot less drama from them, so she made quick exits and went back to her room. She got her own act together and slipped into bed. She had enjoyed such a nice evening with Don. It didn't seem fair that she had to come home to an attitude from her daughter. Rachel blamed Steve for these issues. He needed to be a lot less selfish and concentrate on his children. Right before sliding into dreamland, she decided that she was going to have to confront Steve about everything.

Chapter Twenty-Three

The morning brought an alarm clock that Rachel didn't want to respond to, as well as thunderstorms. She wasn't in the mood to get out of bed, but she didn't have a choice. Unlike her ex, she had to get the children ready for school. She couldn't shirk her responsibilities because she didn't feel motivated to function. Rachel's feet hit the floor as though lead had just been dropped on her lap. She had slept restlessly, and she was paying the price. Rachel rubbed her eyes, and slowly moved toward the bathroom.

Okay, time to be cheerful, she thought as she went downstairs to prepare breakfast. To her surprise, Sarah was standing at the stove scrambling eggs. The kitchen table was set, the juice and milk cartons were in the middle, and toast had popped out of the toaster. Rachel wondered if she should rub her eyes one more time. She thought she had to be dreaming.

Sarah turned around to see her mother standing there, looking quite bewildered. One side of Sarah's mouth turned up in a grin, as though she had something entertaining on her mind. Neither spoke for a moment. Rachel's silence was due mostly to shock, and Sarah's because of amusement.

Finally, after taking in the entire kitchen scene, Rachel sputtered out a comment. "I...I don't...I don't understand. What's going on here?" She looked as though she had witnessed something that didn't make any sense.

"And good morning to you too, Mother." Sarah still had a mischievous grin on her face.

"Oh, yes. Good morning. I just don't...okay what *is* going on here?" Rachel ran her hands through her somewhat tangled hair.

"I'm making breakfast." Sarah had responded as though she made breakfast every morning.

"Yeah, I can see that. But WHY? What don't I know?" Now Rachel was suspicious.

Sarah began to plate the eggs. "Why not? I was up early and when I came downstairs, I thought I would do this. If that's okay with you?" She looked innocently at Rachel.

Rachel blinked a bit, trying to understand this unusual turn of events. "It's perfectly okay with me. You just have to realize that, YOU'VE NEVER DONE THIS BEFORE!" Rachel had cupped her mouth to make the point that this didn't make sense.

Sarah actually giggled. Rachel joined in the laughter.

"Mom, it's really not that big of a deal. I had fun doing this."

"Well, terrific then. That works for me." She looked at Sarah with pride and respect. "I guess you're growing up. It's nice."

"Yeah, whatever."

Rachel wondered if this was Sarah's way of apologizing to her for her nastiness the previous evening. Sarah would never say she was sorry, but her actions this morning spoke loudly.

David and Rebecca came downstairs, and their mouths gaped open upon seeing their sister taking care of everything. They had a look of bewilderment as they turned to each other, but then they happily sat down ready to eat what their sister had prepared. It was best not to ask questions. Just eat and enjoy. Everyone was talking and consuming the delicious breakfast, and then the three of them finished and actually cleaned up after themselves. Rachel sat at the kitchen table, sipping her coffee. This was a very happy start to her day.

The children went upstairs to get ready to go to the bus. Rachel waited downstairs, and then watched them all come enthusiastically downstairs. *They had more energy than she did*, thought Rachel. They put on their raincoats, hugged her goodbye and tore out of the front door. She closed the door and felt the pittance of energy she did have drain right out. She was going to call Steve, but she decided that what she needed was a good workout and a nice hot shower before confronting her children's father. She would call him during his lunch hour.

She exercised and showered and, after running some errands, she returned and called her ex. He answered his phone immediately.

"Hi, Rachel! How's it going?" Rachel could hear him chewing.

"Hi. I'm fine. I guess I caught you while you're eating."

"No problem." Rachel heard him swallow his food. "What's up? How was your evening?"

"It was wonderful. I called to ask you the same question."

"Huh? Oh, it was fine." Then he seemed to change his normally

267

casual tone into one of suspicion. "Why are you asking?"

"It seems you were mentally preoccupied."

"What? Rachel, what are you getting at?" Steve sounded bewildered.

"Steve, I believe that you weren't really *with* the kids."

Steve sounded agitated now. "Yes I was! I was there! I brought them Chinese food. What did they tell you? That I never showed up?"

"That's not what I mean. I know you were physically here, I just don't think you were connecting with them."

"Oh, come on Rachel. This is crazy. I was there, with them, and we were fine. Maybe I'll take them out this weekend. Spend time with them again. Would that be better?"

"That's fine with me. As long as you actually talk with them. By the way, I hate to ask, but what's the situation with Linda?"

Steve was silent for a moment. "I don't know. I don't want to think about that right now."

"Are you still with her? I just want to know if you're living in the same house right."

"No, I'm not living with her at the moment." Steve became sarcastic with Rachel. "Is that okay with you? Did I answer your question?"

"Yes. By the way, I saw her sister last night."

"Lori? You saw Lori?"

"That's right. Lori and John."

"That's interesting. I haven't seen either of them for quite a while."

"They were at our table. She was sitting next to me."

"So, did you talk much with her?"

"Yes. She asked me if I was the Rachel Blum who was married to Steve."

"That had to be awkward."

"Not really. She's a very nice person. She's not a real fan of her sister. We do hope things work out for you and Linda, though."

"Really? Why?"

"Why not? She's your wife."

"So were you." Steve's comment went like a shot through the phone.

"That doesn't matter. What matters is that Linda needs you, and you've both made mistakes. Maybe cut her some slack."

Steve was baffled. "I am stunned here, Rache. I would never have expected you to advocate for Linda. Why are you doing this?"

Rachel sighed, uncertain about her own motives. "I don't know. I guess there's been so much that has happened. We all need to shape up and get our acts together. There's been enough drama already."

"You seem to have gotten your act together."

"Maybe that's given me some perspective. Just try to do the right thing, Steve."

"Yep. Hey, I was thinking that maybe I could take the kids to see your mom this weekend."

Rachel's guard went up. "Why? You don't need to see my mother."

"I don't *mind* visiting with her. I think the kids would have fun with me coming along with them to see her. That might give you and Don more time together. Instead of you having to visit your mom."

Rachel sensed some ulterior motive. She also wasn't about to go along with his plan. "No, I don't think that's a good idea. Thanks, but no thanks."

"Why not? What's the problem?" Steve sounded hurt.

"Steve, I don't think my mother really wants to see YOU. I don't mean to be cruel, but you are her EX son in-law. Got it?"

Steve was perturbed. "Yes. I've got it. I'm just trying to be helpful."

Rachel didn't buy that for a second, but she wasn't about to tell him that. "Thanks for your offer, but maybe take the kids out for meals. Or wherever they want to go. Okay?"

"Okay. Whatever you say. I guess you want me to do a lot of things right now."

"What does THAT mean?"

"Stay with Linda, don't see your mom, take the kids somewhere. Anything else I can do for you?" Steve was dripping with sarcasm.

Rachel was annoyed now. "Yeah, how about you stop being a jerk. Gosh, I give you some advice and ask you to be with your kids, and you give me a hard time. Give me a break."

"Sorry. You're right. I didn't mean to be difficult. I'm just amazed that you want me to be with Linda. Would you feel the

269

same way if she wasn't pregnant? What if you weren't with Don? You'd still want me to stay with her?"

What an ego he has! Does he honestly think that I want him back? "Trust me; I'd still feel this way. You need each other." She thought that was a good way to put it.

"Hmm. Well, we'll see. Anyway, I have to get going here. I have a lunch to finish and work to do."

"Yes, I know you do. Hey, you mentioned you're not living with Linda right now. Where are you?"

"I'm in the house. Where would you think I'd be?"

"I wasn't sure if you meant that *you* had moved out."

"Not a chance. This is my home. I bought it."

"Just out of curiosity, where did Linda go?" Rachel could only imagine how Linda was handling this.

"She's with a single friend."

"Interesting. Well, I'll talk with you soon. I'll let the kids know that you'll be seeing them this weekend."

"Sounds good."

Rachel felt worn out. Although there were times when she had to talk with him, she always felt a bit drained after the conversations. She wondered why she hadn't felt that way during the good years. *Was it her youth? The initial feelings of love and having carefree days? Life happens, as they say.*

Rachel thought she should visit her mother before the weekend. Rachel would be pretty busy and then the school year was coming to a close at the end of the following week. She called Delores, but the answering machine came on.

"This is Delores. I'm not available right now, but please leave a message, and I will return your call." Then, there was a loud beep.

"Hi, Mom. It's Rachel. Um, well, I was going to come out for an hour or so, but I guess you're busy right now. I hope you're having fun. Let's see, I was thinking maybe I could come out tomorrow. In the morning sometime? Let me know if that sounds good to you. Bye."

Rachel then called Grace to see if she'd like to join her for lunch the following week. This would be the last chance she would have before school was ending, and then Rachel and the kids would be leaving for California. Grace answered.

"Hello?"

"Hi, Grace! It's Rachel. How are you doing?"

"Well, hello! I'm fine! How's life with you?"

"Not too bad. I was wondering if we could get together for lunch next week?

"You bet we can! We'll need this get together before the kids are out of school. Help each other get strong for the long haul." Grace laughed at her own comment.

"I think you're right. Although, you know, we certainly can see each other during the summer. Why deprive ourselves of fun?"

"True. The kids will be busy anyway. You're going to California, right?"

"Yeah, but that will only be for a week."

"Okay. Next week sounds great to me. Uh, let's see." Grace was looking at her calendar. "Would Tuesday work for you?"

"Perfect. Around noon?"

"Sounds good. I'll see you Tuesday!"

Rachel clicked off the phone, and when she did, her phone rang. She checked the Caller ID, and it was her mother.

"Hello?"

"Rachel. It's your mother. I got your message. I just returned from a lecture."

"That sounds nice. What was it about?"

"Life in the Golden Years. It was okay. Nothing I didn't already know."

"Still, it was probably good to go."

"I guess. So, if you want to come here tomorrow, that would be lovely."

"Okay. I can be there around ten?"

"Of course. And you can tell me how things are going with you and Don."

"I can tell you right now. Things are fine."

"I expect many more details than that. 'Fine' sounds like something your children would say. You're too mature for that."

Rachel smiled at her mother's observant critique. "We'll discuss everything tomorrow."

"Yes, we will. See you at ten."

Rachel pressed the button to end the call. She looked at the phone and rolled her eyes. *Boy, Mom really wants my relationship to work*, thought Rachel. *I wouldn't mind if things continue to go well.* Rachel smiled and put the phone back in its holder.

271

Rachel was about to get up from the chair when the phone rang again. *Geez, this is annoying.* However, when Rachel looked at the caller information, she got excited. This time, she'd be talking with Don.

"Hello?

"Rachel! Hi! It's Don. How are you today?" He always sounded so happy to talk with her.

"Hi! I'm doing great now that I'm talking with you. What's up?"

"I want to go over our plans for the weekend."

"Sounds wonderful. I'm fine with anything you want to do." Rachel realized that she had just uttered a loaded comment, although she wasn't sure that Don would take it in any odd way.

"Well, now, let me see. What should we do?" He had taken her comment the way that it sounded.

"Hmm. I assume you already had devised a plan before you called, Mister." Rachel laughed.

Don laughed as well. "Yes, yes I did. There's a play that I thought we might want to see. It's a comedy, if you're interested."

"Sure. That sounds like a great idea."

"I thought we could have dinner before the show, and then after the show, maybe we could go somewhere for dessert and coffee. Is that okay?"

"Don, that's more than okay. I love it!"

"All right then. I'll get the tickets and make the dinner reservations. Then I'll let you know what time I'll come to your house."

"I can't wait. Thanks for thinking of this." Rachel loved that Don enjoyed making plans for them.

"I'm just glad I'll be seeing you soon. Anything fun going on with you?"

"Not really. I'm just looking forward to the weekend."

"Same here."

They said their goodbyes, and Rachel felt very content.

Rachel enjoyed the rest of her day. The children came home and were wound up. Excitement was in the air, and they couldn't stop talking about the end of school and upcoming activities. Rachel was very pleased to see all three children feeling so upbeat. There had been enough problems in their lives already, so this feeling of joy was long overdue. She got a kick out of watching them being so animated. The girls were giggling and gesturing wildly at times. David joined in, and whatever he said had them grabbing their stomachs with intense laughter.

The evening wore on as Rachel and the kids sat in the family room. The phone rang for the umpteenth time, and Rachel happily answered seeing that it was Don. She got up immediately to take the call into the living room.

"Hello!" Rachel sat down in one of the chairs and faced the wall, wanting to have some privacy. She felt like a teenager taking a call while her parents were in the other room. It was all very secretive.

"Hi Rachel! How's your evening going?"

"All is well at Casa de Blum. The children are happy, so life is good."

"I'm glad to hear that. I've arranged everything for Saturday night."

Rachel was excited. "Fantastic! This is going to be fun!"

"I'd say so. Is it okay if I come by around 5:15? I know that sounds early, but our dinner reservation is at 5:45, and we'll want to be out of the restaurant around 7:30 or so."

"It's not too early at all. Thank you so much for arranging all of this. I know you have a busy schedule, so it's so nice of you to take the time to plan our evening."

"Oh, it's nothing. I consider myself a lucky man that you want to go out with me. I'm enjoying sharing life with you, Rachel."

Rachel couldn't believe her luck. "I like sharing my life with you too, Don." She felt practically giddy.

At that moment, she turned to see Sarah standing with her arms folded and her head tilted to the side, wondering what her mother was talking about and with whom. Sarah did not look happy. Rachel felt like she had just been caught doing something naughty.

Rachel spoke very softly into the phone. "Uh, Don, I think I'd better get going. Number One daughter is glaring at me."

"Uh, oh, I hope everything is okay."

"Don't worry. I'll be fine. So, I'll see you Saturday at 5:15?"

Don started whispering into the phone as though he was in on Rachel's conspiracy. "Absolutely. And maybe tomorrow night too? Just to go out and grab a cup of coffee and something sweet? If that works for you. I realize that you have a life at home."

"I'd love that. I'm sure I could escape for a little while. Would you like to come here around eight?"

"Sure. That would be great. I'll let you go now. Good luck."

Rachel and Don said goodbye to each other, and Rachel clicked off her phone. She looked at Sarah, as if questioning her reason to be standing there spying on her.

"Yes? Is there something I can do for you?" Rachel remained seated, wanting to look calm and casual about everything.

Sarah looked at her mother, then at the wall, then back at her mother again. She had her typical obstinate, disgusted look on her face, so Rachel braced for whatever comment was forthcoming.

"You know, Mom. That wasn't funny calling me your 'Number One' daughter. Isn't that a bit racist? Like saying, 'Ah, Numba One Son?" She was imitating the old Chinese expression.

Rachel looked shocked by Sarah's reprimand. "Sarah, I was being funny, not racist. Also, I shouldn't have even needed to make that comment because I had come into this room for a little privacy. I guess that was too much to ask for."

Sarah stood silently for a moment, realizing that her mother's rebuke was justified. Even Sarah knew that privacy was important. She would have been very angry had her mother been standing there listening to her conversation. She tried to deflect the comment.

"I was just wondering what was going on. I guess you're seeing Lover Boy this weekend."

Rachel stood up and walked towards Sarah. Her daughter's tone and comment were unacceptable. "Sarah, I know you're not thrilled that I'm seeing someone, but don't use that name when referring to Don. He's a very nice man. We're just having a good time socializing."

Sarah looked at Rachel very skeptically. "Yeah, well, Daddy was 'having a good time 'socializing' as well, wasn't he?" She had put her fingers up to do the quotation.

Rachel felt the heat pulse in her face. "No, this is not the same as Daddy. Not even remotely. Don and I go out to have fun. AND, neither of us is married."

Sarah seemed to be willing to concede this notion. However, Rachel didn't think that her daughter, or any of her children, should dictate what her life should be or how she should behave. She had gone from trying to be calm and understanding to feeling like she was being judged and ridiculed. She decided to put a stop to this right now. Sarah was walking away, so Rachel spoke up.

"Sarah." She stopped and turned around; giving a look that indicated that she didn't know why she was being bothered right now.

"I want to make something very clear to you right here and right now. I don't mind you asking me questions about my relationship with Don or anybody else. That's fine. What I won't allow is your lousy attitude."

Sarah looked stunned by her mother's overt honesty. Her eyes shot wide open like she had just witnessed a crime.

"That's right. You will not EVER dictate what my life should be. I will always do my best to be a good mother to you, Rebecca and David. I love you all very much. However, I have a right to have fun, just like the three of you do. I'm a good, decent person, and I will not have you make what I do seem tawdry. I'm sorry for what has happened to this family in the past. It wasn't my fault, but I'm sorry you all had to suffer and learn to deal with things that no child should have to. I will do what I want, and I will be honorable and I will be respected. Okay?"

Sarah swallowed hard. Her face reddened a bit as well, not because of anger but because of shame. She was mature enough to understand that what her mother said was true. Deep down, she also knew her mother was a decent woman, and that she loved Sarah and her siblings. Maybe it was time to cut her mother some slack. Sarah cleared her throat before she responded. "Yes, I guess it is okay."

"So, I made myself clear? You understand what I just said, right?" All Sarah could do was nod.

"Okay, then. I guess that's it." They both left the living room, and soon after, the day came to a calm end.

Chapter Twenty-Four

The next morning, Rachel readied herself to visit Delores. Because of the talk she had with Sarah the previous evening, Rachel felt more confident in dealing with her mother. Rachel found that she was feeling strong and happy, and her relationship with Don was going better than she would ever have expected. As she drove leisurely toward the home, the sky was a bit cloudy with a slight threat of rain. That didn't dampen Rachel's spirit one bit. She was upbeat because the weekend would bring Don into her world again.

Rachel easily found a parking space, so she maneuvered her car between the lines, turned off the car, got out and locked the vehicle. She had a bounce in her step as she entered the home, arriving about ten minutes early. She didn't see her mother yet, but as she glanced around, she did see Don in the distance. Rachel would have gone towards him to say hello, but he wasn't alone, and he wasn't talking with his father. He was chatting with a lovely young lady. She was sharply dressed in a tailored black pantsuit, had wavy long black hair and a smile that looked dazzling enough to illuminate the room. Rachel couldn't hear a thing, but she saw them sitting next to each other on one of the couches. Don was leaning towards the woman, riveted to what she was saying. At one point, she touched his arm. Rachel didn't want to see more. She looked the other way, her heart beating wildly in her chest, and practically sprinted towards her mother's apartment.

Before Rachel knocked on her mother's door, she took a deep breath to try to collect herself. Her stomach had tightened, and she knew she had to relax. Just as she put her fist up to tap on the door, her mother opened it, not expecting to see Rachel on the other side.

Delores was startled. "Oh my goodness! Rachel, you scared me half to death!"

"Sorry, Mom." Rachel was also feeling a bit rattled.

"I thought I was going to meet you in the lobby."

"I arrived a little early and decided it would be fine for us to enjoy a quiet time right here. How does that sound to you?" Rachel felt unnerved.

"It's fine with me." She looked at her daughter suspiciously.

"Is everything okay?"

"Yeah, Mom, everything is fine." Rachel sounded a bit too high pitched and chipper to her own ears. She smiled, and hoped that would be the end of it.

Delores still looked uncertain, but she didn't press anymore. She turned back into her apartment. "Well, come in. Can I get you anything? Coffee? Tea?"

Rachel wasn't sure she could hold a cup or sip a drink right now. "No. No thanks. You have something if you want."

"I've already had my cup of tea."

They sat down, and Delores looked at Rachel, waiting for her to speak. Rachel wished she hadn't seen Don and that woman sitting together. It threw her too easily. *Perhaps I should have gone over to say hello?* She now thought it was a mistake to have avoided Don. Should she tell her mother that maybe they should go sit in the lobby? No, that would be strange. Rachel's expression must have seemed odd. Delores looked at her, wondering what was on her mind.

"Rachel? *Is* something wrong? You don't seem quite like yourself right now. You're a bit distracted."

Rachel brought herself back to reality. "Oh, no Mom, I'm fine. Really. Everything is fine." Rachel presented her fixed smile to Delores, hoping that would deflect any further discussion.

Delores studied her, not believing a word that Rachel said. She leaned towards Rachel, not about to let her escape scrutiny. "Rachel, I KNOW something is wrong. I can see that you have something bothering you. Fess up, my dear. Please. Let me see if I can help you." Delores's expression emitted real concern. Rachel was both surprised and appreciative.

"Truly, it's nothing. I'm sure it's nothing. I…I just wasn't sure about something I saw, that's all." Rachel wanted to downplay this for her own sake.

Delores sat back in her seat appearing ready to examine the situation. "Rachel. What does all of that mean? I don't understand what you're trying to tell me. So just spit it out."

277

Rachel feared exposing her thoughts. She didn't want to give them any credence, and she believed that by divulging them, she would make her concerns real. However, she realized she should tell her mother. If they were going to have a closer relationship, it was time to let her in on the important details of her life. Even if it left Rachel feeling vulnerable.

Rachel let out a big sigh and dove in. "Okay. Here goes. I'm SURE I'm overreacting. I'm SURE that I must be." She looked at her mother, wondering how she was going to let it all out.

Delores waved her arms out as if to say, "And?" She wanted Rachel to tell her everything.

Rachel didn't look at her mother as she spoke. She fixed her gaze on a wall with a painting of her mother's garden that a local artist had done years ago. Delores had faithfully tended to her precious flowers, plants, herbs and vegetables. Her garden was exquisite and the artist skillfully created a lovely oil paint rendering of the land, capturing the details of the colors and the style.

"I came into the lobby, and I looked for you, even though I was slightly early. So…" Rachel took another deep breath. "As I looked around, I happened to see Don at a distance." She looked at her mother now.

"Yes? You saw Don at a distance." Delores was waiting for the rest of the story.

Rachel blurted out the rest of her thought. "He was sitting on a couch talking with a woman." She looked down for a moment, expelling her pent up breath as though she had exhausted herself by this confession.

Silence filtered through the room. But only for a few seconds.

"AND?" Delores seemed to still want more.

Rachel was perplexed. She looked incredulously at her mother. "What do you mean 'AND?'"

Delores looked confused. "Well, there simply must be more to this story. You haven't told me everything, have you?"

Rachel couldn't believe her mother. *How much more did she need?* "I believe that I have, Mother."

Delores looked befuddled. "I don't understand what the problem is. My dear daughter, what IS going on here? Tell me!"

Rachel's jaw had dropped. *How dense could Delores be?* "Mother, isn't it all obvious? Don was sitting on a couch with some woman." Rachel's expression looked like she was saying *duh!*

"No, I'm afraid this isn't all obvious. So, I guess you'll need to spell it out to your stupid mother." Delores looked annoyed.

Rachel collected her thoughts as if she was now going to try to explain something to a child. She spoke softly. "Mother, Don was sitting with a woman. I have never seen this woman. She even touched his arm." She paused, looking for any recognition of understanding from her mother. She wasn't seeing it. "Mom! He seems to be hanging out with this person!" She figured that after shouting this, her mother would now get it.

Delores gave Rachel a look she used to see sometimes as a young girl. The one where Delores always thought that Rachel was making a mountain out of a mole hill. Like, *Come on, dear. Get over it. Stop exaggerating.* "Rachel. Are you honestly telling me that you think Don is seeing someone else?" It wasn't really so much of a question as a skeptical comment.

"I don't know. He's sitting there all chummy with this pretty young lady. I have no way of knowing what's going on here." She folded her arms in defense.

Delores stood up. "Well, okay then. Let's go find out."

Rachel leaned forward in her chair. "What? What are you talking about?"

"I'm saying we should go find out. Let's see if they're still out there."

"Mother, we can't just go out there and go up to him."

"Why not? We can do anything we want. I live here. If I want to see people, then I will." Delores sounded indignant.

Rachel stood up frantically. Now she was trying to reason with Delores. "Mom, we really can't do this. I don't feel comfortable approaching them. It could be very awkward."

Delores shoed away her concern. "Nonsense. We're going, and that's that." When Delores set her mind to something, nothing more needed to be said.

Rachel felt very insecure about any confrontation, but she and her mother were already heading out of the door and walking towards the lobby. Delores was practically marching there and her troop, Rachel, was right there with her, not feeling quite ready for the battlefield. They both saw Don at the same time. Even though Rachel already knew where he was sitting, it was as though Delores had "Don-radar." He was still sitting with the woman even now. Rachel's stomach lurched a bit and her heart pounded.

Upon their approach to the couch, Don saw them and smiled his usual warm and open smile. There was no expression of shock, surprise or embarrassment on his face. He stood to greet them.

"Delores! Rachel! How are you? It's great to see both of you." Don gave them both a hug.

The lady sitting next to Don stood up. Don looked at her, and said, "Abby, I'd like to introduce you to these lovely ladies." He pointed to Delores first. "This is Delores Weinstein. She lives here, and she's a friend of my father's." Abby nodded her head and smiled as though an important piece of information had been revealed to her, and she understood everything now. He looked at Rachel with a loving expression. "And this. This is Rachel Blum, my girlfriend." He was beaming from ear-to-ear.

Rachel was flattered and confused all at once. Then Don made the all-important introduction. "Ladies, this is Abby Shapiro. She's involved with the activities area of the home." Abby said hello to both women, and Rachel breathed a sigh of relief.

"I asked her if I could speak with her to find out about all of the resident activities as well as to offer some ideas that I have for promoting the home." He looked at Delores. "I know that you and my dad enjoy certain hobbies, and I thought it would be nice to see if those interests could be incorporated into the routine here. I may even be able to help with their website."

So, this was a business meeting. Rachel felt foolish, and Delores raised her eyebrows and smirked giving her a look that said, *See! What were you so worried about?*

Don noticed the look that passed between them. "Is everything okay?"

Rachel blurted out a response before her mother had a chance to say anything. "Everything is fine!" She looked at Abby. "It's so nice to meet you. I'm sure that Don will be able to help you. And I'm glad that my mom and Ben will have an even more fulfilling time here than they already do." She wasn't sure what to say, but she felt what she had already said sounded foolish.

Don looked at her, suspecting something was up, but he didn't pursue his thoughts. "Maybe I'll see you in a bit? Abby and I still need to cover some ground here."

"Of course. Mother and I will go to her apartment and chat." All Rachel could feel was relief. Her tone indicated how fine she was with everything.

They said goodbye, and Rachel and Delores went back to the apartment. Neither said a word until the door was closed. They sat down just as before.

"So? Tell me. What do you think now?" Delores was looking Rachel squarely in the eye.

"I'm not sure what you're asking me?" Rachel really didn't know what Delores was thinking.

"Do you think you can trust him now?"

Rachel looked a bit sheepish. "Yes. I think so." Then she continued emphatically. "Not that he can't see anybody else. I mean, that would be his decision. I wouldn't want to stop him from dating other women."

Delores didn't believe her. "Oh, come on Rachel. You're not fooling me. You have already fallen for him. And I believe he has fallen for you. I understand that you have built these defensive walls around you. I don't blame you. You were hurt, and you certainly don't want to go through that again. But I really do think you can trust him. Don is a nice man. I don't think he would betray you."

Rachel looked at her mother, almost not believing the conversation that they were having. This was a real mother/daughter relationship happening. Her mother actually understood what Rachel was feeling and what she had dealt with in the past. Maybe it was time for Rachel to let down her guard. Rachel's eyes became teary and she began to pour out everything that she had bottled up inside for all these years.

"I know I have to start trusting again. I just have a hard time not looking back. The pain that I felt was awful. I had to deal with so many things. I was forced to hear what Steve had done, and I also had to make sure that the kids would be okay. There was never much time for me to take care of my own emotional issues. To know what I was feeling. I didn't believe I could ever, nor should ever, love again. I didn't even want to trust my own judgment." Rachel grabbed a tissue from her purse. "Then, here's Don. I come to visit you, and I meet this kind, fun, handsome man, and I tried so hard to keep my head on my shoulders. I wanted to be rooted firmly in the ground." Rachel blew her nose

281

and dabbed her eyes. "It's exhausting trying to go through my days, deal with the kids, and hope I can trust him and be happy." She blew her nose again, and then began twisting the tissue in her hands.

Delores got up and moved her chair closer to Rachel. The phone rang, but Delores chose not to hear it. Her focus was completely on her daughter. She put her arm around Rachel, but she didn't say a word. She just held her. The dam broke loose. Rachel began sobbing. She had never even slightly cried in front of her mother, but now the tears wouldn't stop. She sounded like she was in agony, but it didn't matter. Years of built up emotions cascaded from Rachel, and her mother wasn't about to stop the waterfall. Delores and Rachel had never been this close. It was a special moment for both of them. Rachel continued to sob until she was spent. She gulped in air, and then she was quiet. Her tears had streamed down her face, blurring her vision. She didn't care and neither did her mother.

Rachel turned her watery eyes to Delores, and gave her a weak smile. Her mother returned the smile with one of her own. Then, there was a knock on the door. They both looked at the door, startled to realize it might very well be Don on the other side.

"I can't let him see me like this!" Rachel was horrified.

"Okay. Why don't you go to the bathroom and pull yourself together, and I'll try to think of a way to keep him out of here until you're ready to see him. I'll do my best to give you enough time. How does that sound?" Delores was a good conspirator.

"I guess it will have to do. Thanks, Mom." Rachel loved having her mother in her corner. It felt good to have her support.

"I'm happy to help. Always." She grabbed Rachel's hand and gave it a nice squeeze.

Rachel ran into the bathroom, and Delores opened the door to her waiting guest. Don was standing there.

"Hello, Don."

"Hi, Delores. I figured I would come by and say a quick hello to you and Rachel before going back to work."

At that point Delores realized that his time was limited, and she needed to think fast. She couldn't think of any excuses to bring him outside of her apartment. She was ready to let him come in, and then they both heard a hearty hello. Ben was in the hallway.

"Dad! Hi. I thought you were participating in a card game this morning. Otherwise I would have come by your place."

"We postponed the game because Charlie is a bit under the weather, Ned's family is visiting today, and Gus is out of town. Bill and I decided that we might as well reschedule the game. I was coming here to see if Delores wanted to go for a walk. It's not raining right now."

Delores looked back into the apartment, not sure of what to do. Then she turned back to the two men. "Ben, that sounds like a wonderful idea. Rachel is in the restroom at the moment, so maybe the three of us can go take a look at..." *Delores scrambled to come up with something. Anything. Suddenly an idea came to her,* "at the new mural that was painted near the auditorium. I haven't been over there yet, and I'd love to see it. Then we can come back and see Rachel."

The men looked at each other thinking this sounded like an odd idea, but then they nodded their agreement to see the mural.

"Should we wait for Rachel?" The always considerate Don spoke with concern.

"No. I think she had something in her eye, so she may need a moment or two."

"Is she okay? Should I see if I can help her?"

"No, no. That won't be necessary. She's fine, I'm sure." Delores couldn't believe how hard it was to try to fib her way through.

"Well, okay. If you're sure." Don't didn't sound convinced by what Delores was saying.

"Absolutely. And we won't take long. Anyway, I don't think she'd want us hovering." Delores felt like she was really pulling at strings. "We should just go now." She felt a little sense of panic, wanting them all to get out of the apartment until Rachel was ready to be seen.

Delores shut the door, and the three of them took off. Within another minute, Rachel came out of the bathroom. She looked less puffy around the eyes, although she still had a glassy-eyed look about her. Her nose wasn't too red because she had used a cool cloth all over her face. She felt she had done enough to get by. Rachel had no idea as to what Delores said, so she'd have to play along with her story as best she could.

A few minutes later, the door opened, and Delores peeked in.

She looked at Rachel, and Rachel gave her the thumbs up sign. Delores breathed a sigh of relief, knowing that the charade was over and the pressure was off. She allowed the men to come in with her.

Don went over to Rachel to give her a hug. "You okay?" He seemed to notice that she wasn't her usual self.

"Yes, I'm fine." She smiled brightly.

"How's your eye?"

Delores spoke up immediately. "Yes, Rachel. Is your eye better? Was there anything in it?" She prayed Rachel would catch on.

"I think it was just a speck of something. Who knows? Anything could have irritated it. Sometimes I think it's an allergy that dries out my eye, and then I start tearing."

Don gave Rachel a look that indicated he wasn't quite sure what was going on. She tugged at her eye a little, even though she knew she shouldn't. That could cause wrinkles. She didn't want those, but she did want to make it seem like she had been dealing with her eye.

Don needed to be on his way. "I'm going to have to head out. I've got to get back to my business, but it was great seeing all of you, even if it was only for a few minutes."

Rachel was a bit spent from her emotional outburst. "I probably should get going also. I'll walk out with you." Rachel and Don gave their final hugs to their parents, left the apartment and walked towards the lobby. Abby was discussing something with someone, but then she saw Don and waved. She excused herself from the other person, and came towards Don and Rachel.

"Don, I want to thank you again for everything. You're so helpful!" She touched his arm again, the same way that she did before. Rachel didn't know if this was just her way or if she was flirting with Don. *Although, she wouldn't do that in front of his girlfriend, would she?*

"Thank *you* for taking the time to meet with me. I think we accomplished a lot."

"We sure did! Maybe we can talk about more of this sometime soon?"

"Uh, yeah. That would be fine." It almost seemed like Don wasn't sure it was necessary to talk about anything in the immediate future, but he would politely go along with Abby's idea. That's when Rachel cut in.

"Actually, I'd be more than happy to help too." She grabbed Don by the arm, and held him close to her, as though she was staking her claim on him. "I'm sure you could always use more assistance." Rachel smiled at Abby like she had never smiled before!

Abby gave her a closed-mouth smile. "That's very kind of you. You're right. We can use all the help we can get." Once again, because Rachel didn't know her, she had no way of knowing whether Abby was being sincere or if she was bothered by Rachel's offer to help.

"So, the next time you and Don meet, would you like me to join in?" Rachel looked very innocent, wanting to know if she could also be useful.

This time, Don jumped into the conversation. "Rachel, I think that's a wonderful idea. I know *I'd* like to have you with me. I'm sure Abby wouldn't mind that at all. Right, Abby?"

Abby nodded her agreement. She didn't seem overjoyed by the concept of Rachel assisting, but she wasn't about to say no to the couple. Rachel still couldn't decide if Abby just didn't show much emotion or if she really didn't want Rachel to be included, but she didn't care. She wanted to make sure this woman knew the score.

"I really appreciate that you're both so willing to help. Having just started working at the home, I love receiving as much input as possible. So, Don, I'll be in touch because I have your number, and you can pass everything along to Rachel. We'll meet soon.

"Sounds perfect to me." Don looked at Rachel with those loving eyes of his. "Well, Rachel and I will be on our way." He then turned to Abby. "Have a nice day."

"Thanks. You too. Nice to meet you Rachel." She waved at both of them, and Rachel nodded and quickly noticed that Abby was not wearing an engagement or wedding ring. Well, she wasn't about to give Abby a chance to have one presented to her by Don. She and Don left the home and walked into the parking lot.

Don looked at Rachel. "I must say that this has been an interesting day so far."

"How so?"

"Well, between your *eye* issue and Abby, I'm not sure what's going on." Don looked more than amused.

Rachel tried to look innocent. "I don't know what you mean."

"You don't, hmm?" He stopped before they approached Rachel's car. Don folded his arms across his chest trying to assess the day. "Let me see. Your mom covered for you very well today. I don't know why you couldn't be seen, although when Dad and I did see you, well, you weren't quite yourself. Now, this whole thing with Abby. What gives?"

Rachel was very surprised that Don had caught on so well, although she wasn't sure she wanted to tell him much. *How embarrassing would it be if he knew how upset she* had *become when she saw him sitting with Abby?* However, knowing that he was so tuned into her made her feel very special. He was observant, not oblivious.

Rachel looked down at the walkway, uncertain as to how to proceed. "I don't know what to tell you. I guess it's just one of those days." She looked up and gave him her best eye contact. "Mom and I were chatting about various things. Sometimes I get thrown off my game with her. As far as Abby is concerned, let's not talk about her." Rachel had been honest. She and Delores had spoken, and the conversation impacted Rachel greatly.

Don furrowed his brow. "What's the problem with Abby? I know you said we shouldn't talk about her, but I am curious. I don't get it." Don was not sure what to think at the moment.

Rachel laughed cynically. "Oh boy, Don. I just don't know about that girl. I think she wants more than volunteer work out of you." Rachel grinned mischievously at Don.

Don laughed. "Oh, come on Rachel. I don't think so. We were literally just talking business. I swear."

"YOU may have been talking business, but I think she was talking monkey business. Just my woman's intuition. And I don't think she was too pleased to have me jump on board with the two of you."

Don shook his head, finding it hard to believe what Rachel was thinking. "This is really fascinating to me. Well, I don't think you're right about this, but even if you are, I'm not interested in her. I hope you believe me. Really, I do only have eyes for you."

Rachel was very moved by his statement. She felt very reassured. "I am really glad to hear that. I do believe you. Absolutely, positively." She touched his arm in a loving gesture.

"So, I will see you tonight? We can go out for dessert?"

"Yes, that would be delightful."

"I'll come by at eight."

"That's great."

"Okay. I'll see you then."

Rachel got into her car, and Don walked to his car. She sat in hers for a moment, just collecting her thoughts before concentrating on driving home. She was pleased by Don's sincere statement of only noticing her and no other women. Of course, she would have believed the same thing about Steve years ago as well. She had promised herself she wouldn't fall for Don, or any other man for that matter. Yet, she couldn't help herself. They were having fun spending time together, and that was all wonderful. It bothered her that she was so thrown by Abby. If Don did want to see that woman, he could do so and it shouldn't bother her. It *really* shouldn't. And yet, it did. Somehow, the thought of Don being with any other woman shook Rachel to her core. She had her hands on the steering wheel and she laid her forehead against the wheel. She needed to stop thinking like this. After a moment, there was a thumping noise on her car window. Rachel's heart banged wildly, and she looked up. Don was standing there, looking very alarmed. Rachel turned on the car and pushed the button to roll down the window.

"Rachel? Are you okay?" Don bent down leaning slightly into her window.

Rachel wasn't sure what had happened. "Yes, Don, I'm fine. What's wrong?" Her heart was still thumping, and she was scared. *Had something happened somewhere near her car and she wasn't aware of it?*

"I was pulling out of my parking space, and I saw you leaning against the steering wheel. I thought maybe you were sick or you passed out." His hand went to his heart which was also pumping rapidly.

Rachel leaned back in her seat, relieved that everything was okay. "I'm so sorry, Don. I didn't mean to scare you. I'm fine, but I do appreciate your concern. Are YOU okay?"

"Yeah. I'm fine. I was just very worried about you. Why WERE you leaning against the steering wheel?" Don looked very perplexed. She had made this day very confusing for him.

"I don't know." Then, Rachel lied. "I'm just a bit worn out today, and I have to gear myself up to do stuff before the kids come home." Rachel smiled easily at Don, hoping that he would believe her.

Don was grateful that she was okay, but his expression indicated his uncertainty regarding her answer. "Is there anything I can do to help you? Do you need anything?"

Rachel always appreciated his kindness. Here she was worrying about the potential for other women in his life, and he couldn't do enough for her. "That's so sweet, but no. I think I've got it together. I should get going. No loitering in the parking lot." Rachel smiled, trying to be amused by her own joke.

Don seemed hesitant to leave her, but he backed away slightly from the car. "You'll let me know if you need anything, right?"

"Yes, I will. It's just the end of the school year, and things get a little crazy. Mom needs a break." She smiled again, hoping to reassure him that she was fine.

"Okay. I'll let you go, but you have to promise me that you'll call me if you're not okay and if you need any help. Promise?"

"Yes, I promise." She nodded her head in agreement indicating her understanding of his request.

Don looked very serious. "Rachel, I want you to know that I'm not a guy who only wants to be around for all the fun stuff. I know life isn't always easy. Sometimes we need to be there for each other when things get tough."

Rachel shouldn't have been surprised by anything he said, but she was awed by his statement. 'Don, you are so good to me. And I hope you know that I'm there if you need me. I don't want you to ever think my life is all about my kids. I mean, yes, much of it is, but you can count on me too."

He smiled, knowing that Rachel meant was she said. "I'll see you tonight."

"Definitely."

Don backed away from her car completely, and Rachel pulled out of her spot. She waved and Don waved back, smiling. As she looked in the rearview mirror, she saw Don still standing there, watching her drive off towards home. He appeared smaller as the distance increased between them, but Rachel's heart was getting bigger, making room for all of the feelings she was harboring for him.

Chapter Twenty-Five

Rachel's day was relatively normal after all of the unsettling moments at the home. The kids had a good day at school and she was finishing folding some of their clothes so they would be ready to be with their dad for the weekend. The phone rang.

Rachel shouted downstairs to the family room. "Hey. Would someone find out who it is, and if it's someone we know please answer it."

David shouted back. "Okay, Mom. Um, it's Grandma. I'll answer it."

Rachel stopped her folding and listened for David. She assumed her mother wanted to talk with her and not David, and she soon found out that was the case.

"Mom, get the phone. Grandma wants to talk to you!"

"Thanks, David! I'll get it upstairs!"

Rachel picked up the phone, and she heard David click off the other phone. "Hi, Mom."

"Hello, Rachel. My, oh my, there certainly was a lot of yelling about me being on the phone!"

"I'm upstairs folding clothes and the kids are in the family room. Shouting has become our intercom system."

Delores actually found that funny and she laughed. "Rachel, I want to know how you're doing. Is everything okay with you at this point?"

"Well, yeah. Why wouldn't it be?" Rachel was confused.

"You're kidding? Have you forgotten today's events? All the worries about Don and this other lady?"

"No, I haven't forgotten, but everything is fine. I spoke with her a little as Don and I were leaving the home. I'm going to join Don in helping Abby in whatever way I can with activities at the home."

"Really? Well, that's very interesting. So, she's not a problem? She's not his new girlfriend?" Delores was joking, knowing that Abby was actually an employee of the home and no threat to Rachel.

289

Rachel knew her mother thought she had been a bit silly about the whole thing. "No, she's not. It's all fine. And I'm okay now." Rachel paused for a moment, realizing how much her mom had done for her. "Mom, I want to thank you for being there for me today. Your comfort meant the world to me."

"No need to thank me. That's what mothers are supposed to do. I'm just happy I could help."

"Okay, well, still. It was nice." Rachel sighed, suddenly feeling very tired. "I need to get going, but thanks for calling to check up on me."

"I'll talk with you soon, dear."

Rachel was pleased that Delores wanted to be a mother to her. She realized that part of the issue here was Don, and not just a desire to make her daughter feel better. Delores adored Don, and at this point, Rachel wasn't sure her mother would be able to handle it if Don went out of Rachel's life. For that matter, Rachel wasn't sure she could handle it either. However, everything seemed fine right now. Don not only hadn't given her any reason to think they wouldn't continue to be a couple; he had actually continuously reassured Rachel that he wanted to be with her and only her.

The phone rang again, and it was Steve. She hoped he wasn't backing out of his plan to be with the kids.

"Hey, Rache. It's Steve. How's everything?"

"Everything is fine. What's up?" At the moment, Rachel didn't care how he was doing, she just wanted to make sure he was on his way and there wasn't some problem.

"I wanted to call before getting the kids. I assume they're ready for me?"

"Yes they are." She had to ask her burning question. "What's up with you and Linda?" Rachel wanted Steve to concentrate on his life with Linda and perhaps stop bothering her about Don.

"Not much."

"That's not an answer."

"I guess it's not, but hat's really all I can tell you."

"So, I take it she's not with you? I mean living with you?"

"Got that right. I'm not so sure I want her back."

"So, that's that. It's over?"

"Don't know yet. I'll have to take some time to figure that out." Steve was sounding very cool and collected about all of this.

"Does *she* want to come back?"

Steve laughed rather wickedly. "Hell, yes she'd want to come back. If she did, she'd be supported by me again. Linda loves the lap of luxury. Can't get enough of it. Why she acted like a damn fool, I just don't know."

"I think that question could be asked of a lot of people." Rachel wondered if Steve would realize that she had directed that comment squarely at him.

"Well, isn't that just so funny?" Steve did get her dig. Clearly he wasn't very amused. "I know I screwed up. I get that. I made a huge mistake. That doesn't mean that I want to forgive her. And, why would I want to raise another kid? Especially one who isn't mine?"

"I don't know. I say do whatever you want to do. I don't care. However, I will tell the kids they'll be spending time with you and only you. They'll like that."

"So, you're not going to make me try to see the error of my ways if I divorce Linda?"

"Nope, I'm not."

"Okay! That's great. It's nice to know that you won't read me the riot act for being insensitive. Not that I think *I'm* being insensitive. I would just think you'd see it all differently."

"It doesn't matter what I think. This is your life. Should I tell the kids you're on your way?" Rachel was getting tired of talking with Steve.

"Yes. Aren't you and your man getting together this weekend?"

"Yes, DON and I ARE getting together. I enjoy every moment with him." Rachel wanted to hurt Steve. She was tired of trying to always keep it together and not be nasty to him. The gloves were coming off.

"I'll just bet you do." Steve paused and then became reflective. "Well, he does seem like a nice guy. And he's never been married? Hard to understand that."

Rachel didn't like Steve's tone. "What does THAT mean?"

"Nothing. I just think it's amazing that he's never bitten the bullet."

"Well, you don't need to be amazed by any of it. He's been reluctant, and I can't say I blame him." Rachel oozed sarcasm.

"Aw, come on. Our marriage wasn't THAT bad. At least not until I lost my mind. We had good times together. I'll always

291

regret what I did."

Rachel wasn't sure if he was suddenly being very honest that he did regret hurting her or that he regretted getting involved with Linda. Not that it mattered now. This was definitely water under the bridge.

"Rachel? Would you ever consider marrying Don?"

Rachel hadn't even thought about that, and hearing Steve ask the question threw her off her game a bit. "Uh…well…I don't know. It's way too soon to think about that."

"But you haven't ruled out marriage?"

"Steve, why are you asking me about this?" Rachel wasn't thrilled that he was probing so deeply into her life. She wasn't the one who went from one marriage immediately into another. She took her time to think, and was just now enjoying another man's company.

"I'm curious. Just like you want to know everything that's going on with Linda and me, I want to know what the future holds for you. Believe it or not, Rache, I want what's best for you. I haven't always shown that, but I really feel that way."

Steve sounded sincere, but Rachel had lost her trust in him as soon as she heard about his affair. She didn't have any need to trust him again. As long as he was good to the children, that was all she cared about. Rachel didn't want to continue this discussion.

"However you feel, it doesn't matter to me. I've got to get going, but I'll tell the kids you'll be here soon." She was getting tired of repeating herself. He needed to stop talking with her and come pick up the kids.

"Okay. That's fine. I guess there's no problem with you questioning every move I make, but your life is off limits. Sure. Makes sense to me." Steve was now annoyed.

Rachel was getting worn down. "You're right. You're right. Your life and what you do with it isn't any of my business. I'm sorry that I pressed you about your marriage. I promise I won't do that again. I'll live my life without your questions, and you'll live your life without my questions. I only ask certain things because I know it impacts the children." Rachel suddenly found her second wind and let it rip. "Of course, I'M the parent who deals with the day to day stuff. Not that I don't have fun times, but those are not the only times that I have with the children. I have responsibility for them. I get to clean up the messes you create. It's my job to

292

make sure there's stability for them."

There was a long pause, and for a moment Rachel wondered if Steve had hung up on her. She thought her brutal honesty might have angered him to the point of him ending the call. However, she heard him clear his throat and sigh.

"Okay. I get it. I'm a jerk. That's probably not a news flash to you, but if you want to think I'm a bad guy, there's not much I can do about it."

"Actually, that's not really true. I mean the part about there not being much you can do about it."

Steve snickered at the obvious contempt Rachel felt towards him. "Oh, so you think I can change my ways, do you? How kind of you!"

"Steve, all I'm saying is you might want to step up and realize that you're a responsible adult now. You've made choices all along that only seem to benefit you. When it doesn't work out, you toss the bad away and move on."

"Hey, wait just a minute! You're the one who moved on. After I told you about the affair, you called a lawyer right away. So, don't tell ME that I just move on!"

"Well, what was I going to do? You were with Linda. That was that. And why would I want to stay with you when you cheated on me? I'm not really a glutton for punishment. I think you made your choice long before I called a lawyer. You tossed our family and me aside."

"I wasn't going to do that. I mean, yes. I had the affair. Grow up, Rache, it happens. It didn't mean I wanted to end everything with you and the kids."

Rachel was furious now. "YOU grow up! You clearly wanted Linda. I deserved better than that and so did our children! You're the one who acted like an immature jerk. I didn't tell you to go out and have your stupid affair. Besides, you seemed like you were quite in love with her, at least from what you told me. You wanted it all. Well, you got it!"

Steve responded in an almost pleading tone. "Rachel, I didn't want what happened. Honestly. I mean maybe I thought I was in love. I don't know. All I'm saying is that if you had given us half a chance, I think things might have turned out differently. I really wasn't in love with Linda. She was a mistake that I made."

"Oh, so it was up to me to forgive and forget? Is that right? I don't think so. I'm not the one who screwed up. You need to take the blame and be a better person from now on. I don't care if you shouldn't have married Linda. You did, and that's that. Yes. She made a huge mistake, the same way as you did. I'm just sick of your whining and her bitchiness. You both act like a bunch of babies sometimes, but I can tell you that I don't want to be part of your drama. I respect myself too much to get in the middle of every crisis you have. Just come get the children."

"Fine. I'm coming." Steve did click off, and he clearly wasn't happy. Rachel prayed that his mood would improve by the time he arrived at the house to get the kids.

Rachel felt drained but she also felt a sense of relief. The thoughts that she expressed to Steve allowed the pain that she had felt from his infidelity to melt away like ice on a hot day. In the past she had only sarcastically and subtly said things here and there. She knew Steve probably felt wounded at times by some of her opinions about him. However, this conversation went deeper than the others. She wanted him to reflect upon his own behavior and to acknowledge that something needed to change. It wasn't only about her anger over his behavior. She was sure he knew that he had caused her heartache. This was about his character and the future of his own life.

David must have heard some of what she said because after a moment, he poked his head in her bedroom door. "Mom?" He looked at her with big eyes of uncertainty.

Rachel smiled at him, trying to send a message of reassurance in case he had heard her side of the argument. She motioned for him to come towards her. "Hi, sweetie. What are you up to?"

"Um, nothin' much." He looked down at the floor. "I heard you talking."

"Yes, I was on the phone with your dad." Rachel wanted to sound pleasant and upbeat.

David looked up slowly, but would not meet Rachel's eye "Yeah. I thought that's who it was."

Rachel wanted to offer words of solace to minimize her son's troubled gaze. Once again, it was her responsibility to deal with the problem. Steve was off the hook. "Your dad and I had some things that needed to be said. Now he's on his way over here to get you and your sisters. This weekend you all won't even be sharing him. It will be the three of you and your dad. No one

294

else." She put her arm around David.

He looked at her with a glimmer of happiness. "Really? Linda won't be around?"

"No, she won't. She's got some other things going on this weekend. You all can do whatever you want with your dad. Eat out. Maybe go to a movie. Really, whatever you want to do, just tell him."

David looked down again. "That's not all you were talking about. Was it?"

"No, it wasn't. We were talking about life and the future. How you all matter so much to both of us."

David still didn't look at her. "It sounded a bit intense." His head shot up suddenly, and his eyes widened as he was looking at her. "Not that I was listening in. Honest. I was just in the hall at one point, and I heard your raised voice. I didn't hear much."

"It's okay David. I'm not mad. You know, sometimes adults have discussions. Loud discussions. We're all not always going to agree with each other. Just like you and your friends or you and your sisters have arguments. It's nothing to worry about. Your dad is fine and I'm fine."

David seemed somewhat reassured. "Okay. I guess I'll tell Sarah and Rebecca that we'll have a lot of time with dad." He gave a disgusted look, "and we won't have to be with Linda."

Rachel laughed at his obvious distaste for his step-mother. "Go talk with your sisters. I'll finish getting your things together, and I'll come downstairs soon."

David left the room, and Rachel was proud that she was able to dodge another bullet. Steve didn't make it easy for her, but she was getting better every day at dealing with life.

Rachel heard the doorbell ring. Steve had arrived, and she heard the girls talking downstairs.

"Mom! Dad's here!"

"Okay! I'll be down in a minute!"

Rachel was almost finished with packing David's clothes when Steve came into the room. She was startled, not expecting to see him.

He waved at her. "Hello."

"Hello?" She was clearly questioning what he was doing upstairs.

"Rachel. I want to apologize and not have the kids hear me.

I'm sorry about my raised voice during our talk. I get upset sometimes."

"Yeah. Well, David heard my end of the conversation. I had to talk him through some of the things he heard, as gently as possible."

"Oh, no. Is he okay?" Steve seemed genuinely concerned.

"Yeah, he's fine. I told him that you and I both care a lot about him and his sisters, and that sometimes people discuss things loudly."

Steve shook his head in amazement. "You always know how to save the day."

Rachel shrugged. "I try. I may not always succeed, but I do the best that I can. Really, Steve, that's all anybody can do. You don't have to be perfect. Just be there for them."

Steve nodded as though he understood. "Well, I'm ready to take them whenever you're ready for them to go."

Rachel put the last of the David's clothes into his duffle bag. She zipped it, and handed it to Steve. "I'm ready."

They went downstairs, and the kids were patiently standing there, Sarah and Rebecca both holding their necessary weekend clothing and toiletries.

Rachel went to hug each kid, even if the gesture wasn't warmly received by her daughters. "Have a great time!"

"We will now that we have dad all to ourselves." David boasted his joy and then realized how thoughtless he might have sounded. He looked at his father in horror. "I didn't mean it that way! I mean, I do want us to just have time with you, but…"

"It's okay, David. I understand." Steve smiled lovingly at his son. "I'm happy to have some alone-time with all of you as well. This is a treat for me."

They headed for the door, and Steve guided the children outside. He then turned to Rachel.

"I hope you have a nice weekend. You *and* Don."

Rachel heard sincerity in his voice. "Thanks. I'm sure we will. And you have fun with the kids. I know they're happy to spend time with you."

Steve walked out and shut the door. Rachel enjoyed the immediate silence and felt the calm descending over her. It was good. It was as though she had shut the door on the past. At least for the moment, the grudges against Steve were gone, and the

296

future looked wide open to her. A barrier was broken down now that Steve had forced her emotions to gush forth. It had been as though a soda bottle, with its cap on, had always been shaken. A lot at first especially after learning about her ex's affair. Then, she would always try to find a sense of calm, mostly for their children's sake. The bottle continued to shake throughout the years. But tonight, the cap popped off, and the emotions bubbled, pouring out until the angry fizz had stopped.

Rachel took her time getting herself together for her date with Don. As she looked at herself in her bathroom mirror, she shook her head in amazement. She never would have guessed that she'd be at this moment now or ever. She had taken her marriage seriously and was crushed when it fell apart behind her back. After moving away from the rubble as quickly as she could, she had vowed to be a good mother and to make the day to day life as pleasant and stress free as possible for the children and for herself. Rachel had no desire for a relationship and was content just having her routine.

So, now she found this all amusing. Don had ever so gently worked at taking down the emotional defensive walls. He had chipped away at the barriers, not just for Rachel but for himself. She had actually met a man who had a perfect understanding of the wounds that she suffered, and he was happy to be with her. She knew now that Don was a good man, and she would not be hurt.

Rachel finished applying her muted shade of red lipstick, and then she dabbed a little perfume on her wrists and put a brush through her hair. She felt good about herself. Her gut was telling her that things were going well. It was a feeling she hadn't experienced in a very long time.

The doorbell rang, ripping her away from her revelry. It was too early for the visitor to be Don. Maybe the kids had forgotten some things, and Steve was bringing the children back to get the items. The doorbell rang again, three times in a row, sounding fierce and demanding that the door be opened instantly. Rachel went quickly down the stairs and opened the front door, annoyed by the insistence of attention by the person waiting for her acknowledgement. Linda was standing there, looking drawn and upset, eyes bloodshot from a recent crying jag. She looked utterly helpless, but Rachel didn't feel like dealing with her. Not now, not ever. Rachel's disdained expression gave her away immediately.

Linda's eyes blazed in frustration. She put her hands on her hips in defiance. "I know! You're not thrilled that I've shown up on your doorstep." She looked Rachel up and down, giving her a surprised look. "You're going out somewhere? Lucky you to be having so much fun. I guess your ex jerk took the brats for the weekend."

Rachel had gone from feeling intruded upon to very angry in ten seconds. "And so nice to see you too." Rachel paused, trying to figure out what brought this witch to her doorstep. "What can you possibly want from *me?*" Rachel stood solidly at the door, refusing to succumb to her normally hospitable nature of inviting people into her home. Linda was not welcome.

Linda's shoulders slouched as though Rachel's chilly reception had stripped her off all of her strength. "I know you talked with my sister. She called Steve to ask where I was living. I guess she feels sorry for me and wants to help."

Rachel still wasn't sure why the chat with her sister had brought Linda to her house. "And?"

Linda sighed loudly because she felt irritation at having to further explain things. "I thought you might want to talk with me too." Linda noticed Rachel's eyes widen in shock. "So, you're not going to invite me in to discuss my problems?"

Rachel could not believe what she was hearing. *The nerve of this woman!* She motioned with her hand to the interior of her house, but didn't move an inch. "Does this look like a therapist's office to you?"

Linda looked away, trying to collect her thoughts for an appropriate response. Then she looked at Rachel again, half way pleading and half way demanding something more. Through gritted teeth she spoke. "Listen. I thought we were doing okay when we saw each other at the store the one day. You were actually nice to me. Remember? You seemed to want to understand my predicament."

Rachel thought that predicament seemed like an awfully big word for this ding bat of a woman. "Linda, I don't want to talk with you anymore. I have a life to live, and your sister seems concerned. Talk to her. Talk to someone whose life you haven't turned upside down."

Rachel turned around ready to leave Linda at the door, but

Linda wasn't done cajoling for help yet. She spoke quickly. "You thought Steve would forgive me. You believed he might show some understanding. Well, he hasn't so far. He won't even talk to me." Linda's voice shook giving indications that another crying jag was about to commence. Rachel rolled her eyes, and turned around to face Linda. It was time to end this battle.

"Linda, I don't know Steve anymore. Yes, he's the father of my wonderful children. *Brats* as you call them." Linda looked down, knowing that she shouldn't have called them that if she was going to elicit any kindness from Rachel. "However, I don't know what goes on in his mind. You're both selfish, and it seems you're the one who's going to pay the price for both of your faults. That's not my problem. I have talked with Steve, very briefly. I told him to try to be kind to you. But Steve is his own person. No one is going to get through to him. Really, I'm the LAST person you should be discussing this with. *A*, because I can't help you, and *B*, because I don't give a damn what you do." Rachel turned, and walked back inside, gently closing the door in Linda's face. She locked the door, and went into the family room to watch television until Don arrived.

At eight o'clock, the doorbell rang. This time, Rachel was more than happy to dash to the front door and see the welcome caller. She opened the door. Don was very casually leaning again the frame, holding a lovely floral bouquet. His smile was intoxicating.

"Hello. How are you?" Don kissed Rachel, and handed the flowers to her. She happily led him into the house.

"I am fine! Thank you so much for these gorgeous flowers!" She put her nose into the arrangement, sniffing in the sweet aroma. The flowers looked as though they had been plucked directly from a Monet painting.

"You are more than welcome. I couldn't resist getting lovely flowers for a lovely lady."

Rachel felt as though she was on top of the world. Don's sincerity was always evident. He spoke with honesty and his actions were always full of integrity.

"I can't believe how lucky I am to have you in my life." Rachel wanted to express how much she felt for him. She kissed him again, and then proceeded to put the bouquet in a beautiful vase.

"I'm more than happy to be in your life. So, anything fun going on with you?"

"Not really anything fun per se. I just had an interesting encounter with Linda." Rachel face grimaced.

"With Linda? Why?"

"Good question. Why *would* Linda bother me? I guess because she thinks she can. However, I did put a stop to it. She came over here after Steve left with the kids. Said she knew that I had spoken to her sister because her sister contacted her. Linda actually thought I could still help her get through to Steve. Like I want to get involved at all!"

"So, you're done with her."

"Yes, I am. I didn't even let her in the house. I told her good riddance, closed the door in her face and locked it." Rachel pretended to slap the dirt of Linda off of her hands.

Don laughed. "You are good! I'm impressed. You're letting people know what's what now, aren't you." It wasn't a question. Don was clearly amazed by Rachel's determination to be happy and not to be manipulated.

"I guess it's about time." Rachel looked at Don with a huge smile. "So, the weekend is ours. Nice, huh?"

Don came closer to Rachel and put his arms around her. "Yes, it is VERY nice!" He gave her a lingering kiss. Rachel felt so happy that she could have stayed like this forever. After a moment, they came up for air.

"I think the weekend is going to be an enjoyable one." Don grinned like a school boy.

"I must say that I've been in the mood for..." Rachel looked mischievously at Don, and he looked expectantly back at her.

"Chocolate! Delicious, decadent chocolate!"

"Well, okay then. Milady, your wish is my command, and you shall have chocolate!"

They left Rachel's house and headed to the French restaurant where Rachel had taken her mother. The place was known for its homemade desserts. They shared chocolate mousse and chocolate éclairs, along with coffee and great conversation. Rachel wanted to pinch herself because she couldn't believe that life was going so well. She was free to have fun.

After indulging themselves in the luxury of sweets and good conversation, she and Don went back to her house. They sat on the couch enjoying the time spent together. Don had his arm around Rachel's shoulder

Don looked happily at Rachel. "I am having the time of my life with you."

"I know what you mean. I'm enjoying every moment with you. I guess we should be thanking our parents for getting us together. If it wasn't for them being at the retirement home, this would never have happened."

Don shook his head in wonderment. "Weird, huh? Meeting at an old folk's home. However, in this case, weird is good." Don paused for a moment to collect his thoughts. "I know that you're going to California soon. I can tell you that I'm really going to miss you. *Really* going to miss you." Don wanted to make sure that Rachel knew how much her absence would affect him as he stroked her hair gently.

Rachel's head leaned against Don's shoulder. "I'm going to miss you too." She looked up again, meeting his dark eyes. "But, I won't be gone long. Not that I don't want to see my sister and her family. I truly do. But at least I have something to look forward to when I return. Some ONE to look forward to being with. I've never been able to say that before."

Don smiled, showing his perfect pearly whites. "I have a feeling that I'll be counting the days." He almost seemed embarrassed. "I know. That sounds so sappy. But it's how I feel."

"I like sappy."

They both laughed. Then, Don became a bit more serious. "Rachel, is that what it felt like when you were with your ex. I mean when you were dating or when you were married?"

Rachel gave him a curious look. "Well, maybe. Kind of. I'm not sure what you're getting at."

Don looked away, trying to form his thoughts. "As you know, I was close to getting married. I believe I loved her. I just feel something different with you. It feels...I don't know...really special. I can't even verbalize it." He looked back at her with a concerned expression.

Rachel appreciated his candor. "I do understand, and I think you're stating it very well. However, I think you're wondering that, if I felt this with Steve, can it be okay? Is that right?" She wanted to make sure she was getting his correct thought process.

"I think so. Let's face it. I know that we're not teenagers or young twenties either."

Rachel gave a disgusted look. "Or thirties or…I'll stop there!" She shuttered at the thought.

Don smiled. "Sorry. I didn't mean to be such a downer."

Rachel's expression indicated that all was well. "I know. I was just going down the long memory lane. I'll need directions before too long."

Don enjoyed her sense of humor. "Okay. So what I'm trying to say is that we have maturity and some wisdom on our sides. That's got to help us, right? And we've both been cautious. You definitely weren't running towards anything serious with me, and I admit I've always been hesitant about having a committed relationship. However, that's all changed. At least for me. And I think for you as well." He looked at her for reassurance.

Rachel instantly nodded her agreement. Don appreciated her quick positive response, and he kissed her.

"So. Where does that leave us?

Rachel was confused again. "What do you mean?"

"I mean, are we a serious couple? Where do we want this to go?"

Rachel squirmed a bit on the couch. She edged forward, and then settled in again leaning back as comfortable as possible. "Hmm. I don't know. Tell me what you're thinking." Rachel honestly didn't know how to answer him. On the one hand, she was getting a little nervous at the direction of the conversation. On the other hand, she was pleased that Don wanted to express his feelings and actually discuss their future.

"Okay." Don seemed to be wading into untested waters. But he forced himself to stay afloat. "I'm thinking that I may want to be in this for the long haul. I only want to be with you, and I hope you only want to be with me. I'll admit that I've considered what a lifetime with you would be like. And the thought makes me very happy." He looked at her, hesitantly, praying that Rachel wouldn't want to flee for the hills.

Rachel considered what Don said. Her mouth suddenly felt a bit dry, but she ignored the fear. She licked her lips and swallowed, trying not to give away the sudden tremors that she was feeling inside. "Don, that's very nice. I mean, I am blown away by your feelings. And, I can tell you that I only want to see you as well.

Heck, you're the first and only man I've dated since my divorce, so that would be even since I started seeing Steve back in college. Clearly, it's been a while for me." Rachel paused before stating another all-important thought. "Now, I do want to remind you that I have three children. Teens and pre-teen. I'm not sure how you feel about that."

Don shrugged, seemingly unconcerned by the prospect of dealing with the kids. "That doesn't bother me. They're fine. I'm sure it's not easy dealing with them all the time, but maybe the two of us could spend time together with them."

Rachel thought that sounded like an interesting idea. *Maybe it was time for the kids to really get to know Don. Hiding them from him and hiding him from them didn't make sense. Don and her kids were a big part of her life. The biggest parts of her life.* "Okay. I can arrange that. Maybe after we all get back from California. Does that sound like a good plan?"

"Sure. That sounds perfect. So, you don't mind looking into the future with me? It's not too alarming, is it?"

Rachel leaned her head against Don's shoulder, indicating that all was well.

Then they both looked at each other. They kissed each other softly at first. Then their passion began to build. They rose from the couch and, hand in hand, they climbed the stairs to Rachel's bedroom.

Chapter Twenty-Six

The next morning, Don and Rachel lingered in bed for a while. They had shared a blissful night together, and Rachel contentedly stretched her arms over her head, so happy to be waking up next to Don. They enjoyed a leisurely breakfast together, and then he decided he should return to his condo. They kissed goodbye, Rachel showered and then called Leah. She felt so happy and wanted to talk about her feelings with her sister.

"Hello?" Bob, Leah's husband answered the phone.

"Bob! It's Rachel. How are you?" She hadn't spoken with him for a while, and it was good to hear his voice.

"Hey, Rachel! I'm great! How's by you?"

"Life is good. Even better knowing that I'll be visiting all of you soon."

"We're all looking forward to seeing you and the kids. We'll be sure to make it a nice time for you."

"No worries there. Just hanging out with your family is all that we want."

Bob laughed. "Oh, we're quite the bunch. You might need a vacation after being here."

"I don't think so. It's been too long since we've seen all of you. It was nice having Leah here, even if it was too short a visit. I really appreciate that you didn't mind her coming here."

"Of course I don't mind. You two are close, and I think that's wonderful. Besides, the kids and I do fine together. We missed her, but it was good for her to see you too."

"Thanks." Rachel always appreciated Bob's warmth and kindness. *Yes, indeed, her sister had chosen the right spouse.*

"So, I assume you want to talk with your sister?"

"Yes, that would be great. Nice talking with you, though."

"We'll talk more soon, Sis. Have fun."

Rachel loved that Bob called her "Sis." Just as Leah always did. It made her feel like she was a part of their family. She and Leah were tightly knit, but having a "brother" felt pretty special too.

"Hi! How's life treating you?" Leah sounded a little breathless.

"I'm doing very well. Are you okay? You sound like you've been running."

"I have. Just doing stuff with the kids, or should I say *for* the kids. They take a lot out of me, but clearly it's a good cardio workout."

Rachel chuckled. "I know what you mean. I want to tell you that I'm your very happy sister these days."

"Oh, really? Pray tell?" Leah sounded very intrigued.

"I'm having a really great time with a certain man." Rachel's voice inflected coyness.

"That's very nice! Tell me more!" Leah was practically salivating over the phone.

"Suffice it to say that we are very happy together. I'll keep the rest of the information to myself, but you can assume that things have been progressing nicely." Rachel smiled, even though Leah couldn't see her.

Leah happily understood what her sister had conveyed. "It's nice to hear you sounding so content. I can tell that any doubts you've had are ebbing away. Am I right?" Leah hoped her sister was feeling more confident about being in a relationship now.

Rachel responded with a calmest of tones. "I guess. I had always felt comfortable having my guard up, but I feel even better having torn the wall down. I trust him, Leah. I really do."

"Rachel, Um…well… are you kind of falling for him? I mean, deeply?" Leah wanted to exercise caution in asking her sister how much she really felt.

Rachel cradled the phone comfortably against her ear. She was relaxing on her bed, just thinking. She let out a big sigh. "I don't know. Maybe?" Rachel closed her eyes, still pondering her feelings and remembering the previous night. "He is amazing. It's so easy to be with him, and I can't wait to see him, to talk with him. I just don't know."

"I think you do know. Has he expressed his feelings to you?" Leah held her breath, hoping that Don was thinking the same way as Rachel. There was no room for doubt here. Rachel's heart had opened wide, and any wrong move could cause it to shut down permanently.

Rachel spoke softly. "Yes, he has, which is refreshing. He's always saying nice things to me, and he's very open about everything."

Leah exhaled quietly. "That is good. Very good. You know, I have to wonder if it might be very good timing for you to be coming out here soon. Maybe some distance will make all of this much clearer."

Rachel couldn't contain a burst of laughter. "That is really something. Everyone, well, you and Mom, couldn't help but encourage me to get involved with Don. Now, absence from him would be good. Make up your mind."

"Ha, ha. You know what I mean. Of course I want you to be with him seeing as how he makes you so happy. I just think time away might answer questions. For both of you."

"I you say so. Believe me. I am definitely not rushing into anything. We love each other, but I'm not pining away to be married again. It's not some desperate need, so no worries there."

"That's fine, but…." There was a pause. "Yes? Can't you see that I'm on the phone?" Leah had obviously been distracted by one of the children. "Sorry about that. Aaron doesn't seem to want to give me any privacy at the moment."

"No problem. You probably should tend to him. I just wanted to share my joy with you."

"And I'm very glad you did! I want to know everything. I feel like I have a billion other things I want to talk with you about, but I guess I'll put them on hold for now. Duty calls!"

"Understood. At least I'll be seeing you very soon. I can't believe how quickly time is passing."

"I can't either. By the way, how's Mom?"

"She's doing well. I think as long as Don and I are together, she'll be one happy lady."

"Hmm. Well, maybe she'll always be happy then?"

"Okay, enough. I better let you go. I'm not ready to walk down the aisle right now. However, I am going out with him tonight. Dinner and a show. Who knows what else?"

"Sounds like fun! Enjoy every moment!"

"I will. Have a good weekend!"

"You too. Talk to you soon."

Rachel clicked off the phone, put it back in the unit, and slumped down in her bed. She wanted to think about everything that was happening with Don. She remembered the emotions of her youth when she thought about dating. It was kind of fun being able to relive those enjoyable moments of being in love. However, having an adult perspective made the idea seem even better. If nothing else, the divorce from Steve gave her that. She could experience the wonder all over again. She felt as though she was at the right place at the right time. Even if Rachel had met Don at some earlier point, she doubted she would have been ready to accept him in her life. She was barely at that point when she was introduced to him. However, it seemed as if both she and Don were now open to exploring the possibilities. They were even going at the same pace, so everything was flowing naturally. There was no pressure, no uncertainty. Rachel closed her eyes, savoring the joy that she felt.

Rachel had dozed off into a nap when the phone rang. She was a bit out of it when she answered the phone.

Hello?"

"Rachel?"

She sat up abruptly hearing Don's frantic voice. "Don? What is it?" Her heart was racing.

"Sorry, I didn't mean to scare you. I received a call that my dad wasn't feeling quite right. They've taken him to the hospital. I'm not sure what's going on, but I'm going over there right now. I…I just thought I should let you know. I'm not sure what's happening and if we'll even be able to go out tonight. I just don't know."

Rachel was very glad that Don had called. She didn't care about their plans. She only wanted Ben to be okay. "Don, I'll meet you at the hospital. Try not to worry"

Don let out a huge sigh. "Thanks Rachel. I can't tell you how much I appreciate this."

"Don't even think about it. We'll find out what's happening. I'll see you soon."

They said their goodbyes, and Rachel jumped out of bed, brushed her teeth and hair, dressed as quickly as possible and ran downstairs to go to the garage. She was feeling a bit panicky. Rachel prayed that Ben would be okay. She knew exactly how Don was feeling. She's been down this road before, and it never felt good. Of course the last time this happened was when she and Don were having dinner and Delores had been taken to the hospital. She hoped that Ben's problem wouldn't be more serious than what had transpired that time.

Rachel concentrated on driving, and she arrived at the hospital. She walked quickly into the building and headed straight for the ER, assuming that's where she'd find Don. That area of the hospital was a bit too familiar to Rachel. Both parents had spent time there, and her father had been brought there when he had his fatal heart attack. No good memories came from an ER, but she braced herself as she approached the stark room.

Rachel saw Don standing at the reception area. A woman, perhaps in her early thirties, was talking with him. Dressed in hospital issued burgundy slacks and a matching V-neck top, she exuded a professional air. The two appeared calm, so Rachel was hopeful that Ben wasn't in danger. She came up behind Don. He sensed someone there, and turned to see Rachel.

He smiled gently at her, but there was a wariness in his eyes that was unmistakable. Rachel tensed, waiting to know what this all meant. She hugged him gently and then smiled politely at the woman.

"Rachel, this is dad's ER nurse, Jessica. Jessica, this is my girlfriend Rachel."

Rachel loved hearing herself described as his girlfriend. She was still getting used to that description. However, now was not the time to be analyzing her relationship title.

Jessica smiled at Rachel. "Hi, Rachel. It's nice to meet you." Rachel responded in kind.

"So, what's the situation with Ben?" Rachel almost felt afraid to know, but reality called for hearing the facts. She was praying that Jessica had good answers.

"Well, as I was telling Mr. Levy…"

Don interrupted her. "Please, call me Don."

"Thank you. His father is okay. It seems he suffered a very mild stroke. Not all that serious." She turned to Don, focusing on telling him everything because this was about his father. "That's why the home wasn't sure what was going on. They said that something didn't seem right. His words were slightly slurred, but he didn't appear to be ill exactly. They acted correctly in having him come here immediately."

Don looked somewhat confused. "So, is he able to speak?"

"Oh, yes. As a matter-of-fact, right now, you wouldn't even know he had a problem. His actions are perfectly normal. Hence, a mild stroke as opposed to anything severe."

"Where do we go from here?" Don still sounded concerned.

"We want to monitor him overnight. He'll need to be on some medication, and we'll discuss a health regimen with his doctor. But really, there's no cause for alarm. It is good that he came here because it's hard to know anything unless a person has been tested. He might have been able to recover without anyone even knowing this had happened. Sometimes mild strokes go unnoticed."

Both Rachel and Don were visibly relieved and were able relax upon hearing the diagnosis.

"Is it okay if I see my dad?"

"Of course. He's alert."

"Is Rachel allowed to come with me?"

"Sure., that's not a problem." Jessica smiled at them, sensing that their relationship was more than a casual one.

She led them out of the reception area and into a room with beds. Light blue curtains were partially surrounding most of the beds, and then they found Ben. He was lying there, relaxing with his eyes closed.

Jessica quietly approached him. "Mr. Levy? You have visitors."

Ben lazily opened his eyes. Upon seeing Don and Rachel, he became fully awake and smiled. "Hi, you two. It's wonderful to see you." His always present smile exploded on his face.

Don came over to the side of the bed. "It's good to see YOU. How are you feeling?"

"I'm fine. Don't worry about me. No fussing. Okay?"

Don laughed lightly. "Okay, no fussing. We were worried, but we understand that you're going to be perfectly okay."

"Of course I am. I didn't mean to scare you." He turned his head to look at Rachel. "How are you doing?"

"I'm fine now that I know you're okay."

Ben chuckled. "You're a sweet girl. Just like your mother." Ben became serious. "Rachel, be sure to let your mother know that I am okay. Word gets around quickly at the home, and I don't want her fretting over this."

"I will let her know immediately. Just take care of yourself. By the way, I think it would be nice if the four of us could all get together soon. How does that sound to you?"

Ben and Don had huge smiles.

"That sounds wonderful! Something for me to look forward to."

Jessica chimed in. "I think it's time to let Mr. Levy rest." She looked at Don. "There's really nothing you need to do right now."

Don debated asking her a question. She could sense that he wanted to say something.

"Don, is there something else?"

Don came closer to Jessica and whispered, not wanting his father to hear anything. Rachel and I were planning on going out this evening. Dinner and a show. Do you think it would be okay if we do that or should I cancel the plans? I can be here if it's necessary."

Jessica looked amused. "It's fine for you to go out and have a nice evening. Your father is in good hands, and he'll probably be going back home sometime tomorrow. Truly, there's nothing for you to worry about. Just enjoy yourselves." She looked at Rachel and smiled.

"Okay. Thanks. I will have my cell phone with me, and I'll check it as often as I can. So if there's anything that happens or you need me, just call."

"That's fine. We'll take your number, and we'll call you if it's necessary. But I really don't think it will be necessary. So, have fun." Jessica was practically prodding Don to go out on the date.

Don and Rachel laughed at her insistence that they enjoy their evening. He gave Jessica his cell phone number, they said goodbye to Ben, and left the ER.

As Don and Rachel walked outside, they agreed that the weather was picture perfect. They were both glad to be able to take a moment to appreciate the mild temperature, light wind and blue sky. Both of them had dashed into the building so quickly on the way in that they hadn't noticed or thought about anything other than finding out if Ben was okay. Don walked Rachel to her car. She pulled her car keys out of her purse and then Rachel paused before opening the car door.

"Don, I am beyond relieved that Ben is going to be okay. I admit that I was scared."

"Same here. Rachel I can't thank you enough for wanting to be here. You were under no obligation to come. It means a lot to me." Don's eyes were darkly serious.

"I'm glad you called me. No need to thank me for anything. I care so much about both of you, and it was good for me to be able to support you and know what was happening. I love you and I

310

want everything to be okay."

Don looked at her, almost not believing what he had heard her say. However, Rachel had made her last statement so casually and easily that she didn't even realize the word she had uttered. It simply slipped out as though she had been saying it all along. Rachel noticed his intense gaze, and was somewhat confused.

"Is everything okay? Did Jessica tell you something else before I came in?" Rachel was concerned that Ben was in more serious condition than they had let on.

"No, everything is fine. Really great." Don stopped talking for a moment. He smiled slyly at Rachel. "You don't even know what you just said, do you?"

"Huh? What do you mean? What did I say?" Rachel covered her mouth with her hand thinking she had said the wrong thing somehow, but Don's pleased expression told her that she had not made a faux pas.

"So, you really don't know what you said?" He had a mischievous grin on his face.

Rachel still had her hand on her mouth, trying to figure out what she could possibly have told him. Then she removed her hand to speak. "Honestly, I don't know. But from the look on your face, it must have been shocking. Or amusing. Maybe both?"

"Well, let me tell you what you said. Will that work?"

Don was having fun toying with her, but she really wanted to know what unbelievable statement came out of her mouth. She nodded, hoping that she wouldn't be embarrassed by whatever it was.

Don looked up as though trying to formulate his thoughts. He was going to draw this out, even though she was going crazy.

"Okay, just tell me. Please."

"Weelll. You said…hmm. What was it now?" Don scratched his head as though trying to remember.

"You're very funny. Now TELL me!"

"Okay, okay. Now, you're not going to believe this. I mean, I'm amazed. Thrilled, but just so surprised. Who knew?"

Rachel was giving him the evil eye.

"Whoa! Okay. Here goes. You said, and I quote. 'I love you.'" Don looked at her with a very satisfied expression.

Rachel's mouth dropped open. Her face immediately turned red. Her heart started to pound, and for one moment, she was

311

grateful that the hospital emergency room was within walking distance. Rachel was speechless. *What made her say that, especially without even realizing it?* She was mortified.

"You okay?" Don knew that he had startled her.

"Uh...yeah...I guess. Kind of funny, isn't it? I mean, not funny, but...wow."

"Yeah. Wow. A good wow, I hope?" He gave her a questioning look.

"Sure. What do you think? Did I freak you out?" Rachel sincerely prayed that she didn't frighten him. She still couldn't get over the fact that she had said she loved him.

Don didn't look rattled at all. "No, you didn't freak me out. It was nice to hear you say that."

"It was? Really?" Rachel was stunned.

"Yes." Don's demeanor suddenly changed. He looked away for a moment. "Unless you didn't really mean what you said." He looked back at her, questioning her innermost thoughts. A lot was riding on what Rachel said next.

Rachel looked away, but she smiled sincerely. After shocking herself, she had to be honest and admit her true feelings. She gazed directly into his eyes.

"I always mean what I say. Maybe I didn't want to admit to you or to myself that I *have* strong feelings, but my subconscious won't let me get away with being coy." She spread out her arms as if to surrender. "So, there you have it. I bared my soul to you. HOWEVER, we can leave it at that. Nothing more needs to be said right now. Especially here." Rachel pointed to the fact that they were standing in a hospital parking lot.

Don put his hands in his jeans pockets. "I'm not sure I want to drop this topic, even if we are standing here. Maybe, for now, I should just say that I feel the same way. About you. You've made it impossible for me not to love you, Rachel Blum."

Out of the corner of their eyes, they noticed people nearby. When they turned to see who was there, they spotted a younger woman walking with an older woman who was using a cane. The duo smiled at Don and Rachel having heard every word that was spoken. After realizing they had been caught spying, the ladies turned away and pretended that they hadn't been eavesdropping.

Rachel and Don gave embarrassed grins, realizing that any parking lot probably wasn't the best place to declare undying love.

"So, should we continue this conversation elsewhere?" Don seemed intent on delving into the depths of their feelings a bit longer.

"Is that what you want to do? Is there more to be said? I mean, right now?" Rachel wasn't sure she had it in her to have this discussion. Mostly because she didn't know how to feel at the moment.

"Well, if you'd rather continue this later, I'm fine with that. There's no hurry."

Rachel tried to sound light-hearted about the matter. "Later then. That's great. We have plenty of time this weekend."

"Okay." Don looked at his watch. "So, I'll see you at 5:15, right?"

"Definitely."

Don leaned in to kiss Rachel goodbye. She could tell by the pressure of his kiss how much her declaration of love meant to him. Maybe it was her word of love along with the fact that she made it clear about her desire to be with him at the hospital. Whatever it was, she had no complaints about the sweet intimacy.

Rachel unlocked her car door, and Don held it open for her as she got into her seat. He closed it after she buckled herself in, and they waved goodbye to each other. She was glad that it wouldn't be long before she saw him that evening.

When Rachel arrived home, she wanted to talk with Leah, but she knew she needed to call her mother about Ben. She threw down her purse, and reached for the phone.

Delores answered immediately. She sounded upset. "Hello?"

"Mom. Hi, it's Rachel."

"Oh, Rachel!" Her mother sounded on the verge of tears.

"Mom, I hope you're okay. I want to let you know about Ben."

"I'm okay, but I'm so upset about him being taken to the hospital." She paused for a second. "Wait a minute. What do you know about him?"

"Don called me, and told me that Ben had been brought to the hospital. I went over there, and I can tell you that he's going to be fine. He specifically wanted me to tell you not to worry about him. He actually said 'fret.' I thought that was cute."

"Yes, that is cute. So what was wrong with him?"

"A very mild stroke. VERY mild. Nothing to be concerned about. He'll be there overnight, but then he'll come back

313

tomorrow. He was his usual wonderful self."

Delores breathed a sigh of relief. "Thank Goodness! I heard some residents saying that Ben had been taken to the hospital, but no one would tell us what had happened. Privacy laws and all that. I'm telling you we've lost the human touch. But I guess that's not the important issue right now. I'm just so happy that he's going to be okay."

Rachel was touched by her mother's concern. She was so fond of Ben, and she needed his company. Rachel was glad that she could put her mother's mind at ease. "We're all happy about that. So, you're doing okay?"

"I am now. Rachel, thank you so much for letting me know. I appreciate your concerns for me."

"Of course I'm concerned about you. But, it's clear that Ben cares about you."

"He's a good man. Just like his son. How is Don, by the way?"

"He's fine. We're going out tonight."

"Very nice. What are you doing? If you don't mind me asking."

Rachel knew that it wouldn't matter if she did mind, but she was happy to tell her mother the details. "We're going to have dinner and see a show."

"That sounds delightful. So wonderfully civilized."

Rachel laughed. "What does THAT mean?"

"Nothing. I just think it's nice that you're having a dinner and going to the theatre. That is what you mean when you said you're seeing a show? You're going to a play, right? Not a movie."

"Yes, that's what I mean, although we do like movies as well. Nothing wrong with that, right?"

"Of course there's nothing wrong with that. I remember the days when your father and I would go to a nice dinner and see a play. Everyone was dressed to the nines, and it made for a wonderful evening."

"I can imagine. I'm happy you have those memories. By the way, I did tell Ben that I'd love it if the four of us got together sometime. I could have lunch or dinner at my house. Would you like that?"

"Very much! What a nice plan that is! We'll all have a fun time."

"I'll be in touch with you soon. I just wanted to let you know about Ben."

"Thank you, dear. Tell Don I say hello, and you two have a nice time."

"Okay, thanks Mom."

They said goodbye, and Rachel was itching to call Leah. She'd wonder what was happening if her sister was calling again, but Rachel had to tell her everything. She immediately clicked the phone number.

"Hello?" Aaron answered the phone. Just like David, she loved his adorable voice.

"Hi, Aaron. It's Aunt Rachel. How are you?"

"I'm fine. How are you Aunt Rachel?"

"I'm doing well, thank you. What are you doing?"

"Talking to you." Aaron laughed at his own humor. "Actually, I'm ready to go to my friend's house."

"That sounds like fun."

"Yep. He's my best friend."

"That's very nice. The kids and I will be seeing you soon. We're looking forward to spending time with you."

"Yeah. We're all excited about that. It's going to be fun!"

Rachel was pleased to hear the joy in his voice. "Yes, it definitely will be. Is your mom there?"

"Yeah. She'll be taking me to Tommy's house soon. So don't talk too long. Okay?"

Rachel thought that was very funny, but she tried not to laugh. "Okay. I promise I won't keep your mom too long."

"Great. I'll go get her."

"Thanks. See you soon!"

Rachel heard his loud young boy's voice. Mom! Aunt Rachel's on the phone."

Leah answered immediately. "Hello! Two calls so close together. Everything okay?" She sounded slightly alarmed.

"Oh, everything is fine. I think."

"That sounds loaded."

"Well, let me fill you in."

Rachel proceeded to tell Leah about Ben and the talk at the hospital parking lot. After giving her monologue, Rachel paused to hear her sister's thoughts.

"I don't see any problem here. I think it was wonderful that Don chose to call you about his dad. It seems clear that he feels close enough to bring you into his life at every turn. Nothing wrong with that at all. I also think you have to realize you have fallen for him. Once again, nothing wrong with that. And it appears that Don doesn't have any issue with your declaration of love. I think this is all quite nice. Don't you?"

"I guess." Rachel sounded tentative.

"What does that mean? Why the uncertain feelings?" Leah hated hearing the doubt in Rachel's voice.

"I'm just so afraid to become part of a serious relationship. Then again, I have no interest in seeing anyone else. I do care about Don, I enjoy his company, and he's a wonderful man."

"So, where does that leave you? I mean, do you or do you not want to be in a committed relationship?"

"Hmm." Rachel paused for a moment to think. "Yes and no."

Leah laughed. "Okay, my sister wants it both ways. That could be challenging."

"All I'm saying is that I'm not really ready for marriage."

"Oh, well, if that's all you mean, then it's fine."

"How is that fine?"

"Because there's a difference between being with Don in a good, serious relationship and being married to him. It's not as though you have to leap towards a lifetime commitment. Not right now. What does he think?"

"I don't completely know what he thinks. We didn't talk long, although we agreed to continue our discussion later. I suppose I shouldn't assume that he wants to be married right now either."

"I agree. He may just be pleased to know how much you care about him. And that you do love him. That's a first step, not necessarily a final step. Cut yourself some slack and don't worry about this so much. Okay?"

"You're right, you're right. I need to chill out here. I just can't believe I blurted that out. In a hospital parking lot, no less. I hope California clears my head."

"Sis, you're doing fine. You need to stop being so hard on yourself. Declarations of love are not crimes. He didn't blanch and run away screaming."

Rachel laughed loudly at her sister's comment. "True. He seems quite happy with what I said. He wanted to talk more, but I wasn't ready."

"You have all weekend and then some. Just keep having fun."

"I will. And I thank you for your sisterly wisdom. Okay, you'd

316

better get going and take Aaron to Tommy's house."

"You know about that?"

"Oh, yes. Your son is ready to go. It seems we all want to have a good time."

"I guess so. I'm glad you called. I hope everything goes well for you. I want you to be happy."

"Thanks, I know you do. I want that too. To be as happy as my sister."

"Just be happy. Don't ever compare your life to anyone else's. I know I'm lucky, but you have to find happiness on your own terms and in your own way."

"I know. It's just that finding happiness has been a bit of a task for me."

"It seems to me that you're working hard at it and accomplishing a lot. You're stronger and more capable than you realize."

"Let's hope. Thanks again for letting me bend your ear."

"I'm always here for you! Call me soon, okay?"

"Oh, you can be sure you'll know the details."

Rachel, as usual, felt better now that she had spoken with her beloved sister. Even though Leah was younger, she had always been wise beyond her years. She loved life and always knew what she wanted. She didn't compromise and try to make everyone else feel better at her own expense. Though compassionate in nature, she saw things without blinders. That's why she was always good at seeing the whole picture.

Rachel relaxed for the remainder of the day, and then by four, she started getting ready for her evening with Don. She was excited about seeing the play. She hadn't been to the theatre in a long time. Well, not with a man anyway. Grace and Rachel would sometimes enjoy a weekday matinee, but there wasn't a lot of time for that. Rachel put on a peach colored silk dress. She chose to wear an antique locket that belonged to her great-grandmother. The piece was gold and engraved with her great-grandmother's initials. She slid on a gold bangle, her gold watch, and put the finishing touches on her makeup.

As she was walking downstairs at precisely 5:15, the doorbell rang. Her pulse quickened in anticipation of the evening ahead. She opened the door, and Don was standing there, looking as handsome as ever. His broad smile always left her a bit weak, but seeing him in a navy blue suit and a striped multi colored

317

tie practically sent her over the edge. He was holding a box of chocolates. She stood aside for him to enter the house. Don handed her the box.

"For you. I thought that you deserved something sweet and decadent after everything that happened today." He leaned in to kiss her. He smelled so good too!

"Thank you very much! I will happily share these with you later."

Don looked her over. "You look lovely. As always."

"You're not too bad yourself. By the way, any news about your dad?"

"I called the hospital a couple of times today, the second time right before I left to come here. Jessica spoke with me, and she said that Dad is doing very well. He's had food, and he's in good spirits. She told me I can take him back to the home first thing tomorrow morning."

Rachel clapped her hands together in joy. "That is wonderful news! Would you like me to come with you to the hospital? I can help you get him if you'd like."

"You don't have to do that. It's so sweet of you to offer."

"I really don't mind. I could see my mom for a little while when we bring your dad back. Unless that's too much. I don't want you to have to tote me back and forth." Rachel was considering the logistics of everything.

"No, that would be fine. Oh, I can't believe I forgot this, but Abby, you know, the lady who works at the home, wants to meet with me about the activities. I mean, meet with the two of us. I guess with everything that happened with my dad, I completely let it slip my mind."

"Oh, yes. *I* remember *her*." She gave Don a sly look indicating that she remembered this woman very well. "I think we should meet with Abby."

"I'll try to track her down tomorrow. We can BOTH find her tomorrow."

"Are you sure she won't mind me being there?" Rachel was still skeptical about Abby and her decision to have Don involved with the activities.

Don looked at her as if was surprised that Rachel would be saying that. "Rachel, you know better. She's happy to have both of us on board."

"*Sure* she is. Well, we'll see, won't we? She won't have a choice. Besides, I'm very good at assisting. With anything she might need. Anything." Rachel was being silly, and Don laughed.

They left to enjoy their evening out. Don checked for any phone messages during parts of the evening, but there were none. Rachel and he were grateful that Ben was in the clear, and they'd see him the next morning. After the show, they returned to Rachel's home. The evening had been perfect. Just what they both needed. Rachel checked for messages. Unfortunately, there were two. Rebecca had called about fifteen minutes after Rachel and Don left for dinner.

"Mom! Hello! We haven't talked with you since we left the house. We thought you would call to check up on us. Dad seems depressed. I don't mean suicidal depressed, but he's not exactly fun to be around. We don't want to stay here. I mean, there's nothing for us to do." There was a pause and a loud sigh. "Well, I *guess* we could just stay here and watch television. I don't know. Call us!"

The second call, this time from Sarah, came at about eight o'clock.

"Mom! Where ARE you? Rebecca called quite a while ago. Well, whatever. You're obviously out having fun. I guess we'll just have to hang in there."

Rachel felt deflated. She realized that she had not told her children what she'd be doing, and she had forgotten to turn on her cell phone. It didn't even dawn on her to turn it on when Don checked his phone for messages. *Why on earth couldn't Steve be a parent?* She had trusted him to be responsible. Rachel felt very frustrated. Don came towards her, realizing that something was going on.

"Hey, are you okay?"

Rachel looked up at him, not quite sure what to tell him. "I honestly don't know how to answer that question. Two calls from the kids. They're not happy, and their father isn't helping. He is, and I'll quote Rebecca, depressed. I'm certainly not going to call over there now. I don't even think I would have wanted to call three hours ago. I just don't know what his problem is. I'm sick of it." Rachel cocked her head in uncertain amusement. "And you say you don't mind dealing with me and three kids. How sure are you about that now?"

319

Don sat down beside her without any hesitation. He put his arm lovingly around Rachel. She couldn't even look at him in spite of the tenderness he expressed. "You have to believe me, Rachel. I know what I'm doing. Heck, we were kids once ourselves. We both had problems when we were growing up. I understand that it's not always going to be a piece of cake." Then he put his hands on Rachel's face, forcing her to look at him. "But Rachel. you're worth it."

He kissed her tenderly. Rachel knew that he meant what he said. He always did, which was one reason why she felt she could trust him. He didn't seem to want to bolt. They sat back on the couch and were silent for a moment. Rachel collected her thoughts and then spoke.

"Don, you are amazing."

Don played with the top of his tie in jest. "Well, I know I'm a good kisser, but amazing? Thank you so much."

Rachel playfully lightly poked his shoulder. "That's true too, but that's not what I mean. I just can't get over how understanding you always are."

Don shrugged. "Listen, Rachel. Life is challenging. Anyone who thinks that it's supposed to be perfect all the time is deluding himself. So, being understanding shouldn't be difficult for anyone."

"I suppose. I would have just thought that you might have preferred a more normal relationship. You've never been married, and here you are, dealing with a middle-aged woman with three kids. You could have some beautiful, younger, free-wheeling woman. You'd be having the time of your life." Rachel tiredly put her hand through her hair.

"Rachel, I AM having the time of my life. I'm not like your ex-husband. I'm not interested in fluff. I want a real woman with a real life."

Rachel looked at him and smiled. "Okay, you really are too good to be true. I don't know how it is that you turned out to be such a gem of a man, but I'm certainly the lucky beneficiary of your good character."

Don smiled back at her. "So you finally believe that my intentions are honorable? You understand that I'm with you in spite of your misgivings about what you think I can handle?"

Rachel nodded. "I guess you've left me with no choice but

to believe you. And that's not easy for me to do considering my past. I know what you dealt with as a child, when your mom cheated. But I believe the perspective is different when the person is the one being cheated on." Rachel paused to try to formulate her explanation. She stood up and paced for a moment. Then she stopped, and sat back down next to Don.

"You see, I lost faith in myself. I felt that I couldn't trust myself. I mean, I didn't even know that Steve was betraying me. Can you believe that? Talk about being dense." She looked at Don with incredulity.

Don looked as though he was going to interrupt her, but he stopped himself. He was going to tell her that she was being unfair to herself, but he knew she needed to express her feelings, and he was glad to be the one with her, allowing her to let the emotions flow freely.

Rachel stood up again, needing to be in motion. "I know what you're thinking." She put a hand on her hip, and motioned with the other hand. "Rachel, it wasn't your fault that your husband was a jerk. How could you have known what was going on? You trusted him, as one should be able to trust a spouse." Rachel let her hands drop to her side, as if conceding to everything. "Well, you'd be right on all counts. The thing is that it doesn't matter. I wasn't cluing in on anything. My judgment in marrying a man like that wasn't on target. So, when one thinks that one isn't good at choosing the right man to marry, and she gets hurt because of her lack of clarity, that changes her outlook on her decision making capabilities. And, it leaves a huge raw scar on her heart." She paused again, and sat back down. But there was still more to be said, so she continued as Don looked at her with compassion.

"So then, I have no choice but to divorce him. I mean, I have my dignity after all. Or is it just that I can't stand the sight of him anymore? Hard to say because I also have three children whom I need to raise. That becomes an all-consuming activity. One that I, most of the time, have happily taken on as my responsibility. I have let them be my whole life partly because I have been too afraid to allow myself to open up to any other kind of existence."

Rachel looked at Don and gestured towards him. "Then there you are. This kind, fun, good-looking man. But I didn't think I could ever trust again, and I certainly didn't think you could possibly be interested in me. Yet…you seem to be."

Rachel became silent. For a moment, Don wasn't sure whether or not she was finished talking. He just looked at her, allowing her to say more if she chose. When the silence lingered, he spoke.

"I can promise you that I am. Interested. In you. No question about it. And, I do understand much better now how you and I would see the infidelities that we have experienced from different perspectives. I'm just sorry that you were so wounded."

"So am I. But I know the pain that you must have felt was probably similar. And trust becomes a big issue. Still, you have never really had a reason to doubt *yourself. You* didn't make the bad choices."

"We *all* make bad choices in our lifetimes, but I get what you're saying. Of course, I still don't really think that my dad or you made bad judgments. Your *spouses* did." Don's eyes pierced her own.

Rachel appreciated his astute remark. She knew that he was correct about the spouse aspect, so she nodded her head in agreement. Still, she felt that she had every reason to question herself. Maybe back then, but maybe not anymore. "You are so right about that, and I guess it's time I stop berating myself for my own character failings." She looked at Don, questioning if she should allow herself to do that now.

"We have to. Otherwise, how do we move on? It's not fair to punish yourself for the rest of your life for something that you didn't even do." Don leaned in closely to Rachel. "Let it go, Rachel. Give yourself the gift of living the way you want to live."

Rachel's eyes became moist. She was finally going to give herself permission to trust again. Without questioning every move.

"You're right. It's time for me to let go of the doubts and the fears." She sat up, determined to be strong. "I'm an adult, I can handle that." She laughed.

"I couldn't agree more. So, where do we go from here?"

"I don't know. Where do you want to go from here?" Rachel tried not to be nervous, but she still wasn't ready for any major commitment.

"Well, you already said that you love me." Don had a smile that was larger than life.

Rachel tried not to cringe when remembering her strange outburst. "I did indeed."

"And I love you too."

Rachel's eyes widened in surprise. "Really? You love me?" Then she turned skeptical. "Are you saying that because I already said it to you?" She eyed him with suspicion.

"Rachel! Of course not. I'm saying what's in my heart. You've got to believe me." Don almost seemed hurt that she would doubt him about his feelings.

"Okay, okay. I believe you. Please don't be upset."

"I'm not upset. It's just that I never want you to think I would say something that I didn't feel. I'm not like that, although I think you already know that." He was looking at her, wanting reassurance.

"You're right. I DO know that. And I'm glad." Rachel patted his arm to comfort any wounded feelings.

"Good. So…?"

"I think we have some steps to go through before making any radical decisions."

"I'm listening."

"The kids and I will be leaving soon to visit my sister and her family. You know that. Then, as you and I agreed would be a good idea, we'll spend some time with my kids. Then we'll take it from there. How does that sound?" Rachel grinned, looking hopeful.

Don looked away for a moment to think about what Rachel had said. He nodded. "I can live with that." Then Don became very serious. "But Rachel, there's something you need to understand."

Rachel's heart pounded from a fear of what he was about to tell her that she didn't already know.

"I want to make sure you realize that I want to spend my life with you. I don't have any misgivings. Time away from you while you're in California isn't going to change how I feel about you. Time spent with your children isn't going to make me want to walk away. So, we can run some tests to see how we're doing at points A, B and C, but it isn't going to matter. At least not to me. And I hope not to you either."

Rachel got the picture. She was pleased by what he said. Still, she had to be sure of everything. She wasn't in a hurry, although she had to admit that a lifetime with Don was more than appealing.

"I understand. I think we're on the same page. But still, let's give it a little while, and then we'll know what we know." That sounded vague to her ears, but Don's grin indicated that he was fine with what she said.

It was getting late, and they would be picking Ben up at the hospital in the morning. Rachel thanked Don for the wonderful evening. He responded with a passionate kiss and told her he'd get her at eight o'clock if that was okay with her. He wanted his dad back at the home as soon as possible. Rachel agreed and they said their goodbyes.

She closed and locked the front door. After getting a glass of water, she went upstairs, quickly changed into her nightgown, and then completed her bedtime routine. Coming back into the bedroom, she set her alarm clock for seven o'clock, although she knew she might be up even earlier than that because her body was accustomed to rising early. Rachel climbed into bed, and closed her eyes. Unlike some nights when problems weighed heavily on her mind, tonight she immediately drifted into a very peaceful sleep.

Chapter Twenty-Seven

As she predicted to herself the night before, Rachel woke up about a half an hour before her alarm went off. She was wide awake and ready to move into her day. She showered and had a quick breakfast. Rachel thought about calling the kids to let them know where she'd be going, but she knew that she would only wake them. Rachel suspected she would be dealing with three unhappy children later in the day. She really needed to talk with Steve before hearing what the kids had to say. Everyone's behavior needed to change, and it had to happen sooner rather than later.

At 7:57, the doorbell rang. Rachel went running for the door, already anxious to see her man. She opened it and there he was. No longer so formally dressed, he was wearing khakis and a thin striped beige and white dress shirt, which complemented Rachel's choice of brown slacks and a cream colored blouse. Even Don's casual ways always looked smart. He kissed her hello.

Rachel knew that he was in a hurry to see his dad. She quickly grabbed her tan leather purse. "We should get going now, right?"

"If you're ready, and you appear to be, I think that would be great."

They walked briskly to the car and took off for the hospital. They made small talk during the short drive. Don found a parking spot not too far away from the entrance, and they walked hurriedly into the building. Don had already been told where to find Ben, so he led the way to the area. He approached the nurse's station and told a nurse he was there to pick up his father.

A happy voice came from behind. "Well, of course you're here to get your father!"

Don and Rachel turned around to see Ben being wheeled towards them. The woman wheeling him, who must have been around fifty, had a big smile across her face. She was somewhat overweight and was dressed in the same hospital attire that Jessica from the ER wore the day before. This person was also wearing a simple gray sweater and had her hair up in a bun. She had black rimmed glasses and a name tag on her sweater that stated that she was Pauline.

"Dad! What timing! How'd you know we'd be here right at this moment?"

"I didn't, although they told me you'd be here first thing this morning. I've been ready to go for a while. Pauline has kindly been keeping me company while I've been waiting."

Pauline affectionately patted Ben's shoulder. "It's been my pleasure, Mr. Levy." She looked kindly at Don. "Your father is a delightful man, but I'm sure you've always known that."

"I have, thank you." Don appreciated her sweet manner.

Ben smiled at Rachel. "Hello to you too, Rachel. It's quite nice to see you here this morning. You did tell your mother about me?"

"I did, and she was very relieved to know that you're okay." Rachel beamed a bright smile.

Ben looked at Don and Rachel with a sly expression. "Interesting that you're BOTH here. And so early."

Don looked at Ben as if to lecture him. "Dad, Rachel said she wanted to come with me. Isn't that nice?"

"Oh, it is! Very nice! I have no problem with seeing her. I just think it's very early for her to have to be here."

"Nope, it's not. I'm happy to accompany Don. And I'm always glad to see you." Rachel was going to say that Don had picked her up this morning, but she didn't want to start babbling about anything. Ben didn't need to know anything overly personal.

Ben waved their thoughts away. "Okay. I've got it. I should mind my own business. Shall we go?" He was still smiling broadly.

"Dad, Rachel and I merely went to dinner and a show last night." Don looked pointedly at his father now. "When I was leaving her house, she said she'd like to come with me to pick you up. Got it?" Don didn't like the idea of his father thinking about his son's sex life, although he was being truthful about the previous evening.

"Yep. Got it. Are we going now?" Ben was still smiling. Rachel wasn't sure she'd ever seen him frown.

Pauline looked amused by the exchange. She thought they were all adorable. She also thought that Don and Rachel looked like a darling couple. Pauline gathered that Rachel was not Don's wife. Not yet anyway.

Pauline pushed Ben's wheelchair, and Don and Rachel followed them like a mini entourage. As they were heading towards the entryway of the hospital, Don said that he was going to get the car and bring it around. Rachel waited with Ben and Pauline, and within a minute, they were piling into Don's car. In spite of Ben's objections, Rachel chose to sit in the backseat. They all thanked the nurse for her amiable assistance, and she kindly wished them all well. She closed Ben's passenger side door, and they all waved goodbye.

"So, Dad. You seem like you're doing fine. Were you scared when this happened to you at the home?"

"I wasn't scared exactly. Maybe a little confused. I couldn't understand what was happening. I didn't feel sick, but I knew something didn't seem quite right."

Rachel piped up. "That's also why it's so great that you and my mother are at there, immediate assistance."

"That's very true. Living alone isn't always the best thing, is it?" It was a rhetorical question, and Ben left the thought hanging in the air.

Neither Rachel nor Don responded to his pointed question. Rachel wished that she hadn't said anything. She was merely grateful that elderly people had somewhere to live where others were around to assist if necessary. Being older and alone could be frightening. Being younger and alone was something else entirely. Of course, Ben had no idea of the previous night's commitment conversation between his son and Rachel.

Don talked with his dad as Rachel relaxed in the back and gazed out of the window. It was a beautiful clear morning, and people were driving with their windows down. Spring would be turning into summer very soon.

Rachel had been daydreaming so deeply that she suddenly realized that the car was in the circular driveway of the home. She sprang to action, opening her door right before Don opened his door to get out and help Ben. They both went to the passenger side, and Ben came out. He stood with Rachel for a moment, as his son went to park his car. Don then came over to join his father and Rachel. Ben seemed spry enough to charge ahead through the doors, so Don and Rachel followed his step. Many residents may very well have been awaiting Ben's return because a number of people were in the lobby, looking expectantly at the door. When the three of them came through, they started hearing comments like, "There's Ben! He looks fine. Glad it wasn't serious." Residents greeted him, and Don and Rachel stepped aside so Ben's friends could speak with their beloved neighbor.

Within a moment, Rachel saw her mother coming towards the lobby. Delores hurried her step a bit when she saw who all was there. Rachel walked towards her, and they hugged.

"Mom, how are you?"

"I'm doing very well. It's so good to see you and Don, and I'm glad that Ben is back." Delores perused the onlookers. "It seems we've all missed him even though he wasn't at the hospital too long. I don't recall getting this much attention when I had my little mishap and returned the next day." Delores seemed to be trying to take this all lightly, although there was some jealousy in her tone.

"I think there were people talking with you as well when I brought you back." Rachel didn't really remember, but she wanted to make Delores feel better. The simple fact was that Ben had the type of personality people were drawn to. Delores was a bit more reserved. People were fine being with her, but she wasn't as much of a people person as Ben.

Delores sighed contentedly. "I'm just happy that Ben is doing well. That's really the important thing. I want to say hello to him."

Rachel moved out of her mother's way, and Delores headed over to her friend. Don then edged towards Rachel. They both stood with their arms folded looking at the scene.

"Your dad is very popular."

"Yes, he is. He's a good guy."

"Definitely. Just like his son." She smiled but just kept looking forward in an amused fashion.

Don turned and looked appreciatively at Rachel. "Thank you. Okay, while the crowd is being so attentive towards him, should we try to find Abby and see if she has a moment to talk with us?"

"You're a buzz kill, Don, but okay." Rachel smirked at him.

Don laughed. "Oh, come on. It won't be that bad."

"We'll see."

They walked off together, and asked someone at the reception desk where they could find Miss Shapiro. They were directed to take the elevator to the third floor and turn right. The receptionist said she would call and make sure that Miss Shapiro was there. After asking for their names, the lady spoke with Abby. They were told to go on ahead.

Rachel had secretly hoped that Miss Shapiro wouldn't be available. She wasn't sure she was in the mood to deal with her. However, she also knew that she had no reason to dislike her. Don didn't have his sights set on Abby at all. He had professed his love for Rachel. And Abby hadn't done anything wrong. Oh, sure, she appeared to have been flirting with Don, but Rachel wasn't positive that had actually happened.

Don and Rachel walked into the elevator, and he pressed the button for the third floor. He smiled at Rachel, and She smiled back. They were happy to be together. The elevator door opened, and they walked out, turning to the right. They saw her name plate on the first office door that they encountered. Don poked his head in first, and Rachel heard Abby's voice.

"Mr. Levy! I mean, Don. Come in!"

Rachel came in behind him, hoping to get the same excited greeting.

"Rachel. How are you?"

Well, it wasn't quite the same tone, but Rachel forgave her.

"I'm fine thank you. And you?"

"Very well, thanks. Please, take a seat. May I offer you something to drink?"

Both Don and Rachel declined her offer.

Abby sat in her chair, and faced Don. She looked concerned. "How's your father today?"

"Oh, he's much better. Thank you for asking."

"Is he back here now?"

"Yes. Rachel and I went to the hospital to pick him up, and then we brought him home. He's glad to be back." Don smiled.

Abby turned to Rachel. "It's so nice of you to have helped. You must care about Mr. Levy very much. I mean, Ben. Of course Don as well." She laughed a little uncomfortably. There was the slightest hint of a blush. Rachel believed that Abby thought she had already said too much. Rachel still couldn't help but notice again Abby's very bare ring finger.

"I definitely do care about both Levy men. Very much. I told Don last night that I would be happy to accompany him to the

329

hospital to get Ben." Rachel wanted to make it clear that she and Don had been together the prior evening. Abby hadn't asked for any details, but Rachel needed to supply the information.

Although Rachel didn't take her sincere eye contact away from Abby, she could peripherally see Don glance at her. Okay, so she was jousting a little with Abby. *So what?* As long as she could make it clear that Don and she were, without question, a couple, then she was happy.

Abby smiled pleasantly at Rachel and then turned back to Don. "Okay. So I guess we're here to talk about the activities at the home. And also your ability to help me with the website. Shall we do that?"

Rachel and Don conversed with Abby for a little less than an hour. Rachel offered thoughts here and there, but she let Don and Abby do most of the talking. By the end of the meeting, they had accomplished a great deal. The three stood up to say goodbye. Don and Rachel thanked Abby for her time, and Abby said how much she appreciated their help and their interest. Rachel was in front of Don as they were heading out the door. She was just outside when Abby spoke up again.

"Uh, Don? Would it be possible for you to come here again to help me with some other ideas for the home's website? There are a number of things that I'll need to have you deal with, but I don't want to take up anymore of your time right now. This meeting was really about the activities, and I'm sure you'd like to get back to your father right now. Could you call me to set up a meeting?"

Rachel turned around, not sure what to make of Abby's request. Rachel didn't want to feel insecure. This was business, pure and simple. Don was going to deal with some women in his business. It's just that this request for another meeting seemed very blatant to Rachel. Abby was making it clear that Rachel need not attend the next appointment.

"Sure. If there's more help that you'll need, I'd be happy to come back."

"Of course you'd be paid for your time. I mean, this is your business after all."

"No, that's not necessary. My father lives here, so consider this a charitable contribution. Besides, I don't think we'll need to take up too much time with this. I've seen the site, and it actually is very good. It might only need a little tweaking here and there."

"I'm glad to know that. I'll expect your call to name the date."

Ooh, Rachel didn't like her using the word *date*. Still, she knew she shouldn't be upset about this. She trusted Don. She just wasn't a fan of Miss Shapiro at the moment.

"Okay, I'll call soon." Don turned around and nearly bumped right into Rachel. She felt flustered for one moment, and then she turned around and walked out with Don following her.

As they walked to the elevator to go back down and see their parents, Rachel was silent. She wasn't angry. She was just trying to work quickly through what had occurred.

Don put his arm around her. "You okay? You're quiet."

"Sure. I'm fine." Rachel didn't sound very convincing.

"Uh, oh. Someone isn't really fine. What is it?"

The elevator door opened, and they stepped forward. Don pushed the button for the first floor.

Rachel folded her arms, a sure indication to Don that something was bothering her. He waited for her to tell him what she was feeling.

"Really, it's nothing." She smiled at him. "I'm just being silly."

Don didn't look like he was buying her comment at all. "I don't think I'd ever use the word *silly* to describe you, Rachel. I suspect there's more to all of this, but you don't have to tell me."

"Really. There's nothing to tell." She blew out air which caused a strand of hair on her forehead to move. "I just don't like that woman." Rachel was irritated with herself for feeling this way.

The elevator door opened. They walked out, but Don gently pulled her aside. "So, please explain." He wasn't about to let this go.

"Explain what?" Rachel had a feeling she knew what he wanted her to explain, but she was buying time for herself.

"I think you know. What is it about Abby that bothers you? I don't want to work with her if you're sensing something awkward. It's not worth it if she upsets you."

Rachel's mouth instantly gaped open. She couldn't believe that Don would be willing not to do business with Abby merely because it was a problem for her. Most men would figure that Rachel needed to get over her juvenile concerns and jealousy.

"You mean if I didn't want you to see her, for business, you wouldn't? Are you serious?"

Don gave Rachel a look that meant this should be obvious.

"Of course I wouldn't. Your feelings mean more to me than doing business with her. Why would I want to do something that makes you unhappy?" He was surprised that Rachel would even pose the question.

Rachel shook her head in disbelief. In happy disbelief. *How was it possible that there wasn't a woman out there who caught this man a long time ago?* "Well, aren't you incredible?"

Don looked concerned. "Please believe me, Rachel. I'm serious. I'd never want to do anything to upset you."

Rachel realized that Don had completely misunderstood her surprise. She reached out to hug him. "I *know* that, Don. I believe you. I really meant it when I said that you're incredible. I wasn't being sarcastic. No wonder I love you so much!" She could feel Don relax. They embraced for a moment longer.

"So you don't want me to do business with Abby. Is that correct?"

"No. That is NOT correct. You do what you need to do. Just because I'm bothered by her doesn't mean that you shouldn't deal with her. It's okay." She truly meant it.

"But Rachel, if you feel uncomfortable about this…"

Rachel grabbed him and kissed him hard. She didn't want him to worry about a thing. She knew that she didn't need to be insecure anymore. After a lengthy kiss, they pulled apart.

Don took a deep, satisfied breath. "Well, I guess you're okay with everything now."

"I guess so. Should we say hello to our parents now?"

After visiting for a while with Ben and Delores, Rachel figured she should get back home. The children were returning in the evening, and the upcoming week was their last week of school. She needed to gear up for everything. So Don and she left the home and headed back to Rachel's.

They pulled up to Rachel's house, and Don walked her to the door. He kissed her tenderly.

"Rachel, I know you don't need me to say this, but I need to say this." He took her hands in his. Rachel looked at him, wondering what he needed to tell her.

"Thank you. Thank you for wanting to come with me today to get my dad. Thank you for joining me at the meeting with Abby. Thank you for wanting to be such a big part of my life. I just needed to express how much everything you've done has meant to me."

Rachel looked lovingly into his eyes. "Don, you're right. I don't need any thanks for doing things that I am happy to do. I'm glad my actions mean so much to you, but I'm grateful to be involved with the things that matter to you. I should be thanking YOU for opening up my world. You get the biggest thanks for making me realize that I could love someone again."

Don looked sheepish, but he was happy with what Rachel said. "Heck, Rachel. You made me realize that I could *truly* love someone. Period."

Rachel smiled at his comment. "Seems we've both found our ways. It's a good feeling."

"I guess I should let you get to everything. I know you have a lot going on. Rachel, I am going to see you this week, right? Obviously I'm going to want to see you before you head off to California."

"Absolutely! Maybe we could get together for lunch? I'm seeing my friend, Grace, on Tuesday, but the rest of the days should be open."

"Okay, then. I'll call you. We'll figure something out for sure." He kissed her again.

They said goodbye, and Rachel felt a little pang of sadness. She really did want to keep spending time with him. However, she knew she needed to get things done before the children came home. She checked for messages, and found she had some. The kids were getting desperate to hear from her, so she called Steve's house. Sarah answered.

"Mom, it's about time that you called!"

"And hello to you too. So, what is going on?"

"Didn't you get our messages?"

"Yes, of course I did. I just don't understand why you all can't spend some time with your dad. This shouldn't be so challenging."

Sarah grunted her disgust. "Guess again. Maybe you want to talk to Dad?"

"There's nothing for me to say to him."

"Yes there is! Tell him he's not being very attentive to us."

"Have you all told him that?" Rachel felt that her children should be open and honest with their father.

"Mom, we talk with him, but he's just not into being with

us. You come over, talk with him, and then Rebecca, David and I should come back home. I think that would be the best plan. Okay?" Sarah was practically pleading with her mother.

Rachel didn't want to have to talk with Steve yet again, but clearly she was back in the thick of it. And now was the time to end it. She would have to find a way to deal with the problem once and for all.

"Okay. You've got it. I'm coming over right now."

Sarah let out a huge, grateful sigh. "Thank you!"

Rachel realized that things must be tense if Sarah sounded *that* appreciative. She grabbed her purse, got in the car and made her way to Steve's house. The kids saw her pull up, so the front door was open before Rachel turned off the car. She got out, and walked towards them.

Rebecca came to her and gave her a hug. "Mom, it's SO good to see you!"

Rachel was stunned. *How bad had it been?* "It's good to see you too. All of you. So, where's your dad?"

David answered her. "Upstairs in his bedroom."

They all walked in together, and Rachel went directly upstairs leaving three hopeful children tentatively watching her climb the stairs. Rachel walked towards Steve's bedroom. The door was open, so she peeked in. He was sitting at his desk, looking at the computer.

"Steve? What's going on? What are you doing?" Rachel was very confused.

He turned around quickly as Rachel had been so quiet in coming in that he was startled. "Rachel? What are you doing here?"

"What do you mean, what am I doing here? Didn't the kids tell you I was coming?"

Steve looked annoyed. "No. No, they didn't."

Rachel folded her arms, ready for a confrontation. "Well, I'm *here* because I've been getting calls since last night that there seems to be a problem."

Steve stood up, and walked away from his desk to talk with Rachel. "Problem? I don't understand." He actually seemed mystified.

"Apparently you don't. Steve, this has got to stop. Whenever you're with the kids, they're unhappy. I constantly hear that

334

you're not paying attention to them and that you're distant. What is going on?"

Steve looked ashamed. "Rachel. I'm sorry. Really I am. It's just that…well…I've had other things on my mind."

Rachel was now getting angry. "So? You think it's an excuse that you have other things on your mind? Who doesn't? I always have other things on my mind, but it doesn't mean that I'm allowed to stop parenting. The kids have got to be your first priority. You should WANT to spend time with them!" Rachel felt like she was lecturing a child.

"Rachel. I DO want to spend time with them. I want to spend time with…with ALL of you. Rachel, the reason that I've been preoccupied is that I've been thinking. About US. Rachel, I want US back. I want our family back. I want to stop screwing up and get this right. Bring it back to what we had. You. Me. The kids. I know we can do this if we try. The desperate look on Steve's face only made Rachel angrier. She looked at him as though she was ready to throw a poison dart at him.

"You have GOT to be kidding? I can't believe you! There are so many parts to this that bother me, so where do I begin? Oh, yes. I know where. There's no way that I'd EVER want to resume our relationship. I divorced you for a reason, in case you forgot. Also, I'm in a very good relationship." Steve turned away in disgust. "I know you can't deal with the fact that I've moved on, and that I'm happy with a good and decent man. But I have. Also, why does your preoccupation mean that you can't give your children the attention they deserve? You don't want your family back. You've turned your back on your own children!"

Steve turned around to look at her. "I have NOT turned my back on them! I've been trying to think of a way to have us all come back together."

"According to what they tell me, you're not paying attention to them. So, I don't know what your little game is here, but we're not playing it anymore. Got it?" Rachel was getting angrier by the second.

"Damn it, Rachel, I'm not playing a game! Why can't you understand that I know that I've hurt you in the past, but I'm trying to make it right again?"

"Maybe for YOU, but clearly not for your children. What don't YOU understand? Do I need to spell it out better for you?"

Rachel put her arms out to her side to draw attention to her point. "I don't want you back. I only want you to be a good father for your children. This can't be that difficult to comprehend." They both stood silent for a moment. Rachel knew that she needed to calm down. She didn't want the children to hear them arguing.

Steve started to nod his head up and down. "Okay. So, you're telling me, without a doubt in your mind, that you don't want to give us another chance? Not even for the sake of the kids?" Steve was making a final desperate attempt to get her back.

Rachel shook her head from side to side, not believing what she was hearing. "For the sake of the kids? I'VE done everything for the sake of OUR children. What have YOU done? You're the one who ruined everything because of your self-serving needs. So, don't you dare put this on me! How about you just concentrate on being the best father that your children could possibly have? Leave me out of your equation. I'm happier than I've ever been, and I intend to stay that way."

Steve responded coldly. "Well, I guess you've made your decision."

"Steve, I made my decision the moment I found out about the choice you made to be unfaithful. Seems like you're always wanting to be the one making the decisions, and that's finally worked for me. Because of your selfish action, I found a wonderful man."

Without any kindness or emotion, Steve responded. "Glad to hear it." He walked past her, out of the room, and went downstairs.

Rachel took a deep, cleansing breath. She too proceeded downstairs to take the children home. Sarah, Rebecca and David were standing side by side, looking at their parents. Each had a different expression. Sarah's was one of simmering anger, Rebecca's face indicated uncertainty, and David looked slightly concerned. Rachel hated that they had been affected by any of this. She knew she couldn't protect them from every bad thing in life, but she wanted to shield them from problems that should never have happened. She tried to reassure them with a smile.

Steve had his hands in his pockets as he stood looking at his children. His jaw clenched, and then he addressed them. "Kids, I'm very sorry that you haven't been too happy with me recently. I want to apologize for not being with you enough. I guess my head has been somewhere else these last weeks." He looked briefly at Rachel. "And that's not fair to all of you. I promise you that I will do better." He didn't smile. He just seemed worn down.

The kids looked at each other and then at Rachel, as if to seek reassurance. The only thing that Rachel could do was nod and smile. She didn't know if Steve could remain faithful to his promise to them. He hadn't to her, so she had no idea what to expect from him in regards to his children.

"Dad, is Linda coming back at some point?" David seemed to want answers to more than one problem at this point. Rachel couldn't blame him for his curiosity. She wanted to know the answer as well.

Steve looked down for a moment, not sure how to respond. "Well, David, I can't answer that question right now. It's possible, but there are things to be worked out. Don't you worry, though. She's not going to be a problem for you. I'm going to be there for you, no matter what. Okay?" He tried to look reassuring.

David looked down and nodded. He wasn't so convinced. Rachel's heart felt heavy. When she was younger, before being married, she never envisioned she'd be dealing with this type of situation. The guilt she felt was powerful, even if none of this was her fault. She loved her children, and they felt vulnerable. Rachel wanted to break the tension.

"Kids, why don't I take you home? You'll see your dad before we go to California. And, I'm sure a phone call or two back and forth will happen." Rachel looked hopefully at Steve. He could keep in touch, even if he wasn't physically with them.

The kids picked up their belongings, and Steve hugged each of them. There was no feeling of joy in the air. Questions and concerns loomed, but Rachel knew it was going to take time to sort everything out. In the meantime, she'd do what she could to make her children feel wanted and loved.

Rachel drove home, and although the kids talked a bit, they were not their usual animated selves. They arrived home, and the children took their bags upstairs. Rachel decided that it would be a good idea to talk with them. She called the children downstairs.

They sat around the kitchen table, where Rachel had placed a dish of cookies and had glasses of milk for them. She wanted this conversation to be as stress-free and casual as possible.

"I want to find out how you're all feeling. I know this has been a challenging time for you. I'll tell you why I wasn't here as much this weekend. One of the reasons was that Don's father was briefly hospitalized."

The children actually gave looks of surprised concern.

She quickly put their minds at ease. "He's fine now, but I went to the hospital a couple of times with Don, the second time to take his dad back to the home. I saw Grandma as well. Don and I also went out during the weekend. However, that's not why I wanted to talk with you. I want to know what's on your minds."

For a moment, the kids appeared uneasy and unsure of what to say. David chose to start the conversation. "Mom, we don't have fun with dad anymore. He tries to pretend like he wants us around, but he kind of...well...he drifts off. You know what I mean?"

"I think I do. Is that how you two see it?" She looked at Sarah and Rebecca, hoping to have them open up to her.

They nodded in agreement, and then Sarah began talking. "It's not like we don't *want* to spend time with Dad. It's just that it seems like he doesn't want to spend time with *us*. I don't know what his problem is, but I don't want to be bothered with him if he doesn't care about me. Or us." She pointed to her siblings. She was obviously hurting.

Rachel folded her hands together on the table. This wasn't going to be easy, but parenting wasn't always a walk in the meadow. "I know that he cares about you. The thing is that, sometimes, when adults are having their own issues, they don't always know how to handle anything else. Problems can become all-consuming. It's not good, but it's life."

"But, what IS his problem?" Rebecca seemed adamant to know the truth. "I assume it has something to do with Linda." Rebecca spit out her step-mother's name like it was poison.

Rachel slid her fingers through her hair. She didn't know if she should tell them the truth. It seemed like it wasn't her place to do that, and yet her children had a right to know what was happening in their father's life. She looked at them, seeing their questioning eyes drilling into her own. Damn Steve for not being open with them. Once again, his issues fell on her lap.

"Okay, I'm going to fill you in on more details. Just keep in mind that adults are human beings too, and we make lots of mistakes." Rachel already regretted her comment. *Why set it up like this? Oh, well, she couldn't take it back now.* She whooshed her hand around as if to erase what she just said.

Rachel wanted to pull her thoughts together. "Let's see. Okay. Your dad found out that Linda is pregnant." The kids looked shocked. This would not make their lives any easier in their minds. When Rachel realized the impact and assumption of her statement, she wanted to clear things up quickly. "Actually, there's more to this than you think. Unfortunately, the child is not your father's."

The children looked stunned. The thing that Rachel feared was that this was too much information for them, especially for young David. However, there was nothing she could do about the circumstances.

"I know. This is a lot to take in. However, maybe this information makes your dad's mood seem more understandable." Rachel wasn't happy that she had to be the buffer between the children and their father. She really had no desire to explain his problems or to make the children feel sorry for him.

"So, is he done with Linda?" Sarah looked hopeful.

"I honestly don't know, Honey."

"You know, Mom. Dad seems to want you back." Rebecca looked for a reaction from her mother.

Rachel gave a direct response. "I think that might be the case, but it isn't going to happen."

"Why not?" David put forth his own question.

Rachel hated having to be this open, but she had to stay strong and keep steady with the inquisition. "Because I don't want to be with him now. And, I'm very happy with Don, although he isn't the reason that I am not going back with your dad." She didn't want the kids to think that Don was preventing their family unit from coming together again.

"So, you don't love Daddy anymore?" Sarah always looked at her with suspicion.

Rachel was trying to remain steady. "Not like I used to. I care about him, and I always will because he's your father. But sometimes a person falls in love with someone and that person turns out not to have the character the other person thought he had." Rachel knew that her comment didn't come out as clearly as she would have hoped, and her thoughts were confirmed by the confused expression on three faces staring at her.

339

"Are you in love with Don?" Rebecca was trying to figure this all out.

Rachel was hesitant, but she had to be completely honest. With her children and with herself. "Yes. I am." She shocked herself by verbalizing her feelings.

Her children were speechless, and this alarmed Rachel. "I know you're all a bit surprised. I am as well. I didn't expect this to happen to me. What I will tell you is that, after our trip to California, we're all going to spend some time together. Just hanging out. Don wants you to get to know him better, and so do I. I'm not rushing into anything, so don't worry about that. I would never bring someone into your lives if I didn't feel that it was okay." She looked at them, wondering what they were thinking.

Sarah muttered. "Like Daddy did."

Rachel looked directly at her oldest child. "Sarah, I know that what your dad did wasn't the best thing for any of us. But like I said, we all make mistakes. He may realize that now, and he'll have to find his way in life. He'll have to make some choices. We all do. It's not always fun or easy. However, hopefully you'll all learn from your father and from me, and you won't go down the same road we did. Although you will have your own issues, and that's okay. We all have to navigate as best we can. I can tell you that, in spite of everything that has gone on in my life, I'm truly happy. I have all of you, and I have Don. If we think about what we're doing, and what we want for our futures, life can be wonderful."

The children seemed to be absorbing what their mother said. And, as opposed to the beginning of their conversation, they now appeared to be more relaxed. Maybe Rachel was getting through to them and helping them. She hoped that was the case.

"I like Don. He seems nice." David chimed in. The girls looked at him, and they seemed to be in agreement. They simply nodded slightly like they thought what their brother said was probably true.

"Are you going to marry him?" Rebecca still needed more information.

"I'm glad that you all seem to be okay with him. I suspect we might get married at some point, but let's not think about that right now. I just want your last week of school to be good, and we'll all enjoy being with our family in California. You have your summer activities. So there's plenty to keep us all occupied for the next few months."

The phone rang, and Sarah jumped up to find out who was calling. She looked at the Caller ID, and answered it. Rachel assumed that it was for Sarah.

"Hello?" Pause. "I'm fine thank you. How are you?" Pause. "Yes, she's right here. Just a moment please." Sarah held her hand over the phone. "Mom, it's for you. It's Don."

Rachel looked very surprised. She was impressed by Sarah's civility. She got up to get the phone.

"Thank you, Sarah." Her daughter actually smiled at her.

Rachel put the phone to her ear. "Hello? Don? How are you?"

"I'm fine. Was that Sarah?"

Rachel laughed lightly. "Yes, it was."

"She was very polite."

"Thank you. We've all been talking here. About a lot of things."

"Oh? You sound very cryptic."

"Yeah. Well, I'll talk with you soon about everything." The children had left the kitchen, so Rachel felt that she could at least imply that there was plenty going on.

"That sounds good. That's why I'm calling. I'd like to have lunch with you this week. Does Wednesday work for you?"

"That would be great."

"So, I'll come by at noon. I'm looking forward to seeing you!"

Rachel smiled. "I'm looking forward to seeing you also. Like I said, there's a lot to tell you. And it's all pretty good."

"Excellent! I'll let you go. But I'll see you soon."

"Okay. Take care."

Rachel got off the phone, and took a deep breath. The kids were somewhat noisy in the family room, and she was grateful for that. She watched them for a moment as she was standing in the kitchen. They were talking and watching television. Everything, at least for the moment, was normal again.

Chapter Twenty-Eight

The early part of the week brought an excitement that was taking over the household. The children were chomping at the bit that school was almost over. Rachel had to keep them contained because they had final exams as well. She kept reminding them that, soon enough, they'd be on summer vacation, so this was the final push to the end.

Tuesday's lunch with Grace was wonderful for both of them. Rachel prepared a lot of food for them, so for a few hours, they talked and ate. Grace was thrilled to know how happy Rachel was with Don. Grace had worried that Rachel would never allow herself to be happy with any man, and now it appeared that she had waited to date until she found the perfect companion. Rachel told Grace that she wanted her to meet Don, and they both decided that a couple's dinner out would be good. Rachel suspected that Mike and Don would enjoy getting to know each other. Mike was a fun, smart guy, and the two could easily become friends.

Wednesday came around, and Rachel was happy knowing she'd see Don for lunch. After the kids left for school, she exercised, showered and ran a couple of errands. Rachel came back to the house at 11:30, giving herself just a short time to freshen up before Don came to take her to lunch. She had just finished brushing her hair when the doorbell rang. Rachel threw down the brush and practically ran down the stairs. She opened the door, and Don came in. After leaning in to kiss her, he brought his hands from behind his back, and revealed a present. The item was wrapped in red glossy paper with a white ribbon. Rachel looked at it, and then looked at Don. She was intrigued, figuring it had to be jewelry.

"Here, take it."

Rachel took it, and just held it, still looking at Don.

"Go ahead. Open it."

They went into the living room and sat down.

Rachel smiled mischievously at Don. Her voice was alluring.

"What have *you* done?" She began to take off the ribbon and the paper.

Don looked playfully back at her. "Open it and find out."

Rachel finally made her way to a pretty red velvet box. She opened it, and found a gold link bracelet with a gold heart charm, diamond encrusted around the border on both sides of the heart. She gasped at its beauty and at its sentiment. "Don, this is *lovely*!" She removed the bracelet from the soft lining, and looked more closely at the charm. There was an inscription engraved in cursive lettering that said "Love's Journey" and the current year. The back of the heart was inscribed with their names. Rachel's eyes misted as she held the bracelet. She reached out to Don and hugged him with all of her strength.

"So, I guess you like it?"

"Indeed I do. It's incredible. Not just how pretty it is. But it's the meaning that moves me the most."

"It means a lot to me as well. This year has been our beginning. I intend to have many more with you, Rachel, and I'm going to want to fill that bracelet with more charms." He looked at her with his kind eyes. "I wanted you to have this before you left for California."

Rachel looked at it again. "Thank you SO much!" Don helped her clasp the bracelet to her wrist. It was a perfect fit. They kissed passionately, and then they both looked at the charm dangling from its link.

"I don't want to cut this moment short, but I think we should get some lunch."

"That's fine." Rachel kept staring at her bracelet.

They left the house and headed to an Italian restaurant which wasn't too far from Rachel's house. The place was founded by two Italian brothers, and the food was wonderfully authentic. Although it was packed when they arrived, the hostess found a little corner table, which was perfect for Don and Rachel. As always, Don pulled out the chair for Rachel, and she sat down. He then took his seat, and the hostess gave them their menus. As they checked out the selections, they talked.

"So, you said that there were some interesting things going on? What's all happened since I last saw you?" Don had been curious since their phone conversation on Sunday.

"Oh, boy. Where do I begin?"

343

Don put his menu aside. "Really? This must be quite something."

Rachel put her menu down as well. She looked at her bracelet again, and shook her wrist to watch the charm dance. They both laughed at the whimsy of it all. Then the waitress came to take their orders. After they ordered pasta and red wine, Rachel continued.

"I talked with the kids after you left the other day. They weren't happy, and I came over to Steve's to get them." Rachel took a deep breath before finishing the story. "The kids said he was upstairs, and they wanted me to talk with him. Seems he'd been a bit down. So, I went upstairs to ask him what's going on, and I find out that he wants me back."

Don jolted a bit in his seat, and his mouth dropped open.

"No need to worry. I wouldn't go back with him for anything. Even if you weren't in the picture." Don relaxed after hearing that, although he already knew her feelings. Still, even he needed reassurance every now and then.

"I had a few things to say to him, and that ended it. So, I brought the kids home, and we talked. They wanted to know what was going on with their dad. Why he was behaving in such a distant manner. I told them. Everything. All about Linda. That wasn't easy, but I had to be honest. Then, I was asked about you." She looked at Don with intensity.

Don leaned in a little closer to Rachel, as if being nearer to her would allow him to know even more.

"I told them that I love you." Rachel stopped speaking. The two stared into each other's eyes. Then they smiled lovingly at each other.

"I'm happy to hear those words," Don said it plainly but beautifully.

"I thought you would be. So, I told them that you and I will be spending time with them during the summer."

"How did that go over?" Don was counting on that not being a problem.

"Very well actually. The first impression that you gave was a good one. They seem to like you, and Sarah's polite tone with you when you spoke on the phone indicates that we may all have a nice time together."

"I am relieved, to say the least. I really want to get to know them."

"I know you do."

Their food was presented, so they ate and talked through the remainder of their time together. Rachel insisted on paying when the bill arrived, and Don reluctantly acquiesced. Don drove Rachel back to her house, and went inside briefly. They sat and talked for a little longer.

"I guess this is it until you come back from seeing your family?" Don sounded melancholy about her upcoming absence.

"Yes, I think so. There's just so much to be done between now and when we leave. However, we won't be gone long, and you and I will see each other when I return."

"I know how much you're looking forward to this trip, so enjoy every moment. Don't wish it away just because we'll miss each other."

"You're right. This trip is a real treat. For the kids and for me. However, you WILL be missed. And I do want to see you soon after I get back."

"I'm glad. We'll have dinner when you get back. And then maybe you, the kids, and I can have a day together."

"I love that thought. It's nice to have someone to come back to."

Don and Rachel stood to say goodbye. He kissed her passionately and hugged her. Rachel walked with him out to his car, and they kissed again. Then Rachel realized that her next door neighbor was outside tending to her flowers. Don and Rachel laughed at having been caught. They shouted hello to the lady, and she said hello back. Don got in his car, and they waved goodbye to each other. Rachel went back inside, and closed the door. Yes, she was very happy that she would be with her family. But, she was missing Don already.

Chapter Twenty-Nine

The next day Rachel decided that before departing for California, she should visit her mother. She phoned her, and Delores told her that she'd be happy to spend time with her. Rachel drove to the home, walked into the lobby and was heading towards her mother's apartment when someone called out to her from behind.

"Rachel?" The voice was unmistakably Abby's. Rachel stopped cold, wishing that she had arrived either earlier or later to avoid seeing this woman. She knew she was being foolish, but since seeing this woman the first time, Rachel couldn't shake the bad feelings that she had toward Abby. And Rachel knew it really wasn't Abby's fault. She worked at the home, and Don was doing some business with her. *So what? Just because she was young and attractive didn't mean a thing.* Still, there was just something about Abby that grated on Rachel. However, she turned around; trying to pretend that she wasn't sure who had just spoken her name. When she saw Abby, she put on her best game face and walked towards her.

"Hi, Abby! How *are* you?" She reached out her hand to professionally shake Abby's.

"I'm fine, thanks. And you?"

Rachel was uncomfortable, but she would manage. "I'm doing very well, thank you."

"I guess you're here to see your mom?"

Rachel clutched her purse tightly; it gave her a feeling of security. "I am. I'll be leaving town shortly, to visit my sister and her family, and I want to see my mother before I leave." *Damn! Why did I just tell this woman that I won't be around? Don may get a phone call or two from her before I return.* Rachel wanted to kick herself for even thinking these things.

Abby nodded as though she thought this was the best idea in the world. "That's nice! Getting a chance to see the family. Where do they live?"

346

"In California."

"How fun! Not a bad place to go at all."

"That's true. I'm looking so forward to seeing my sister and her family. We're very close." And then Rachel couldn't stop herself. "And, I have a lot to tell my sister." Rachel smiled knowingly and shook the bracelet on her wrist.

Abby saw the bracelet, but there was no way for her to understand what Rachel was indicating. "Oh? What does that mean?"

"My sister knows how close Don and I are, but she doesn't know the *entire* situation. So, it will be nice to let her in on how things are going right now." Rachel was still smiling slyly. She literally couldn't help it.

Abby stood, eying the bracelet. One arm was bent across her body, while the other arm rested under her chin. She seemed to be trying to assess the situation. "Interesting. Are congratulations in order? I realize that I'm seeing the bracelet and not a diamond ring, but...?"

Rachel started feeling very foolish. It's not like Don had literally proposed, and Rachel was the one who told him that they shouldn't be in a hurry. Still, their relationship was heading towards marriage. Rachel knew it. And she was darn well going to make sure that Abby knew it as well.

Rachel confirmed her thoughts "I'd say congratulations would be acceptable. According to Don, this bracelet is the first step. I think he'd rather have given me a ring, but I told him we should wait until I return from California. And we both want to spend time with my children over their summer break. After that, I think we'll be set to head down the aisle." In her own mind Rachel was wondering what she was thinking by divulging all of this information. This was way too much to share with Abby.

Abby kept nodding. "That's truly wonderful, and I'm very happy for both of you. I guess I'll give Don my congratulations the next time I see him?" She looked at Rachel as though to question if she should do that.

Rachel acted like it wasn't necessary. "It's not like you *have* to do that. Maybe just when we make the official announcement." *How big a shovel will I need to get myself out of this?* Rachel wanted to jump out of her skin. She needed to escape.

"I understand."

Rachel wasn't sure what tone Abby was taking with her. She was being cool, but it seemed like there was something else, like she understood that nothing was happening at the moment.

"Well, I told my mom that I was coming, so I guess I had better be on my way to her apartment. So nice to see you, Abby." Rachel was glad that her own name wasn't *Pinocchio*.

"Tell her I said hello. Have fun in California!"

Rachel took long strides to get to her mother's apartment. She couldn't believe how she had behaved and she debated as to whether or not she should share this encounter with Don. She arrived at her mother's door and knocked. Delores opened the door.

"Hello. How are you, Rachel?" Delores gave her daughter a little hug.

"I'm fine, Mom, how are you?" She walked into the living room.

"I'm doing very well. Would you like some tea? I'm having a cup."

"Sure, that sounds nice."

They sat at the dinette table where Delores had placed a silver tray she had received as a wedding gift with a pot of tea which was being kept warm by a pink and yellow floral patterned cozy. There were a couple of floral pale pink and light blue bone china tea cups and saucers accompanying the teapot. Also on the tray were two tiny sterling silver spoons, sugar and milk. Delores always presented everything in a lovely, refined manner. Rachel poured the tea into the delicate cups, and took a sip of tea. It was flavored very delicately with vanilla. Rachel instantly relaxed.

"So, I'm sure you're looking forward to seeing Leah and the family." Delores smiled thinking about the fun Rachel and her children would have.

"Yes I am. It's going to be wonderful." Rachel lifted her tea cup again, and Delores zoomed in on her wrist.

"Rachel? What a lovely bracelet! I don't think I've seen you wear that one before."

Rachel put down her cup of tea and smiled. She looked at it for the hundredth time. "It is new."

Delores looked at Rachel and saw the shy sweet smile that had spread across her face. Delores was curious.

"Oh? So tell me about it."

Rachel rolled it around and around her wrist, letting the charm dance back and forth as the bracelet whirled around. Still smiling, she let Delores in on her thoughts. "Well, Mom, it's from Don."

Delores looked pleasantly surprised. "Really?"

Rachel nodded affirmatively. "Yes. Really."

"Okay? So, are you going to tell me more about it?" Delores's heart was pounding softly.

Rachel laughed easily. "I can. Don wanted me to have this before I left for California."

"There's a heart on the bracelet."

"Yes, that's right, Mom. There is a heart. And there's a lot of meaning within that heart." Rachel hadn't even been looking at her mother, only at the bracelet. It's as if there was something hypnotic about it that drew her to continuously gaze at it.

"It's certainly lovely. He has fine taste."

"It's more than lovely. It's precious."

Delores's heart filled with love and happiness for her daughter. She hadn't seen her like this in years. Probably not since the birth of David.

"Rachel? What does this mean?" Delores didn't want to grill Rachel, so she was speaking very calmly to her. Maybe the cup of tea was soothing to her as well.

Rachel looked at Delores. "It means that things are going very well for Don and me. It means that life is good."

"I would say so." She paused for a few seconds. "Rachel, are you and Don in love?" Delores practically held her breath, waiting hopefully for the answer that she desired. She wanted Rachel to live happily ever after.

Rachel looked down and smiled. Then she looked at her mother again. "Yes. We love each other very much."

For the first time since her own husband passed away, Delores felt like crying. However, this time, the tears would not be filled with sorrow but with joy. She contained the tears, but she lovingly patted Rachel's hand from across the table.

"I couldn't be more delighted. He's a good man, and you're a wonderful woman. You're a good team." Rachel was happy to hear her mother say these things. She had become a very positive person since Rachel had been seeing Don. "Do you think you'll be wearing more jewelry than a heart charm bracelet in the near future?" Delores decided it was okay to do a little digging.

Rachel pushed a lock of hair behind her ear. "I think there's a pretty good chance." Rachel thought back to the things she said to Abby. She winced, and Delores immediately noticed.

"What is it, Rachel?"

"Nothing horrible. I was just thinking of something I said that was kind of stupid."

"Would you be willing to tell me what it is?" Delores looked unsure that Rachel would share everything.

Rachel turned up the side of her mouth. She truly felt foolish. "Okay, but I'm warning you. What I did was plain silly." She checked her mother's expression to see if she should continue to tell her what she did.

Delores quickly reassured her daughter. "It's okay. We've all done silly things."

Rachel wasn't sure that her mother actually ever had, but she decided to tell her what had happened. After completing her story, she stopped and looked at Delores, hoping that she hadn't made her mother think her daughter was a total dolt. To her great surprise, Delores started laughing. Laughing so hard that she started coughing. Rachel sat stunned, looking at her mother with concern and bafflement.

Delores finally collected herself. "Oh, Rachel! I enjoyed every bit of that story!" She was patting her chest where her heart was located, calming herself down.

Rachel leaned across the table, looking at Delores as if she had lost her mind. "Mom. What on *earth* could you possibly have found so funny about this? I mean, I really went overboard, don't you think?" Rachel was very serious.

"Rachel, my dear child. Maybe you went overboard. Maybe. But it shows you how much you want Don in your life and ONLY in your life. I think it's adorable. You are so smitten, and you're going to protect what's yours." Delores started chuckling again. "I only wish I could have heard the conversation."

Rachel leaned back in her chair and folded her arms. She didn't think it was quite as amusing as her mother apparently did. Well, it wasn't her mother who nearly made a complete fool out of herself.

"Do you think I should let Don know about this?" Rachel really needed help figuring out this whole mess.

Delores leaned towards Rachel. "Well of course you should!

Why wouldn't you? I think he'll just love you all the more for what you did. It's darling."

Rachel rolled her eyes. "Darling? I don't think that's quite what I'd call it. I just hope that he doesn't think I'm so insecure."

Delores raised her eyebrows at Rachel. "And you're not?" She took a sip of her tea.

"Well, maybe I am." Rachel sat up and looked adamant. "But Abby seems predatory." Rachel slouched. "Maybe I'm just more attuned to these signs now."

Delores looked with pity at Rachel. "There's no need to be attuned to that now that Don is the man in your life. He's given you no reason to worry, and he never will."

Rachel sat up quickly, eyeing her mother with suspicion. "And how can you be so sure? What do you know that I don't? Did you know that Steve would succumb to another woman?"

"Of course I didn't know that Steve would have an affair. But Steve was never like Don. Steve was…" Delores was ready to reveal her thoughts but then stopped herself. She wasn't sure that it was a good idea to state her true feelings about Rachel's previous choice of a husband.

"Yes? Go on." Rachel wanted to hear everything that her mother had to say about Steve.

Delores took another sip of tea, and looked at Rachel over the rim of her cup. Then she put the cup down and allowed the liquid to grow colder.

"Okay. I'll tell you what I thought of Steve." She sighed, pausing to collecting her thoughts. "He always seemed charming, and not in a good way. A bit self-centered too, acting like he was the expert to guide you through life. I never felt that he wanted to *share* life with you so much as he wanted to determine how you were going to live it with him and through him. I always knew that you were smart and capable, and then you chose a man who only wanted to have fun but not take you too seriously. I think you were caught up in the glitz of Steve, but you didn't seem to realize that he had no substance. Nothing about him ever set right with me. I'm sorry to say these things, but that's how I saw it at the time." Delores looked at Rachel, praying she hadn't gone too far and hurt her.

Rachel was frozen. Not that there was a chill in the air. She just couldn't believe that her mother had felt all of these things.

After sitting in shock for just a moment, Rachel became a bit confrontational.

"Mom, why didn't you share these thoughts with me when I was first seeing Steve? Surely you could have said *something* before I married him?" Rachel was tempted to blame her mother for everything that happened.

Delores looked at Rachel with a great deal of skepticism. "Rachel, come on. How was I possibly going to say any of those things to you back then? You didn't give two hoots about what I thought. I couldn't do or say anything right as far as you were concerned. I knew if I said anything to you, I would have faced a very cold shoulder. You were always a stubborn young lady, and that came from your intelligence. I discussed my thoughts with your father, but he felt I shouldn't interfere. That you had to make your own decisions." Delores appeared reflective. "I know your father loved you very much, but I think he was wrong. I should have said something." Then Delores looked pointedly at her daughter. "However, I don't think you would have done anything differently. Would you?"

Rachel's face changed from contorted frustration to capitulation. "I doubt it. I thought I was in love. I *was* in love. I just felt that way about the wrong man."

Delores's expression softened and she patted Rachel's hand again. "You know that it's okay? It doesn't matter now. Look where you are today." Delores held out her arms to indicate the vastness of Rachel's world. "Three wonderful children, a mother and a sister who think the world of you, and a fantastic man who loves you as well. Not bad at all!"

Rachel was stunned by her mother's kindness. To have her mother state these incredible things about Rachel's life just bowled her over. She was very moved by the entire conversation.

"Thanks, Mom. I really appreciate what you've said. I guess everything has turned out pretty well."

"I'd say so."

Rachel was looking at her mother in a different light now. She debated speaking her mind, and they had come so far that Rachel felt it would be okay to disclose more of her deepest feelings. "For so much of my life I've felt that you and I didn't get along very well. You didn't understand me, or so I thought. I was always trying to please you, and I would become frustrated by your lack of interest in my life."

Delores eyed Rachel wistfully. "I'm sorry, Rachel. I didn't mean to behave that way. I always understood you. I was always interested in you." Delores took a sip of her now cold tea and then poured more of the hot tea in her cup.

"Maybe you did understand me more than I thought. It just always seemed that Leah was the good and special child and that you two connected so much better than you and I did."

"Leah *was* a good and special child. But so were you. I suppose it's natural at times to feel closer to one child than the other. I'm sorry if that's how it appeared." Delores seemed a bit sad.

This time, Rachel patted her mother's hand. "That's okay, Mom. I think what I was feeling was normal. There's bound to be sibling rivalry in every family. However, the good thing is that Leah and I have always been very close."

"I don't like that I may not have been the best mother to you. I know that you and your father always got along well. I must have been distant." Delores was contemplative now. "Sometimes we don't realize our own behavior." She looked directly at Rachel. "Now that you're happy with a good man, it seems that my ways have improved. He's been a good influence."

"I'm happy to give Don some of the credit, but we've worked on our relationship together. We've come a long way."

Delores smiled with contentment. "I like being part of a happy family. It's a good feeling."

Delores stood, and went around the little table to stand by Rachel. Delores then held out her arms ready to embrace her daughter. Rachel stood, and they held onto each other. They had never been closer, and now their bond was strong.

They talked for a few more minutes about Rachel and the children's upcoming trip. Rachel told her mother that there would be a dinner with Don and Ben upon Rachel's return from California. Rachel left the home and returned to her own.

Before the children came home from school, Rachel wrote a note to Don, thanking him for the bracelet and sending words of love. She decided she would mail the letter on the day she was leaving, just to surprise him with words from her heart as she was away. Then she began preparing for the trip, deciding what clothes should be packed. She heard the murmur of kids downstairs, so she stopped her activities and went to them.

They were congregating in the kitchen, eating chips and talking loudly. The end of school always brought a higher decibel of noise into the house, but Rachel was pleased that they were so happy. There was a lot for everyone in the house to look forward to in the upcoming months. The phone rang and the sound broke its way into the party-like atmosphere. Rachel answered, noticing that it was Steve.

"Hello?"

"Hi, Rachel. I was wondering if it would be okay if I took the kids out to dinner tonight. I figure with them leaving soon to see your sister and her family that I would like to spend a little time with them before they depart. Is that okay with you?"

Rachel was surprised by his sudden interest in being with the kids, but it was fine with her. Maybe she had finally gotten through to him about his responsibilities. "Sure. That would be great. What time will you come to pick them up?"

"I would like to come over now. Does that work?"

"Yes, of course. I'll let them know."

After saying goodbye to Steve, Rachel told the kids about their plans. It was as though she deflated a balloon right in front of them.

"I thought you would enjoy this. Your dad specifically called here because he wants to see you." Rachel didn't understand their lack of enthusiasm.

They nodded. "I guess that it's okay. I hope he's in a better mood now." Sarah wasn't going to waste her time on a parent who didn't want to be involved in her life. Rachel didn't blame her.

Within a short time, Steve rang the doorbell. David went to open the door, and his father was standing there with a nice smile, ready to greet his children. He stepped into the foyer.

"Hey, David! How are you?"

David smiled, a bit unsurely, but he responded. "I'm fine. How are you, Dad?"

"Doing well. Just glad that we can have some fun tonight."

The girls came to say hello. Rachel stood there as well. They all looked at him, checking for a strange mood or anything about their father that would seem off.

"So, where do you kids want to go for dinner? I'm up for anything."

The children looked at each other, pondering the question. Rebecca smiled. "I know! There's this great new Mexican restaurant that Julie told me about." Julie and Rebecca had known each other for years. They were as thick as thieves, liking the same things and sharing every thought that they had.

Steve looked at the other two. "It sounds great to me. How 'bout you two?"

Sarah and David were on board with the selection. Nothing more was said, other than the polite goodbyes. The four of them left Rachel in her quiet house. She prepared her dinner, and left it to cook in the oven while she called Leah.

"Hey! How are you?"

"I'm fine! I have an empty house because Steve has taken the kids out to dinner. Figured he should see them before we all leave for California."

"That's very nice. I'm glad that he's interested in spending time with them. So, you're not with your man tonight?"

Rachel laughed at her sister's way of speaking. "No. Besides, this was a last minute thing. Steve called to ask if he could do this, and he came to get them. I'm going to eat my dinner and get things ready for the trip."

"Sounds good. So, how is our wonderful Mr. Levy doing these days?"

"He's doing quite well. He gave me a gift." Rachel sounded playful.

"Oh? Is it any of my business what he gave you?"

"I think so. Mom saw it today."

"Really? Oh…is it…well…oh." Leah wasn't sure how much she should say considering she thought the gift was possibly an engagement ring.

Rachel laughed. "Silly. It's a very pretty heart charm bracelet. The sentiment is beyond belief, and I will be wearing it when I see you."

"Okay. I just wasn't sure where you were heading with this. I guess you'll have quite a bit to tell me when you get here. At least that's what I hope."

"I will. I have to say that life is going well. Who knows? Maybe you'll be coming here for a visit again. You might be part of a special event."

"Okay, NOW you have to tell me. Is the bracelet an appetizer and a diamond ring is the entrée?"

Rachel laughed again. "Perhaps. I suppose that I shouldn't jump the gun with this. I'm really the one who has been drawing out the relationship. But it's all going very well. Don and I will be spending time together with the kids. He wants to get to know them better, and I think they should get to know him better as well."

"This is all incredible! Has he proposed to you?" Rachel could tell that Leah was on the edge of her seat, provided she could be calm enough to sit.

"Nothing official. But like I said, that's more because of me. I'm really not ready to walk down the aisle. Not just yet."

"Oh? You certainly sound like you are. I just can't believe this! It's so exciting!"

"Don't get too excited. I've probably said more than I should at this point. There are no guarantees right now." Rachel didn't want to set up any false hope for her beloved sister. She knew that Leah wanted her to be happy, and Leah was practically planning the wedding for her right now.

"I understand. I need to take a deep breath and let things happen as they will. SO, anything else going on?" Leah was trying hard to move on.

"This and that. But I'll share everything with you in person."

"That will be wonderful. So, I'll see you soon. I'll be the one picking you and the kids up at the airport. We figured that there wouldn't be enough room in the car for all of us, you, your kids, and the luggage."

"That's fine. The kids are looking very forward to seeing their cousins. Really, this trip was such a good idea. I love that we're going to be able to spend time with all of you."

"And I suppose that you're right about the possibility of us coming to see you rather than you coming to see us during the winter holiday. Or...oh, my! You might even be on your honeymoon at that point!"

"Leah, let's take this slow. One step at a time. Got it?" Rachel lightly admonished her overly excited sister.

"Yes. Yes, you're right. I need another cleansing breath." Rachel heard Leah literally take a deep breath.

"I guess I better let you go so that you can calm down a bit."

Leah laughed. "Okay, I understand. I need to stop thinking

about this for now. Anyway, safe travels, and tell the kids we're all looking forward to seeing them."

"Thanks. I'll do that. I love you, sis!"

"Right back at you!"

Rachel ate her dinner in the quiet house and then continued the travel preparations. By around 8:30, Steve had returned with the children. Everyone looked very happy and there was a great deal of chatter in the air. Sarah, Rebecca and David said their goodbyes to their dad. That left Rachel and Steve standing near the stairs, watching the kids run up to their rooms.

"Looks like everything went well tonight." Rachel had a happy lilt to her voice.

Steve looked happy and content. "It did. We all had a good time together." He stood looking at Rachel, and then continued talking. "I think I'm finally getting my life back in order, no small thanks to your efforts."

Rachel looked surprised. She didn't understand what Steve was talking about. "What did I do?"

Steve looked like he couldn't believe she didn't get it. "Rachel, are you serious? You've been trying to get through to me for months. And you succeeded. You made me take a painfully hard look at myself."

Rachel led him to take a seat in the family room. If this was confession time, he might as well be somewhat comfortable. She sat down, and he shared his thoughts.

"I've always known that I was a major jerk to do what I did." He checked for Rachel's expression to confirm what he already thought about himself. She just sat and listened. He was grateful not to face more recriminations from her. "However my bad behavior never meant that I stopped loving you. In my own way." Rachel looked downward, not wanting to show her distaste for what her ex was stating.

"I know. It doesn't make sense to you. I'm not sure it makes sense to me either. I wanted to have my fun, and I paid a heavy price. Unlike other guys' wives, you didn't want me back after what I had done. Can't say that I blame you, but I figured that I'd just tell you that Linda and I loved each other and we were getting married. So, I've been unhappy for a while. BUT, I'm changing my ways now."

Rachel wanted to hear more. Steve was ready to reveal his new life plan, and she was curious to know what it would be.

"I have asked Linda to come back." Seeing Rachel's eyes widen in happy surprise was very satisfying to Steve. He was turning over a new leaf, and his ex-wife was taken by surprise by his revelation. "Hard to believe, huh? So, here's the plan. She is going to have the baby. But we're not going to raise the child. When you met her sister, she told you that she and her husband work for a couple who own a children's bookstore. The couple has always wanted to have children, but they have not been able. They've recently considered adopting. So, Lori told them about Linda."

Rachel was stunned. The world worked in mysterious ways. "This is incredible."

"Yeah, can you believe it? Linda's bad judgment has turned into a blessing for this couple. We've seen a lawyer, and we're drawing up papers now. Linda and I have been given another chance to make things right. We're also going to see a marriage counselor. I'm hoping that everything will start to fall into place given time and the healing process."

"I hope so too. I think that we should stop squandering the time that we've got and try to enjoy life. Maybe we're all finally growing up and realizing what's important."

"Perhaps. I'm not sure that we'll ever have it completely figured out, but then we wouldn't be living if there were no challenges or questions."

Rachel noticed that Steve seemed calmer and more accepting of his future. As far as she was concerned, he was heading in the right direction. Maybe because she was at a better place in her own life, she wanted that for Steve also.

They sat in a contemplative mood, and then Steve noticed Rachel's charm bracelet dangling below her sleeve. He raised an eyebrow.

"So, I see you have a pretty bracelet there." He pointed to her wrist.

Rachel, as if caught with a stolen item, quickly moved her other hand over the bracelet to hide Don's precious gift. She became very possessive of her new love token, and she didn't want Steve encroaching on the romantic bond that she shared with Don. The bracelet, though worn publicly, was Rachel's alone to gaze upon and admire. Rachel nodded an affirmative response to Steve. She wasn't sure what to say.

"From the look on your face, I'd say there's a lot of meaning behind that lovely bracelet, yes?"

Rachel looked up from her hidden wrist. She looked sheepishly at Steve. "Yes."

He appeared fine with it. "That's wonderful, Rachel. I mean it. If you've found true love with Don, then that's great. I'm very happy for you."

Rachel looked at him, not sure if she could believe what he said. He could tell that she was unsure about his proclamation.

Steve crossed his heart. "Honest, Rache. I'm serious. I WANT you to be happy. And it seems that Don has made you feel that way again. I should be shaking his hand and thanking him for cleaning up my mess."

Rachel laughed at his joke. Then Steve laughed with her, realizing that things were okay. He knew she did believe that he was sincere.

"Would it be okay if I talked with the kids, maybe just once, while they're visiting with the family?"

"Of course it's okay. You can talk with them as often as you'd like. I'm sure they'd love to hear from you."

Steve stood up. Rachel did the same, and they headed to the front door. He gave her a little brotherly hug.

"Thanks Rachel. I appreciate your guidance and your willingness to listen to me tonight. It appears that we may both be headed on the right track towards our futures."

"That's what it looks like. Let's keep our fingers crossed." Rachel did just that, and the heart on her bracelet danced. Steve left and Rachel finished tidying the kitchen. Then she went upstairs to check on the kids.

She poked her head into David's room. "Hi, sweetie! How's everything going?"

David looked up from his reclining position on the bed. He shoved his comic book aside. "Everything is great!"

"So, you had a nice time with your dad?"

"Sure did! The food was tasty, and we all talked a lot. It was kinda like it used to be."

Rachel couldn't have been happier. Seeing her son's shining eyes and hearing the upbeat tone in his voice was a welcome exchange for all of the recent troubling days. She went to him and gave him a big hug and a kiss.

"I'm so glad that you all had fun. I think you need to get ready for bed. Okay?"

David's smile still illuminated his face. "Okay."

Rachel closed his door and headed to Rebecca's. She knocked on the slightly ajar door, respecting a teenage girl's need for privacy.

"Come in!"

Rachel opened the door, and Rebecca smiled a little. "Hey, Mom."

"Hey. So, everything is going well?"

Rebecca's expression indicated that she wasn't sure why everything wouldn't be going well. "Yeah. I guess."

"I just wanted to make sure you're doing okay and that you had a nice dinner." Rachel still stood at the door.

"Dinner was great. Julie was right about the place. She knows so much!" Rebecca had a far-away look of admiration for her best friend.

"Good. I'm glad. Well, get some sleep, I'll see you tomorrow morning."

Rachel closed her door, and went to Sarah's. Her door was completely closed, so Rachel knocked.

"Yeah?"

Rachel called through the closed door. "It's Mom." Rachel had no intention of asking permission to go into any part of the house. She simply opened the door. Sarah was reading, a tradition she had almost always had before settling down into bed at night.

"Just wondering how everything is going."

Sarah responded without emotion. "Everything's fine."

"Nothing fun to report, huh?"

Sarah looked at her mother, wondering if she was digging to try to find out something. "No. Not that I can think of."

"I hope that you had a good time with your dad."

"I did. I think we all did."

"Okay. I just wanted to make sure that you're okay with everything."

"I am."

"Well, goodnight."

Rachel closed the door. She went into her own room thinking how it was always the same with her kids. The girls never once asked how their own mother was doing. She knew that this was typical, but she felt that it wasn't right. Mothers are human beings too. Still, for now, she'd simply have to accept the lack of consideration. She was just happy that life was improving each day.

Chapter Thirty

Rachel was beyond ready to head to California. She did have one more thing to do before the kids came home from their final day at school. Rachel picked up the phone to call Don.

"Hello?" Oh, how she always loved hearing that man's voice!

"Hello, Mr. Levy. How are you?"

"I'm fine, now that I'm taking a break to talk with you!"

Rachel gave a girlish laugh. "I wanted to say goodbye again before the kids and I take off for California."

"I appreciate that." Rachel could hear a bit of sadness in his tone. It made her happy to know that she would be so missed, but she didn't want him to actually be sad.

"My bracelet and I will be back before you know it."

Don laughed. "I guess I did well with that gift. You obviously like it very much."

"I do, but it's the man who gave it to me whom I love very much."

"I like the sound of that! As you know, it was given with lots of love."

"I know." Rachel soaked in Don's sweetness. "Is it okay if I call you while I'm away?"

"Is it okay? Heck, yes! I'd be thrilled to hear your voice and know how things are going. But, no matter how much I want that, and how much I'm going to miss you, I want you to concentrate on enjoying every moment with your family. That's what's important."

"I can think of you and spend time with my other loved-ones too. I multi-task very well."

"I like that. Your comment about your *other* loved ones. I can't tell you how nice that sounds to my ears that I'm one of your loved ones too."

"I just want to make sure you know how I feel about you."

"I *do* know. Rachel, you mean the world to me. I'm looking forward to spending a lot of time with you when you return, and with your kids."

"It's going to be great." Rachel sighed. "I guess it's time for me to get going. I just needed to hear your voice."

Don's voice was gentle. "That's nice. It's good to hear yours too. And, as you said, we'll talk. But just have a fantastic time. That's what I want for you. Always."

"I promise you that I will have a fabulous time."

"Well, I'll let you go. Rachel. I love you very much."

"I love you too."

They said goodbye, and Rachel clicked off the phone. Strangely enough, she had an emotional lump in her throat. It surprised her. She so wanted to see Leah and her family, but another part of her didn't want to go. She wanted to be with Don. Forever.

The school year had finally ended, and in the days before their departure to California, Rachel had three over-the-moon children in her house. There were peals of laughter, music blaring from rooms, and conversations with each other as well as with friends on the phone. Rachel called Grace to say goodbye and to let her know that she'd want to get together soon after returning from the trip. The night before leaving was filled with excitement, final preparations, and eventually the household shut down for the evening. They were all ready to head to the coast.

Rachel and the kids arrived at the airport. Going through security was never fun, but they all managed and knew that once they were at the gate, the vacation had begun. They boarded the plane when their zone number was announced. The children sat together, and Rachel had a seat on the aisle across from them. The flight was smooth, and they actually arrived at the gate a few minutes early. After collecting their carry-on items, they deplaned and headed with determination towards the baggage claim area. The moment they arrived, they saw Leah waving wildly at them. She walked quickly towards them and they moved towards her. All carry-on items landed with a thud on the floor as the five embraced. People looking in their direction would have thought that they hadn't seen each other in years. That wasn't the case, but it didn't matter. They were all happy to be together. The kids led the way to the baggage carrousel as Rachel and Leah walked arm in arm behind them. Bags were coming out of the chute, and everyone was waiting patiently for their belongings. Leah grabbed Rachel's arm. She looked at the bracelet.

"Very nice!" Leah looked more closely at the charm. "Oh,

Rachel! This is incredible!" She gave her another huge hug.

"Thanks. I happen to love it very much. And the man who gave it to me."

Leah looked at her with wonder. "I am simply stunned. It wasn't all that long ago that I could barely mention anything remotely close to you being in a relationship. And now look at you! Miss *I'm in love*. I am just so happy for you. For both of you." Leah actually looked a bit misty as she hugged Rachel once more.

"I know. It's all strange to me, but I'm enjoying every moment of it. Things have definitely improved all around."

"When we get to the house, you and I are going to sit down in the sunroom with cookies and a cup of coffee, and we're going to gab, gab, gab. Does that sound like a plan?"

"It sounds like a perfect plan."

The bags arrived, and Leah led them to her van. They all got into the car, and the kids were talking and watching the scenery go by. Rachel and Leah talked non-stop, and then they arrived at Leah's neighborhood. Being California, it was vastly different than the mid-western terrain where Rachel and her kids lived. There were palm trees and other luscious landscaping. Leah's family lived very well, and there was plenty of evidence of their success when the van pulled into the long brick-paved driveway. Rachel and her family were located in a very nice upper-middle class neighborhood, but Leah's home was in a completely different league.

It had been awhile since Rachel had visited, so she had almost forgotten the grandeur of the house. In the front yard, there was a lovely ornamental fountain with water spouting from the mouths of a variety of stone fish, and the landscaping was perfectly done by professionals. Color abounded, and the tropical flare was prevalent.

Leah pushed a button, and the 4-door garage opened, revealing two other cars, both luxury. Leah turned off the car, and the passengers all climbed out, a bit wearily but happy to be at their destination. They lugged their travel items in, with Leah assisting. She opened the door to the house.

"Hello? Anybody home?"

Rachel and the kids came in behind Leah, entering into the grand kitchen. It was completely modern and chic. Stainless steel gleamed around the kitchen and was overshadowed only by the massive red and black colored granite island. It was like looking at a gem in the middle of the kitchen. The range against the wall was used by the family, but when there were social gatherings, the gas burners on the island could easily accommodate more cooking. The floor consisted of blue, green, red and burnt orange Mexican tiles, giving the room a colorful, warm feel.

The kitchen opened widely into the great room, this time the floor casually consisting of massive sand colored tiles covered in places with bold, colorful rugs. Dark brown leather couches with colorful decorative pillows and cozy cream colored chairs dotted the room. A floor-to-ceiling stone fireplace was sandwiched between floor-to-ceiling windows. The statement that the room made was bold and relaxed at the same time.

Leah's husband came sprinting down the stairs. He was a very fit man, but not in the sense of being muscular. He was of average height, but very trim. His brown hair was short and combed to the side of his forehead. His features were average, but behind his wire rimmed glasses were blue eyes that smiled. In that sense, he reminded Rachel of Don. They both exuded the warmth of their personalities through their eyes.

He came over to Rachel, and gave her a hug. "So good to see you, sis! We've had an excited household waiting for your arrival!" He looked at the children as well. "And, needless to say, your visit has much been much anticipated also. We're thrilled to have you here!"

The kids looked at him and smiled. They responded with their thanks at being invited. Just as they were all greeting each other with loving words and laughter, the front door flew open, and Aaron and Amy dashed in.

"Hi! We're here! We were at our friend's house, and we saw the car pull in."

It had been a while since the cousins had seen each other. Sarah, Rebecca and David were a bit shy at first, and probably somewhat frazzled by their travels and being in unfamiliar surroundings, beautiful though it was. However, Leah's children were as perceptive as she always had been, and they immediately came over and hugged their guests. It was a sweet picture. Aaron and Amy grabbed as much of the luggage as they could, and Rachel's kids followed them upstairs to their rooms. Sarah and

Rebecca would share one room, and David and Aaron would share Aaron's room.

"It's so wonderful to be here! Thanks for opening your home to us for the week."

"It's our pleasure. What can I get you? Anything to drink?" Bob was a good host. His job required that he be one, but it was also in his nature to be kind and helpful. He was just a good guy. It was as simple as that.

Leah was arm-in-arm with Rachel and directed her gaze at Bob. "YOU may take her belongings upstairs to her room. I will take care of the rest. We will be in the sunroom if anyone needs us. Although I'm sure no one will." Leah was pretending to have airs, and they all laughed at her dramatic ways.

"Gotcha! Have fun, ladies!" Bob bowed to them.

Leah first took Rachel into the kitchen to get their sustenance. Rachel was happy watching her sister move around and get everything together. In spite of the grandeur of the life that she was living, Leah was as down-to-earth as she could be. So were Bob and their children. Because of his business, being an executive of a major corporation, this was the life they led. They were comfortable with it, and it showed in the coziness of their existence. The home was not big and sterile. It was large and full of life. They entertained frequently, hence the size of the home. But it was clear that they made the home fit them, not the other way around.

Leah brewed the coffee, placed a variety of cookies on a white china plate, and placed mugs, cream and sugar on a large silver tray. She poured the coffee into a carafe, and Rachel took that. They made their way to the sunroom, which was exactly what it was. A lovely sun-filled room. White wicker chairs with pink and yellow cushions were set around a yellow round wooden table. The floor was tiled in stark white, and pots were overflowing with colorful plants and flowers. Rachel felt as though she had entered Eden. The floor to ceiling windows allowed the lovely backyard to come to them. The home sat on two acres of land, some of which was taken up by an in-ground pool. There were chaise lounges and umbrellas set up, ready for anyone to come out and swim or relax by the pool. It was a serene setting.

Rachel and Leah settled in, and Rachel took a heavenly sip of coffee. "Ooh, this hits the spot!" She closed her eyes in rapture.

"I figured you could use a boost after your travels. We'll have a nice dinner tonight. We're eating here, but I have everything set to go. I just have to heat up a couple of things. That way, we can all relax. You may want to eat and then go to sleep."

"You may be right. This works for now, though." Rachel lifted her mug as though saluting.

"So, tell me everything!"

And that's just what Rachel did. She filled Leah in on the relationship with Don. She told her about Steve and Linda, and about how things were coming along with Delores. After sitting for longer than they realized, five children appeared in the sunroom.

"Mom, I think you should start getting dinner ready." Aaron looked pleadingly at Leah.

Leah glanced at her watch. "Oh! I guess I should at that. Thanks for letting me know. We want our guests to think we're hospitable, don't we?"

Aaron smiled with the same boyish nature as David did. Rachel wished that the two families could always be together.

The kids went back upstairs to do whatever it was they were doing. Leah told Rachel that she could certainly go to her room and relax for a while. Rachel freshened up a bit, but then came back down to be with her sister. Rachel thought that if she took a nap, she'd sleep until morning, so it was best to be with her sister and then she would enjoy the nice dinner with the entire family.

Within an hour, Leah was ready to serve up the fine meal. The family came together and went into the dining room. This room wasn't grand. It would easily seat a party of twelve, and probably more, but it wasn't a huge room. Though somewhat formal with its red walls, crystal chandelier and ornately carved wood display case for the china and silverware, this eating area could be used by the family every night if that was the desire.

Leah had placed white china plates at each setting, along with black napkins, silver cutlery and crystal glassware. A lovely bouquet of flowers sat in three separate shorter square glass vases, one pink set, one white set and one red set, adding a touch of elegance without getting in the way of everyone seeing each other allowing for good conversation.

Rachel and the children were seated, Leah refusing help from her houseguests. Bob filled the glasses with water, and offered a glass of wine to Rachel which she happily accepted. Leah began, with Bob's help, bringing out the meal. There was a platter of aromatic sage, thyme and lemon-scented chicken pieces surrounded by glazed carrots, caramelized onions and asparagus. A casserole dish containing scalloped potatoes was also placed on the table. There were also homemade rolls and butter. They were having a feast!

Bob pulled out Leah's chair, and she sat at the head of the table next to Rachel. Bob sat at the other end. Everyone was suddenly quiet, and Bob raised his wine glass to make a toast.

"To our wonderful family. We are grateful for the arrival of our loved ones, and we look forward to many days of fun with all of you. Thank you for gracing our home with your presence."

Leah and her children murmured their happy agreement. Rachel was touched by Bob's kind words. She and her children felt welcomed and loved. In turn, she thanked them for their invitation and for being such a loving family to her and to her children.

They ate and talked, and laughter filled the room. By the end of the meal, which included a chocolate cream cake, everyone was tired from the excitement of the day. Leah hugged Rachel and her children, and told them to go to sleep. She, Bob and their kids would clean up. Rachel was too tired to argue, so she and the kids tromped up the stairs. Rachel said a pleasantly weary goodnight to her children, and she went into her designated room.

The room was, not surprisingly, very comfortable. The walls were off white with a light blue and green wallpaper border of seashells. There was an inviting queen-size bed with a tan duvet and luxurious pillows. An armoire with a flat screen television and shelves containing glass sculptures and seashells graced the wall. There was also a framed black and white photo of Leah and Rachel when they were children. Rachel went to the armoire, and looked more closely at the picture. They were smiling, Leah with two missing teeth. They had their arms around each other like they were pals. And they were. *Still are*, thought Rachel. It must have been summer because their arms were bare, and their hair looked a bit damp, as though they had been swimming before the photo was taken. Rachel shook her head. How far they both had come. The photo looked like it had been taken in another lifetime. Rachel supposed that it was a whole other lifetime ago. So much had happened, but those sisters were still the same in many ways. Their love for each other had only intensified over the years.

Rachel looked around the room. So lovely, with its sitting area and, as in Rachel's home, an attached bathroom so that a person could have complete privacy. It was like a bed and breakfast type of room. Yes, her sister's life had turned out well. Rachel thought of her own life, and then she looked at her bracelet. Things had turned out all right. Through all of the turbulence, she had found a steady path. Not so long ago, she didn't think it was possible that she would be where she was today. There was a knock on her door, breaking her reverie.

"Yes. Come in."

The door opened, and Rachel's kids were standing there, dressed in their nightwear.

"Hi. Come in."

The kids looked at her room and were awed. "Our rooms are really great, and this room is amazing too! Mom, we *love* this house!" Sarah was impressed.

"It is beautiful. No question about it."

"Our home is nice too." Rebecca was going to stick up for their digs back home.

Rachel smiled. "I think our home is quite lovely. The best thing is that both are filled with a lot of love. We're all very fortunate."

"We just wanted to say goodnight. We're so happy to be here. Thanks for making this trip happen." Rachel couldn't believe that Sarah had spoken in such an appreciative way. *Maybe this house had some kind of magical power.* Rachel wanted to laugh at her own thoughts, but she didn't dare. She was just so happy that her kids were enjoying their time here. Enough so that they were coming to her to say goodnight. This had to be a first.

Rachel gave them all hugs. "It's my pleasure. I'm happy we're all having such a nice time. I wish you all a goodnight, and I'll see you in the morning."

They scurried out, back to their rooms. Rachel closed the door, savoring the utter joy she was feeling.

Chapter Thirty-One

Rachel slept the sleep of the dead. She woke up, and stretched like a cat. She almost felt like purring. After looking at the clock, she was amazed that she had slumbered so long. She got out of bed slowly, and went to the bathroom to prepare for the day. Dressed in casual navy slacks and a thin lighter blue cotton sweater, she headed downstairs. She could already smell the wonderful scents wafting from the kitchen.

Leah and Bob were in the kitchen, cooking what appeared to be another feast. Bob was making waffles; Leah had scrambled eggs with herbs which were now in a pan, and bacon and sausage were sizzling in another pan. There was a large bowl of cut up fruit, juice in a pitcher, and coffee was brewing. Rachel was salivating. Leah turned around, sensing that someone was there. She waved a spatula in Rachel's direction.

"Good morning! How are you?"

"Good morning to both of you. I'm wonderful, and you two look adorable with your matching aprons."

"Ah, yes, aren't we just precious?" Leah fluttered her lashes.

"I hope you're hungry. We have a culinary masterpiece for you." Bob placed the waffles on a plate with flare.

"Actually, even in spite of the incredible dinner last night, I am hungry. What can I do to help?"

"Nothing. You are not to lift a finger while you're here. Got it?" Leah issued her command in the sweetest tone possible.

"Okay, if you insist. You know, I may never leave. This lifestyle could become addictive."

"So stay. Works for us, doesn't it Bob." Leah stated it as an agreement between husband and wife, not a question.

"Absolutely! Seriously, Rachel, we'd love you to stay here with us anytime."

Rachel had been kidding, as they were fully aware, but she was touched by the sincerity of their pronouncements. By the looks on their faces, she knew they meant every word.

"I appreciate that. What would I do without you?" She came to Leah and then to Bob, giving them both big hugs.

The children must have heard the commotion in the kitchen because, one after another, they all began to appear. Aaron was first to show up, looking eagerly at the variety of food that he would be happily consuming. The last to show was Sarah, yawning but looking like she was glad to be part of the happy group.

Without being asked, each child carried something into the dining room. Upon entering the room this morning, Rachel's eyes opened wide in amazement to see the room transformed from the dinner ambiance of last night's meal to the new beauty of the breakfast appearance. Different tableware was being used at this hour, with white plates enameled with pink and yellow flowers and yellow placemats and napkins adorning each setting. Spring was flowing throughout the room.

Similar to the previous meal, everyone chatted and laughed. The family bond was evident. There were no awkward pauses, only constant chatter. Everyone discussed the plans for the day, as well as most of the plans for the entire time together. Rachel was happy to let the rest of them figure out the activities during their time in California. Whatever anyone wanted to do was perfectly fine with her.

And that's how the week progressed. They went to stores, galleries, botanical gardens and great restaurants. Sometimes the family went together, sometimes just Leah and Rachel went out. Bob took time off from work to take the kids places while Leah and Rachel would go out to lunch and talk for hours. The days were idyllic for Rachel. She phoned Don once, and he was thrilled to hear her voice. He could tell how relaxed and happy she was, and it made him feel good to know that Rachel was doing so well. The kids spoke with their dad almost every day.

The day before Rachel and the kids were to depart was a bittersweet one. They had enjoyed their time more than they could say, but the thought of parting was heartbreaking. Leah assured all of them that there would be more visits, and she was certain that Rachel and the kids would be able to come back to California before too long. She didn't express it openly, but it was her opinion that Don would be accompanying her sister on the next visit. After talking with Rachel about everything, Leah truly

371

believed that Don would be her sister's future husband. Leah couldn't have been more pleased.

The family dinner was special, as everything had been during the entire time that Rachel and her children had been visiting with the family. Bob took great joy in preparing food as much as any chef did, so while Rachel and Leah had been reveling in their last afternoon out; he was busy cooking up a storm. When the family sat down at the dining room table that final evening, Bob presented his creations. Cheese puffs and salads started the meal in a most delicious manner. That was followed by beef tenderloin and roasted herbed new potatoes. He had made a wine sauce to go with that, although the beef was so delicious and tender, it really didn't need anything else. Haricot vert with minced garlic and olive oil accompanied the entrée. The dessert, a vanilla cake with macerated strawberries was bakery bought, and a favorite of the family's.

After the dinner was completed, the children went their own way. Bob, Leah and Rachel sat comfortably full sipping cordials and continuing their conversation. Rachel sat back lazily in her chair.

"Bob and Leah, the children and I have had the best time with you and the kids. I honestly can't even express what this visit has meant to us."

Bob responded. "Sis, WE'VE had the best time, and we're grateful that you and the children have been able to spend time with us. You've all been missed. It was wonderful that Leah was able to spend time with you on her visit, but the kids and I wanted to be with all of you as well."

"Thanks. I hope that we can do this more often."

Leah spoke softly. "I know we will. Life has taken many turns, and it seems that the path is a bit calmer these days. It would be great if Mom could come with you next time. And Don." Leah took a sip of her drink, and looked at Rachel's expression.

Rachel had an easy smile on her face. "Yes. I'd agree. That would be very nice." Rachel didn't look at her sister. She twirled the stem of the glass around her fingers.

The three chatted for a bit more, and then Bob rose to clear the plates and clean up. Once again, he chose to do the work himself. Rachel and Leah retreated to the sunroom. Leah turned on the lights, and they sat in the same seats where they had begun their time together during the visit. They let their eyes set on the lit landscaped yard, and were quiet for a moment.

Leah spoke, gently fluttering away the silence. "Bob and I will miss you, and I know the kids will be sad to see you go."

Rachel looked at her sister. "Your kids are wonderful. I don't think I've told you that yet, but you should know what a fabulous job you and Bob have done raising them. I think they've probably influenced my own kids during our stay. Their attitudes seemed to have improved while we've been here."

"You're sweet to say these things. Bob and I love and *like* our children very much. Don't get me wrong, they have their moments. Your kids are great also. I hope you know that. You're a loving parent to them, and it hasn't been easy for you."

"Nope, it hasn't always been easy. My kids should have had an upbringing with parents who loved each other and were always married. Whenever I have troubles with them, I try to keep in mind that they haven't had the most ideal home life. It should have been better."

"I don't think you need to excuse their bad behavior when it happens. Children can have the most wonderful home lives in the world. That doesn't mean that they're always going to behave."

"I know. It's just that I'm sure they're acting out their frustrations at times. I can't blame them for that. I can't completely blame myself either, but Steve isn't normally the one dealing with the more arduous moments."

"Where do you see the family dynamic going? You've said that Steve and Linda will be attempting to work things out. Does that mean she's going to be a bit nicer to the children? And, what will you and Don be doing?

Rachel's eyes had settled on the beauty of the nighttime sky, but upon hearing Leah mention Don, her head turned to her sister. "I don't know about Linda or Don."

"What do you mean?" Leah looked very perplexed.

Rachel shrugged. "I don't know how Linda will behave. I hope she's nicer to the kids, but I have no clue about that. And I don't know what you mean about Don."

Leah looked at Rachel, not sure of what to make of her sister's thoughts. "Okay. I mean, is Don ready to be in a household with your kids? Is he ready to take on family life?"

Rachel swallowed hard. "I don't know. I mean, I think so, but

373

I'm not totally sure. He says he is ready. You know, Leah, we haven't set a wedding date. So, let's not rush anything." Rachel suddenly wasn't comfortable with these ideas.

"Sweetie, I'm not trying to rush anything. But you've made it clear that there's a future with you and Don." Leah looked at Rachel's wrist where the charm bracelet had been dangling for the entire trip. She doubted that Rachel had removed it even to bathe. "That lovely charm means something. Right?"

Rachel looked at the heart, and smiled. "Yes. I'd say it does." Then she looked more serious. "Still, Don and I haven't discussed a wedding. I know that he wants to spend time with the kids over the summer break. I suppose we'll know more when we see how that goes.

Leah appeared confident. "I think *that* means something for sure. Don wants to get to know them and have them get to know him. Clearly, he's thinking marriage." Rachel looked concerned again. Leah wasn't sure why her sister's emotions were all over the map right now. "Rachel? What is it? What's bothering you?"

Rachel sat very still for a moment, her eyes focused straight ahead at the pool area. She licked her lips, suddenly experiencing some fear. "What if he can't deal with the children? What if they *are* too much for him? There are three of them, and the two girls, being teens, can be challenging." She turned to face Leah dead on. "I wouldn't blame him for not being ready for them. He's a warm-hearted caring man. But this might be too much to ask him to handle."

Leah placed her hand on her sister's arm in a comforting gesture. "Rachel, I can't guarantee anything, but I can tell you that I believe that Don can manage the situation. He's always known that they're part of the package. I really think that everything is going to be okay."

Rachel's body tension eased immediately. She trusted her sister's instincts, and in her own heart, she did believe that Don wouldn't bolt. Rachel didn't say anything. She merely nodded, and Leah knew her sister would be okay.

Chapter Thirty-Two

The next morning, everyone rose early. Rachel and her kids had to be at the airport for a morning flight. Bob and Leah, per usual, were in the kitchen, whipping up an easy breakfast. Rachel didn't want the kids or herself being gourmands before sitting for hours on a plane. They had indulged in all kinds of wonderful foods while they had been in California, although they had also been so active that Rachel didn't think she gained too many extra pounds.

Even though Amy and Aaron weren't going to the airport, and therefore didn't have to be up so early, they too came down and joined their aunt and their cousins for the going away meal. The kids were awake, but they looked a bit sad, making them appear somewhat tired. Rachel felt that they were not happy to see their cousins leave. She was glad they had enjoyed each other's company.

The family sat down to eat, although unlike other meals, there wasn't quite as much chatter. Maybe they were all a bit sleepy still, but there was an air of melancholy that was palpable. Had Rachel been able to suddenly state that they were all staying in California, she suspected that there would be hoots and hollers enough to be heard throughout the neighborhood.

After eating rather quickly, Rachel and her kids finished getting ready and were downstairs with suitcases and carry-on bags within fifteen minutes.

Bob came to Rachel and gave her a big bear hug. "We're all going to miss you, sis. I hope we'll see you very soon."

Rachel suddenly felt choked up, but she wasn't about to cry. "We're all sad to be leaving. I'm sure we'll be together before too long."

All of the kids hugged each other, and then the kids hugged the adults. It was a beautiful scene of love all around. Bob, Aaron and Amy helped them get the luggage into Leah's car, and they all said more goodbyes. They waved to each other as Leah backed the car out of the garage. There was mostly silence through the ride to the airport. It seemed that Rachel and her children wanted to take in the last views of their surroundings. Leah said some things here and there, and then they arrived at the passenger drop off area.

Rachel distracted herself by getting luggage out of the car. She didn't want to feel the ache of leaving her sister. She convinced herself that she would see Leah soon, and that there was a good reason to be returning to her life. Don would be waiting, and the future looked bright.

When there was nothing more to be done than say goodbye, Rachel stood looking at the sister she cherished beyond words. She could see tears well up in Leah's eyes, but they were both smiling at each other, trying their hardest not to experience the sad pang of departing each other's company. The children looked on in respectful silence, understanding and appreciating what their aunt and mother were feeling. Leah and Rachel hugged each other hard, and then pulled away. A tiny tear escaped from Leah's eye, and she brushed it away impatiently. She looked like she refused to have any more droplets escape. Rachel held onto her emotions, knowing that if she responded in kind to Leah's feelings, she herself would lose all control.

"Call me when you get home."

"You know that I will." Rachel turned to look at her children, who were standing patiently, not wanting to interfere in the heartfelt moment that they were witnessing. "We all thank you for your wonderful hospitality, don't we kids?" They smiled tentatively and nodded.

"You're all more than welcome. Have a safe and easy trip." Leah's voice was shaky, so Rachel decided it was time to go. Her heart felt heavy, and she wanted to break away from the emotional tension that she and her sister were feeling. She gave a wave, and turned around with the children following right behind. They headed inside towards the check-in kiosks, and Leah went to her car, unable to control the slight stream of tears that were now flowing freely down her face like rain falling down a window pane.

The flight went smoothly and the plane landed with ease. Rachel and her children wearily walked off and slowly made their way to pick up their baggage. The mood was a bit somber within their family both because of the tired feeling they were experiencing and the continuing sadness of ending their perfect trip. The excitement for the children was gone, but Rachel suddenly got her second wind when she realized she'd probably be talking to Don before the day came to a close.

Their luggage arrived, and they walked to the garage to get in the car. Not a word was spoken by the children all the way home. Rachel had started to say something, and then she realized that they had all fallen asleep. They had experienced so much in a week, and she knew they were probably exhausted. The emotional distress of leaving California, their family, and the lovely home, had all taken its toll.

Rachel felt a bit disoriented as she came closer to home. She felt as though she had been gone much longer than a week, and she knew that getting back into the swing of things would take some effort. She drove the car onto their driveway and into the garage. Somehow the children must have sensed that they were home because they began to stir. With bleary eyes, they got out of the car, and dragged their belongings into the house.

"Mom, is it okay if I leave my stuff down here? I think I'm going to lie down." Sarah was very mellow right now.

"Sure. That's fine. Why don't all of you just not worry about your bags right now? Relax for a while."

The children gratefully climbed the stairs, and Rachel heard the sounds of doors being closed. She wasn't quite as worn out as they were, so she decided to call Leah to inform her they'd made it back without any glitches. Rachel heard one ring, and the phone on the other end was answered.

"Hello? Rachel?"

Rachel laughed. "Yes, Leah, it's your sister. You were already eager to hear from me, huh?"

"Of course! So, how was the flight?"

"Everything went fine, although you wore my children out completely. I need to thank you for that!"

They both laughed. "Our pleasure. How are you faring right now?"

"I'm a little tired, but not too much worse for wear." Rachel paused. "I miss you already."

"I know what you mean. My drive back home felt lonely. When I came back, Bob sensed my down mood, and he took me out for a walk and an ice cream cone. And we hadn't even had lunch yet!"

"You've got a good man there, Leah."

"I know I do. And fortunately, you have a good man THERE."

"That's true."

"So, is he your next call? Of course I'm assuming that you called me first."

"You assume correctly. I will call him soon."

"And Mom. Don't forget to call her. Tell her that I said hello, and I'll be in touch before too long."

"Will do. Take care of yourself, and give our thanks again to your family. Honestly, we all had the best time with you guys."

"Let's hope we get together again soon. Tell your kids we all say hello."

Rachel and Leah hung up reluctantly. Rachel didn't want to wait any longer to call Don. Her heart did a little skip as she punched in his phone number. As Leah, had done, he answered immediately.

"Hello?"

"Hello, Don. How's life?" Rachel amused herself with her casual introduction.

Don chuckled. "Life is better now that I hear your voice. You have returned!"

"Yes, we're back, and I missed you."

"Glad to hear that. I missed you as well. But I hope that you had a good time."

"I did. We all did. We were quite sad to leave, but I can tell you that the thought of coming back and seeing you made the return visit much more pleasant for me."

"Hmm. So absence *does* make the heart grow fonder?"

"I suppose that's true. I can tell you that, absence or not, my heart has grown fonder for you."

"Rachel, that really is nice to hear. I can't wait to see you. When will we be able to get together?"

Rachel was delighted that Don was so eager to see her. "I bet I can make an escape tomorrow for lunch. How will that work for you?"

"It will work perfectly. I'll come by at noon?"

"Yes, that would be great. And I'll come up with a dinner date for us to have with our parents. I promised everyone that I would

378

make this happen."

"Okay. You're ambitious! Planning things already. I'd like for just us to go out for dinner some night. And, I want to get together with you and your kids too."

"We'll arrange everything this week then. I guess I had better call my mom now."

"Oh, you called me first?"

"Well, actually I called Leah before calling you, just to let her know that we arrived safely. However, I did call you right after I spoke with her."

"I'm honored. Well, you get going, and I'll see you tomorrow. I love you, Rachel."

Rachel easily returned the sentiment. "I love you too, Don. See you tomorrow." Rachel sighed happily. She called her mother next.

"Hello?"

"Hi, Mom. It's Rachel."

"Well, of course it's you! How are you and the kids? How's everyone in California?" Delores sounded very happy to hear from Rachel.

"We're all doing great. Everyone had fun, and they say hello. Leah will be in touch with you soon."

"I'll look forward to hearing from her. So, it was a nice getaway for you and the kids?"

"Yes, it certainly was. It's nice to be back, though. Even though we already miss them. How are things with you? What have you done while I've been away?"

"Just the usual. Everything is going well." Delores paused for just a moment. "Have you spoken with Don yet?" Delores sounded hopeful.

Rachel smiled knowing that her mother had obviously been waiting to know how that part of Rachel's life was going. "Yes, I just spoke with him. Are you happy now?"

Delores actually laughed. "I was just wondering, that's all. How's he doing? Did he miss you?"

"He's fine, and he missed me. I'll be seeing him tomorrow."

"Very nice! Tell him I said hello."

"I will. I told him that the four of us will have to get together soon. For dinner some night. I promised that we would, remember?"

"I do remember. Ben and I will wait to hear from you about that."

"Okay. I think I should get going here. The kids are tired, and so am I. It's been a long day."

"I can imagine. It's good to hear your voice. Give the kids hugs from me, and I hope I'll see you soon."

Rachel was thrilled to hear her mother's enthusiasm about everything. Positive changes had been happening recently, and this all felt right. Rachel decided that she should also let Steve know that she and the kids had returned. So, she called his home.

"Hello?" Linda answered.

"Hello? Linda? It's Rachel."

"Hi." Linda didn't sound annoyed, but she sounded hesitant.

Rachel wasn't sure what to say. She thought she should say something to Linda before asking to speak with Steve. "So, how are you?" Rachel wasn't sure how to proceed.

"I'm okay. Coming along, I guess."

"I'm glad. Is Steve there?" Rachel was literally at a loss for words.

"Yes, I'll get him." Linda sounded calmer than ever. Maybe she was changing for the better.

"Hello? Rachel?"

"Yes, it's Rachel. How are you?"

"I'm fine. How was the trip? The kids sounded very happy whenever I spoke with them."

"We all had a great time. It wasn't easy to leave. Hey, I guess there have been some changes since I left. Linda seems to be doing okay."

"Yep. Like I told you before you left, we have plans to work everything out. So far, we're managing, although, with the pregnancy, she doesn't feel so great every day. She's doing well, though."

"That's good. I'm happy for both of you."

"I assume that your sister and her family are doing well? And Don probably missed you."

"Yes on all counts."

"That's good. That's good." Rachel wasn't sure if he really thought it was so good that Don missed her, considering that he repeated the sentence twice. Still, it really didn't matter.

"I just wanted to let you know that we were back safe and

sound. The kids are resting, but I'll have them call you when they feel a bit more awake."

"Thanks. I'd appreciate that."

"Okay. Good luck with everything."

"You too."

The conversation was easy and without rancor. That was a win as far as Rachel was concerned.

Rachel did a little unpacking and started some laundry. She feared that she would never get caught up with it all, but she knew it would just take time to get through the piles. As one load of wash was in the machine, she decided to lie down on the couch for just a moment. She fell soundly asleep.

"Mom!" David had startled Rachel out of a deep sleep. She jumped up, not quite being sure where she was. She looked around, trying to understand her surroundings with the little light that she had coming from a table lamp.

"David! What is it?" Rachel was alarmed thinking something must be terribly wrong.

"I'm starving!" He looked at his mother as though he wondered why his food had not magically appeared on the kitchen table. Rachel knew that she was officially back home, taking on the full-time role of motherhood.

She dropped her head down, relieved that everything was okay. Everything except her son's empty stomach. "I think I'm just going to order a pizza. Is that okay?" She raised her head again and rubbed her neck, praying he would give a positive answer. She was not disappointed.

David raised his hand in the air in victory. "Yes! What kind can we have?"

"Whatever kind you want." Rachel got up slowly from the couch, and hobbled towards the kitchen to get the menu from their favorite pizza parlor. Suddenly, the doorbell rang. Rachel's brain was still a bit foggy, and she was sure that she probably didn't look all that great either. She felt disheveled. "David, would you answer the door, please?"

As she was trying to find the pizza menu in the kitchen, Rachel could hear a slight murmuring. Then she heard David shout. "This is awesome! Thanks, Don!" Rachel froze as though she had seen a ghost. *Don? Right now?* She smoothed out her hair, and quickly found a mint in a bag in the cupboard. Well, she thought, this is what he'll see every now and then if he actually does marry me. She viewed her appearance quickly in the chrome toaster, and thought that, although she was a bit bedraggled, she wasn't hideous. Rachel came out of the kitchen to see both David and Don smiling as though they had found a treasure. Don because he was so happy to see Rachel and David because his eyes were focused on the huge pizza box that Don was holding in his capable hands.

Rachel smiled, placing her hands on her hips in amusement. "How did you know that we wanted pizza right now? Literally, David just woke me up, and I was going into the kitchen to get the pizza menu. What are you, a mind-reader?"

"Trust me; I was hoping that I wasn't making a big mistake by just showing up with a pizza. I tried to time this correctly, knowing you'd want dinner, but that you wouldn't feel up to making it. If David's reaction is any indication, it seems like I had a good idea." Don looked lovingly at Rachel. Without taking his eyes off of Rachel, he held out the pizza box and said, "David, would you take this into the kitchen and get some plates for everyone?" David grabbed the pizza, and ran into the kitchen.

Rachel approached Don. "Thank you. I mean that from the bottom of my heart. You have no idea how much this means to me."

"I think I do." Don put his hands on Rachel's face and kissed her passionately. Rachel now knew for sure that she had been greatly missed. He pulled away after a moment. "I decided that if I brought pizza, I'd be able to see you. I really didn't want to wait until tomorrow."

"I'm glad that you didn't wait. I know the kids will be as well."

Just as Rachel said that, Sarah and Rebecca walked slowly down the steps. They looked like they weren't sure what planet they were on.

"What's going on? Hi, Don." Sarah was polite, and Rachel appreciated her acknowledgement of Don.

"Hi. How are both of you doing? You had a nice time in California?"

Both girls smiled, happy that Don asked them about their trip. "It was wonderful! We had the best time!" Rebecca couldn't contain her joy. She went from being lethargic to being elated.

"I'm glad to hear that. I'm sure you enjoyed spending time

with your family. If you're hungry, there's pizza in the kitchen. Your brother is in there now."

They all went into the kitchen. David had done as Don requested, putting plates, napkins and glasses on the table. Rachel brought out drinks, and they all sat down, devouring the delicious slices. Rachel was so impressed that Don had taken it upon himself to bring dinner. It was such a simple gesture, yet it was so thoughtful. He had considered her needs, and her children's needs. Rachel was also pleased that they were all with each other. Maybe this would be the first of many times like this.

They continued eating and talking, and then Don noticed that Rachel was wearing the charm bracelet. He smiled, and then she realized why. She smiled back, and playfully shook her wrist. She leaned closer to him and whispered. "I haven't taken it off. Not once." Don grinned, nodding his head up and down indicating approval.

There were still two pieces of pizza left, but everyone's was full. The kids must have still been tired. Rachel watched in amazement as they placed their dirty dishes and glasses into the dishwasher. They all sincerely thanked Don for bringing the pizza, and he told them that they were welcome and he was happy to supply it. They excused themselves, said goodnight, and went upstairs.

When all was quiet in the kitchen, Don kissed Rachel again. She savored the moment. "I missed you SO much, Rachel. I was happy for you because you were doing something good for yourself and for your family. But I wanted you with me. Selfish, huh?"

"Not at all. I felt the same way. I was thrilled to be spending time with my family. I miss them now. But I also want to be with you."

"I'd say that everything went well tonight. The kids are responding positively to my presence."

"That is true. I couldn't be happier that things are going so well." Rachel stretched her legs out a bit, and sat back comfortably in her kitchen chair. "I feel like we're all in a better place. The children were so happy being in California and spending time with the family. They seem to be appreciating my efforts." Then Rachel looked wary. "I almost get scared wondering when the other shoe is going to drop. I mean, things have been SO good. I'm not used to this." She smiled at Don.

"I'm not used to this." He motioned to her. "Rachel, you have changed my world. Yes, I have been happy. I guess. But I have more now. It feels really good."

Rachel leaned forward, and in the quiet surroundings, she kissed Don. After a moment, she spoke. "I think I need to set up our date. The one with our parents. Yes?" She looked at Don, wondering if he thought that he was ready for the event.

"Yes. I think that's a good idea. I can tell you that they're both looking forward to an evening with us. When I visited with my dad a few days ago, he told me that he can't wait to see us. Your mother said the same thing to me." Rachel looked surprised. Don explained. "Your mother was around as well. I came in and saw them both sitting in the lobby. So, we all talked."

Rachel rolled her eyes. "Oh, brother. How did that visit go?" She wasn't sure if she should be horrified or not.

"Now, now. It went fine. They've both simply made their feelings clear."

Rachel now looked perplexed. "What feelings?"

Don cleared his throat, not sure how to proceed. "How shall I put this?" He looked up as though trying to find divine inspiration to help him explain everything.

Rachel folded her arms. "Just put it out there. You have me worried."

Don laughed. "No need to worry. I think they'd just like to be witnessing us exchanging vows."

Rachel slumped down in her chair, embarrassed, and covered her face with her hands. "Oh. My. God."

Don patted her arm in comfort. "It's okay Rachel. It's not like it was even just your mom making the inference. It's as though they're in cahoots. I thought it was kind of cute."

Rachel sprang up in her chair. "Cute? Apparently you're a lot more understanding than I am." Rachel looked disgusted.

Don questioned her reaction. "So, the idea of exchanging vows with me holds no appeal to you?"

Rachel changed to a softer demeanor. "Oh, don't think that. I didn't mean that at all. It holds a great appeal to me." Don smiled his reassurance. "I just don't want them pushing us."

"I know." Don looked away for a moment in reflection. Then he turned his gaze back to Rachel. "It's just that I've thought a lot about this, Rachel. In my heart I know what I want. Marriage to

384

you is something that I'm in favor of."

Rachel didn't even blink. She sat very still. Finding the breath to speak, Rachel responded. "Wow. That's quite a bold statement. I...I'm glad to know how you feel. I feel the same way. I just figured that you'd want to be sure of things. You know, be sure that you'd be okay taking on three kids. Do you even feel like you know me well enough?" Rachel felt that she had to make him ask questions of himself.

"As a matter-of-fact, I think I do know you very well." He paused. "I know you've been through a lot." He looked at her, trying to figure out any hesitancy on her part. Is trust still an issue with you?"

Rachel had no problem answering the question. "No. It's not. I trust you completely. I guess I'm more worried for your sake. Not that you can't trust ME. That's not what I mean. I just think it might be asking a lot to deal with me and three children. You're okay with all of that?" Rachel figured she should find out where he really stood on the matter.

"I know it seems crazy for a bachelor to want to suddenly find himself with three children, but it doesn't bother me at all. Maybe that's because I love YOU so much. I kind of feel like we can do this, and do this well together. They really are good kids."

"So, even dealing with moodiness, teenage angst, a screaming mother, and constant drama you'd be fine?" Rachel wanted to challenge his idealistic view.

Don folded his hands in front of him as if being cross-examined. "Definitely. It's not like I never went through stuff myself. I was raised in a bit of drama too." He reached out his hands to hold Rachel's. "Honestly. I just want to be with you. It's really that simple. With love, I believe anything is possible. We'd have each other through it all."

Rachel looked down at his strong hands. She felt that anything would be possible with Don by her side. Then she looked up at him again. "Are you saying that you don't need to spend more time with the children before making a life-altering decision?"

"I really don't, although I realize they might need more time to get to know me. I don't want to make waves for them. I guess what I'm trying to say is that, if and when they are okay with me then I'd like to make it official. Rachel, I want to marry you."

Rachel's heart pounded. Not that what Don said was

unexpected. It just sounded strange to hear him say the words. She was speechless. Don kept looking for signs of anything she was thinking. She knew that she needed to respond to him. "Wow! You really ARE serious!" Rachel instantly wanted to clarify her comment, realizing that what she had said wasn't what he probably wanted to hear. Nor was it what she necessarily intended to say. "I mean, I'm glad. If you don't have any doubts about entering permanently into my life, then I'd like to marry you too."

Don's smile went a mile wide. But only for a second. He bent his neck down and shook his head back and forth. Rachel held her breath, wondering what she might have said or what he was thinking. *Was he already regretting what he had said to her?*

Rachel was alarmed. "Don? What is it?" She didn't want to sound shrill, but she was convinced that was how her voice sounded.

He looked up at her, and she suddenly felt faint from her pounding heart. Everything was falling apart. He didn't look happy. *What could have happened in a split second?*

"Rachel. You're going to marry an idiot. I HOPE."

Rachel was very confused. "Huh?" It was the only word she could muster.

"That wasn't much of a proposal I gave you. *I want to marry you* was the best I could do? Somehow I think you deserve better than that."

Rachel's heart stopped its wild pounding. She smiled at him and gave him a big kiss. "It sounded perfect to my ears. Coming from you, it sounded like music."

"So, you're still okay with this? I didn't get down on bended knee, and I didn't bring a ring to present to you. I'm not sure how romantic this all was for you."

Rachel looked at him with sincere eyes. "Don, it couldn't have been MORE romantic. This is all I need. Just you, wanting to spend your life with me."

They stood up and hugged each other. Don kissed her, and Rachel felt like melting. For a moment, they just looked at each other, two happy people with a bright future.

"So, where do we go from here?" Don sounded very relaxed.

"Good question." Rachel sat back down, and so did Don. "I still think that we need to keep this to ourselves for just a little while. I want the children to spend more time with you. I'VE had time, but they haven't. I owe them that, although I don't think we'll have to wait too long."

"That's perfectly reasonable. I want them to get used to me being around." Don paused for a just a moment. "I assume you'll still want to live here?"

"Yes. Is that okay with you?"

"Absolutely." He paused, thinking about more things. "Small wedding?"

"Yes. Small. If that works for you?"

"It does. I would like to see you walk down the aisle. Maybe on my dad's arm?"

"Oh, Don. That would be wonderful! I love him like a father. I hope he'll want to do this."

"He will. I know how much he loves you."

Rachel looked questioningly at Don.

"He's told me. He really does love you like a daughter."

Rachel swallowed hard. She was quite moved knowing that's how Ben thought of her. She had loved her own father so much, and the thought of having a man as nice as Ben treat her as though she was his own daughter made her feel very fortunate.

"This is all very good. I still can't believe how far we've come. Maybe just how far I'VE come." She put her hand on the table, hearing the light tinkling of her charm bracelet.

"We have both come a long way. However, I suppose we should continue this conversation another day. You need sleep. You didn't expect me to show up at your front door, and then to have me tell you that I want to marry you. That's a lot after you've just returned from California." Don stood up, preparing to leave. Rachel stood as well, and went to his side.

"I can tell you that this is the best welcome home I've ever had. The joy of the trip has only been surpassed by your declaration of wanting to marry me. Honestly, Don, you've made me so happy."

They shared a lingering kiss at the door. "Don't forget to arrange our double date with your mom and my dad." Don smiled, finding the concept amusing.

"How does Friday night sound to you? I almost wonder if this should be a family gathering. I could include the kids."

Don looked admiringly at Rachel. "I think that's a brilliant idea."

387

"What can I say? You've inspired me tonight!"

"Is it okay if I still see you tomorrow? Whenever it works for you?"

"It's more than okay. I'll call you in the morning when I know more of what's going on."

"Great. Even a coffee with you would be fine. I just want to be with you." He kissed her again, and he went to his car.

Rachel closed the door, appreciating every moment she had with Don. She still had to let it sink in that he wanted to marry her. It seemed too good to be true. And, yet, she knew it was true. She loved him, and he loved her. It was that simple. She turned off the lights, not even caring about tidying up the kitchen. Slowly, Rachel climbed the stairs, and went to her room. After quickly getting herself ready for bed, she settled in for the night.

Chapter Thirty-Three

The kids woke up before Rachel, but they didn't disturb her. They went downstairs, and saw, with surprise, the kitchen that was left in slight disarray. Each pitched in to finish cleaning.

"Mom must have been really worn out to leave the kitchen untidy." Rebecca was merely making a statement of fact.

Sarah was wiping off the table with a cloth. "Yeah, I'm sure she was tired. We all had a long day yesterday." She stopped cleaning, and held the cloth in her hands. "It was really nice of Don to bring that pizza, doncha' think?" She was looking at her sister as if seeking confirmation to her question.

"It was very nice of him. That was good pizza!"

"I like Don." David was placing a glass in the dishwasher. Both sisters looked at him, almost as if they were surprised that he would offer any comment. "Well I *do*. He's always nice. He talks with us."

Rebecca and Sarah looked at each other and nodded. They couldn't argue with anything their brother had said. "And Mom does seem very happy when he's around." Sarah was analyzing the situation.

"She's not just happy. It's obvious that she's REALLY happy." Rebecca's eyes gleamed as though she'd just revealed a secret.

The children finished cleaning in silence. Sarah then asked the burning question. "Do you guys think that Mom and Don will get married?"

David's face lit up, but he waited for Rebecca's response. She raised her eyebrows and looked as if she felt that the marriage possibility was not a bad idea. "Perhaps. I think it would be fine, don't you?" She looked at Sarah, forgetting that David was even in the room and should be part of the discussion. His eyes focused on Sarah, hoping her answer would be a positive one.

Sarah returned the facial expression that had been on Rebecca's face. "I suppose. I mean, if they love each other, I think it would be great."

"I'm sure they love each other!" David was practically busting to give his opinion on the subject. "I hope they get married."

Once again, the sisters turned to look at their brother. "You HOPE they get married? Why's that?" Sarah now wanted David's input.

"I just think it would be good for Mom and for us. She'd be happy and we'd be happy." For David, it was all that simple.

The girls shrugged, thinking that what he had said made sense. There really was no need for further discussion.

They went into the family room to watch television. Within fifteen minutes, Rachel was coming down the stairs, looking bright eyed and ready to start her day.

"Good morning! How are you all doing today? Refreshed?"

"Yep. How are you this morning, Mom?" David sounded chipper.

"I'm doing great, thanks for asking."

"Mom, we all thought it was it was very nice of Don to bring that pizza last night. He's very thoughtful." Rachel sensed that Sarah's meaning was a bit deeper than the comment she posed.

"Yes. It was very nice. He's a very kind man." Rachel eyed her daughter with a bit of suspicion.

"What? Why are you looking at me that way? We really do think he's a nice guy!"

"Okay. Sorry." Rachel put up her hands in defense. "It just sounded like there was more to what you were saying."

"All she's trying to say is that we think Don is a good man, and that if you love each other, we don't mind if you get married." Rebecca had her feet on the table and her eyes were focused on the television screen. It clearly impacted everyone in the room because three sets of eyes were looking at Rebecca as if she'd just said the most shocking thing ever heard.

"Wh...what? What did you say? I mean, I *heard* what you said, but...what?" Rachel was in shock.

Rebecca took her feet off the table, and turned to face her mother. "Mom, we know that you and Don love each other. There's no point in denying it, and nor should you want to. We think he's a good guy, and we like him. He makes you happy, and it seems that you make him happy. We're perfectly okay if you marry him."

Rachel was stunned. Stunned by Rebecca's young teenage

390

sensitivity, and stunned by her children's absolute acceptance of including Don in their lives. For all of her worry about handling everything carefully for them, it seemed that they were fine with the situation right now. She was speechless.

"Yeah, Mom. We're perfectly okay." David's sweet voice permeated Rachel's thoughts.

Rachel stared at all of them with incredulity. Then, out of the blue, she broke into tears. They looked at each other, not knowing what the problem was or what they should do. Rebecca had assumed her statement would make her mother happy. Tears were not supposed to be part of the equation.

Sarah went to her mother, and she patted her shoulder. "Mom? What's wrong?" The unexpected kindness of her daughter's gesture made it almost impossible for Rachel to stop crying. She did attempt to pull herself together.

She blew her nose into a tissue, always having those readily available in her pants' pocket. "Nothing is wrong. That's why I'm crying." She blew her nose again, and tried to make light of her emotions by chuckling. "Really, I'm okay. I just appreciate all of you so much. You've taken me by surprise, that's all. Yes, Don and I do love each other, and we do want to get married. I wanted to give you all time to get to know him. I guess I didn't realize how you already felt about him, and that you had already accepted him." Rachel blew her nose again. Oddly enough, Sarah was still standing there, patting her mother's shoulder. When Rachel was able to see clearly again through her watery eyes, she looked at her children and saw smiles. She planned to keep this memory in her mind's eye forever.

"So, you and Don DO want to get married? Maybe you should set the date. We'll help you with the plans." Ever practical Rebecca was ready to assist.

"Okay. I appreciate that. But before any plans are made, I need to let Don know about this. And, once I do that, I'd like to have a dinner here with all of you, Grandma, and Don's dad. We'll share the good news with them then." She paused for a moment, her head reeling with information. Then she looked at the three again. "So, you really *are* okay with this? You don't need more time?"

"More time for what?" Sarah didn't know what Rachel was talking about.

"I don't know. More time spent with Don to get to know him?

Time to adjust? I don't know." Rachel really didn't know. She never expected their absolute approval so quickly, so she wasn't quite sure how to handle something that was this easy.

"We know him. We like him. And, we'll be able to hang around with him. Right?" David cut to the chase.

"Right. I'm glad you're all okay with this. Really. I can't even express the joy that I'm feeling. Come here." The other two came to her, and the four shared a big group hug.

After holding on for a few moments, the happy group broke up, and Rachel called Don.

"Hi, Rachel! How's everything? Did you sleep well last night?"

"I did, and things are beyond wonderful right now. I am busting out with information, and I can't even wait until I see you to tell you. Okay?"

"Okay." Don sounded unsure, although he had heard her say the word wonderful. *So how bad could it be?*

Rachel took a deep breath. "Okay. Here goes. The kids want us to get married. They know how we feel, they like you, and they're fine with everything."

There was a moment of silence, and Rachel wasn't sure how to take the void. But then Don responded. "This is incredible! Rachel, your kids have made me the happiest man in the world! Would it be okay if I come over right now?"

"Yes! That would be great! I'll let them know that you're coming. Should I find out if my mom and your dad can come over tonight?"

"Definitely. I don't want us to have to wait to tell them the good news. I'll hang up, and you call your mom. I'll call my dad."

"Okay. I'll see you soon."

"Yes, you will!"

Rachel felt giddy, but she wanted to control her emotions so that Delores wouldn't suspect anything. She called her apartment.

"Hello?"

"Mom, it's Rachel. How are you?"

"I'm fine, dear. How are you? Are you rested now?"

"Pretty much. I was wondering if you'd like to come here for dinner tonight. Don is going to ask his dad if tonight works for him." Rachel couldn't believe how calmly she was speaking.

"I'd be happy to come tonight! I've been looking forward to this occasion since it was mentioned."

"Wonderful. The kids will be here too. I assume that's okay?"
"Of course it's okay! Goodness, Rachel, I'm always happy to see my grandchildren."

"Okay. I'll ask Don to pick up you and Ben. Maybe around six or so."

"Whatever you'd like. Six is fine with me. This is so exciting!"

Rachel was pleased by her mother's enthusiasm, but Rachel knew that her mother would even be more excited when she heard the good news. "It will be fun. So, I'll see you tonight."

"Okay, dear. I'll see you soon."

Rachel told the kids about Don coming over and that the dinner was being arranged. Within twenty minutes, the doorbell rang. David ran to the door to open it.

"Hi, Don! Congratulations!" David was quick to say the right thing.

"Thanks, David! I appreciate that!"

David opened the door wide for Don to come in. Rachel beamed at him, and he couldn't contain himself. In front of the children, he went towards Rachel, grabbed her, lifted her up off the floor, and kissed her. The three kids actually clapped and hooted. It was a fun and wonderful moment.

Rachel felt somewhat breathless. "So, did you get a hold of your dad? Can he come? My mom can."

"Yes to both questions."

"I told Mom you'd get the two of them at around six. Is that okay?"

"That's fine. So, what will we do about dinner? I don't want you to have to cook. You need a break, so where should we pick up some grub for us?"

"I'm sure I could whip up some pasta and sauce. That's easy enough. I can put together a salad as well. I have plenty of time, although I do need to get to the grocery store."

"Would you like me to go for you? You could give me a list of what you need, and I'll get the items."

Rachel looked surprised. "You could do that?"

Don looked amused. "Yes, Rachel, my love. I do go to the grocery store. You see, even single men need to eat every now and then."

Rachel laughed. "Yes, that's true. Okay. I don't need many things. I'm going to do my regular shopping at another time."

"I can get everything you need. Why go if you don't have to?"

Rachel couldn't think of a reason not to have him do the shopping. He was going to be her husband soon. Partners shared responsibilities. "Okay. If that's what you want to do. I'll compile a list."

Don chatted with the kids while she went into the kitchen. As she wrote on a notepad, she heard happy sounds of laughter from the family room. She could faintly hear them talking, but she couldn't quite discern the subject matter. It was nice to know that this would be a regular occurrence in her house. Having Don with them would make life wonderful.

She left the kitchen, and handed him the list. "Thank you for doing this for me."

"My pleasure. I'm happy to do whatever I can for you."

"I know. That's just one of the many reasons that I love you so much."

She saw Sarah roll her eyes in an amused manner. "Okay. I know. Mother can be lame sometimes." Rachel gave her a sly smile, and Sarah laughed.

'I don't think your mother is lame at all." And with that, he kissed her, and bid adieu.

As Don was shopping, Rachel was doing laundry, and the kids were setting the dining room table. There was a hubbub of activity. Rachel wanted to take a moment to call Leah. She had to let her know what was happening.

"Hi, Rachel! How are you? What's up?" Leah was very happy to be talking with her sister again.

"I want to let you know that life is great. Oh, and one other thing. Don and I are going to be married." Rachel couldn't resist sounding so casual about it.

Leah screamed with joy. Rachel had to take the phone away from her ear for a moment. "I am SO happy for you both!! This is incredible! Tell me everything!"

Rachel laughed. "Okay. But let me tell you first that Mom and Ben are coming here tonight, and we're telling them then. So don't call Mom about this."

"I promise I won't. She is going to flip out!"

"I suspect she will." Rachel proceeded to tell Leah all of the details. At the end of the story, Rachel heard Leah sniffling. "Leah? Are you okay?"

"I'm fine. I'm just so happy. My sister is getting married to a wonderful man. Your dreams are coming true!"

Rachel appreciated her sister's sentiments. "Yes, my dreams are coming true. Who would have figured?"

"So, have you set the date yet?"

"No, but we will shortly. We just want a simple wedding."

"That's fine, but I have to be there. I have to share this momentous occasion with you."

"Definitely. I want you right here with us."

"It's okay if I tell Bob and the kids?"

"I think that should be fine."

"Let me know how it all goes tonight. Are you nervous?"

"About what?"

"Telling mom. Getting married. I hope that you're not nervous, because there's nothing to be nervous about. I was just wondering." Leah didn't want to plant the thought in Rachel's head that she should be nervous. She regretted having said anything.

"You know, I'm *not* nervous. Mom will be happy this time, unlike when I told her I was marrying Steve. Ben will be thrilled as well, and I do feel like I'm making a good decision this time. I guess it really didn't take me long to know what I wanted and that Don was a good man. Everything feels right."

"That's what I want to hear! Okay, I'll let you go, but keep me posted."

"Will do. We'll talk more about life very soon. I want to know what's happening in your life as well."

"Not much to tell. Just go have fun."

Rachel was so happy. She and the kids were doing chores, and then Don came back saying that there were bags in the car if the kids would like to help bring them in. Oddly enough, they ran outside to get them. She couldn't believe how willing they were to assist. Don wasn't demanding anything of them. He just politely asked for their help. He went back outside, claiming that he was going to get more bags. Instead, he came in with a lovely floral display. There were a variety of flowers in colors of red, pink, yellow, lilac, and baby's breath was placed strategically as well. Rachel thanked him with a kiss, and she put them on the dining room table.

The kids, along with Don, brought in the rest of the grocery bags. They took items out, and everything was put away.

395

Somehow, with Don around, everything was easy, and hearing the chatter and the laughter made Rachel feel content.

Once the kids had helped, they went upstairs, figuring that their mom and their future step-father would want some privacy. Don and Rachel stood in the kitchen.

"Well, I had better get going. I know you have a lot to do. I'll pick up my dad and your mom at six."

"Don, thanks so much for all of your help. I know we were going to just get a cup of coffee and relax today, but I'm looking so forward to tonight. It's going to feel great to tell your dad and my mom the good news."

Don came to Rachel and put his loving arms around her. "I'm so happy that I could help you today. And, I'm thrilled that we'll be able to have the family together to share our happiness." He kissed her warmly.

After Don left, Rachel made a simple breakfast for her family, did more laundry and prepared the pasta sauce. She and the kids had a quick bite to eat for lunch, and before Rachel knew it, she needed to get her own act together. She showered, put on navy slacks and a pink silk shell. She chose a spring floral print cardigan sweater to wear over the shell. She gazed at herself in her bathroom mirror and smiled. She looked radiant and happy. This was a look she was sure to have for years to come.

Rachel and the kids were downstairs when the doorbell rang a little after six. Rachel's heart pounded intensely. She didn't expect to react that way, so she knew she was a bit nervous. Good nervous, though.

David ran to the door, knowing that everyone was going to have a fun evening.

"Hi, Grandma! Mr. Levy. Don. Come on in!"

Delores hugged David, and Rachel was pleased to see the familial gesture. Delores introduced Ben to the family. He said hello to the children, and came over to greet Rachel, giving her a big hug and a kiss on the cheek.

"My, oh, my, it smells wonderful in here! I know I'm going to like this dinner! And the company." Ben's eyes glimmered with happiness. No wonder Rachel loved him so much. He was always kind and happy.

Don came over to Rachel and gave her a little kiss. He smiled at her, knowing they shared a great secret.

Delores hugged Rachel and then Don. "Rachel, this is so nice! I can't tell you how happy Ben and I are to be here tonight!"

Rachel knew that she meant it. "I'm happy to have everyone here. Dinner is ready, so why don't we head into the dining room." Ben escorted Delores, and Don did the same with Rachel. The children, nicely dressed and well-mannered, followed them all.

Ben, Delores and Don remarked about the lovely table arrangement. Rachel would have credited Don with bringing the pretty flowers, but she didn't want Delores or Ben to know that he had been there that morning.

Everyone sat down, and the food was passed around the table. Rachel had a large platter of linguini tossed in a tomato, garlic and meat sauce. There was also crusty bread to be dipped in olive oil, and a huge chopped salad. After everyone had eaten and talked for a while, Don looked at Rachel to get a sign of approval for making the announcement. Rachel blushed slightly and nodded. Her heart was pounding again.

"Delores? Dad?" The two looked at Don, sensing a different tone to his voice. "I want to put this as simply as possible. Rachel and I are going to be married."

Delores and Ben were stunned. Their mouths were wide open, and then they looked at each other. After the moment of pleasant shock wore off, everyone stood up and hugged each other, offering a multitude of congratulations.

Rachel and Don had their arms around each other, and they were laughing and smiling amidst all of the excitement.

"There's one other thing. I have something for Rachel." She looked at him, wondering what he was talking about. He pulled out a black velvet box. She now knew what he meant. Rachel looked at him as if to say, "You didn't have to do that." Don smiled, and opened the box. Inside was a sparkling two carat heart shaped diamond ring set in platinum. Rachel stood looking at it, not believing what her eyes were seeing. Delores gazed at the gleaming diamond, unable to take her eyes off of it. Even Sarah and Rebecca were stunned into silence.

"Here. Let me put it on your finger." He slid it on easily. How he knew the size of her finger, Rachel didn't know, and she didn't care. It was the most beautiful thing she had ever seen. Aside from the bracelet he had given her. He kissed her, and everyone clapped.

"Don, this is exquisite." Rachel kept staring at her hand, tilting it back and forth to admire its perfect glimmer.

"Not as exquisite as you are." He kissed her again, and everyone said, "Ahh."

"I hope you don't mind me explaining why I chose this ring." Rachel indicated that he should continue. "The heart shape speaks volumes in the same way as the heart charm on the bracelet. I want to give you a two carat heart which represents the two of us." Delores held her hand to her chest in amazement of her future son-in-law's sentiment. "Also, it's set in platinum. The rarest of metals because we have something very rare in today's world. True, heartfelt love."

Rachel wanted to cry, but she contained her emotions. She leaned against him, appreciating every word he had said. Everyone else stood quietly, letting the special moment sink in. Rachel then, very quietly, gave her thanks to Don. She wasn't sure she could say anything more.

The family sat back down, talking quietly. Don and Rachel held hands for a moment, just happy to have told everyone their news.

"Not to be pushy, but have you thought of a date?" Delores wanted this marriage to happen quickly.

"No, but soon is good. And something simple." Rachel wanted to make sure her mother knew that this would not be an elaborate party. Getting married to Don was the only thing that mattered. "I know that Leah will want to be here, but otherwise, we don't want many people at the ceremony."

"Don, are you okay with this? It is your first marriage. Your ONLY marriage." Everyone laughed at Delores's bold comment.

"I'm more than okay with this. I just want to marry your daughter. That's all that matters to me." He looked at Rachel with love in his eyes and kissed her again.

"And I want my son to marry you too, my dear future daughter-in-law." Ben wanted to make his declaration as well.

Rachel smiled at her future father-in-law. "I'd like you to walk me down the aisle. If that's okay with you?"

Ben looked at her with a surprised expression. "I'd be honored to do that." He took out a handkerchief and quietly blew his nose.

The evening continued, and in the time between the announcement being made, and dessert, coffee and tea being consumed, a wedding date had been set. Rachel decided to call Leah immediately because the wedding was only a month away. She phoned her while Ben, Don and Delores were still there. Leah happily listened to the details that Rachel shared, and she was ready to book the trip. Leah's children had summer activities, and she really wanted to focus completely on Rachel. She didn't want any distractions, so leaving her children at home with Bob just made sense.

Rachel and Delores planned to shop for dresses during the week. Don was going to arrange the venue for the ceremony, and Rachel would get the flowers. She intended to tell Grace about this tomorrow, and she knew that Grace would want to take photos. Don had a friend in New York who would be his Best Man.

Don kissed Rachel goodbye, and took Ben and Delores back to their residence. This had been an eventful evening, and Rachel didn't want to overwhelm either one of them. After the three left, the girls kept admiring their mother's engagement ring. Then Sarah mentioned something.

"Mom. You'll need to let Dad know about this."

The thought hadn't even occurred to Rachel, but she knew that her daughter was correct. "I will. I think it's too late to call him tonight, but I'll call him tomorrow."

They all cleaned up the dishes, Rachel having refused the help of Don, Ben and Delores to assist with the job. After they were finished, she and the children collapsed on the family room sofa.

"Mom, what should we call Don?" David looked a little concerned.

Rachel hadn't considered that either. "What would you like to call him?"

"I think Don would be fine. We have a dad already. I might feel funny calling Don 'dad' too."

Rachel nodded in agreement. "Okay, then. Don it is. We'll ask him, just to make sure he's comfortable with that too."

After talking for a bit longer, Rachel and the children decided that it was time for bed. It had been a long and exciting day, and they were exhausted.

Chapter Thirty-Four

The next morning, Rachel was up bright and early. She picked up the phone to call Steve.

He answered, and they made small talk for about a minute. Then Rachel decided it was time to share her good news.

"Steve, I wanted to let you know that Don and I are getting married."

There was a long pause, and Rachel wasn't sure that he had heard her. She was about to repeat what she had said, but Steve finally responded.

"So, it's happening. Congratulations, Rache. I hope you'll be very happy." There was very little emotion to his tone. He was just trying to be polite.

"Th…Thank you. I appreciate that. I'm already happy." Rachel was uncomfortable now. It wasn't her duty to make sure that her ex was okay about her upcoming event, but she didn't want to have this tension between them either.

"I'm sure you are. Don is a lucky man."

"Thanks. I consider myself to be a lucky woman." She figured she would try to broaden the happiness. "I guess we're both doing well now. You and Linda are working things out, and I have someone in my life. It's all good." Rachel tried to sound peppy, in spite of the gloomy attitude that Steve had taken on.

"So, when's the big day?" Steve said in a monotone.

"It's in a month. We're having a small, simple wedding." Rachel didn't feel the need to invite Steve and Linda to her happy occasion.

"Makes sense. There's no point in having some elaborate shindig the second time around."

"That's what I figured."

"Are the kids happy?"

"Yes. Very." This was all very terse, but information needed to be given. Rachel wasn't in the mood to continue talking. "Okay, well, I just wanted to let you know. Enjoy your day."

"Will do. Thanks for calling."

They hung up, and Rachel felt a bit weary. However, she refused to allow him to deflate her upbeat feelings. She had given him her news, and that was that. He had put her through plenty of garbage in the past. Now, it was her turn to finally be happy.

Rachel's next call was to Grace. He friend was very excited for Rachel, and she suggested that she and her husband get together with Rachel and Don for dinner some night. Grace was thrilled to be part of the wedding, and she marked the date on her calendar.

As the weeks went by, Rachel and Delores shopped for their dresses, and Rachel took her children shopping to find outfits. Rachel saw Don nearly every day, and it was a surprisingly relaxed time for both of them. Don was in the process of selling his condo, and he and Rachel had a nice dinner with Grace and Mike. The men hit it off splendidly, and Rachel knew there would be many more fun times ahead for both couples.

Leah came to town a few days before the wedding. To save time, she purchased her silky pink and pale yellow dress in California, and was enjoying hanging out with Rachel for a while. Leah was planning on staying at the house for the few days that Rachel and Don would be away on their honeymoon. She could spend time with the children and get Rebecca and David to their summer activities. Rachel felt that, with Steve working, the kids were better off being in their own home.

A couple of nights before the wedding, Don and Rachel went out for a quiet dinner. All of the plans were set, and it was only a matter of showing up at the hall and exchanging their vows. They ordered glasses of champagne to toast each other.

"Rachel, I love you so much. I have one more thing that I want to give you before our wedding." Rachel couldn't imagine what he would be bestowing upon her now. The charm bracelet was so meaningful, and then the incredible engagement ring was such a special piece as well. Don handed Rachel a glossy red little bag. She reached inside it, and pulled out a tiny red velvet pouch. Inside the soft pouch was another gold heart. This one had their wedding date inscribed, and their birthstones bezel set in the gold. It had a large spring ring clasp so that she could immediately attach it to the bracelet.

"Oh, Don! I love this one too! You're always so thoughtful!" She reached across the small table and kissed him. Because, as usual, she was wearing the bracelet, she had him place the heart charm on the link. It was perfect! "I feel like you're spoiling me. But I love it. You're such a romantic man."

"Aw shucks. What can I tell you? I love giving these things to you." He laughed, but then he just looked at Rachel, appreciating everything about her.

"So, I don't think I'll be seeing you tomorrow. I don't know why, but I'm just superstitious."

"I understand. It's fine. Actually, my dad, Ed, and I are having dinner together tomorrow night. We want to spend some time together before the Big Day." Ed was Don's friend from New York, and he had been happy to come and be part of the wedding.

"That's very nice. I'm glad. It seems that we have everything together anyway. I can't tell you how pleased I am that Ben will be walking me down the aisle. I'm happy that he'll be my father-in-law. I couldn't have chosen a better man for the job."

"Rachel, we're both very lucky. We have people who love us, and we have each other. It doesn't get better than that."

They held up their champagne flutes, and clicked them together.

Chapter Thirty-Five

The next day turned out to be a busy one for Rachel. She was spending most of the day with her mother, the kids, and Leah. They went out for lunch, and laughed the day away. As they were all chattering away, Rachel saw Linda at another table. She was with a friend, and as she stood up, Rachel couldn't help but notice her rounded front. Rachel didn't bother to go over and say hello. She merely observed her. Linda looked tired and, as she was walking away from the table, her posture made it seem like she was being prodded in the back. She was clearly uncomfortable, and Rachel actually felt sorry for her. Not that pregnancy was necessarily easy for any woman, but she knew Linda well enough to know that this experience was almost torture for her. She didn't look happy and glowing like most pregnant women.

When Rachel arrived home, there was a loving message from Don. He was so happy that he'd be married to her tomorrow. He hoped she was having a good day.

The next day, Rachel was up early and excited. So were her children and Leah. The sun was shining and the temperature was mild. They couldn't have ordered a more beautiful day. The wedding would take place at noon, and at eleven, they were dressed and ready to get Delores. Don and Ed were picking up Ben, and Grace was coming with her husband Mike to the venue.

When Rachel and her team arrived at the hall, Delores, who was dressed in a silver gray colored silk dress, gave her daughter a big hug. Rachel was dressed in a cream satin three quarter length dress. It had three quarter length sleeves, and therefore she was able to nicely show off her two-charm bracelet. Rachel looked radiant. The girls wore matching floral printed gauzy dresses, and they looked like spring. David was handsome in his black suit and tie.

At 11:45, Rachel was told that the Groom, Ed and Ben had arrived. Her pulse quickened, knowing that in fifteen minutes,

Ben would be walking her down the aisle. There was a lot of talking, and then the judge came in to tell them that it was time. Rachel took a deep breath, and Leah handed her the pretty bouquet of roses that she would be carrying down the aisle. The music started, and everyone nervously got into place.

First, Don went down the aisle. Then Ed and Grace went arm and arm together. After those two were standing near the judge, the children walked down together. Seeing the three of them almost made Rachel cry, but she wouldn't allow herself to do that. Not yet at least. Leah and Delores walked next, and then Ben, as handsome as ever, kissed Rachel on the cheek, and took her arm in his. She was glad to have his loving support beside her.

As they walked slowly, she saw Don gazing at her. His smile was contagious, as she smiled widely too. He was handsome in his suit, waiting for his bride. Ben delivered Rachel to his waiting son, and Don took her hand. They turned to face the judge. In a matter of a few minutes, they had exchanged their vows, wedding bands were placed on their fingers, and the ceremony was completed. They kissed and walked arm and arm back up the aisle. The others followed.

There was a lot of kissing and hugging, and many words of congratulations and best wishes. Delores was dabbing her eyes a bit as well. It had been a lovely day. Rachel and Don headed to his car to go back to Rachel's house. The wedding party would go in the other cars, and join them at the house for lunch. Don opened the passenger side of the car door for Rachel, as he had done so many times during their courtship. He then got in as well. He looked at his lovely wife, finding it hard to believe his good fortune. She looked at him, thinking the same thing about being with him. He kissed her softly.

As he turned the car on, he looked at her again. "Rachel, my love, our journey continues."

Epilogue

"Love's Journey" takes Rachel's 48-year-old heart from being on emotional lockdown to finding the one man whose own wounds would mend with hers. Together Rachel and Don discover that, at any point in life, love is possible.

The story is partly Rachel's and Don's, but it also defines the paths of understanding that Rachel finally achieves with her mother, her daughters, and herself. Through Rachel allowing her heart to go unguarded, she develops stronger and happier relationships with the loved ones who surround her. She finds strength through love, and her loved ones find that as well. Delores listens, shares her insight and becomes more loving, the children appreciate and understand their mother more, and even Rachel's ex and his wife seek a better future. This is a journey about the wonders that come from attaining love.